W9-BPM-910

Other Books In This Series

TESSERACTS FOURTEEN

Edited by
John Robert Colombo
& Brett Alexander Savory

EDGE SCIENCE FICTION AND FANTASY PUBLISHING

AN IMPRINT OF HADES PUBLICATIONS, INC.

CALGARY

EDGE

Edge Science Fiction and Fantasy Publishing
An Imprint of Hades Publications Inc.
P.O. Box 1714, Calgary, Alberta, T2P 2L7, Canada

In-house editing by Laura Pellerine
Interior design by Brian Hades
Cover Design by Erik Mohr

ISBN: 978-1-894063-37-1

EDGE Science Fiction and Fantasy Publishing and Hades Publications, Inc.
acknowledges the ongoing support of the Canada Council for the Arts and the
Alberta Foundation for the Arts for our publishing programme.

Library and Archives Canada Cataloguing in Publication

CIP Data on file with the National Library of Canada

ISBN: 978-1-894063-37-1

FIRST EDITION
(x-20100824)
Printed in Canada
www.edgewebsite.com

Contents

Dedication

To the Memory of

Phyllis Gotlieb (1926-2009)
Jeanne Robinson (1948-2010)

Foreword

John Robert Colombo

Reader, I urge you to read the stories that appear in this rich and varied anthology of strange Canadian fiction. Be sure to read them in the order that they appear here. If you do that you will find yourself caught up in the deceptive charm of the opening sentence of the first story. The sentence goes like this: "Genevieve and Ben examined the map of Italy on a placemat."

What a great beginning for a short work of fiction! It sounds so innocent and yet it seems so...odd. I am sure that you will want to read on...and on...especially when it dawns on you that nobody is traveling to or about the boot of Italy...but that the reader is being led, not cap in hand but hand in hand, through the shadowy side of life in a small community in Canada.

If you continue to read story after story you will inevitably come to the last line of the last story in this anthology. There you will read the following ominous words: "I knew that if she came for us, I would hold Celia back, even if Celia looked up to be saved." What a great ending: ominous, mysterious, meaningful...even if by now you know who is speaking and why Celia is being held back.

Once you have finished reading the stories in this anthology, a contemporary collection of such surmises and surprises, I am sure you will agree with me that story after story probes the darker side of *human nature*, even the darker side of what might be called *inhuman nature*. The stories shed eerie lights on the shadows of realities and existences we only suspect.

Readers of the earlier annual anthologies in this series will appreciate the fact that, in common with its thirteen (fourteen including *Tesseracts "Q"*) predecessors, *Tesseracts 14* is a collection of contemporary Canadian fantastic literature. It is not a reprint anthology or a commissioned collection, but an open collection of stories submitted by the country's most arresting writers. The publisher does not charge for submissions; instead, the publisher pays professional fees for all the literary works that we have accepted for publication. When I write *we* I have in mind myself and my fellow editor Brett Alexander Savory.

We selected twenty stories and twenty-one poems (in three collections)—from a total of some 450 submissions. I found it a great and at times bewildering experience to read, over the course of a few weeks, so many works of the fantastic imagination. After a while I began to yearn for the easy certitudes of reading a new work by a recognized writer like Stephen King or (to keep it Canadian) Robert Charles Wilson. The "easy certitudes" are the fact that from the byline I would know in advance what to expect. I had no idea what to expect when I turned to these manuscripts, manuscripts written by writers new to me and probably new to you too. The stories were contributed by writers—unknown, hardly known, barely known, known, even well known—and I had no idea what they would write about and how they would write about it. That is why the subtitle *Strange Canadian Stories* was chosen. Strangeness is characteristic of this collection...strange almost to the point, the breaking point, of estrangement. At first I wanted to subtitle the anthology *Really Strange Canadian Stories*—it has a ring to it!—but with some reluctance I came to the conclusion that the adjective *really* was inappropriate: The prose in the collection, while vivid and vital, is in no way experimental or subversive or demanding. In fact, the quality that I most detected and admired in the prose is its accessibility, its professionalism. The writing here is the work of professional story-tellers, many of whom reach out for artistry and memorability.

Up to this point I have been using the word *stories* to describe the contents of this collection. I should really stop doing that. Once you have worked your way through the collection, you will realize that not every work that has been included here is a work of fiction, for there are also highly imaginative poems and even one speech (albeit a highly inventive one that only a mature writer would dare to compose and deliver). One of my editorial determinations was to insist that no single poem would be accepted; only groups or suites of poetry would be given serious consideration. Poems would not be used as "fill" but would be treated as full-fledged contributions in their own right. I think the poetry included here needs no excuse: it is an exercise of the fantastic imagination, the same imagination that finds vivid expression in prose fiction.

Now I have been using the words *imagination* and *fantastic* with abandon, for I maintain that they express the dimension that most characterizes all the writing that appears here. The writers themselves are Canadian—by birth, by choice—but that is almost (but not completely) incidental when it comes to works of the imagination. To the degree that a writer is an artisan or an artist, he represents his time and place, and most of the locales of these stories will be seen (I believe) to be imaginatively or intuitively settings that are Canadian. But what is most important is not the nationality of the writer or the region of the world or the zone of space , but the nature of the writing itself. That nature is fantastic.

Now I like to use the words *fantastic literature* because these words refer to writing in the various genres (stories, novels, poetry, documentary) when it is informed by the *fantastic imagination*. This imagination is to be distinguished from the imagination that forms *mainstream fiction* or *mundane writing* which focuses on psychological realism. The literary works here are concerned with psychology, human inevitably, but they are additionally concerned with psychologies that may be distinctly non-real, man-made perhaps, even decidedly non-human. To simplify the discussion, let me suggest that *fantastic literature* includes imaginative writing that is Science Fiction, Fantasy Fiction, and Weird Fiction.

This generic division is three-fold, but is not cast in concrete or scripted in the akashic records. Yet it does seem to permit an *ad hoc* classification of the contributions here: SF is oriented to technological change and the future; FF is confined to peculiar powers and realities in the past or alongside our own in the present; and WF describes our present world and its society altered in one or two specific and irrational ways. It is possible to classify the stories in this anthology using this scheme. I do not recommend doing so, but it is often useful to attempt to determine "the center of gravity" of a given story to see if it is consistent with its premise and genre. Really strange stories might *not* be fully consistent. These stories, while strange, *are* consistent. (Their consistency may well be the single Canadian trait that they share!)

Brett and I had no trouble deciding that the stories included here were well deserving of publication, and we accepted them with close to unanimous agreement, right off the bat. We selected them on the basis of how they affected us, on how well they are written, and on how well they cohere. Some attention was paid to representing all the regions of the country, but no attempt was made to do this on the basis of population. We wish there were more contributions from that quarter of the population that is *francophone*, but stories in French that we read, while interesting, sounded as if they had been rendered into English by "translation generators," as indeed some were. (In the past twenty years, machine-translation has come some distance, but not enough to outpace the skill of the talented translator. Would that there were more translators to match the richly talented writers of French.) As for gender representation, we never kept count of female *vis-à-vis* male writers, so the two editors, being male, are relieved that so many women are represented on the basis of quality.

We are only sorry that so few submissions could be accepted. As it is, we exceeded the publisher-imposed upper limit—the "speed of light" of 100,000 words. Apologies are due to the many talented men and women who were not represented here but who are writing science fiction, fantasy fiction, and weird fiction with distinction. Yet the admission of an editorial basis is in order. We grew weary of stories with such sentences as "When Hassan the Cripple made his way to the sordid but colorful slave quarter..." or "It suddenly dawned on me that the twin lights were those of the eyes of vampires, glowing like hot coals in the night...." An anthology *fully* representative of popular tastes might include a lot of High Fantasy and Vampire Fiction, *de rigueur* in 2010!

What has been chosen for inclusion here leads me to conclude that there is much wisdom in the observation made by the endlessly insightful and inventive writer William Gibson. I have in mind this remark of his: "As I've said many times, the future is already here. It's just not very evenly distributed." That insight is now more than a decade old, for he first said it during a panel discussion broadcast on National Public Radio's "Talk of the Nation," November 20, 1999. It is one of those observations that becomes truer with the passing of the decades. At this very moment the seeds of the future are sprouting all around us, underbrush obscured by the older growth of the past. I believe that Gibson's observation applies to the writers in this anthology. There are writers represented in these pages whom we are reading today and whom we will be reading repeatedly in the years and the decades to come, for they are chroniclers of our present and our future, alas!

Acknowledgements

I am pleased to acknowledge the assistance that I received from my fellow editor Brett Alexander Savory and also from other editors and writers. Brett's acknowledgements appear later on; mine appear right here.

Brian Hades, the publisher of EDGE Science Fiction and Fantasy Publishing, Calgary, Alberta, is to be saluted for his dedication to the publishing of fantastic literature, and expressly for his on-going commitment to the *Tesseracts* series. Erik Mohr created the arresting cover. (Do not let it unduly unnerve you—it depicts no particular story or poem, though it does suggest the "pink-eye" experienced by the editors as they read all these submissions!)

A general and ongoing indebtedness is acknowledged to the *grande dames* of Canadian speculative writing, Phyllis Gotlieb and Judith Merril. Along the way I sought and received advice from a clutch of people (none of whom shall remain anonymous): Carolyn Clink, Cory Doctorow, Christopher Dewdney, Candas Jane Dorsey, Peter Halasz, Don Hutchison, Robert Priest, Robert J. Sawyer, Lorna Toolis. If you have enjoyed reading these literary works, they are to be praised. If you have doubts about the quality of any of these literary works, my colleagues are not to be held responsible!

Every reader will appreciate the fact that in the final analysis, thanks are due to the innumerable writers who submitted their works, to the writers whose works were almost included, and particularly to those writers whose "strange Canadian stories" add excitement to the pages of *Tesseracts 14*.

John Robert Colombo, the co-editor, an author and anthologist, takes pride in the fact that he compiled *Other Canadas* (1979), the first anthology of the country's fantastic literature. He contributed to *Tesseracts 1* and *Tesseracts 4*, and the editors of *Tesseracts 6* dedicated that collection to him. He has edited collections of the short fiction written by Algernon Blackwood, Leslie A. Croutch, Maurice Level, and Stephen Leacock. *Poems of Space and Time* consists of more than three hundred of his "poems and effects" inspired by scientific exploration and the fantastic imagination.

Giant Scorpions Attack

Tony Burgess

Genevieve and Ben examine the map of Italy on a placemat.
"How big are whales?"

A whale with a sunny smile and a jaunty plume sits off the
toe. Genevieve knows that Ben is trying to gauge the size of
things on the map. If the whale is a mile long, then it is about
four miles from Roma to Milano. Ben's first instinct is to trust
what he sees, then try to understand it. Genevieve smiles. She
has no idea how big the boot is, but she knows that there is no
way to tell by looking at this drawing.

"Whales are bigger than any animal. Ever."

Ben studies the map again. "Where's Duntroon?"

Genevieve tosses her hair back with both hands. She's about
to settle for Ben the impossibility of knowing everything when,
as she often does, she decides that Ben's on to something.

Genevieve pulls the paper cup of crayons over and starts
to draw lines across Italy.

"What's that s'posed to be?"

Genevieve takes a stubby pencil and writes Sydenham Trail.
Erie Street. In a heavy cross in the middle she writes 124 and 91.

"Now, it's a map of Duntroon."

"Write that."

Genevieve writes DUNTROON in big blocks across the
word Italy. Making the I an N, the T a bolder T, the A an R, the
L an O. The best she can to with the Y is a Q. Ben sees this and
can now accept that it is a map of their home town.

"Now we have to put stuff from Duntroon on it. We don't
have whales."

Ben looks at her as if she's crazy then puts thinking fingers
under each eye.

"Like what?"

"I dunno."

"Raccoons?"

Genevieve looks out the tall window beside their table. Ben watches her do this, then lays his head down. A heavy truck hammers past. A small red car. Blue. A long white truck with a milk logo. Genevieve sits back as if stung. She points without pointing. Ben turns his head on his arm, then sits up quickly.

"Poo Lady," he whispers.

Poo Lady appears once a day in Duntroon. She pushes an old-fashioned blue baby carriage and wears a green housecoat. She has curlers in her hair. Local children believe she rolls poo that she finds in the park, and maybe even her own, into her hair. They also believe that there is a baby made of poo bouncing around in the pram. There is a literal aura around this woman, a fecal spell, and it is believed that if you even say her name, Poo Lady, or, God forbid, ever spoke to her, that your breath would smell of farts for the rest of your life. Everything about her, the color of green, the thin black wheels, the filthy fart cigarette in her mouth had done something unspeakable to someone at some point. The worst part of her is the lie, the horrible pushing as if a baby was actually in there. Genevieve and Ben shudder. She has passed the window.

"Put the (whispered) Poo Lady on the map."

Genevieve sighs. She suffers for having a younger brother. Ben's forehead lands hard on the back of his hands and stays.

"Okay, okay, I know. I know exactly. We'll do a weird map of Duntroon. All the things that are here that no one talks about. All the stuff *we* know about."

Ben sits up.

"Poo Lady?"

"Poo Lady."

And so they begin to make their map starting with a drawing of the Poo Lady on the 124. She is encircled in light brown. Then there is the House of Cruelty at the end of Erie Street. A pilot lives there who has gone mad because he spends more time in the sky than on the ground. The only way he can keep from killing children is to drown cats in a barrel in his back yard. Then there is the Stab Forest. A heavy tangle of thorn trees down the hill behind the legion on the west route out of town. The body of a woman was found in there five years ago. Her husband was taken away but the children know it was the spikes that got her. Piercing through her clothes and literally pulling out her heart and flinging it to the ground. Then on

Sydenham, the Cherry House. In it lives a giant woman and her daughter who is grown up but only as tall as a two year old. This woman sings songs to God under her breath and the daughter cackles and twists when she walks. Half of her body never came out of her mother, and is still growing inside somewhere, tightening the old woman's shoulders. The mother is in so much pain that she sings to God under her breath every second of every day. The daughter is a kind of devil.

Genevieve and Ben sit silently for a long while trying to think of other things to put on the map.

"The fishing hole."

"That's not weird."

"All the grade sixers pee in it on their way home from school."

"So? That's just gross."

"Yeah. But nobody knows. Might be good to tell them."

Genevieve makes a blue circle and fills it with yellow. Gross alone is too low a standard but gross and informative isn't.

Genevieve and Ben stand on the narrow walkway at the side of their house. Genevieve turns and faces the heavy ivy. She lifts the back of her shirt and instructs her brother to press the map against her bare back then pull the shirt over it.

"Mom and Dad don't need to know about this."

She instructs Ben to hurry. Wasps are emerging from the shadows beneath the leaves. She closes her eyes until he is done.

That night Genevieve lies awake in her bed. The map lies in the dust beneath her box spring. She is waiting, as she does every night, for fear to creep up before falling asleep. She has to select what the fear can rise into safely. Usually a sound, or rather, the space between two sounds. The ductwork snaps somewhere in the house. Too alert, too random to make a proper space. A pump scrolls through water in the basement. Across the hall, Ben is coughing in his sleep. Then she finds it. The electric clock groans and ticks and then is silent. Not silent really, more suspended until the next groan and tick. *That* is the space. Genevieve focuses on the space. She needs to be accurate or the fear will never come and she will never sleep. The space is a hole. A gap. A non-groan and a non-tick. It is a thing covered or a thing removed. She races around it trying to make it what it is. It is a groan breathing in instead of out. It is all the silent ticks awaiting selection. Genevieve feels her ears grow larger than her pillow. It is the thinking about groaning and the remembering about ticking. Her eyes reach down and draw heavy bedding up into her thoughts. Genevieve feels her heart start to plink in the space. It is dying. The space between the groan and the tick is dying. Genevieve's hands release around the bear at her chest and she falls to sleep.

⸝⸝⸝⸝

The next morning, Genevieve checks that Ben's shoes are on the right feet. He stands looking up at her waiting. "Okay, you're good."

"Do you have the map?"

Genevieve nods.

"I gave it a title. It needs to be called something."

Ben grabs his cheeks, agreeing.

"What is it called? What? What?"

"Shhh. Outside."

Genevieve looks back into the house as the storm door slaps closed behind Ben.

Ben waits outside, standing in a puddle. He feels dirty water wick up his instep. Genevieve emerges and carefully turns to close the door. She points to the end of the driveway then follows her brother, avoiding the puddle and stepping between the faint shades of his wet footprints.

"Keep going. Don't act weird."

They reach end of Erie Street and stop. Duntroon sits on top of the Niagara escarpment and from here they can see all of Clearview Township. From Creemore out to Cashtown. The steeples of Stayner and the entire Nottawasaga Bay including the beaches of Tiny Township. The view is sweeping and the perspective so odd that it translates to your eye like wallpaper in a Chinese restaurant. Genevieve turns her back and casts a quick shadow, her head darkens the center of Christian Island some eighty kilometers away. She carefully rolls up the back of her shirt and Ben draws the map off her skin.

"It's called 'The Evil Tour of Duntroon'," she tells him.

Ben closes an eye to think. Genevieve watches.

"Anyway, that's what it is."

Ben's face falls.

"It's mine too. I thought of it."

Genevieve remembers.

"Okay, okay. What do you think?"

Ben closes his eye again and Genevieve patiently looks at her map.

"What about Giant Scorpion Attacks?"

"What about *what*?"

"Giant Scorpion Attacks."

Genevieve controls herself. Ben holds his chin and stares at the map. He is the decider.

"Okay. We go with your one. What was it again?"

"The Evil Tour of Duntroon."

Genevieve pulls out a drawing pencil and begins to write the title in block letters at the top.

Neither child is aware that a man has approached. He has come down from the crest of the high street and is stopped, stooped over them as Genevieve finishes.

"The Evil Tour of Duntroon."

The children jump towards each other as if to pounce on the words written that they have just heard spoken.

The man laughs and pulls his hat back off his face.

"Don't worry! The secret's safe—is it a secret?"

Genevieve is too upset to speak. Ben grins and nods. He believes the map's importance has now begun.

"Can I see your map?"

The man's hand falls open against Genevieve's arm. She knows him. She has seen him. Not his name, but him. He sits on the stool beside the antique tractors at the fair in October. He sits beside a barrel fire with a yellow dog resting by his feet. At the fair his hat is light colored. He holds the map up close to his face and studies it.

"The Poo Lady. Hmmm."

Genevieve feels fire move around her throat. Ben claps both hands to his mouth. He's too nervous to actually laugh but he thinks this could be funny.

"Astounding. I didn't know children could still see her."

Genevieve looks at his face. He is serious. She dislikes being patronized and can tell quickly when that's happening.

"It's an impressive tour. I will never tell a soul. You have my word."

He reaches his hand out and after a pause Genevieve takes it and they shake firmly once. The man looks slightly nervous. Surprised.

"I look forward to seeing it completed."

He bows and turns. Ben is suddenly overcome with the sensation that the police will come. He repeats his phone number and address carefully in his head. Genevieve calls after the man.

"But it is. It is done."

The man stops and pauses before turning around. He looks at the children and slowly removes his hat. A long strip of gray wires spring up out of his head and point away from the bay. He takes a step towards them and stops.

"Okay. You're done then. It's a terrific map."

Genevieve walks up to him before he can turn to go.

"No, it's not. It's not done. Is it?"

The man looks down at the girl. His eyes are wide. She has caught him at something.

"Why isn't it done?"

For a moment she thinks the man is going to cry, but breathes deep, accepting a responsibility, and leans in close to speak. There's something too grown up about him now. Genevieve regrets her question.

"If your map is complete you must include the rabbit place behind the community center."

Genevieve blinks and looks down at her map. *Rabbit place*?

"When we were kids the family raised rabbits there. It's right there."

His finger stabs at the map. Genevieve looks back to check for Ben. He hasn't moved.

"Why should we? What's weird about that place?"

"Evil. Your map is the evil tour. This place is."

"Is what?"

"Is evil."

The man scans the street around him and looks out into the bay.

"Just don't go there. Just put it on your map."

"I WILL go there."

"I said don't. You listen to me."

"Then tell me what's there."

The man might yell. He's drawing himself up to yell.

"Please, Mister."

His shoulders fall in as if something substantial has just escaped from him. He pushes his mouth hard into the back of his hand then speaks in a long single breath.

"I didn't see it well myself. But there's a head on the couch at the top of the stairs."

He glares wanting this to sink in. Genevieve takes a step back.

"There's a what on a what?

"A head on a couch. I saw it from half way up the stairs, and that day, three of my friends who did get to the top never came back down."

"What happened?"

"I ran away before I could see. They were missing from that moment on. Other kids too. That summer and the next."

Ben is now beside Genevieve. He asks her instead of the man.

"What kind of head?"

The man closes his eyes tightly.

"An old woman's head, I think. There was no body."

Again to his sister.

"Was she dead?"

"Actually, no. She wasn't. It was yelling at us from the couch."

The man takes a deep shivery breath, wipes his face then stands straight. He is looking down now and Genevieve can tell that he's finished playing this game, whatever it is.

"And so, I told you and that's that. Put it in your map or don't."

Genevieve feels sharply that there is real meanness in this story. She knows that when strangers try to scare children very bad things are involved.

Genevieve and Ben watch the man walking quickly down the hill to the long road that rolls over farmland to Stayner.

From that moment on Genevieve stopped hiding the map. She wasn't sure what had happened to it but was aware that it had lost something. It had lost its pull. It was something that adults do. They have no sense of proportion, of size. It wasn't that he was trying to lure the children into a derelict building; to Genevieve, that was garden variety grown-up shenanigans and not her problem. Her problem was that the map had been deformed. An old woman's head on a couch that somehow removed children from the world—this is more than just a lie. It forced everything else on the map to be true and she wasn't sure, now that the map had lost its voice, that these things were true. The half baby growing inside the mother. The cherry tree tearing out the lady's heart. None of it stays together if it isn't said in a certain way by certain people at a certain time. Genevieve pictures the whale smiling as it rests on the water by the Italian toe. It is its second nature that is sunny and insane and probably twenty miles long.

Genevieve and Ben play in the park until lunchtime. They don't speak of the map again. They pretend they are apes for a while, then they walk on the moon and then, and she doesn't know how or why, they pretend to steal straw from the baby

Jesus' manger. At home Genevieve lays the map on the counter for her mom to find. It will end up on the fridge beside drawings of her stick family beneath the sun.

Ben scoops up his tomato soup in a spoon too big for his mouth. Genevieve thinks he's no smarter than a dog. She blows on her soup until it cools then pushes it away.

"I'm going to my room."

Ben turns his heavy spoon and the rash colored soup drops to the table. He is a puppy standing in its water dish. Genevieve leaves him.

She lies on her bed for an hour looking up at the glow in the dark stars on her ceiling. The room is sunny so the stars are taking light and not giving it. In time she becomes aware of an odd sensation. A shift in the sunlight. A cloud probably passed over the sun, but it triggers a mild panic in her. Genevieve sits up on the edge of her bed. Her shadow waves across the floor as if time has sped up. Something is wrong.

The map is gone. Genevieve slaps her hand on the counter where she left it.

"Ben?"

She calls from the middle of the room.

"Ben?"

From the middle of the house.

"Ben?"

From the middle of the yard.

"Ben!"

The top of the street.

"Ben!"

Oh no he didn't. He didn't. He didn't.

Genevieve dashes to the end of Erie Street and runs through the intersection below the community hall. Gravel trucks and seagulls shred the sky around her. A row of rusted barrels hold back the cherry trees in the alley. A bath tub sits on bare dirt. A Christmas decoration. Rudolph. Santa.

The house is a frightening face, dark and grinning, but Genevieve doesn't notice this as she leaps across the porch and trips through the screen door.

"Ben!"

A stove in the middle of the sitting room to the right.

"Ben!"

A pigeon in the kitchen. A pigeon!

"Ben!"

Genevieve stands at the bottom of the stairs. She can't see the top but knows this is where it happens. Each step is bowed and worn smooth as a shin. Halfway up she can see the top of the couch. Then the arm rests. It sits against the wall below a painting of a boathouse. The cushions are heavy and settled deep and empty. No old lady's head. No head.

"Ben!"

Genevieve stands for a moment listening to silence and leaning in the mote pricked sunlight at the top of the stairs.

"Help."

Ben. Downstairs. Genevieve makes it half way down and stops. It is here. A head hovers eight feet in the air.

"Help."

A head without a body. An old woman's head. Her eyes are looking and the lips are moving.

Genevieve folds her hands over her head as she runs beneath it. A blood dancing scream rips through the air as she runs. She is screaming. Ben is screaming. The head is screaming.

She skids across the ground. Nothing can stop her. She is fleeing death. A monster is screaming at her.

At the end of the alley she tries to stop. But she is too late and she slams into the side of a pale blue pram and tumbles through its upended wheels. A gravel truck grinds its breaks into the clouds and a long white pupa unravels under Genevieve. The baby's face is twisted in a cry and it is rust and yellow with spidery veins breaking on its cheeks. The baby throws a small hand up that falls off. Dung bones separate from dung flesh as a thousand curls of fetid air become unbreathable clumps of light.

Tony Burgess is the author of several book-length fictions. He is also a frequent contributor of short fiction to periodicals, magazines, and anthologies. He recently adapted his novel *Pontypool Changes Everything* into a radio play for the CBC and a feature film, directed by Bruce McDonald. Tony lives in Stayner, Ontario, with his wife, Rachel, and their children, Griffin and Camille. Griffin supplied the title "Giant Scorpions Attack."

The Director's Cut

Susan Forest

Night pooled on the bed in a tangle of starlight and shadow and Lasha cried out, "Is he coming? Jim, is he—"

"Who? Is who coming?"

"Is he—"

I fumbled for my glasses. My good ones, the horn rims, were gone from the nightstand. I pulled the wire-rims with the cracked left lens from the drawer.

"I can't get out!"

"Hush—" I worried away at the sheets until Lasha slid free. She trembled, damp in the heat, lingering in some other world, and I gathered her into my arms as if she were a child and vulnerable. As if I were the strong one. "Shhh. Tell me."

She folded her angles into me in unfamiliar softness. "There was—a jacket. Made of every fabric—cotton and taffeta and acetate and burlap—hand-sewn with the tiniest stitches. White, all white." She huddled in my arms. "It was too tight. It—it frightened me."

"You came to bed late." I toyed with a strand of her hair, a curl of crimson that tickled and teased my arm. "You were playing at divination. Your dreams are full of fancy." Her image, split by the crack in my left lens, overlapped with her solid image in my right.

"And the sleeves." Her hair tumbled forward as she rested her head on my shoulder. "Crocheted like a spider web, all sticky paths looping back on one another. But long, too long."

"It's the reefer," I soothed. "Come. Sleep."

But she would not sleep. "It closed with big, square buttons of horn and ivory. And the lining was pure silk, Jim. Nothing softer." Lasha stretched and wrapped her legs around my waist. "And for standing up to ruthless Suits, nothing harder. Bullet-proof at close range."

"It's the wine and the tarot, Lasha. Come. I'll hold you. Sleep." Dusk and night trifled with star shimmer, played across the pillows, a wreath of fog. And in the center of the black and gray, Lasha lay back on the bed, her red hair cascading like blood over the rumpled duvet, her arms reaching out.

"It was a gift." A tiny wrinkle appeared between her brows and for an instant she became the Lasha I knew, assured and determined. "From you."

"It's the heat."

Starlight fell on her hair and bare shoulder, but shadows clung to her face and neck and breasts. She wore an old muscle shirt from somewhere, not mine, that clung to her bony frame. She peered at me from beneath heavy lids. "You never fuck me."

"No, Lasha."

"But what if I wanted it?"

"That's not what we do."

The frost light of summer stars stole across her shoulders. "What would you do if I left you?"

"You're free, Lasha. No one can hold down Lightning."

She stretched her arms restlessly over the edge of the bed and her agitation crept between us. "I'm still trapped here. Why, I wonder?"

"You love the business."

"The business is out there," she argued. "Hollywood."

"You used to think our work was better than that."

She lowered her lashes, peering at me through them, inscrutable.

I softened my voice with temptation. "We film Ophelia tomorrow."

She shifted, floating on some other sea, focusing on nothing. "You didn't stay for the Ouija."

"Ophelia needs to be buried. I had a grave to dig."

But her spirit had drifted beyond reach, moved on, leaving me trapped in a web of words unsaid.

"The jacket." She whispered, as if to the stars beyond the skylight. "In my dream. It had a small stain."

"Hush." I lay at her side, draped an arm across her stomach. "The tarot's tangled your imagination."

"A blood stain."

A zephyr lifted the gossamer over the window; touched my neck and a shiver scuttled over my skin. "You've been reading Washington Irving." I diverted, distracted, but sleep was banished now from our bed.

"A devil's blemish."

"You're still high, Lasha. Come. Sleep."

"Do you know what his price is?"

"Too high. Go to sleep."

She nestled into me in the tangle of damp sheets, seeing some dark and distant place within her thoughts. "The collar. The collar I couldn't see. I could feel it, though. Soft. Oh, so soft, like fur. Like long, luxurious fur." She tucked herself into me. "I wanted that jacket, Jim, even though it choked me."

"It was only a dream."

She twisted the covers into a chaste cocoon. "They say..." She yawned, a cat; lazy, eyes closed. "You can call the devil with the Ouija."

⸻

We made movies in those days. Lasha did everything. She woke at dawn, made lists and organized, calling people, always calling people. We lived upstairs, she and I, intimate as lovers, celibate as eunuchs, in the warehouse where the filming was done, where the fantasies played out. I did nothing but what Lasha told me to do, which was everything. I went for coffee. Answered emails. Painted sets, hung lights, sewed costumes, picked up.

Mostly, I dressed Lasha. I made her clothes. I styled her hair. Lasha had wonderful hair then, long and kinky and willfully wild. I lived to touch it, smell it, adorn it. I was the only one to work with her hair. She didn't want the natural look. No, the red was a dye, a lie, different with every mood. "Put more orange in it," she'd say. "Streaks along the top." Then she'd lay all the way back in the barber's chair and give herself up completely to me. "More burgundy. More *red*."

Then she would be gone.

Doing things, being with people. Because people were what Lasha was all about. Actors, designers, musicians. Long-haired technicians in ripped jeans with wrenches in their pockets climbing ladders to tighten the nuts on big tin-can lights. Makeup artists smoking Camels in back rooms, swathed in chenille and rehearsal socks. Government arts funders with pale fingers and obscure forms, rigid with ass-tight loopholes. And executive producers who didn't really matter, because Lasha was in charge. She fought for every scrap of film that ever came out under her name. A bullet-proof vest might have helped her to bear the world.

We existed in perpetual deep night, and brilliant day. Lights seared the stage so it became a desert, barren and dry. They broiled the actors, who walked through *The Sandbox* and *Waiting for Godot* and *No Exit*. But in the cool dark, behind the sandbags and dollies, behind the folding chairs and empty beer cans, there was a richness, of furtive movement and silent cues, the smell of greasepaint and spirit gum. Costumes fluttered on racks, cigarettes glowed in ballet hands. Paper cups emoted on overturned oilcan coffee tables, and ropy wires slithered across the floor or hung like vines from impossibly high catwalks.

Lasha's life was a spotlight. Intense. Hot. Forever struggling to spill beyond the black box eclipsing her. But, as her movies leaked into the world, cracks appeared in our warehouse, admitting strangers and fear. We saw how they knocked at the doors, and we huddled inside, in curiosity and despair, she and I.

When the work was done, and it was never done, the play began, which never stopped. The actors came off stage and into the fantasy to smoke and strip out of costume and gossip. The lights dimmed then, and candles appeared, and the bottles and joints, and the Ouija and tarot. Hands, gracefully dancing in smoky glow, gestured, illustrated, slowed. Tongues loosened and names dropped, and grand ambitions flowed. They'd trade their souls for a chance at Hollywood. And it was Lasha who summoned the séance.

Other things happened, too; secretive things, in dark corners. Love-making in broom closets or overstuffed couches or deserted kitchen tables on top of the silverware and grapes, beating the table, moaning, crying.

I watched her.

From the space between the counter and the window, beneath the hanging pots, bypassed by moonlight and candle-light, I watched her jerk to the rhythm of a faceless stunt man. She watched back, eyes on mine, fever bright. Lightning current pulsed in the space between us, sharpening, demanding, insisting, until we quivered and throbbed and burst.

A small director arrived one morning, with a Gordian script, towing an actor with a name. Through my binoculars I saw them, standing in the oversized barn doors, silhouetted, black against brilliant day. The director strutted onto our mock wooden "O" to the gravedigger's pit where I dressed the set, and I let the binoculars fall back on their lanyard. House lights at half power glinted from his sunglasses.

"They say I need Lasha," his words shackled, coerced, colluded. "Or she needs me."

"We're in the middle of *Hamlet*. We don't need you."

"'Course you do, baby." His smile was a fisherman's, eyeing a fat sturgeon, calculating strategy and the worth of my atheist soul. "Or you *will*." He passed his hand through the air as if drawing a curtain, and in that instant the world faded to grays and murmurs. Only the small, dark man and I existed, facing one another at opposite ends of conduit, black as Hell. Nauseous memories of my uncle in the night crawled out of my skin.

"Now, where can I find the little producer? I have a piece for her. Candy."

He wanted Lasha?

"Lasha, that's right." He spoke as if we had known each other for years. As if I'd asked the question aloud.

Clammy fingers like past shame slid down my groin.

"You know who I am."

My stomach heaved.

"Now. Lasha summoned me." He produced the Tower of the Major Arcana by way of evidence. "And I have a gift for her. Or, shall we say, a trade."

Lasha summoned him? For God's sake, why?

"Why? Trapped, isn't that what she said? Can't get out?"

"We don't want you. We—" The words blistered my lips.

"We?" His voice flowed around me, soothing, explaining; intimate as unwanted touch. "You can't hold quicksilver, Jim. It's like a film. You create an artifact to play over and over until the pictures fade to nothing. But that moment between the actors? It's gone. You should know that, baby." His grip lessened. "You might see things more clearly if your lens wasn't cracked."

I swallowed, massaged my throat, tried to breathe.

"But I can help you, even to capture mercury. Bring me something of hers." He smiled, soft pink lips peeking from his black goatee. "When you're ready."

The best boy slumped by and noticed the newcomers. "Need a hand?"

"Two. Clever ones." The small man laughed, a pitch too high. His gaze shifted from me, and I fell from the nightmare as Lasha had, panting and chilled with sweat. "She wants more, Jim." His whisper rattled in my thoughts.

"Lasha!" The boy hoisted electrical cable over his shoulder and slouched off toward her office.

I stumbled to the shower to scrub myself clean.

When she saw the actor, Lasha's eyes grew large and dark. She wore her wild curls coiled on top of her head then, and sported fake glasses and a clip board; but she wrapped *Hamlet* and scheduled the new script for the following week. Funding was in place, so sets were designed and built. Pyrotechnics and mirrors appeared, thespians rehearsed and mimes mimed. Lasha's laugh became softer for the actor, and she tossed her head more. She sprinkled herself near him, a glitter of sunlight on wet fur, and the heat of her smile left me.

"Jim, get Colin a coffee."

"Jim, run to the store for cigarettes."

"Jim, run the bath."

The shower sprayed a glittering mist before a scrim of night, fogging my glasses. The tub, high porcelain sides and rolled top, perched on claw feet. Hairs like fine lines lifted from the surface to bob on the rising water, a film of grit and soap scum.

Lasha glistened like a seal, climbing out, all sheen, lampside, and shadow, my side. She toweled away the film until the tiny hairs stood out from her skin, haloed in light. She spritzed spray and gathered chiffon.

I coiled cable in the bedroom. Tonight she would star for me on the silverware and grapes and I didn't care if it was with the big name actor. Tonight we, Lasha and I, would quiver and throb and burst.

She stepped out of the spot, silhouette against white-lit mist, her eyes picking me out of the dark. "Colin is taking me to Hollywood."

The cables tangled about my feet.

"He has a part for me in *The American Dream*."

Her words, a hammer. "You're not an actress."

"I could be." She adjusted the sash restraining the springy coils on her head.

"You never wanted to be an actress."

"I could act. I could write, do props. It's a foot in the door. An exit."

"You could never do props. You'd go out of your mind—"

"I'm obscured here, Jim!"

"Obscured?" I wiped the mist from my glasses but beads of moisture wept from them, blurring her.

"Shadowed. Occulted. Overcast."

Hollywood. And what would remain? Sound stage without sound? Camera without lens? Moth without flame?

She slid into the barber's chair, bright-lit by bare bulbs. When Lasha decided a thing, it was done.

"Well, then." Damn her. Damn him.

"You understand."

"I don't, no." Panic fingered my gut and I dropped the cables.

"Jim. No hysterics." Cool. Cold, even. Changed.

Words blanched from my tongue. I loosed the red silk tie that bound her mane and buried my hands in the masses of kinky hair, soothing my panic, finding release.

I had to keep her.

"You'll get along. You always were the strong one."

"No. No, not me." I tilted the chair back and wound the sash around my hands. I laid the silky red across her throat, a gash. "All that hair has to go."

"You think?"

"Definitely." I tilted my head so her neck appeared broken, refracted in my left lens. My fingers trembled on the sash in a fantasy of indecision. I tugged, and it slithered into my hands.

"Eye-catching, then. I have to be noticed."

"Cut. Short." I used the sash to tie her wrists to the arms of the chair. "Smooth on top and spiked at the back." The shears lay before the mirror, glinting, brilliant, honed.

"But still red; red, and orange and burgundy."

"Crimson."

Lasha lay back, eyes closed, tendrils falling from forehead to floor. Her throat gleamed, white in the brilliant light, naked to her breasts. "Asymmetrical," she said. "You have to be unique in Hollywood."

I opened the scissors, gripped a blade against its handle and felt the edge bite my palm. Razor pain to relieve anguish. I knelt beside her. Pain. That was what was needed.

Her hair smelled of violets.

The open blade pressed into the flesh of her neck and the soft skin yielded. My eyes stung. "This short?"

"Do it." Her voice was low, seductive. "Here, on the barber chair."

A drop of blood wrung from my hand appeared on her chest. She arched her back, pressing herself into my wrist and the red trickle snaked between her breasts. She turned to look at me, twisting her neck into the blade. Eyes, black, all pupil. Lashes inked with kohl and mascara, lips ruby, a blurring together of Lasha and remembrance of Lasha.

Leaving.

A half-moan slithered from my throat and I had to push myself with a force of will to stand astride her, hard up against her hips. She lay in the chair, bound, unresisting.

"Fuck me."

And would she stay, if I did? Renege on her contract with the director?

"Do it to me, Jim."

I drew the point of the shears down her chest, tracing the red line.

Her back lifted, nipples erect. "Once. Before Hollywood."

I leaned over her, took the rope of her hair, my creation, and pulled her head hard against the head rest. In one shear, I snipped the strands from their roots. "This short?" I backed from her, arms upraised, trophy in one hand, bloody scissors in the other.

"Do it!"

"On the silverware and grapes? Like the stunt man?" The scissors clattered to the floor.

"Why won't you fuck me?"

I clamped her severed mane in a clip. "On the catwalk stairs, like a gaffer?"

"Jim!"

I traced a stain of crimson down her torso with my slashed hand. "On the bar from Virginia Woolf, like a patron?"

"Finish it!"

"And spoil what's special between us?"

She tugged at the sash at her wrists.

I knelt beside the barber chair and the down of her shoulder brushed my cheek. "This is not goodbye." I clipped the letter "A" into the scalp above her ear. "Asymmetrical," I whispered, and left to clean the blood from my hands.

But in the studio below, the sound technician blasted the cast with *In-A-Godda-Da-Vida*. The small director planned his cuts; the actor with the name read blockbuster scripts; the carpenter hung flats; the stage manager counted headsets; the bookkeeper tallied sums; the actors promised undying fealty; the bit players hugged one another; and the best boy lit a joint.

The costume girl looked for Lasha, and finding her, untied the red silk around her wrists.

I hid in the sound booth and beat on the silent glass. Lasha was leaving. I caressed the shank of hair. Lasha was leaving.

In the empty night, Lasha came to where I sat alone on the edge of the unmade bed, her carpetbag in the doorway. She looked at me with pale lamp eyes, bare of kohl and mascara. "I'm going."

"You're stepping under an arc light."

She picked up her shaggy coat woven with wools of llama and goat, with raw fleece and herb-dyed down, and pulled it over one shoulder.

I struggled to cry out, to stop her. As easily try to put the stars out of joint.

She left, and the rooms we'd lived in let out a breath like a spotlight cooling after the spectacle is over and the playgoers have left the theater for another life. Moonlight dripped through the cracks in the skylight, fluorescence dying.

For, what was the warehouse without her? What was the soundstage, the paint cans, the dimmers, the front office, without her? What was the moonlight without her?

What was I without her?

I picked up used paper cups.

The shadows followed me.

I dusted the prop shelf.

The candles flickered and went out as I passed.

I stacked brooms in the closet.

The warehouse sighed.

And, so, now in this hour before dawn, when all secrets are kept and revealed, I climbed the ladder to the catwalk, knowing where to go as certainly as I knew the ending of *Hamlet*. Up, to the rafters, to deliver the mane of hair.

The small director waited. "As I said." My horn rims peeked from his breast pocket.

"You need a hand. I heard."

"Two. Clever ones. Good with scissors."

I held out my arms. He took my hands and turned them over. "One is damaged."

"It works."

He shrugged. "Very well." He squeezed. "For my collection."

My hands vanished. Shocks seared my forearms, pierced to my shoulders and shot down my back. I fell gasping to my knees.

"The pain won't lessen, but you'll get used to it." He reached into a pool of shadow, produced a box and laid it before me. "I keep my promises, if not my word."

I gathered the smooth, white cardboard, whispering and heavy, into my arms. My gift for Lasha.

"Pity." The voice whispered in the air around me, or in my mind, but the director had vanished along with my hands.

I brought the box, in arms that ended in jagged, wrinkled scars, to the ghost-gray light that fell onto the center of our bed. I nudged the unruly sheets away and sat at the edge of the halo to slide the lid back.

I poked the white jacket from the tissue and spread it across the bed. Hand stitched. My hands. It glowed in the moonlight, silky threads winding their way across the sheen. I touched the ivory buttons, my buttons, and ran my stump across the lining, downy as a baby's velvet crown. I crushed my face into the collar, soft with the curls of red I had stolen. I breathed in Lasha's scent, after the lovemaking, after the wine, after the cigarettes, when her eyes were black and wet, and she was yielding and mine.

And so. She returned to me.

A step on the floor, the perfume of her breath on my neck, her hand on my shoulder. I felt the bedsprings creak; she pressed her body into mine.

"What did you give him, Lasha? For Hollywood?"

But I knew the answer. "Love." She blinked and turned to me with the expression of one who fought her way up from the depths of a dream. "I gave up you, Jim."

I smiled. Because she hadn't given up love at all. She was back. I turned and gave her the jacket. Drew it around her shoulders and crossed the long sleeves over her waist and fastened them behind her back.

Her eyes were bright and distant, lingering for one wistful, uncomprehending moment on the skylight, then gone again to another plane. I didn't mind. We all had a price to pay. The padded shoulders looked fine on her. She needed them to bear the world.

Susan J. Forest is a member of the Science Fiction Writers of America. She was a finalist for the 2008 the Prix Aurora Award in the Short Fiction category for "Back," (*Analog*). Recent sales include, "Paid in Full" and "Immunity" (*Asimov's*) and "The Right Chemistry" (*On Spec*). Other stories have been published in *On Spec*, *Tesseracts 10* and *11*. Her YA novel, *The Dragon Prince*, was awarded the Children's Circle Book Choice Award.

Rocketship Red

Michael R. Colangelo

Eagan runs through a field of wheat. A long string tied at his wrist traces away from him and vanishes into the sky, ending in a bright red kite.

He often daydreams that he's up there, that his kite is not made of fabric and bound together with vinyl twine. It is, in fact, a bright red rocket made of steel and he's not Eagan the sixth of eleven farming children. He's Captain Eagan, an American rocket pilot.

But then Mother calls him for dinner off the back porch of the farmhouse. They're having soy again. Her shrill call distracts him and the kite loses its jet stream.

It falls to the dirt and he hurries inside. They're a soy farm. He's always eating soy.

There are men from the city that drive out to Eagan's farm to buy soy from them. Two of these men are from the United States Air Force. They're interested in supplying soy-based food products for their boys and their colonization efforts in space.

One of the men, Captain Campbell, is unfriendly with Eagan. But the other, Captain Sampson, is tremendously pleased to talk with him about joining the Air Force.

Captain Sampson used to fly a rocket in space, but now he works behind a desk. He laughs off the blood pressure cuff that he wears beneath the sleeve of his uniform and his ever-shaking hands.

He's handsome enough to be in the movies, which is why they use him in the commercials. He tells Eagan to look him up in the city once he turns seventeen. That's the age that boys can go to rocket flying school.

Eagan solemnly promises Captain Sampson that he will.

⇒⊶⟨⟨ ᷡ — ᷡ ⟩⟩⊷⇐

When he does turn seventeen, he hasn't forgotten the conversation. There's some static from his family about his decision. His Dad doesn't understand. He is, after all, a proud soy farmer. The farm is doing very well. There's plenty of work and money to go around for Eagan and all of his siblings.

Still, Eagan persists, and his father finally lets it go. There's a small sliver of pride in his voice when he tells the boys down at the Legion Hall where his sixth boy plans on going.

⇒⊶⟨⟨ ᷡ — ᷡ ⟩⟩⊷⇐

Captain Sampson is true to his word. Soon, Eagan finds himself set up in the dormitories at the Flight Academy.

The school is exciting, the city is exciting, and the eclectic mix of people he meets is exciting too.

One month stretches into six months, and one year stretches into four years. Eagan graduates with good enough scores to become a genuine rocket pilot. It's the best year of his life.

There is some sadness to his victory, though. Captain Sampson's ailments finally catch up to him and he dies shortly after Eagan graduates. Still, the loss of the man who helped him realize his dreams only galvanizes his resolve to succeed.

He's stationed on the moon at the Bravo moon base. There, he continues his training while waiting for deployment to further away outstations.

⇒⊶⟨⟨ ᷡ — ᷡ ⟩⟩⊷⇐

Space exploration and expansion is great for the human race, up to a point. They colonize asteroids and build orbital structures and mine for important metals and fuels and other key commodities. Things are easy for a very long time.

Things are what Captain Sampson might have called "swell".

But like all things, man's luck and good fortune comes to an end. At the dark corners of the universe, they start looking to cultivate the antimatter that flows into a temporal rift created at the end of the universe.

They find it out in the fringes, but they also discover something else. It's sentient and hostile and so alien in nature, that they can't classify it properly under their current scientific guidelines.

⇒⊶⟨⟨ ᷡ — ᷡ ⟩⟩⊷⇐

Men die along the outskirts of the rift. They die screaming into Eagan's communication module. He can hear the fate that awaits him.

Sometimes their rockets return to base on autopilot with the men inside them destroyed from the mind outward, like microwaved eggs. These men have sensed whatever lurks in the rift. The impossibility of it, so far from human comprehension, has destroyed them.

The antimatter farming projects are put on hold and new initiatives are defined. Now, they are more interested in what it is that lives in the dark zones at the edge of the world.

Comparisons in the newspapers are made to the old New World explorations.

Everybody worries about sailing off the edge of the world.

To combat the madness-inducing effects of the rift, all pilots are required to sign up for mind-strengthening exercises. This involves pushing colored blocks of wood around on a piece of linoleum floor mat.

⊷⊶⟵ ⊰ ⸺ ⊱ ⟶⊷⊶

Eagan discovers it for himself one day while engaging in a solo exercise along the border of the rift.

Because there are new initiatives, he has been forced to learn new flight paths. Everything is routine until it isn't anymore.

There's a sudden burst of static over the communications module, and then Captain Sampson's voice comes through loud and clear over the headset.

The voice tells him what he needs to do next.

⊷⊶⟵ ⊰ ⸺ ⊱ ⟶⊷⊶

It is nothing at all like flying a kite.

Michael R. Colangelo is a writer from Toronto.

Soil From My Fingers

L. L. Hannett

I could convince falconers to trade six hawks for two of my hens. I could navigate borderlands without steering the caravan into Meito ghost fields. I could ford winter rivers, violent with fast-moving ice, without losing any of my stock. If duty called I could lead the Pasha's warriors into battle, and guide most of them back out again. My clan was ten wagons strong; my brothers' sons would add three more to that count before we set out on our next traveling days. Some believed I could make dead vines bear fruit or teach lame goats to walk, if only I wielded the right tools. Had the right ingredients. Spoke the right words. These things I could do and more. But it all meant nothing if no one remembered me, if I couldn't give my wife a child.

It wasn't for lack of trying. When we were first married, mystery and excitement drove me to Astrith's wagon every night. I'd walk past the campfires above which spitted hares roasted, ignoring the rumble in my belly in favor of a lower hunger, earning smiles from my cousins and brothers. It was bad luck for husbands to live with their brides until after a first child was born; skittish young ghosts shy away from wombs when men are forever booming into them. I was determined to get Astrith with child, so we could start our life together. Properly. Without risking barrenness, or worse, being cursed with the unnatural offspring breaking this taboo would bring.

Astrith's laugh gave me shivers, her touch was assured, her embrace was open and warm. I couldn't wait to join her in bed each night, to renew our efforts at giving our House an heir. The clanwives would serenade me with a chorus of luck-giving whistles as I stepped out of the flickering light into evening's deepening shadows; more often than not, my mother would give me a skin of fermented mare's milk to bring as a gift. Thus armed, my hands and face and cock scrubbed clean, I would knock on the fresh green paint of my wife's door, and wait for her to invite me in.

Deep yellow candle glow spilled down the wooden steps leading up to her caravan when she opened the door that first night. Astrith had been beautiful then. Her fair skin was made tawny in the ambient light, her black hair unplaited, her blouse unlaced and revealing. I nearly dropped the skin of milk when I saw her. Nearly tumbled back down the stairs and into the familiar sounds of falling night: cook pots clinking on heated stones, knives being honed by the fireside, axes splitting enough logs to keep darkness at bay, stories being told in murmurs. Closing the door, I'd turned to Astrith and blamed my clumsiness on the green-eyed cat winding itself around my ankles. I'd had a reputation among traders and warriors to uphold. Never let it be said that Tomaken is a stumbler.

Astrith had laughed at my excuses; a resonant, healthy sound. She'd bent down and shooed Sorokin, her favorite cat, away from my feet. While she was down there, she'd made quick work of my pants' drawstring. Within moments, I was praying to the Meitoshi, thanking them for blessing me with such joy.

⟿⟸⟼ — ⟻⟾⟾

My knuckles were stained green from three years of nightly knockings. One thousand nights joining my wife, observed by her broods of kittens; one thousand days of tears marking Astrith's wan features, and mine, as the cradle I'd built remained empty. She continued to welcome me, with arms and legs and heart; but after she'd twice expelled the bloody husk of a baby long before it was due in this world, Astrith's enthusiasm for my affections grew thin.

"Keep trying", my mother said, her breath visible in the late winter air. She took my hands, gave me a milk-skin kept warm by the fire. I placed it beneath my thick woolen vest; its heat did little to thaw the block of ice in my chest. "The moon is waxing, the stars are spinning. The time for growth and change is at hand." When she patted my cheek, her hand was shaky. The whistle she sounded as I shuffled to Astrith's wagon was more than a little forced.

My wife was sitting at the small fold-out table in the caravan's far end, next to a potbellied stove that exuded more heat than was needed for such a small space. Her doeskin mantle was bundled in her lap, wrapped around something I couldn't quite see. *Not the baby*, I prayed, when I noticed Astrith's eyes were red from crying. Six months she had kept this one; I dreaded seeing the infant's lifeless form, shrivelled in her lap. But there was no blood-stained nightdress, the woven floor-coverings hadn't been rolled back to expose scrubbable boards, the tin chamber pot was still empty and tucked away in a corner. I held the door open, thinking Sorokin would want to escape the stifling heat—she had grown to be an outside cat, one who preferred being cold. When she didn't appear, I closed the door and took a few halting steps toward my wife.

"I've looked everywhere," she said, staring down at the mewling, writhing mass in her arms. "Beneath the mattress, in all the cupboards, behind curtains. In the footlocker, the undercarriage, in the crawlspace above the bed. I even pried slats away from the walls" —I saw two wooden boards, leaning next to Astrith's horse-head fiddle— " but I couldn't find it anywhere."

"Couldn't find what, Breath of My Heart?"

Dark circles ringed her eyes, and her voice broke when she said, "The curse against mothers that plagues this house. There must be a hidden fetish, a poisoned charm in these walls. How will I carry this child to term when even poor Sorokin has been taken from me?"

My heartbeat quickened. I loosened Astrith's grip on the cloak, pulled its covering folds away, revealed Sorokin's still form. Six naked kittens squirmed at their mother's cold teats, blinking blindly and struggling for supremacy. The two smallest ones looked like they wouldn't endure the next five minutes; the four others weren't faring much better.

"Only one need survive," I said, plucking the strongest kitten from the litter, shifting the rest to the floor. I whispered life-giving words, pierced a small hole in the milk-skin with my teeth, then pressed the charmed liquid to the creature's mouth. She snuffled and gulped greedily.

"We'll defy this curse as a family. You and me, and Katla here." Astrith smiled at the name. "The moon has changed for us three, My Breath. You'll see."

—◆◁◦——◦▷◆—

The baby seemed reluctant to join us. Our clan had journeyed throughout the traveling days: we'd crossed the heart of the grasslands; we'd scaled the steppes (avoiding the bandits that roamed those lands); and our path had reached the wooded foothills surrounding Zhureem Ordon, the Pasha's mountain-top fortress, when my daughter declared she was ready to be born.

She was more than two weeks late; Astrith's confinement was long and painful. The midwives earned their keep all day— their cheeks grew ruddy, their summer tunics stained with sweat, as they ran to and from the river carrying canteens of water for boiling or for rinsing blood-soaked rags. They wouldn't cut the child from her mother's womb, no matter how badly it pained them to see Astrith struggle: to remove a creature thus would deem it unborn. The ancestors would keep its spirit, leaving only the shell of an infant behind. It would be better for mother and child to die than to bring such an abomination into the world. Our clan prided itself on its band of heirs; we had yet to lose any of our offspring to the ghost fields. With the Meitoshi behind me, we wouldn't start with my child.

I remained at our camp while my men went hunting in the forest. They nodded their approval when I volunteered to tend the horses, beasts renowned for their wiliness, before they disappeared into the trees. For hours I dug post-holes for the animals' temporary pens in the clearing opposite our wagons and tents. I could hear Astrith's cries even there. They'd started off strong, but had grown weaker and weaker until my spade, ringing against rocky soil, drowned them out.

The sun had passed her torch to night's guardian before Chinta, the eldest midwife, came to collect me. She placed her wizened hand on my shoulder, not flinching at the filth and sweat she found there, and whispered, "It's time for you to come."

Her expression was unreadable. I dropped the spade, grabbed my sheepskin jerkin, and followed Chinta to Astrith's caravan. The camp was quiet. The men were only now starting to return from their hunt; the women hovered in hushed circles near my wife's dwelling, waiting for news of the birth. The crunch of my boots on brittle grass echoed in my ears, the beads dangling from my long black braid clicked together with each step I took. Chinta left me at the stairs, her head bowed. I'm sure I heard voices rise in speculation as soon as the door snicked shut behind me.

Astrith sat up in bed, nestled beneath a mound of quilts and furs. Wet tendrils of hair clung to her cheeks, which were the grayish white of old teeth and dewy from her labor. Her head was propped up against stained pillows; her eyes were open but moved sleepily as I approached. Two large bowls filled with crimson water had been abandoned at the foot of her bed. In her arms a bundle, not unlike the one she'd held three months earlier.

"We've a beautiful girl," my wife said. A smile wavered at the edges of her lips.

"A girl," I breathed. I perched on the edge of the mattress, trying to disturb my girls as little as possible. "A daughter." Astrith's nod was barely perceptible. "May I?" I asked, then scooped the bundle into my arms before my wife had a chance to respond.

The baby was much smaller than I'd expected. Her skin was also bluer than seemed normal. She was so tightly swaddled all that was visible was her head, which was topped with a shock of black fuzz. Full lips, tiny nose, two delicate ears, two puffy eyes. Each feature appeared in its proper place. Her eyes were closed for the most part, but she'd peeked at me long enough to show off the deep brown of her irises. Flecked with gold, just like my mother's. "She's stunning," I whispered.

Katla wound through my legs, just like Sorokin used to, and meowed to get my attention. "Look, Katla," I said, crouching down to the cat. "A perfect little sister for you." But I felt uneasy as I said it. The cat recoiled at the sight of my daughter; she swatted at the baby with claws extended. The girl didn't react in the slightest. Her breathing shallowed.

"Something's wrong," I said to Astrith. "This infant is too cold."

Tears spilled over my wife's pale cheeks, but she remained silent.

"We must get the midwives, get them back here to fix her—"

Astrith shook her head. "They know she's not right, Tomaken. Why else would they have summoned you? You know a husband doesn't see his child until it's been named."

I'd forgotten, in my excitement.

"You are here to say goodbye, nothing more," she said.

"No," I replied. "No," as the baby grew still. "Nothing's wrong with her, Breath of My Heart. All she needs is to get some fresh air." I chuckled, tried to keep my voice even as I scoured the room for ingredients. "I've told you not to keep your stove so warm," —*there's blood*, grabbing a handful of soaked rags from the bowls— "and in the middle of summer no less,"—*there's hair*, snatching a few inky strands from my wife's bone-handled brush— "but I'm sure you'll learn these things," —*there's dirt aplenty outside*— "when you've had more time as a mother."

All I need now, I thought, *is an appropriate vessel...*

The cat yowled as I stepped on her tail. I smiled, shook my head at her. "Come here, my Katla. We're going for a little walk."

All eyes were averted as I exited the caravan. Yet even a blind man would have seen the burden I carried, would have noticed the speed with which I left the enclosure of our camp. Not many would have paid attention to the cat-shaped flicker of darkness at my heels, or would have thought it unusual if they had. No one stopped me as I blended in with the shadows; it was only fitting I bury the child before its spirit grew too accustomed to the warmth of our homes, the taste of our breath.

And I had every intention of putting my girl in the earth, but none of leaving her there.

First, I took her to the river where the waters thrummed like ancestral voices. I immersed my daughter, ridding all traces of her human birth. Then I gathered my supplies in one arm, the baby and Katla in the other. The cat fought against me until I pinned her to my side, trapped her small head in my large hand; she wailed like a newborn, which I took as a good sign. I hoped the fight would stay in her until it was needed most.

I returned to the site of my afternoon's toils. Without hesitation, I dropped the baby and accompanying magics into the freshly turned earth, which was rich brown and smelled of horse dung. I lifted the cat up, looked her straight in the eyes: they were as vibrant an emerald as her dam's had been. "Thank you, my Katla," I said—and with a silent prayer for the Meito to send a strong spirit, I snapped the cat's neck and buried her in the same pit as my daughter.

I could have left it there, and almost did. One final element was needed, to quicken the spell, but I didn't think I had the will to provide it. *If it took this long to work the proper way*, I thought, *there's no chance it's going to work now.* My mind made up, I turned toward the river, ready to cleanse myself of the night's events. To wash everything away.

I'd gone no more than three steps when a picture of Astrith, exhausted and probably barren, flitted across my mind. It was for her I was doing this. For her, and my heir. I walked back to the mound of tamped dirt, used the spade handle to drill a deep hole in its center. Bile rose in the back of my throat. I took a deep breath, let the chill breeze soothe me. Exhaling, I reminded myself that Tomaken is no stumbler. I knelt, not to bury my girl but to bring her back.

Almost a fortnight had passed since I'd had a night visit with my wife; it wasn't long before my stroking hand coaxed warm spurts of semen onto the earth. There was no pleasure in this act, only need. When my racing pulse slowed, I pulled up my trousers, watched my seed seep into the ground, then cried until my head pounded.

⊶❦⟿ — ❧⟿⊷

Astrith didn't question where I'd found our green-eyed daughter. She didn't mention the filth I'd carried into the room on my boots, merely brushed crumbs of dirt off our wriggling infant as I placed her on the bed. We'd been married long enough now for her to know my secrets. To know what I was capable of doing. I slipped into bed beside her in the gray twilight that masquerades as daybreak, and tucked the girl snugly between us.

"We'll have to give her a name," Astrith said. It was clear from my wife's expression that she was already besotted. "Before we can introduce her to the rest of the clan."

"Her name is Katla," I said. "You'll find she won't answer to anything else."

Astrith looked at me for a moment too long, but didn't say anything. My strong wife, always proving I was lucky to love her. I kissed her full on the lips then, as I hadn't done in weeks. She responded in kind, though we were both so exhausted our mouths soon parted. I ran my finger along her smooth brow, traced the line of her high cheekbones, then cradled her square jaw in my palm. "Get some rest," I said. Her contented smile was a welcome pressure against my hand. "We'll give our Katla the introduction she deserves when the rooster has properly greeted morning."

I looked down at Katla as Astrith slept. The baby was restless, her eyes wide open. She gave off an incredible heat. In my fatigue, I thought I saw her frown as if concentrating. Darkness pooled around her head, making her hair appear longer than it had been when we were outside. The air seemed to shimmer around her; in my mind I chastised my wife for insisting on stoking the fire so fervently. But the coals had been banked hours ago.

Katla's struggles subsided and with them my worries. My head was leaden with weariness, so I laid it on the edge of Astrith's pillow, telling myself I'd hear the cock's crow soon enough. I just needed to rest my eyes.

The sun was well above the horizon, her rusty light streaming through the caravan's west-facing windows, when I was woken by Astrith's insistent shaking. I blinked to clear away the sleep, rolled over to discover that Katla was no longer on the bed beside me.

"What's wrong?" I asked, instantly awake. "What's wrong with the baby?"

Astrith clucked her tongue at me, like a practiced mother already. Her voice wasn't nearly so assured. "Nothing's wrong, Tomaken. Not really. It's just... Do you think it's possible for a child to be *too* healthy?"

As she stepped aside I got a clear view of the cradle. I didn't have to ask what she meant.

Katla was sitting up.

My daughter blinked at me as I met her gaze—her knowing, flashing green gaze. She stretched her mouth wide in a yawn. Her gums, glistening with dribble, were studded with the tips of white teeth.

My stomach clenched as I looked at the child I'd created. Less than a day on this earth, and already more robust than my brother's two-year-old son. I knew the color was draining from my tanned face: I could tell this by the look of fear on my wife's.

"Perhaps it's always this way," I said, sitting up, my mind racing. "Growth-spurts aren't uncommon—"

A knock at the door interrupted my flawed explanations.

"I've brought some dried curds for you, Tomaken." My mother's scratchy voice barely penetrated the wagon's thick paneling. Words must be whispered around a house of the dead, for fear of calling the spirit's attention before it reaches the ghost fields. "And some *bantan* for Astrith, to help her regain her strength." I tapped three times on the wall, a sign of thanks that wouldn't invite further conversation.

I waited until the sound of my mother's shuffling bootsteps had moved beyond earshot before I dared speak again. "Do you think she heard us?"

Astrith ignored the question, silenced me with a sharp gesture. "We mustn't introduce Katla like this."

I got out of bed, paced over to the cradle, took Katla up in my arms. She was heavy, and smelled of sour milk. Her skin was pale to the point of translucence. And she was enchanting, no matter her size.

"But what if she cries?" I asked. "What will we do with the clothes she soils? They'll know she's here eventually, and I'd rather not enrage the ancestors. Not when we've become a real family at last."

My wife, always sensible, shook her head. "The clan won't see her now, not without suspecting—as we do, My Breath—that the Meito are playing tricks with us."

Once again I looked at my daughter, knowing full well it wasn't the guardians who were responsible. Not this time.

"Give me a day to think," I said. I pressed a kiss on my wife's forehead and the child into her arms. "Just keep her quiet until I return."

⌖⌖

I avoided my kin as I left Astrith's caravan. Head down, I skirted the clearing and broke a new path through the forest. Walking would do me good; it clears the mind, gives a man the distance he needs to think. The air was still, pungent with the scent of damp leaves. Fresh, with an undertone of rot. I felt my blood pumping as I blazed the trail, filling me with good energy, releasing the bad. My face, chest, armpits, crotch all grew moist with sweat—still I walked. Over the river, whispering now that it was day; through the copse of silver birch, where I gathered strips of bark for luck; past the sentinel pines whose needles seemed tipped with flames, silhouetted against the setting sun; until the moon had risen high overhead, burnishing leaves and branches and animal eyes with silver.

My pulse throbbed in my ears as I emerged on the other side of the woods. The plains stretched out before me, a vast sea of gray and black. Long blades of sweet-grass undulated in an unfelt wind; the ancestors busily moved from place to place, shifting grasses the only sign of their passing. Hours of walking had taken me far away from my problem, but no closer to a solution. I crouched down, caught my breath, and dug my fingers into the earth.

The grasses waved in a hypnotic rhythm. Night predators rustled in the undergrowth behind me. Clouds streamed past the moon, strobing its soft light. Treetops swayed, shushed. My heartbeat slowed, evened out. Loose soil streamed through my fingers. The night was filled with echoes of the ancestors' busy feet.

I must have dozed, then. A waking sleep in which time passed but I remained frozen, eyes open. A kestrel swooped down before me; the yellow ring around her eyes, the bright cere of her beak, and her dangerous feet were luminous in the waning moonlight. In a flash, she snatched a vole, who had innocently poked his head out of the ground not two feet in front of me. Her shrill cry of triumph shook me out of my stupor, set my heart pounding once more.

As I stood, my joints stiff and aching, my boots covered in dew, I noticed a russet feather sticking up out of the earth where the kestrel had made her kill. Smiling, I plucked it like a flower. The Meito had given me a sign—and signs, unlike the swift growth of cat-infants, could easily be deciphered.

I would consult with Temudzhin, the Meito's interpreter. My smile broadened. Clutching the feather tightly in my fist, I turned back to the woods, my heart and footsteps light.

—◆◄ ⟡ — ⟡ ►◆—

They did not remain so for long.

I arrived back at our encampment by mid-afternoon, only to notice a flattened patch of grass where Temudzhin's wagon and supply tent should have been. My cousin, Chuluun, walked past as I stood gaping at the deep ruts Temudzhin's caravan had left in the ground. Chuluun bowed his head, touched fingers to brow by way of greeting.

"How long has he been gone?" I asked, pointing at the white scattering of Temudzhin's fire, noticing new shoots of grass already sprouting where the tent had been staked. His departure was clearly not recent.

"Four sunrises ago," Chuluun replied. "The Pasha wanted an audience with him before the autumn markets get too hectic." Chuluun looked up at the sky, gauging the sun's path. "If his journey has gone smoothly, he shouldn't be too long in reaching Zhureem Ordon."

I thanked my cousin, then headed for Astrith's wagon. If anything, my heart was heavier now than it had been yesterday. Even if I left right away, I'd never catch Temudzhin before he ascended the Pasha's mountain, before he passed the palace's bronze gates. And if I tried, there was no doubt the clan would discover Katla before my return. They would see what I'd done, and they would banish me for it. It's one thing to heal a wounded yak, to encourage horses to stud or to provide supplies from next to nothing—it was another thing altogether to invite ghosts into our community and to make one my heir.

Astrith opened the caravan's door before my foot had made contact with the bottom step. She looked as frantic as I felt.

"Hurry, Tomaken," she whispered. "Get inside."

Her hands were shaking, but still she closed the door gently to avoid waking the child curled up on our bed. And she was a child now, no longer an infant. One who didn't know better would think she was a girl of four or five years. Her hair was glossy, long and black, just like her namesake's. Astrith had tied it back with red ribbons, as was custom for girls of that age. The tips of the ribbons were frayed and wet; Katla was chewing one in her sleep. She was wrapped in one of my wife's old shifts, which was too big by far. Her pale shoulders and long, sinewy legs were exposed but Katla didn't seem to mind the cold. A soft rumble, like purring, escaped her throat as she exhaled.

"Get rid of it," Astrith snapped. "We can't care for it, Tomaken. I can't."

I looked at my wife, my mouth pressed firmly shut.

"Get rid of it," she repeated.

I breathed out slowly. Closed my eyes. A plan started to form in my mind.

Four days to reach the Pasha's markets. Four days to send a bird ahead, to organize an audience with my lord. Four days for the girl to grow.

I opened my eyes again, and nodded.

⟶⟶❖❖ — ❖❖⟵⟵

No bride would ever be as pure as my Katla. She had never been stained with moon blood; she had hardly yet learned to speak. *This last trait alone will increase her value*, I thought.

My sturdy horse seemed delighted to be free of the wagon's halter. He sped us across hills, his footing sure and steadfast as wooded knolls grew into stony mountains. I gave him free rein, adjusting his course only when his exuberance threatened to lead us away from the Pasha's territory. The horse's unshod hooves were swift; we reached Yangjugol, the valley curving around the cliff-top palace, by the time Katla had stretched into a beautiful girl of twelve. I had hoped she would've reached sixteen after four days' time; that her hips and breasts would have become more pronounced. Softer and more enticingly full.

But my horse was too fleet—we'd arrived along with the third sunrise, carried on gusts of wintry mountain air—and Katla's growth spurts were erratic and slowing. Still, I had no doubt she would appeal to my lord. The transaction would be brief; she would be purchased instantly. I would be back on my horse before the ache of three days' riding had had a chance to leave my legs.

As we rode through the valley, I realized a few dozen merchants must've had the same idea as me: reach Yangjugol early enough to prise the fattest coins from our Pasha's tight grasp, make a profit before the chill settled in too securely, leave before the autumn markets began in earnest. All the men, regardless of clan or age, stopped their work as we passed and openly stared at Katla, sitting in the saddle before me. In their place, I too would have stared.

Several stalls had already been erected in the shadow of Zhureem Ordon. The palace's blood-red rooftops and peaked gables were barely visible from the mountain's base, hidden as they were behind a high impenetrable wall. A road switch backed up the mountain face, ending in a closed bronze gate; it would take us more than a few hours' hard walking to reach it.

I tethered my horse by the snow leopards' enclosure, which stood taller than the height of two men and, as far as I could see, ran the length of the mountain. These great felines were the Pasha's pride, his favorite possessions; and like all treasures, kept under lock and key. I had no fondness for leopards. Their crystal blue eyes were too knowing, like they'd seen my misdeeds and were only keeping silent to torment me. I slapped Katla's hand when she looked ready to reach through the cage's evenly spaced bars. She blinked, but did not cry out as a normal child would. Her hand fell limply to her side.

"She's a frigid little thing isn't she, Tomaken?"

"Bitter words spoil beauty," I replied, watching Setseh and the Pasha's two other wives approach. "You should bite your tongue before it curdles."

Setseh's hair was streaked with gray, pulled back from her lined face in a loose horse-tail. As first wife, she had earned the silk scarves draped over her burgundy woolens, and poking out of the basket she carried. She had also earned her sharp tongue. Yarmaa and Dzhol walked two paces behind her; the twins had tinted their hair since I saw them last, it was now the hue of dried henna. The color didn't become them. The wives' skirts flapped in the valley's katabatic winds, unhindered by buckles or pride. Their soft cotton shirts gaped unrestrained, the effect too familiar to be tempting. They knew men lusted not for women they had already enjoyed, but for those who were yet unexplored. Even so, they regularly came down to Yangjugol, and strutted around the merchants as if they were still girls of eighteen.

"And how will you be using your tongue today, Tomaken?" Setseh asked. She bent down and placed the basket near the snow leopards' enclosure. "As warrior? Pauper? Supplicant?" She took strips of dried ox-meat out of the basket, slipped them through the bars as she spoke.

I stepped away from the cage as the leopards wrestled over these morsels, their saliva flying in gobbets, their breath rank.

"I approach our lord as a father," I said. "And as a merchant."

Setseh hissed as Katla snatched a strip of meat out of the basket and began nibbling on it. She slapped the girl's face and hands until they were red. Katla dropped the tidbit, but continued to lick the salt from her fingers.

"Are you an imbecile, girl? Stealing from the Pasha's pride?" Yarmaa and Dzhol snorted as Katla's brow furrowed in confusion. "Get this creature out of my sight!"

I gathered Katla into my arms, more to steady myself than to comfort her. She didn't seem disturbed in the least by Setseh's anger. But the first wife's disdain reassured me. The wives always turned vicious when the Pasha was ready to add to their number: Setseh had been unbearable when Yarmaa arrived; and the pair of them were fit to be tied when Dzhol followed her sister to Zhureem Ordon. Looking now at the flush in their weathered faces, I couldn't help but think it was my Katla's icy skin that infuriated them. So translucent, so bruisable, so different from their own brash coloring. Their hides had been worn tough with use, like well-ridden stallions. My Katla wasn't yet broken in. She would be the Pasha's youngest wife yet. The most tender. The most disconcerting.

⊷⊷⦿ — ⦿⊶⊶

"One condition," I said, "and my little daughter will be yours."

The Pasha stood proudly in the fortress' reception hall. A silk vest stretched over his thick robes, a mink hat topped his gray head. He stroked the wealthy expanse of his belly with jewel-encrusted fingers and stared out the window, surveying the lands his father had conquered. I was forced to speak to his back.

"You may buy her now," I informed him, "but you may not enjoy her until she has had her first bloods." It was perhaps an arbitrary rule, but necessary. Prohibition makes all purchases more enticing, and I wanted to be sure the Pasha would bite. It would do none of us any good, seeing her ravished and left unbought. I could not take her home again.

I bowed my head as I spoke, wrapped Katla in my finest embroidered cloak, fastened its toggles tight beneath her chin. My hand lingered there, enjoying her warmth after our cold trek up the mountain, until her unflinching green gaze made me shiver. The Pasha turned at that moment and caught the gesture. He stood with one eyebrow raised.

Let him think I yearn for her, I thought. *That this restriction springs from lust instead of fear. He can think what he likes. Just so long as he believes my act, and takes her. This creature will not be Tomaken's heir.*

"Let me inspect the girl more closely," he said.

Never had a prospective bride approached the Pasha with such a sinuous gait. She hadn't done it intentionally, of that I am sure; but if he hadn't been interested before, my lord certainly was now. He appraised my Katla—by all accounts a chieftain's daughter, a warrior's daughter—as he would the treasures we men had won for him in the wars. Like porcelain or rice, leather saddlebags, or snow leopard tails like the three dangling limply on his banner above the hall's great fireplace. But my Katla was more precious to him than cinnamon, than jade, than ivory.

Good girl, I thought. I was forced to look out the window, beyond the Pasha's bulk. The price I got would be lower if my lord saw me smile.

The forest was a dark smudge at the edge of my vision, sketched beyond the vast valley aproning out before us. Its dense foliage and closely packed trees harbored my clan, kept them hidden in the empire's margins. I yearned to be back with them, for this deal to be done. The clan could use the profit Katla's body would gain for us. And Astrith and I could use some peace.

My lord wanted to keep Katla out of any other man's reach, to balance her firmly on the tip of his tower. I knew this the moment his eyes widened at the sight of her. His coffers were full; his bed empty. He had no use for haggard wives.

So he agreed to my condition.

⊷⊶⊰ ⊱⊷⊶

Snow fell, carried dusk in its wake, as I placed the heavy purse in my saddlebag. The horse was restless, eager to be on the road and away from the mountain's chill climate. I planned to ride through the night, taking rest only when I couldn't avoid it. The summer snows wouldn't last, but their arrival was a harbinger of worse times to come. I was anxious to be on my way; to be back in Astrith's stifling caravan, with her arms and legs wrapped around me. Perhaps there was time yet, to earn a child. To replace Katla. To forget her.

"Aren't you forgetting something?"

Setseh's voice was shrill. Her hand was gripped tightly around the neck of Katla's cloak. She dragged the girl behind her, toward me.

"You do us no favors, Tomaken. Leaving such trash behind."

She pushed the girl in the back, knocked her to the ground at my feet. "Take her. Or else let the Meito take you."

I bent to help Katla stand; took a pinch of earth between my fingertips and scattered it to the winds to counteract the first wife's curse. "I wouldn't let your husband hear such profanity," I said, brushing Katla off. "You of all people should know what the Meito do to those who curse the Pasha's wife."

Yarmaa and Dzhol looked at each other, then at Setseh. As one, the three women approached my Katla, began fussing with her hair, straightening her cloak, smoothing the thin shift she wore beneath it.

"It is done then, is it?"

I nodded and mounted my horse. The sky was growing increasingly dark. I prayed the storm would hold until I was well beyond the Pasha's territory.

Setseh pulled Katla close, placed a gloved hand on her shoulder. She kept her gaze locked on mine and said, "Well, well, little wife. Be sure you lie still when our husband comes to you, else you will feel the pain of his knife."

"A knife in your heart," Yarmaa said, undoing and taking the girl's cloak, poking her slight chest. "To accompany the plunge of his shaft down below." Dzhol smiled, and giggled. Third wives are of little use for much else.

In this way the women tried to taunt me, as if I were a true father. As if I cared what happened to Katla, as if I cared that they threatened her. I was glad to be rid of her, glad to avoid seeing her grow any older. Katla, too, seemed undisturbed. A hint of pink tipped her nose, the ends of her fingers. She held her head high while the women hissed and cooed in her ears. She was rose-colored, but not afraid.

The wives were oblivious to the sound of the Pasha's stately footsteps crunching down the road to Yangjugol. His pace was not hurried but not slow. He descended from Zhureem Ordon with controlled anticipation. Katla watched silently as her new husband slapped his first wife, then tossed her aside like gnawed bones. She did not flinch when Setseh's head clashed against metal bars, nor when Yarmaa and Dzhol began whimpering. She blinked when his voice boomed across the valley, announcing his claim. Declaring her his property, his wife.

A puff of relief escaped my lips, dispersed into the twilight. She was his. No longer my Katla, no longer my concern. His.

The bitter rattle of iron on metal told me I was mistaken to relax so soon. I steered my mount around, just in time to see Setseh throwing open the door to the snow leopards' cage. There was no time for her to scurry out of the way before they sprang; the gleam in her eye revealed that safety came second to her revenge. One leopard wrapped its teeth around the first wife's throat, silencing her venomous words. Years of captivity hadn't slowed the Pasha's pets in the least. Their movements were lithe and swift.

The scant crowd of merchants scattered with fear, several running without being chased. These men were not warriors: they fled like selfish children, saving themselves with no thought for their lord's plight. The Pasha was left to confront a muscular leopard with no army to support him. My lord wielded nothing more than a belt, which he lashed about like a whip. He fought bravely, even when a second cat slinked up behind him and took a great swipe at his hamstrings. A trio of leopards sped toward me; my horse reared but did not unseat me. His nimble hooves danced around slashing paws, striking teeth. He edged us closer to Katla, away from the road. The Pasha now lay wounded at her side, his leg a mess of blood and ligaments. She paid him no attention. Great cats appeared and disappeared in the thinning crowd—she followed them with her eyes.

Her gaze caught mine just as the leopard pounced. The sky twisted. The earth rushed up to meet me. My teeth crashed together, blood poured from my nose. I inhaled in sharp gasps. I looked at my horse, splayed on the ground, his back snapped. Saw my leg twisted in the stirrup, bent at an unnatural angle. I smelled the leopard's stale breath before I felt its paws on my back. Without meaning to, I moaned. Death in battle is honorable; it should not be feared. But only shame can come from a death such as this.

My head snapped up as I heard the soft tread of footsteps. Katla crouched down before me, placed her hand on my head, met the leopard's gaze evenly. I felt the weight of his forelegs leave my back. He snorted, drew closer to the girl I had made.

His pale eyes were a shade darker than Katla's; his composure rivaled a king's. A low growl rumbled from his soft, white throat. There was no threat of a roar from one such as him. It was merely a purr.

She stroked my hair as the leopard coiled its long tail around her. Threaded it around her legs, beneath the thin cloth of her shift. His purrs intensified as he flicked his tail, in and out. Katla's fingers spasmed, dug into my scalp—then went still for a moment. She draped her other arm around the thick fur of the great feline's neck, then resumed gently patting my head. She licked the leopard's cheek, the dark rosettes of his pelt round shadows beneath her wet tongue. Her gaze was fierce, unflinching, as she threw her leg over his back, pulled herself up, away from me. The chaos surrounding us seemed muted and unimportant. She looked down at her steed, then at me. It was the only time I'd see her smile.

The tip of the leopard's tail trailed behind them as they left the clearing together, streaking the snow with moist dirt instead of blood. I watched them blend into the forest, stealthy as only cats can be, blinking as tears filled my eyes.

I could keep clouds at bay with a glance and a well-spoken word. I could outwit a Pasha and survive his snow leopards' attacks. I would see love in my wife's face until the end of my days and, Meitoshi willing, she would see the same. My clan would be strong with men; warriors and traders who would outlive and thrive without me. But only their names would be recorded in our people's annals; their names and their children's. Not mine. The bravest, the strongest, the wiliest clan-child would steal my title, gain control of our family. It was settled the moment Katla and her mate disappeared into the shadows. I knew then, as I had known from the moment I made her: no matter how mighty my deeds or how valiant, I would only ever be remembered as the master of dust and dirt.

Lisa Hannett has sold stories to *Clarkesworld Magazine*, *Fantasy Magazine*, *Weird Tales*, *ChiZine*, *Electric Velocipede*, *On Spec*, and *Midnight Echo*. She is a graduate of the Clarion South. Eight years ago, Lisa moved from Ottawa to Adelaide, South Australia— city of churches, bizarre murders, and pie floaters. She hopes to finish her PhD in medieval Icelandic literature before she grows older than her subject matter.

The Brief Medical Career of Fine Sam Fine

Brent Hayward

Parties, & Promiscuity

Moira had been at figurative loggerheads with her sister for as long as she could remember; she imagined an ending to their relationship that would rival the greatest *tragedies lyriques*. Home life (it could only be termed this with the strongest of ironic intonation) was bickering and bitterness, uneasy silences, drunken rages, crockery smashing. Outings were a different sort of nightmare: fiascoes, each time the girls left their apartment.

But, by far, the most heinous occasions were house parties.

Needless to say, Lucinda had a fondness for attending these sordid affairs with unimaginative regularity.

A cool September night. Leaves crunching under feet and the faint smell of smoke from chimneys returned to the air after a long hot summer, but stuck in this stale basement Moira felt claustrophobic and nauseous, clammy all over. Like she did at every party. Mushed up against the back of a stinky couch (beer, mostly, and mildew), she waited, unseen, appalled.

Perhaps this boy entwined with Lucinda was someone once glimpsed standing, smoking, outside a corner store. Moira imagined her sister descending the stairs to spy him, sitting in the gloom, and then making her way over to where he sat, vapid on the couch, knees wide apart, big dirty football hands hanging between them. She imagined her sister introducing herself (though surely that wasn't necessary: Lucinda was a legend in town).

And now she was draped over him. Or somehow semi-reclined. Without being able to see clearly, Moira, thankfully, could never be exactly sure of the compromising positions her sister achieved. Merciful, too, she could hear very little. Puccini's *Madame Lescault* played in her mind, a baroque feast intended to smother remnants of any external din, such as the incessant *thump-thump* of so-called music and the drone of a drunken voice. Any snippets of conversation she overheard were, for the most part, composed of Lucinda's inane twaddle—the same twaddle Moira had been listening to and feel *hum* up her spine for twenty-one years now!

Moira tried to breathe and choked on thick cigarette smoke; she stopped trying. Twice, inebriated louts had knocked her about. And Lucinda had banged into a wall or something else *really* solid; Moira was bruised pretty good, she was sure.

There was still the inevitable *finale* to look forward to, Lucinda's *fin-de-soiree* on some settee or bed—maybe on this very couch—rolling around with a hormone-mad male.

Moira sighed. Her delicate sensibilities were stripped away at these parties. Such indignities, and all of them suffered cooped within the depths of Lucinda's silly hat.

The Cat in the Hat Hat, & a Close Call

On this particular evening, Lucinda sported the Cat in the Hat hat: tall, unattractive, and ungainly. Striped red and white, it rose a good two feet. Some room inside for movement, but Lucinda had warned Moira against moving.

However, because the Cat in the Hat hat was made of felt it didn't rub Moira's skin raw, like some of the other hats did. But it certainly was rank inside. Moira was sweating.

Through pinholes, she saw unfathomable glimmers.

At one point, a warm, masculine forearm, thrown behind Lucinda, pressed the fabric of her hat up against Moira's face until Lucinda was kind enough to move. Another time, the same boy (Moira hoped it was the same boy) tried to run the fingers of his free hand up the back of Lucinda's head, actually working them under the elastic brim of the Cat in the Hat hat itself! One large, clumsy digit came within half an inch of Moira's pounding breastbone!

From shadow, she watched its dreadful approach—

Lucinda diverted the boy's attention.

Lucinda was good at diverting boys' attentions.

Washrooms

Brief reprieves came when Lucinda went to pee, or to cake on more foundation powder. Or smear on more lipstick. And then only if she remembered, and felt like removing the hat. And if the bathroom door had a functioning lock. And no one was passed out on the floor. Or in the tub.

At this party—thank God!—conditions were met.

Lucinda yanked off the hat, leaving Moira blinking, gasping for the relatively fresh air. Even the dinginess of this water closet was too bright, blinding after several hours of being treated like a mushroom. Lucinda's coarse hair had dragged across Moira's body but Moira had given up complaining about *that* problem long ago.

"Did you see this babe I've been talking to?" Lucinda demanded, peering into a mirror; Moira, of course, watched the wall opposite. "This guy, Sam Fine? Did you see him? Hey, I'm talking to you back there."

Had she seen him? Was there any point in addressing that question? What Moira wanted to say was, *You tell me the same thing at every stupid party: 'Some guy likes me, he really likes me!' Then you let him slobber all over you and grope you and he never calls you again. So you sit at home, getting drunk and watching TV, crying, breaking beer bottles against the wall. You complain about your life as if it's my fault when I refuse to take responsibility!*

But Moira didn't want to fight. She just wanted to go home. So she kept quiet.

Lucinda, meanwhile, popped a zit. When she bent to splash cold water on her face, Moira's view of the wall changed to nothing but ceiling. Two pipes up there, painted green. Peeling. A big yellow stain. Moira wondered if her sister was going to vomit tonight—yet another all-too-common ordeal.

Over the sound of the water's splashing, Lucinda repeated what she had said about Sam Fine. Then she asked, "Are you awake back there? Retard, I'm talking to you."

"Of course I'm awake," Moira finally replied. "You expect me to be sleeping? Maybe you were concerned I had suffocated."

"I should be so lucky. You can't suffocate. I know, I've tried many times. Listen, just do me a favor and answer when I ask you something. At least *try* to be a normal sister." Lucinda fumbled to push her jeans down and then sat heavily upon the toilet. "Anyhow, what I was saying is that this guy is a *babe*. And I think he likes me. His name is Sam Fine and he is fine, fine, fine."

How Moira hated her sister's laugh, which unfortunately filled that tiny room for some time then, shaking her like quaking from Hell itself. (Right there, gray and spongy, dark sea to Moira's tossing ship!)

Some while after her sister had calmed—Moira's shoulder was pressed up painfully against the rusted underside of a cheap medicine cabinet—Moira said, "Could we please get out of here. *Soon.*"

"What?" Lucinda fumbled with the toilet paper. "You little twerp, what did you say?"

"Let's get out of here. You're just going to make a fool out of yourself. Again."

"All that whispering back there. Idiot, speak up, will you? Whisper all the damn time. So negative. Now we just got here, okay? Didn't you hear what I've been saying about Fine Sam Fine? Just relax and enjoy yourself for once. He's in Med School, did I tell you that? *A doctor.* Or at least, he will be soon." Getting up from the toilet, Lucinda had to hold onto the shower curtain to stop from falling into the tub. "Jeez-us," she continued, regaining her balance (such as it was), "if only I *could* leave you at home but look, retard, we're not splitting for a long time so deal with it, okay?"

Before Moira could answer, Lucinda had rudely pulled the Cat in the Hat hat back on and was fumbling at the doorknob with eager hands.

A Few Surprises, Followed
by Some True Music, *En Fin*

The first surprise of the evening came when Moira realized how much the boy with Lucinda was talking. Not only could she detect the drone of his conversation but she could tell quite easily when Lucinda was just *listening*; there was little movement from her sister, except for nodding. Her curiosity piqued by this unorthodox interaction, Moira began to pay more attention, letting the operatic mantra she recited to herself fade. This Sam Fine, it appeared, spoke in reasonable tones, as if he might be actually be expressing ideas, sharing rational thoughts! Was that possible? Had Lucinda selected someone here, at this party, with thoughts of his own? In the darkness of the hat Moira smiled. If what she suspected was true, then the choice must have been an oversight. Serves Lucinda right; she was probably very disappointed!

But other surprises were in store, and they unfolded in succession, near to the end of the evening, the most astonishing being the fact that Sam Fine left the party abruptly, by himself, with nothing more than a hug for his time. And despite this, Lucinda traveled home on the last subway train in an oddly exuberant mood. When she and Moira finally arrived at their apartment (a shabby room, plus kitchenette and bathroom, on the top floor of a tenement situated on a dead-end street), Lucinda was actually *bubbly*. So good was her inexplicable mood that she acquiesced without prompting to change the radio station from Rockin' 92 to Classical 88.2, which at this point was playing the Nightly Opera Hour, Moira's favorite three hours of airwave time. Lucinda even moved the radio so Moira could better hear the wonderful arias!

(The deal the sisters had settled on, long ago, was that if Moira didn't let the cat out of the bag, so to speak, at inopportune times, she would be rewarded with a book of her choice from the library or a few hours of radio, or Lucinda would sit facing away from the TV while some "dumb-ass" show on PBS aired. But rarely was it this easy, and never without some sort of grumbling.)

Lucinda lay upon the bed, talking nonsense about her future life with Fine Sam Fine, strategizing her next move while Moira listened to Schütz's score for the Rinuccini libretto *Dafne,* her entire body pressed up against the thrumming speaker in an unbalanced embrace. How she reveled in that ancient piece (arguably the first opera ever written). The night was ending with a treat...

When Mozart or Lully or even good old Henry Purcell took hold of Moira, she was lifted to a world where she could leave Lucinda, walk away from her sister on legs of her own. When tenor voices swelled, she filled those small lungs of hers and imagined herself standing atop a mountain, the beautiful princess Electra, waiting for the sound of her knight Idamante, who was coming, racing breathlessly along the trail to sweep her up and onto the back of his throbbing stallion...

Thus reveling, Moira gazed dreamily at her treasures, precious items collected over the years and stored neatly in a series of recesses in the wooden headboard of the bed, just within Moira's reach when Lucinda slept or reclined, as she did now, giddy and waffling on and on about Sam Fine while music and the sight of her *objets trouvés* flowed through Moira in ecstatic waves.

A Summary of the Contents of Moira's
Treasure Trove & Brief History Thereof

√ One (1) artificial rose, black in color, petals thread-
   bare. Liberated from a vase in a doctor's office while
   Lucinda bent to tie her boot.

√ Two (2) knitting needles, attached (irony not missed)
   by a nylon tether, with which, one day, hopefully,
   to make a garment (e.g.: custom sleeve/shoulder
   warmer).

√ One (1) creased Technicolor photograph of the ven-
   erable Marilyn Horn, whose flexible vocal range was
   most extraordinary, performing in Handel's *Orlando*
   at the Lincoln Center for the Arts. (A show Lucinda
   had said she "would not be caught dead at," when
   Moira begged her to go.)

√ Seven (7) very shiny brass buttons that distorted
   reflections to the point where one could imagine,
   if one so desired, one's face looking quite different.

√ Two (2) HB pencils (leads broken).

√ One (1) small notepad.

√ One (1) wedge-shaped shard of mirror, perhaps six
   inches in length overall, used to see various parts
   of the room while Lucinda reposed or, sometimes,
   walked around hatless. The item was acquired after
   Lucinda had had a particularly bad tantrum in which
   she accumulated fourteen years of bad luck by
   throwing an ashtray at *two* separate mirrors—picking
   the ashtray up and throwing it a *second* time—while
   screaming phrases such as "you freak," and "you
   parasite." When Lucinda had eventually fallen
   asleep on the floor (for she had been *very* drunk that
   night), said shard was scooped up from the detri-
   tus that lay scattered about them both like a tornado's
   aftermath.

√ One (1) desiccated moth, believed to have traces of
   red on its underwings—too brittle to confirm.

√ One (1) tiny figurine of a dog, glass, within which
   swam wondrous colors stretched like mysterious and
   beautiful taffy.

√ Two (2) se-tenant postage stamps from the United States of America, valued 5¢ each, bearing the likenesses of Frances Farmer, whose dramatic life and death were particularly affecting (even though Farmer was not an opera singer).

Sam Fine's Entrance

Rudely retrieved from *La Bohème* and her mental inventory by, of all things, a knock on the window! Lucinda had fallen asleep in such a manner that Moira could see the silhouette of someone at the glass: pale face peering in from utter darkness. Of their third floor window!

"Lucinda," Moira hissed, quite terrified. "Someone's here! Wake up, cover me! There's an *intruder!*"

Rapping again. Out in the night, the indistinct face shifted, trying to see better, cupped hand to brow. In her drunken slumber, Lucinda moaned and rolled. Then lights from a lost vehicle turning around in the *cul-de-sac* allowed Moira a good, yet brief, look at the intruder and she was taken aback by the face she saw: intelligent eyes, high cheekbones, soft wavy hair. She gazed upon these features as they bloomed and then faded, as if stricken, knowing the peeper could see nothing in the dim room, maybe a few dark shapes against a darker background, at best.

The knocking came a third time, and Lucinda finally woke up, snorting and thrashing about until she discovered where she was and what had caused the disturbance. Then she was on her feet, staggering groggily toward the window when she realized she was hatless and ran back for her nightcap. (This piece of haberdashery wasn't so bad because Moira could easily hear through the thin fabric and even see shapes moving about.) So Lucinda knew this peeping Tom? A suspicion began to bloom in Moira: *My goodness,* she wondered, *could this be Sam Fine, from the party*? A twinge of something she had long ago tried to forever suppress stirred in her: having resigned herself that she could only ever meet family members (who were all long gone now) and the occasional doctor (the services of whom the sisters could no longer afford), Moira was prepared for a life of solitude, with only the opera for company, and her treasures, yet her heart was racing wildly as the window slid up and the boy said, in a deep, mellifluous voice, "Hey there Luce."

"Get in, Sam."

It *was* he! Adonis, beautiful Orestes.

"Get yer ass in here." Lucinda's own voice was crude and breathless and phony.

"I wanted to see you again," Sam explained. "Is that all right? I couldn't sleep or study and I was thinking about what we said. The door downstairs was locked..."

"Yeah, yeah. Come in, come in."

Lucinda stepped aside while Sam clambered through the window. He must have scaled the lilac tree that grew in the front yard. All Moira could see was a gauzy view of Lucinda's *Guns 'n Roses* poster but when she heard Sam's runners thump to the floor it thrilled her to know he was in the same room as her: under the nightcap, she was as naked as the day she (and her sister) had been born.

Carl Maria von Weber's *Der Freischütz*

Lucinda sprawled on the messy bed, trying to look enticing, but Sam, thankfully, was not to be enticed. Against the padded headboard, Moira watched as best she could. Even through the hazy gauze of the nightcap, and at such an obscure angle, Sam was truly gorgeous to behold. As he talked, his large hands moved gracefully. Wonderful hands. The hands of a prince. His eyes and teeth sparkled in the dim light.

Oh, what words he spoke! Yearnings, goals, each phrase reverberating inside Moira, resonating to her very core. The sentiments were familiar, echoing her own or counterpart to them... How these words were wasted on Lucinda, who grunted and uttered her usual stupid contributions. What did Sam Fine see in her? He had already proven to Moira in a short while that he was far from shallow, yet here he was, about to willingly talk through the night with her sister. Moira wanted to shout, *I'm back here Sam! It's me you want to converse with!*

But if she did that, Sam would see her, and then he would run screaming, never to return; Moira bit her tongue.

Soon, Carl Marie von Weber's *Freeshooter* (or *Der Freischütz*) came on the radio—Moira's favorite opera of all time. Sam abruptly ceased talking. Those lovely hands leapt at the opening horn overture.

"Von Weber," he breathed, pronouncing the name properly. His face became even more angelic. "Listen Lucinda. Hear that? Hear the, um, crescendo. And the, the uh... ascending *struggle.*"

Moira's own definition, verbatim! Sam's eyes had closed as he sank back. Trying to stare at him, incredulous, Moira felt her girlish crush turn to pangs of *love!* The boy was her *soul*mate. There could be no doubt. Songs filled her, poignant tunes of Eurydice and Dido. (And not that contemporary British tart!) A protective ice broke away from the tight little bulb that was her heart; green shoots reached up toward the light, burgeoning, alive; hopeful shoots, tender shoots. Feelings so intense ravished Moira that tears sprang to her eyes. She was in *love!*

And then the unthinkable happened.

The Unthinkable

Propped up by pillows, Lucinda had apparently passed out as the opera unfolded—no fan she—and her body now toppled like a felled tree; the nightcap caught on the headboard and was yanked clean from her head! Sam Fine, leaning in quick to catch Lucinda, instead came face to face with Moira, who lay naked and exposed, an ugly boil on the back of her sister's head.

They stared at each other for a long time.

Sam Fine's eyes, so blue, widened slowly. He did not laugh, or scream, or flee. Quietly, he asked, "Who are *you?*"

"Moira," Moira said, her newly expanded heart pounding. "I'm Lucinda's older sister." (Technically, this was true; she *had* emerged first.)

Licking his full lips, Sam reached out to move Lucinda's hair away. He let one finger trail down Moira's arm. In his eyes was a look that could only be described by Moira as one of, well, of *rapture.*

"Please, cover me," Moira said. "I asked Lucinda, to make me a nightdress, but as you can see... she's not yet done so."

"Sorry, sorry..." Fumbling nervously in the bedclothes to arrange the sheet, so that it covered Moira's body but left her face exposed, Sam was visibly embarrassed. He worked quickly, eyes averted, cheeks reddening.

"Thank you," Moira said, when he was done.

"You, uh... been back there all night? Of course, what a stupid question. The hats. The hats. That's why Lucinda always wears those big hats."

Moira nodded, but since most of her head and neck and what little spine she possessed was fused to Lucinda's skull, the movement was imperceptible. She hesitated, then said, "It's not

Lucinda who likes to listen to the opera, Sam. It's me." How delicious it had been to say his name!

Sam Fine smiled. His teeth were big and white and glorious. "Did you like that, uh, von *Weber* piece?"

"I love *Der Freischütz*."

They both said, "That romantic setting," at the same time, and laughed briefly together, and stared again at each other again for a long while, without blinking, searching each other's gaze.

Moira was starting to let herself hope that there was a possibility her new and tender love might be requited...

Lucinda, meanwhile, had begun to snore.

A Little Later

Sam lay on the bed, his body next to Lucinda's, his head tilted so he could whisper to Moira directly. Those lips, inches from her. She could feel the heat of him like a furnace. Never before had Moira felt this alive.

They spoke of the opera, of course, and of literature, the ballet, philosophies. Moira knew she was soon doing most of the talking but Sam seemed engrossed. It was as if floodgates had opened up inside her, releasing an unstoppable torrent. She had never spoken thusly in her life.

After listening attentively for what seemed like hours, Sam said to her, almost breathlessly, "What I want to know is, uh, more about *you*. Tell me... tell me about your family." A bead of sweat ran down Sam's forehead, though it was not hot in the room.

"My family? We were orphaned." Moira wished she could mop his brow. Was proximity to her making him flush?

"Did you, uh, know your mom?" Sam asked.

"I know a bit about her, though we never met."

"Could you tell me, tell me about her?"

The Hopeless Case

Little Ella Mae Bainbridge, twelve years old, was sent out to the corner store, for a quart of milk, on January 26, 1972. Skinny and pig-tailed, Ella Mae was the only child of Reverend Joe Bainbridge and his wife, Victoria. The neighborhood was white, pristine, quiet; the trip to the store, three short blocks.

Skipping along the sidewalk, money clenched in her right fist and singing a merry tune, Ella Mae was pulverized by a huge gold Cadillac that had jumped the curb. The car, driven by fourteen-year-old Sam "Deep Purple" Painscott, who had just stolen it minutes before from the parking lot of the first strip mall to be built in the area, had been found with the keys inside, engine running. The Caddy belonged to old boy Frankish, who was doddering around in the sporting goods retail outlet, searching out a lure for winter pickerel. Just as Frankish paid for his purchase, and addressed complaints concerning inflationary times to the very air about him, his car was coming to rest in a great cloud of brick dust, metal, oil, dirt, and Ella Mae's blood. Pinned somewhere in that mess, bones broken, body sundered, yet miraculously alive, the child had been plunged into a coma from which she would never emerge.

Prone on a cheap hospital bed, in a ward no patient had ever left under his or her own power, Ella Mae lived out the rest of her life. A host of machines kept her body going. Bleeding eventually stopped, and the fractures knitted, and that inert body grew, changed, and entered puberty. Over time, Ella Mae metamorphosed into an adult, albeit atrophied, woman. She would have been an attractive woman—if she were capable of a smile, or even a twitch, any sign of life at all besides those you could read on monitors.

Devices next to her bed beeped. Cylinders hissed up and down in their glass housings. Lights mimicked the patterns of her heart. And years went by.

Over a decade she lay there before a doctor noted a change in Ella Mae's condition—an inexplicable change: the patient appeared to be *swelling*. This doctor, who was new on the ward and had not yet succumbed to the futility of his assignment, speculated that there might be gas trapped in Ella Mae's lower intestines. Subsequent examination later revealed the unsettling fact that a certain visitor to Ella Mae's room, aside from her grieving parents (who had not come by in many months, by this point) had also found the patient attractive. An orderly, perhaps, or a night cleaner. Maybe even a security guard.

It goes without saying that the good Rev. Bainbridge and his wife were Christians, and that they believed in God, and in the wisdom of His ways. This, despite the fact that their only child, their sweet young girl, now needed machines to keep her breathing and had to be flipped on a regular basis to stop bed-sores from rotting the flesh from her bones. They would not hear of terminating this new life growing inside their child; they were appalled at the suggestion. *This pregnancy,* they said, *is God's way of giving us back our daughter. A new chance.*

But the eager young doctor pleaded: *Ella Mae has had a steady stream of drugs administered to her over the past ten years. For her to give birth is madness!*

The Reverend and his wife answered: *We won't hear of it. What you are suggesting is murder in God's eyes.*

So, five months later, after a messy delivery in which their daughter lost a lot of blood but *still* did not die, the pious couple remained adamant, stoic; they would not even consider the proposed operation to separate the newborn twins, for it was obvious that the tiny one—caught by a ring of bone, as if pulling herself out of the larger girl's head with one little arm, legs hidden under the surface of her sister's skull— would surely die.

Two souls, the parents said. But they sounded less convinced now. The Reverend was tired, stubbled. On Victoria's breath was the faintest scent of Bombay Gin. *Two gifts?*

Anyhow, heartbreak soon killed them, Vic and Joe. Ground them down. Too much grief piled up, crushing even their strong beliefs. They went to confront their God.

There followed a series of foster homes, a series of towns. Some rudimentary tutoring, since regular schooling turned out to be an impossibility. Upon reaching sixteen, a government pension. Set up, in a small apartment, on the outskirts of the outskirts of town.

Which brings us up to date.

Sweetest Sorrow

The sun was beginning to rise when Sam finally said he had to leave. It seemed as if the story had made him weepy; his eyes were glazed and unfocused. Moira could feel the tenderness established between them like a palpable tether.

Sam promised, in a strained voice, to return the following night, at eight. They would get Lucinda drunk, and when she fell asleep, he and Moira could talk, and lie next to each other once more.

Sam Fine pulled Lucinda's nightcap back on.

Listening to him clamber over the sill, Moira knew that the prince she had always dreamed of had finally arrived in her life. She imagined the two of them galloping off into the sunset, heading toward a place far from her sister, or perhaps a place from which her sister had vanished altogether.

Love: Day One (1)

At around ten the next morning, Lucinda awoke, hungover. Moira had not slept. Complaining and holding her head, one hand on either side of Moira (who never sympathized with her sister's suffering one whit), Lucinda made a big production of her headache and dehydration. As she drank her coffee, she wanted to know what had happened after she'd passed out. Moira told her that Sam had merely gotten bored watching her sleep and had left. Lucinda grew angry at hearing this and half-heartedly threw a few things around the room. Eventually, though, after a bloody Caesar—hair o' the dog, Lucinda's hangover cure—and listening to a terrible combo called *AC/DC*, she mellowed out somewhat.

For Moira, that day of waiting was bittersweet torture. The paradox was that she wanted to savor every moment of anticipation yet time could not go fast enough. How could these disparate, delicious feelings be sustained?

Just before supper, Lucinda showered. Though her body and face were too close to the source of the spray itself, and when Lucinda washed her hair it was a somewhat uncomfortable, showers were refreshing for Moira. It was also a relief to know that they would smell clean this evening, fresh, for Sam's return. With her tiny arm, Moira rubbed at her body.

Ablutions complete, Lucinda wrapped her head—Moira included—in a towel. Possibly to drown out Moira's humming. Then Lucinda made a telephone call. Moira knew this because she was hit twice by the handset while Lucinda had a rather animated conversation, trying to keep her voice down, which she succeeded in doing, since Moira heard nary a word.

She did, however, feel urgency up her backbone.

When Lucinda took the towel off, an hour or so later, Moira asked whom she'd been talking to; Lucinda denied being on the phone at all.

"Whatever," Moira said, buoyed beyond such vagaries as her sister's bald-faced lies.

Eight o'clock finally arrived and so did Sam, punctual, knocking on the door this time. Lucinda pulled on her puffy Rasta hat. This piece of apparel, though ridiculous, was not too stuffy. It afforded fuzzy visuals yet minimal acoustics.

From what Moira could gather, Sam had brought a bottle with him, the contents of which Lucinda promptly drank.

Before long, Lucinda was out cold and Sam was lifting up the
Rastafarian hat like he was lifting the lid off a frying pan, smiling down at the hash cooking there.

"Hi there," Moira whispered.

"Hi there."

Lucinda was slumped face down at their kitchen table,
which meant that Moira lay on her back, face up. An ideal
position, really. Empty bottle of Dewar's whiskey on the table,
one glass. It was a little odd, even for Lucinda, to drink so
much, so fast, by herself. But fates were clearly pulling strings
to achieve Moira's happy ending.

Where was Sam walking off to? He was over by the bed,
quickly changing the radio station:

"*...that goes out to our two new listeners who called last night
and concludes the request part of our aria program...*"

The Second Conversation

Moira began by asking rather boldly what Sam thought of
Rossini's *La Cenerentola*, which was the story of Angelina—
better known by her nickname, *Cinderella*—and was a story that
Moira associated very strongly with, but Sam didn't seem to
know that particular *opera seria*. Bit of a blank look, in fact, on
his pretty face, which was a little surprising since the piece was
a foundation block of early opera. But never mind.

Then Sam Fine mentioned the Three Tenors; Moira did not
know what to say about this pedestrian offering.

After a brief, nearly awkward pause, Sam changed the subject altogether, telling Moira a little about his own family, all of
whom sounded like good, if somewhat simple, people. Sam
seemed a little nervous. Maybe he wasn't feeling well.

And, since he and Moira felt so close already (Sam explained),
he asked if it was okay to inquire how Moira stayed healthy
under the hats, if she was comfortable in there, what she ate
(indeed, *if* she ate), and other such questions about her makeup, "because your sister doesn't know any of this stuff," he con-
cluded.

"Lucinda?" Moira was confused (though Sam's piercing
gaze may have been the cause). "You've, you've talked with her
about *this*? About *me*?"

"I, uh, no. I mean, it's obvious. I mean, she wouldn't know
about this kind of stuff, would she? About science and all that?
If I did ask her." Smiling somewhat shakily. "That's all I meant."

"No," Moira said slowly, curious about the reddening of Sam's face but not willing to let the evening slip out of her grasp. And since she *had* listened to the doctors while Lucinda flirted with them, Moira actually was able to explain to Sam, without feeling self-conscious at all, about her biology, and about what it was, precisely, that made her tick.

What Makes Moira Tick

Pelvis, lower extremities: absent. Reproductive organs: absent. (Pair of cyst-like growths at the junction of patients represents solidified ovarian tissue?) Spine: present (with severe "corkscrew" abnormalities), but only first 10 anterior vertebrae, all fused to the parietal plate of patient L's skull. Series of nodes along sphenoid plate of patient L's skull indicate vestigial lumbar backbone and sacrum. Left arm: present, though greatly undersized and movement limited. Muscle development and strength: well advanced. Right arm: entirely absent. Extreme microcephala. Head mobility: limited.

Personalities remain distinct. Brainwave activity appears to be at par in both brains (if not somewhat more advanced in patient M!).

Digestive system: incomplete. Sustenance derived from patient L. Circulatory system: limited. Independent heart supplies blood to head but 'body' proper gets oxygen from patient L. Small lungs: present, but do not supply air to this secondary system. They are, for all intents, redundant—

Love: Day One, Abruptly Concluded

Before Moira had completed her descriptions—in terms she thought Sam would appreciate, what with his choice of a medical career path—he appeared to swoon. Then he said he had to leave, though Moira begged him to stay.

"I have to get outta here," he repeated, rather curtly.

"Have I upset you?" Moira was frantic.

"No. Of course not."

"Was I too graphic? I just thought, well..."

"I have an accounting final tomorrow," Sam stammered, and with that he left.

Stunned in the silent room, Moira understood that something had gone awry. Clearly, there were misunderstandings, communication troubles, bridges between their hearts that seemed insufficient to bear the weight of their love. Accounting? Why had Lucinda lied to her about Sam's chosen profession?

Or had *Sam* lied? Was Sam Fine to be a practitioner of Medical science or a bean counter? Moira did not mind which, both being honest professions, but why had she been told falsehoods? And by whom?

Love: Day Two
Lucinda woke, still at the table, in a terrible state. The first thing she did was move a hand up gingerly to touch Moira, whereupon, contacting her sister's body, she began to quietly sob. Then she went and lay on their bed and cried some more while Moira fondled her glass dog figurine and pondered her love, which was wounded already, feeling new pains that were not quite pains cracking around her tender heart.

After a few cans of pop and a pack of Winstons, in a foul mood, Lucinda pulled on the Cat in the Hat hat and went outside for a slow perambulation. Moira could smell the heat of the day and her sister's rising boozy stench. She could see flickers of sunlight but little else. Lucinda walked and walked.

At one point, Moira was sure she heard Lucinda arguing. There was a muffled male voice and she heard her sister shout what sounded like, "No more stalling!"

But when the sisters got home later and the hat finally came off, Moira asked Lucinda about the encounter and Lucinda denied it had happened, saying only that she had gone for a walk down by river because she had wanted to be alone. Moira entertained the suspicion that it might have been Sam Fine, and that Lucinda and he had been discussing problems in their own failed relationship, problems that she, Moira, had caused. Maybe Sam had been stalling in asking Lucinda to go steady?

For once, in this complicated production, with their heartaches, and shared paramour, the sisters had something in common.

A Mysterious Scene (Preceded by an Interlude On the Nature of Love)
Suffering a mayfly's existence, delicate gossamer (though we pretend these comparisons are not true), love cannot stay fierce and burning. No attempts to fan the embers can keep them blazing. Indeed, they flicker out in an instant. Initiated, wearied, Moira understood this all too well now. Opera had forewarned her: Mascagni's *Isabeau*, anything Greek. *Romeo*

and Juliet, of course. Now she felt it first hand. Was Sam ever going to return? He had not said. Uncertainty was agony. There was no way to bond two people together in this life. (A bond of flesh, like the bond between her and her sister, was a sham, a cruel joke.)

Recalling the last conversation she'd had with Sam, Moira could not stop a terrible thought from entering her mind: What if he was already torn from her life? What if their love was over, before it had really begun?

However, in the early evening of that wretched second day, there came a knock at the door; Moira wanted to cry out from where she lay fretting at the rear of her sister's head.

Lucinda picked up the big fedora and tugged it on. The big fedora! Of all nights! Sight and smell gone! Hearing gone! The bitch!

Moira waited in the darkness, heart pounding. How would Lucinda be taken out of the picture this evening? Was her sister dim enough to fall for the same trick two nights in a row? Was Sam even prepared to attempt it?

After opening the door, Lucinda moved about the apartment restlessly, pent-up, pacing. Now Moira had doubts that it had been Sam Fine at the door. She could not be sure of anything. Was that a faint male voice? It seemed insistent at times. Did her sister yell the word "coward"?

Once again, she felt Lucinda drinking heavily, head tilted back. Guzzling straight from the bottle this time.

Abruptly, Lucinda slammed the bottle down and dropped to her knees. Moira thought that maybe she had fallen, or that she was going to vomit, but then after a moment her sister's head began to move backwards and forwards, backwards and forwards, as if she were nodding in time to a tune Moira couldn't hear. During these motions, a hand (Sam's? was that Sam's firm hand?) twice grasped Moira's body briefly yet roughly, fingers caught in Lucinda's hair before releasing her.

When Lucinda stopped the odd motions, she coughed for a while, spat (on the floor!?), and went to lie on their bed. Under the hat Moira was frantic. *What* was going on? Whoever it was in the room with them came and sat on the mattress. Then they, too, reposed.

For a long period, only the rising and falling of Lucinda's breathing. Moira waited but the fedora was never lifted off. Very carefully, Moira worked the hat off herself. The fedora was tight, removing it was difficult, but she had accomplished this feat several times in the past, when Lucinda had fallen asleep without getting undressed.

No attempt was made to stop Moira.

The hat rolled off the bed onto the floor.

On her back, snoring, clothes in disarray, Lucinda lay. She stank of booze.

Next to her, Sam sprawled in a similar disheveled and drunken state.

The Understanding

Getting past the initial confusion, Moira deliberated, frantically putting the pieces together of a working theory:

Sam had arrived, after much soul-searching, with intentions to tell Lucinda of the love he felt for Moira. The previous night he had realized it, following his talk with Moira, and had abruptly left when he found himself unable to deal with the intensity of his emotions.

Upon arrival, he had promptly confessed; Lucinda, listening, paced.

Tormented, they both consumed an abundance of alcoholic beverages.

When Lucinda had heard enough and was being torn asunder, she had dropped to her knees, shaking her head to negate the confession. During this pathetic display—in an attempt to comfort her, or maybe even to keep her at bay?—Sam had felt the need to physically hold Lucinda's head. Since he was so distraught himself, and somewhat tipsy, Sam had momentarily forgotten Moira's unfortunate place of residence and had gripped her slight body, releasing it only when he realized that it was his love he held.

Lucinda had thrown herself onto the bed.

Following, Sam Fine tried to comfort her.

Their clothes became disarrayed during this debacle.

Exhausted by emotions and whiskey, they had both fallen asleep.

Now, Lucinda drooled and Sam (dreaming of Moira?) smiled in repose. How hard it must have been for him to confront Lucinda and tell her the truth. To confess his love, his new, delicate love.

"My sweetness, my sweetness," Moira breathed, feeling much better. "We will be united soon." And with a tear in her eye, she drove her shard of mirror deep into her lover's

jugular vein, pulling it laterally with all the might of her one
tiny arm, trying vainly to turn her face away from the erupting
geyser of Fine Sam Fine's hot and pumping blood as it
sprayed high up into the room.

Curtain

The idea, in keeping with the greatest operatic stories
of all, was to expire together, on that mattress, life-forces
mingling, souls forever as one; Lucinda messed that up by
rolling over (one arm outflung to slap against Sam's still
chest), twisting Moira quickly in such a way that Moira
dropped the shard of mirror. She tried to reach for it but
Lucinda sat up suddenly, gagging as if there were something
caught in her throat. Desperate, Moira swiped up her knitting
needles from their recess in the headboard. She *had* to die
embracing Sam! That was the only way to seal romance forever, to keep it fierce and burning.

But Lucinda was heading toward the bathroom, stum-
bling across the carpet, leaving Moira to watch Sam's cooling,
blood-soaked body recede—

In one hand he grasped a *knife!*

Had his plan been the same, to seal their love with
eternity's kiss? Moira's heart struggled to soar!

And on the bedside table were open medical journals,
vials, and a... a *garbage bag?*

Lucinda washed her face, gargled, spat into the sink. She
did not even notice the gore on her clothes and skin. Moira
frantically told herself that when her sister went back into the
main room she would see Sam's body and surely run to his
side. Then, as Lucinda bent over him, Moira could grab the
mirror shard and finally kill herself. All would be as it should
be, as it is at the end of the greatest love stories.

Heading back to the bed, Lucinda rubbed her eyes and
started mumbling, "What are you waiting for, you loser. You
don't have the guts to do this? You gonna stall another night?
Don't expect another blow—"

And stopped. Halfway across the room she stood there.
"Oh my God," she screamed. "Not tonight! Not tonight! You
were going to, you were going to... Little *freak!*" Her tone rose
to a relentless shriek.

Distraught beyond all reason herself—Moira was only trying to stop the vibrations from shattering her body and frail
sanity—she had to *think*, to regroup her *plan:* the knitting

needles plunged easily into her sister's soft temple. Lucinda stopped screaming but didn't topple onto the bed, like Moira had hoped. Her sister stood very still. Then she said, "Chocolate. Mommy? Want to see my triangle? The sun is hot. Four plus four plus four plus four is shitshit*shit*," and turned, without another word, to flee the apartment.

Moira caught one last glimpse of Fine Sam Fine's body before Lucinda pounded mindlessly down the stairs and galloped outside, past the lilac tree, past the dead-end, hair streaming out, plunging with Moira, who was weeping now, atop her head, beyond the last developments of town and into the dark night.

Brent Hayward is the author of *Filaria*. His short fiction has appeared in several publications, including *On Spec*, *ChiZine*, and *Horizons SF*. He lives in Toronto, where he is working on his second novel.

Harvest Moon

M. L. D. Curelas

Judging by the amount of cider drunk and fresh apple pie eaten, the Johannsens' annual Harvest Festival had been a success. Although the barn had been spiffed up and decorated to handle the party—Harvest Festival was *never cancelled*—the predicted rain hadn't fallen, gifting the weary farming community with mostly clear skies and an unusually warm night.

People trickled off the Johannsen property in groups, loading their children into vehicles sitting on the patchy brown and green lawn. Ginnie's family was one of the last to leave; her dad liked to give his farm hands as much time as possible to enjoy the festivities.

Ginnie grumbled as she clambered into the battered blue pickup truck. Her family lived so close to the Johannsen farm that Ginnie could see the porch lights of her house from here. It was a distant twinkle to be sure, but the flatness of the land aided visibility.

"I don't see why I can't walk home. I could do it," Ginnie said, scooting over to the middle seat of the truck. General rule of thumb in her family: shortest legs sat in the middle. "I'm not a baby, I'm eight."

"Nobody walks on Festival night, Ginnie, you know that, no matter what their age." Her mother leaned into the cab and set her purse and casserole dish on the floor way underneath the glove compartment, then disappeared to go fetch another armful of belongings.

Ginnie snorted. She didn't get some of the traditions her family and neighbors followed. Making corn dollies was another odd one. Her mother had once likened the dolly to a rabbit's foot; Ginnie could almost understand that comparison. She'd made hers tonight along with the other girls; the dolly, wrapped in a swatch of cotton, sat nestled in her mother's voluminous purse.

She glanced out the open door. She was the first one to the truck. One of the farm hands was dancing a tottering jig on the road, but he wasn't looking her way. Ginnie bent over and pulled out the little dolly. She wasn't supposed to play with it; the dolly wasn't a toy.

A corn husk comprised the body. A few leaves were twisted into vestiges of arms and legs, with a string tying off a lump at the top to make a head. Her dolly wore a scrap of blue gingham, kinda like Dorothy from *The Wizard of Oz*, and a few strings of brown yarn were glued to the head. Ginnie tucked the dolly into her pocket and patted it, enjoying its comforting weight.

She swiveled around on her knees to peek out the rear window of the cab. The farm hands climbed into the back of the truck with the slow and fumbling movements of people who'd been imbibing. The dancing farm hand had to be pushed onto the tailgate.

Cider wasn't the only beverage served at the Harvest Festival. Many of the farm wives liked to show off their home-made wines and ales, and their neighbors savored the opportunity to sample the exhibits. Ginnie chanted the names of the men as they crawled across the truck bed, hesitating when Joseph got in.

He was older than most of the farm hands, with thick streaks of gray in his long, flat black braids, and very tall. Ginnie was a little frightened of him, even though he'd never been anything but nice to her. He noticed her watching, and inclined his head in greeting, a smile crinkling his copper face. Joseph did not fumble as he found a place to sit.

Michael hopped into the truck bed with ease, scrambling to the rear corner where he would be sheltered from the wind. Seeing Ginnie, he grinned and waved. Ginnie stuck out her tongue at her older brother, then collapsed back into her seat, turning away before he saw the scowl that creased her face.

When Ginnie's mother reappeared with Baby John cradled in one arm and a small jug of cider in the other, Ginnie said, "Why does Michael get to sit in the back?"

Her mother sighed. "There isn't room for four people in the front, Ginnie." She tucked the jug into the corner on the floor, arranging the purse and casserole dish around it to keep the jug from falling over and spilling its contents.

"Baby John makes four people!"

Mother gave Ginnie a *look*. Ginnie pressed back into the worn vinyl of her seat, feeling pinned by the sudden steel in Mother's eyes. "Baby John rides in my lap, young lady, which you well know." She held up a hand, and Ginnie closed her mouth with a reluctant snap. "And before you ask, no, you may not switch places with Michael."

It was a familiar refrain, and Ginnie didn't bother protesting further. The next exchange would follow along the lines of how Ginnie was a girl and the men in the back of the truck were, well, *men*, and, therefore, unsuitable company for a little girl, especially if they had been drinking Mrs. MacKenzie's plum wine. Last year Ginnie had mouthed along with her mother's explanation and had received a smart swat on the rump and a week without TV for her sass.

"Better get buckled in, your dad's coming."

Ginnie grabbed the ends of her seat belt and clicked them into place. The buckle sagged around her middle, giving her ample room to turn around and spy on the men (*her brother*) in the back.

"Oh, for Heaven's sake, Ginnie." Her mother grabbed the tail of the belt and yanked, pulling the strap snug against Ginnie's stomach.

"It hurts! It's too tight!"

Mother stepped up into the truck, using her free hand for balance, and settled into the passenger seat. She pulled her own shoulder and lap belts across her body and snapped them into place, Baby John snuggled in the crook of her arm. Only then did she turn to her daughter. "Nonsense."

"What's nonsense?" Ginnie's dad opened his door, slid into the cab, and shut the door in a smooth motion that bespoke years of repetition.

"Nothin'!" Ginnie fiddled with the long tail of excess seat belt and strove for an innocent look.

Dad raised one eyebrow, like that alien on the TV show that Michael liked so much. "Uh-huh." He glanced from daughter to wife, and, pleased with what he saw, inserted the keys into the ignition and started the truck.

Unable to lean forward far enough to see around her parents through the side windows, Ginnie contented herself with the view provided by the windshield. In a few seconds she identified her porch lights again, counted them, and then looked up to find the Big Dipper.

The moon overwhelmed everything in the night sky. Orange—not yellow or ghostly white—but muddy orange, a perfect round blob of dried blood, the moon cast its cold light down over the land, illuminating the harvested fields. Ginnie had never seen such a moon before. She gaped at it, all thoughts of picking out star constellations driven from her mind.

Discordant, slurred singing jarred her out of her reverie. The men weren't the world's best vocalists, even when they were sober, but the bouncy rhythm, so different from the plaintive songs that her mother liked, fascinated Ginnie. Michael's high tenor warbled above the other voices, giving the song a sweet tone.

They weren't singing in English, so Ginnie turned to her dad. "What's the song about?"

Dad cleared his throat. "Oh, it's, uh, it's too fast for me to understand, sweetie. Probably about a boyfriend and girlfriend."

He sounded amused. Ginnie eyed him with suspicion, but her dad wasn't smiling, so she relaxed, satisfied that she wasn't being laughed at. "Oh."

"How about we listen to the oldies station? We should hear a couple of songs before we get home," Mother suggested.

Dad smiled. "Good idea." He reached for the radio dial, but his hand froze in mid-air.

The singing abruptly stopped. Into the thick silence an eerie crooning rose, causing the hairs on Ginnie's arm to stand straight up.

She craned her neck, but her head didn't even top the seat so all that she saw was blue-black vinyl patched with duct tape. Ginnie squirmed, tugging at her seat belt, but she failed to create any wriggle room. She couldn't see what was happening behind her, why the men were so quiet, and what was making that weird noise.

Ginnie shivered and wrapped her thin arms around her body.

One of the men banged on the rear window. "Drive faster, sir!"

Dad peered into the rear-view mirror. He cursed and the truck jolted forward. Ginnie's seat belt pressed against her stomach. She kept her eyes focused on the solid lights that represented her house. The lights were getting closer, but, as she'd heard her mother complain many times, the truck was old and didn't go very fast. It would take awhile to get home.

Despite the increased speed of the truck, the crooning grew louder, and Ginnie knew that whatever was making the noise was getting closer. Close enough that her ears parsed the sound better, and she realized that she was hearing howling, not crooning.

Her stomach felt strange, knotted and hard, like it had before her piano recital. She opened her mouth to ask, "what was making the noise," but nothing came out.

"We're in a car, we're supposed to be safe," Mother said. "Michael's back there."

Hearing the quiver in her mother's voice, Ginnie looked over. Her mother's teeth clamped her bottom lip; a drop of blood trickled down her chin.

The choir of howls encased the truck in cotton batting, creating a surreal world for the truck and its passengers. Baby John's tiny face was scrunched into a ferocious scowl, the one he made when he screeched with anger. Ginnie knew she should have been able to hear him, but she didn't.

Something thumped in the back, and there was a distinct sensation of *sinking*. One of the men screamed, the shrill sound piercing the auditory fog.

"They're jumping aboard," Dad hunched over the steering wheel.

Something banged into her mother's door. Ginnie flinched. "Ginnie," her mother said, slamming her hand down on the lock, "undo your belt." The something banged into the door again, which distended into a vaguely animal shape. The truck swerved.

Ginnie's fingers felt fat and far away from her body and she couldn't grasp the buckle.

"Ginnie!" her mother snapped.

"I can't! I don't know how!" Ginnie wailed. Her eyes burned and her throat ached, and her ears rang with the sounds of screams and snarls and wet, ripping noises.

Then her mother's fingers, cool and strong, brushed Ginnie's fat, useless fingers aside. The belt unsnapped with a smart click. "Get on the floor," her mother instructed. "Now."

Ginnie crawled down around her mother's knees and curled into a ball, squeezing into the small space. "Here, hold your brother," her mother's voice drifted down and Ginnie found herself clutching Baby John.

She cradled the infant against her chest, ears pricked, concentrating on the sounds from above. Yelling, *a lot* of yelling, and metallic bangs convinced Ginnie that she didn't want to see anything happening in the truck, but when the sharp tinkle of glass rang out, a chill crept up her back. What if Mother and Dad were hurt?

Biting her lip, Ginnie wedged Baby John into the corner with the cider jug and casserole dish. His face had become an interesting shade of purple, and Ginnie wondered if her baby brother would scream until something popped. She patted him, making sure he wouldn't roll out of his corner, and twisted her legs underneath her. Once kneeling, she leaned forward and peered over the edge of the seat.

The angle wasn't good, but Ginnie could see plenty. Her mother huddled in the corner of the cab, blood trickling down her cheek from a narrow cut. The back window was broken; shards of glass were scattered over the seat.

As Ginnie gawped at the jagged hole, two gigantic gray paws curled over the edges of the opening. A wolf (*not a coyote, too big*) thrust its shaggy, silver head into the cab, snarling and snapping its jaws. Ginnie's mother shouted and smacked its nose with the flat of her hand. The wolf drew back, blinking dirty orange (*moon colored*) eyes.

The wolf lunged again, coming farther into the cab, its teeth missing her dad's shoulder by a hair. Ginnie shrieked, and the wolf turned towards her, rust eyes regarding her with the clinical detachment of children ripping the wings off flies. Its tongue snaked out and ran along its chops.

The wolf wanted to hurt her, she realized. It shifted its paws, preparing for another surge forward. Ginnie felt a prick in her side. She reached into her pocket and closed her fingers around the corn dolly. Rabbit's foot. Good luck. Protection? She hurled the dolly at the wolf. It smacked against the wolf's chest. Something sizzled. The wolf flinched and drew back with a low whine.

A dark shape appeared behind the wolf.

"Joseph," Ginnie whispered.

The farm hand wrapped one arm around the wolf's neck, stilling it, and drove a knife into the wolf's chest. The wolf yelped, a sharp exclamation of pain and protest, dirty orange eyes wide with surprise, then slumped against the window.

Joseph shoved the carcass aside and leaned into the cab, avoiding the spikes of glass. "It was the last one! We managed to push the others off. They've fallen behind now."

"Thank God," Mother said.

"We will need silver to purify the bodies," Joseph said.

Mother shook her head, but didn't say anything.

The truck took a hard right turn, bounced along the driveway for a few seconds, then rolled to a stop. Ginnie rocked back onto her heels, then forward; her forehead bumped into the seat.

Mother and Dad immediately slid out of the truck. Ginnie pulled herself back onto the seat. Her eyes skimmed over the horror of the truck bed, then focused beyond and behind it. Several large four-legged animals milled at the end of the driveway. Their fur glinted orange in the moonlight. One wolf looked up, meeting her gaze; its mouth drew back into a snarl.

"Dad!"

He looked over his shoulder, mouth tightening when he saw the wolves. "They can't come on our land, Ginnie. We're safe."

"Mind the baby," Mother ordered as she shut her door.

Ginnie tore her eyes away from the animals, and forced herself to watch her parents as they joined Joseph on the lawn. She could see everything that was happening, and, thanks to the broken rear window, she could hear everything too.

Mother's voice floated on the still night air. "Joseph—"

"The men think as I do," he said, cutting her off. "It is Harvest night, and we aren't the only beings preparing for winter."

All heads turned towards the road, where the wolves gathered. Ginnie thought that she could hear them snuffling like hounds searching for the trail. As one creature, the wolves sat back on their haunches and howled.

Joseph cleared his throat, dragging attention back to himself. "Purification is necessary, especially for those who were bitten."

"I know that, Joseph." Mother had assumed her don't-try-to-lecture-me-Missy tone. "But given that we were attacked in a group, and none of us have set foot on public ground, I don't believe that purification will work. Especially for those of us who are living. We followed the rules; we were supposed to be safe from Harvest."

Ginnie gnawed on her lip. Rules? Public ground? *Harvest?*

Joseph stiffened. His eyebrows knit together in a disapproving scowl. "We *will* use standard purification procedures on the men who didn't make it." His voice was cold; Ginnie shivered, glad that Joseph wasn't angry with her.

Mother sputtered, but Joseph continued in a low rumble. "As for the rest of us...I have a tincture which will purge the body. It will be...unpleasant...but it should work. Your son is injured. He will need to be purified as well." He removed a small envelope from an inner pocket of his coat, and handed it to her mother. "I don't travel on this night without it."

Ginnie moaned. Michael was *(bitten)* hurt? By one of those...wolves?

Mother tried to put the envelope back into Joseph's hand. "He doesn't need this. He was just cut by the glass, like I was. I saw it."

Joseph frowned. "That big one made a beeline for the boy. With all the blood, it would be safer—"

"If we were wrong about the conditions to ensure our safety," Mother said, "then how can we be sure that the purification rituals are true? We could be wrong about those too! We could cause unnecessary pain to, to the living."

"Of course they're true," Dad said, closing Mother's fingers around the envelope. "Michael will take the treatment, and we'll have to make up more for everyone else. Now, Joseph, about the unlucky ones..."

Joseph and her father stepped farther away from the truck, their heads bent close together. Ginnie couldn't hear their words, so her attention wandered back to the truck. The farm hands were climbing out of the truck bed, many of them bleeding, but a couple didn't move at all. Those still figures were dragged to the edge of the truck bed, passed down to the men waiting there, and then laid out on the ground. Puddles of blackness stained their throats and chests. One of the unmoving men was the dancing farm hand. Ginnie gulped.

Her mother seemed oblivious both to the solemn farm hands and the intense discussion between Dad and Joseph. She fluttered around Michael. Blood oozed down his cheek. "Are you all right, Michael? Let me see that cut." Mother fished a tissue out of a pocket and wiped his face. "I was right; it's just a scratch." She glanced over her shoulder at Joseph and Dad.

She turned back to Michael. "I don't think you'll even need...stitches. Here, let's take you to bed, Okay? I'll fix you a mug of warm milk; it'll help you sleep." She stuffed into her pocket the envelope that Joseph had given to her. Mother wrapped an arm around Michael's shoulder and led him to the house, her voice fading to a murmur.

Ginnie watched them enter the house, peeked down at Baby John, who gurgled at her, and then resumed observing the others through the broken window. The men hadn't bothered with the wolf carcass. It lay in a careless heap in the corner of the truck.

The wolf, the *dead* wolf, shone. Ginnie inched closer to the hole in the window and cautiously poked her head out. The wolf's body flickered and *thinned*, becoming more of a silvery patch of light instead of a silver bundle of fur and flesh with every passing moment. In a few seconds, the wolf dissipated, and nothing remained where it had lain but a brilliant moonbeam.

Ginnie tried to scream, but a hoarse whine was all her throat could manage. She gawked at the spot where the body had been, then looked beyond the tailgate to the road. The wolves stared at her, before they too dissolved into the night sky, their rusty eyes the last to fade away.

Ginnie whipped around to stare at the moon through the windshield. It was still full and orange, the dark spots that made up its face small bloodstains that dotted the surface. As Ginnie watched, the dark spots rearranged themselves and, suddenly, it was a wolf's face grinning down at her, tongue lolling out of its mouth.

Ginnie screamed.

Now she was the one being fussed over. The door swung open and several pairs of hands carried her out, everyone asking: "What's wrong? What's wrong?"

And urgently, someone—her dad? Joseph?—demanded, "Where did the wolf go?"

Ginnie could see it in her mind, the wolves, both dead and alive, *evaporating* in the moonlight, but how could she explain that the moon had somehow absorbed the wolves? That the wolves were the moon? "Disappeared," she mumbled. "It disappeared."

"Maybe it wasn't dead after all," her dad said, pushing her hair out of her face, petting her arms, checking for injuries.

"Perhaps," said Joseph, but he sounded doubtful. He looked uneasily at the moon.

Then Mother returned, and ushered Ginnie into the house. A saucepan of warm milk sat on the stove. Mother poured some into a mug and handed it to Ginnie. "Drink this while I put Baby John to bed."

Ginnie drank quickly. Without cocoa, warm milk didn't taste so good. She placed her empty mug in the sink. Strange herbs rested in a neat heap in the porcelain basin. Michael's mug also sat in the sink, traces of milk, nothing else, ringing the bottom of the mug. Ginnie stared at it for a few seconds, her face blank, before returning to her chair.

Her mother returned, walked with Ginnie upstairs and tucked her into bed.

A few gunshots roared outside.

Her mother sighed and glanced out the window. "Unfortunate, but necessary. Cremation is the next step, I suppose, for their families' sake. Ours too. We can't have any awkward questions about posthumous wounds."

Ginnie nodded, even though she didn't know all the big words.

"An outsider, Ginnie, would call us primitive," her mother continued with a wobbly smile. "They'd look at the silver bullets and laugh. But we know better, don't we?" She turned away from the window and muttered, "Or we thought we did."

Mother took something out of her pocket. "You forgot this." She placed the corn dolly on the bed next to Ginnie. The doll's face had blackened. Bits of yarn had melted, becoming hard and shiny. "It brings luck," Mother said, smoothing her hand over Ginnie's brow. "One thing that worked like it was supposed to. Try to get some sleep, sweetie. I'll be downstairs if you need anything."

Ginnie listened to her mother go downstairs and re-enter the kitchen. In the quiet house, the gush of water roared from the faucet like river rapids. The herbs. Ginnie shuddered.

She yanked the covers over her head so that she wouldn't see the moonlight shining through the window, cutting an orange swath through her bedroom. The thick blankets also muffled noise: the sound of Michael, in the room next to hers, talking to the moon.

M.L.D. Curelas lives in Calgary, Alberta with her beagle, three guinea pigs, and her supportive husband. A career librarian, Margaret currently works as acquisitions editor for EDGE Science Fiction & Fantasy Publishing. A voracious reader, she also plays baritone saxophone, board games with friends, and can occasionally be spotted swing dancing. "*Harvest Moon*" is her second publication.

Heat Death
~ or ~
Answering the
Ouroboros Question

Patrick Johanneson

The ferret draped around my shoulders farted, and I laughed. One of the toga-clad old men turned to glare at me. I grinned back as widely as I could, showing him how I still had all my teeth. Disgusted, he turned back to his conversation. I could just guess what they were discussing in hushed voices: *Why are we here? Who came first? Did we make man, or did man make us?*

You'd think after man vanished, that'd be the end of *that* line of questioning. You'd be wrong, I'm afraid. The old chicken-or-the-egg conversation is about the only one most of these hoary old fuckers seem to be interested in having. No matter how often I point out that it's plainly an ouroboros of a question, a snake endlessly eating its own tail—not to mention it's *irrelevant* besides—they insist on discussing it.

Gods. You gotta love 'em.

I snapped my fingers and made fire. "Hey," I said to my ferret. "Remember when I gave fire to Prometheus?"

He yawned with a movement that threatened to unhinge his jaws, then smacked his lips. Ignoring my question, he said, "I'm hungry."

I glanced around. A golem was approaching, carrying a tray piled high with organs: the livers of jaguars, the spleens of skunks, the tiny hearts of shrews. I made for it, brushing past one of the philosopher gods as I went. I touched my flaming middle finger to his linens as I passed.

"Ah," said my ferret, as the golem stopped and bowed my way, "lovely." He dipped his sharp snout into the carnate pyramid and came out with a veined globe clutched in his teeth,

a minotaur's testicle. It made a distressing snapping sound as
he bit down.

Behind me, angry voices rose. I looked back over my shoulder. Through ferret hair I could see that the god whose robe I'd
lit was now wreathed in flames, his toga nothing but blackened
rags hanging on his unblemished, unimpeachable alabaster
skin. He looked very angry indeed.

"Remember when I gave fire to Prometheus?" I said again,
walking faster.

"As I recall," said my ferret, chewing with his mouth open,
"you *stole* fire from the People, because you thought it'd be
funny to let 'em freeze in the winter like the other animals. But
then Mother Thunder came to you, angry, and you—"

"Yes, enough," I said.

I risked another glance back. One of the Roman gods had
made a little rain cloud above his flaming peer. Somehow it had
failed to improve his mood. I didn't get it. Who *didn't* like being
naked and wet?

"As I recall, you pissed yourself."

"I was a *fox*," I said. "Of *course* I pissed myself. All the time
I pissed anywhere I—"

"You know what I mean," said my ferret.

"I think you need to shut up now," I said.

A bolt of lightning sizzled by overhead. I wasn't sure if that
was bad aim or a mere warning, and I didn't plan to stick
around to find out.

"Besides, nobody *gave* fire to Prometheus. He *stole*—"

"Seriously, shut up."

"Whatever," he said, swallowing the last of the testicle. He
laid his head down and began to snore.

Right in my ear. Hot meat breath snores, *right in my ear*. For
all the gods' sakes.

⚒ ⚒ ⚒

I fetched up next to a marble fountain, cherubs pissing
clear water into a broad white bowl. Glancing back over my
shoulder, I decided I'd run—sorry, *strode*—far enough. I looked
around.

Marble columns vined with ivy marched away down the
sides of the dusty trail. High, wispy clouds skimmed across the
blue, blue sky. All of it fiction, of course, a great lie perpetuated
by sheer force of will. Because who's got more force of will than
a god? No one, baby, except maybe another god. Or, you know,
all of them.

The fountain burbled and gurgled. It sounded like joy. I took a golden chalice from the collection adorning the fountain's wide rim. I held it under the running water, let it fill, then wished for wine. I took a sip and spat it out. "Fuck," I said.

"What?" said my ferret, his voice drowsy.

"Fucking arak." I threw the goblet away. "I *hate* anise."

He yawned and stretched, his little paws kneading my shoulders. "Why'd you ask for it then?"

"I didn't." It's not easy being a trickster sometimes. You can't turn it off. You'll even play tricks on yourself.

"Hey," my ferret said, snapping to attention and pointing like a hunting dog with his tiny black nose, "is that Baldr?"

"No," I said, "can't be, that lot took the easy way out." I squinted against the glare anyway.

"Yeah." He lay down on my shoulders and sighed, contented beyond measure. His breath still stank of raw meat. "Sure looks like him, though."

It wasn't him. It couldn't be. Baldr and the rest of the noble northern pantheon had bit it a long time ago, back when there were still stars and the whorls of galaxies, back when there was still an Earth, back when there was still a reason for we gods to exist.

But that was a long time ago, a trillion years or maybe a trillion trillion years ago. Eternity is damned long and it feels even longer when you're trapped with a bunch of crusty old sons of bitches that gnaw evermore at the puzzles of who came first and what are we and why are we here.

This party goes ever on, knots of gods drinking wine and mead, milk and blood from golden chalices, discussing all the irrelevant ouroboros questions, and meanwhile the universe falls ever deeper into the grand pit of entropic decay. Planets, flung free of their stars, have disintegrated in the yawning interstellar, intergalactic dark. The stars, in their turn, ran down and fell apart; the stellar nurseries having flown apart in the gaping maw of the third law of thermodynamics, no new stars were born to replace them. Even atoms are no more; protons and neutrons have decayed.

Some infinite time ago, on its trillionth birthday, the human race wrote itself into the interstices between the physical constants of the universe, and disappeared. We gods don't know why. Perhaps they did it hoping to emerge someday, in a bright and distant future; perhaps it was a sublime form of racial suicide.

Outside this unending party, all is dark, darker than the grave. The only sound is the X-ray hiss of black holes, devouring the last stray leptons and quarks, crushing them into nothingness. And even when the black holes are gone, evaporated, died of hunger after quintillions of years, this party may linger yet, because it's made of gods' dreams, far stronger than pathetic energy and slipshod matter.

This grand palace of the imagination floats on the cooling corpse of the universe like an algal bloom on a long-lost lake, ignoring the fact of its own impossibility, maintained by the boundless wills of the gods herein assembled. It's a beautiful place, gorgeous beyond comprehension. Great forests of oak and spruce, redwood and aspen reach for the sky, their leaves shivering and whispering in the breezes. Ionic and Doric columns stand in soldier's ranks, and fawns and nymphs dart back and forth among them, racing each other for the pure sweet joy of it. A great stepped pyramid, its angles softened by a two-cubit-thick carpet of green moss, waits at the heart of a jungle filled with the cries and songs of macaws, pumas, birds-of-paradise. Golden fountains everywhere dispense whatever ambrosia your heart might desire. It's the perfect amalgam of any and all of the cultures of human faith, an ecosystem of mythemes and all their attendant imagery.

Existing here is about as dull as watching shit dry in the sun, let me tell you.

⊷►◄ ◄ ⊲ — ▷ ► ►⊶

I went fishing.

There are lakes here, broad flat reaches of water, mirror-still, where you can see clear to the bottom even at the deepest point. I wished a canoe into existence on the rocky verge of one of these lakes, checked it carefully for leaks—you can't be too careful when you're a trickster—then dreamt a paddle into my hands and pushed off. My ferret woke briefly from his doze, looked around at all the water, muttered "Again?", and went back to sleep. He loves fish, but he hates fishing.

I rowed till I could see the fish darting hither and thither, maybe twenty feet below me. I set the paddle down on the curved floor of the canoe and waited.

After a while, a handful of fish swam nearer the surface. I watched and waited. One of them, a big jackfish, broke the surface with his head and gills.

"Hello, Fox," he said.

"Hullo, brother pike," I replied.

"So what's new?"

"Well, there's a bunch of old fogeys goin' on and on about the chicken and the egg on shore," I said. "Care to see?"

"Thanks, but no thanks."

"I set one old fucker's robe on fire."

"I bet you did."

"C'mon, hop up into the boat. I'll give you a better view."

"I'm not falling for that one, trickster," said the fish. Fish can't frown, but I'm pretty sure if they could, he would have frowned at me. "I'll hop into the boat, you'll brain me and cook me, and I'll end up swimming out of your foul ass, in pieces. Not this fish, old son."

"You don't trust me?" I said, putting on a sad face.

"Not as far as I can—" Those were very nearly his last words, because while he was speaking I lunged into the water and grabbed him by his gills, hooking my fingers deep inside. His eyes got big, and he croaked "Fuck you, Fox," and those truly *were* his last words.

My ferret woke up when I dropped the fish into the bottom of the canoe. He sniffed the air, then took a deep breath, savoring the odor. "Got one, did you?"

"Yes," I said, picking up the paddle. "Don't eat any till we get back to shore."

She came walking barefoot down the beach as I cooked my share of the fish over a fire I'd built from the chopped-up wreckage of the canoe. She wore a plain dress of pale silk that brushed her ankles. Her toenails, fingernails, and lips were painted the color of blood.

My ferret chewed his fish head in my ear, wet smacking noises and the crunching of bones. I've learned to ignore it over the past few eternities. He looked up at her, and said, "Who's she?"

"I'm not sure." There are an awful lot of gods and goddesses around here, and most of them don't like me and my kind. Tricksters get on a lot of nerves. It's a gift.

This goddess arrived at fireside and, saying nothing, sat next to me. I gave the spit that impaled the pickerel a quarter-turn. My ferret finished chewing, swallowed, and said, "You got a name?"

I said, "Ignore him. He's got about the worst manners in this place."

She said, "Do *you* have a name, little fur?"

I said, before the ferret could speak, "He's Weasel, and I'm Fox."

"*Ferret*," muttered the ferret, "it's *Ferret*, not Weasel..."

She laughed. "Some called me Moon, in my day," she said. Her eyes were bright green, like jade in the sun. "I've met your kind before, Fox. I don't believe I should quite trust you, should I?"

I gave her my broadest, most charming smile. "Care for some fish?"

⊷⊶◈ — ◈ ⊷⊶

After we ate, we went for a walk. She led, I followed, and my ferret dozed. He sleeps a lot, these days. I can understand.

We came to a fountain, and each of us took a chalice. I could hear a faint sound, like distant thunder, but more regular. We dipped our goblets into the running water, made our wishes, and drank. Mine tasted like mints and chocolate, which was unfortunate, since I'd wished for beer. Hers left red stains on her teeth. I couldn't tell if it was from wine or blood.

We kept walking, toward the thunder-sound. After a while, I realized it wasn't thunder; it was a drumbeat.

The ground under our feet grew spongy, and great shaggy trees arched over us, shading us from the sun. The drumming was hypnotic, a thudding sound that called my body to dance. Moon felt it too, I think; her steps became more rhythmic, more dance-like. Together we danced into the heart of the forest.

We came to a graveyard, a decoration surely, with canted headstones and tilted marble crosses furred with moss, their epitaphs weathered into illegibility. Kudzu climbed the trees, strangling them, and vines hung everywhere. In the shadows and the shades, Loa danced their crazy dances, their Creole chants shivering on top of the drumbeat.

We found a bench at the edge of the empty boneyard and watched them for a while. Someone had set a bouquet of fresh flowers on one of the nearby graves: stargazer lilies, frail orchids, baby's breath, a spray of roses in a shade of red so dark they looked almost black. We sat, saying nothing, letting the rhythms of the dance and the spicy honey smell of the stargazers envelop us. Her bare shoulder was cold against my skin.

One song ended, and another began, a paean on sex and rapture.

Moon said, "Why are we here?"

"Oh for *fuck's* sake," I said, standing. "Not you too." My ferret woke up, but kept his peace. I think I startled him with my vehemence.

"Hear me out, Fox," she said. Her eyes implored me.

"No, seriously," I said. "I am sick and fucking tired of hearing everyone here noodle around that fucking question like it's the only thing of any importance in all the god-damned universe. If I have to—"

She shut me up by standing next to me, laying her fingertip on my lips, and whispering, "Fox, shut up." She sat back down and patted the bench next to her. I stood my ground, glaring at her. The tips of my ears burned.

In the shadows, the drumming and the songs went on, the Loa ignoring us. Perhaps they hadn't even noticed my outburst. They've always been a little different.

Moon said, "It's the only question that bears *asking*, Fox. It's a question that no one out there"—she waved an arm to indicate our backtrail, the elder gods with their togas and their Doric columns and olive boughs—"seems willing to seek a true answer for."

One of the dancers darted toward us, hissed "*Damballah Wedo vous regarde!*" and retreated again to the shade of one of the great trees.

"But I have an answer," she said, ignoring the interruption like it hadn't even happened. "One that's so simple and so obvious, it seems, that no other has come upon it in all the millennia that we've been here at the party."

I looked at her, glared at her, really, and waited.

"We're *gods*, aren't we?" she said. "We're meant to *create*." She smiled at me, and stood up again. "So let's *create*."

She shrugged her shoulders, and her dress slipped off them, slithered down her pale body, and pooled at her feet. She stepped one foot out of it, and with the other kicked it away in among the headstones. Like all proper goddesses she wore nothing underneath.

Taking his cue to leave, my ferret bounded away, deeper into the graveyard, pursuing some small animal.

"Are you coming?" she said.

Nobody had to tell me twice.

She smelled like earth and rain. Her lips tasted like blood, her tongue fought like a snake. When I slid inside her she clenched me with muscles I didn't know existed.

She fucked like a thunderstorm. She bit and scratched and howled like an animal. I did too. I roared like a bear, and she roared like a lioness, almost at the same time.

And then she pushed me off of her and sat up and said, "Like that. Just like that."

I couldn't smell the grave flowers anymore. All there was to smell was the musk of raw god sex.

In a lull in the drumbeat, I heard my ferret say, "So I take it you two are done, then?"

⟶⟵⟶ ⟵⟶⟵

Moon's belly swelled as we walked back. Even over the span of a couple of hours, the change was noticeable. By the time we returned to the stony beach where we'd met, it was time: her water broke, staining the smooth pebbles underfoot.

She gave birth to a brand-new universe, a fledgling bubble of light and heat and space-time. We named it, blessed it, and sent it on its way, out past the event-horizon curve of the endless party, into the heat-death nothingness beyond.

And later, when one of the elder gods asked me which came first, I grinned and said, "I did, but not by much."

Patrick Johanneson was born, raised, and still lives in Manitoba. He works as a webmaster as a small university, volunteers at a second-run/art-house theatre, teaches judo, and writes SF and fantasy. His short stories have appeared in *On Spec* and online in Ecclectica and InterText. He is working on a novel, *Everything that Never Happened*, about sailors and the undead (but not, it must be noted, about pirates and zombies).

Destiny Lives in the Tattoo's Needle

Suzanne Church

I dropped from the airship like a rock, praying for my chute to open.

It did.

The landing jolted me from ankle to jaw, but I remembered my training and hit the ground without snapping any bones.

The enemy was out there, searching for anyone who had survived the wreck, and filling me with the dread that follows a man in war. Especially a Thinker, like me, for whom torture might be worth the effort.

I inhaled as I scanned around. Tall grasses brushed at my thighs. I had absorbed data on the sage grass that grew in this part of Pacifica, a grass that not even goats would eat. The smell was heady, like moldy bark, and I tore off a piece and sipped at the end.

Bile rising, the bitterness spoke volumes on the intellectual brilliance of goats.

To my left, the remnants of a wooden fence lay crumbled along the base of a rolling hill. On the other side, the wild grass looked a little different, more like an intentional crop, though it was overrun with weeds and bushes. I headed for the densest patch, hoping to find some dandelion leaves.

On closer inspection, the fence wasn't rotten so much as carefully broken to appear worn. I climbed over and dropped to all fours. By moonlight, I clawed at a clump of dandelions, brushing the dirt away before I munched on the leaves. The roots looked like carrots so I took a bite. Though bitter, they didn't engage my gag reflex like the sage grass had, so I ate two and saved a bunch for later.

I crawled up the hill and, from the crest, a vista opened up before me. The amber hue of the downed airship caught my attention. Remembering the last course I'd plotted before the ship lost containment, and using the stars, I determined the crash site was north of me. The remains burned bright enough to build a partial day-bubble in the darkness. It called men with weapons like moths to a porch light.

I could see them, some on foot and some on troop transports, gathering around the edges of the wreckage. Worse, the unmistakable hands-in-the-air gestures of prisoners added their dejected silhouettes to the crowd.

Damn.

They'd be searching for me. I carried a plethora of secrets, though not on paper. Every airship had a Thinker. We were worth more in a war than ammunition, more than any grunt or officer for that matter.

Back to crawling, with my rear a little closer to the ground, I headed down the hill, putting some land in the line of sight between the ship and my position. The fence followed a crooked line all the way to the next ridge and beyond. My instincts told me to ditch the field and go my own way, because where there were fences, there were people loyal to the Pacificers. But the wooden construct's clever design spoke to me. Dandelions, sage grass, and grain in beautiful randomness; no simple farmer would build such a marvel.

Past the second ridge, the fence took a sharp turn to the south and ended at a pile of rocks arranged to conceal an opening.

My nerves turned the corner from worried to hyper-alert while my Thinker curiosity drove me forward. I felt more exposed than I had on the high ridge. I might as well have shouted, "I'm an Atlanticer. Come and take me. Free torture material, no waiting!" Yet I kept on crawling.

I paused to slow my breathing. I counted ten inhales before movement near the rocks caught my eye. The guy had a bow pointed at me, making me wonder if I had hopped dimensions to a land where guns and grenades didn't win all the playground fights. On my knees, I raised both hands, hoping I wouldn't learn what it felt like to have a shaft of wood sticking out of me.

"I'm unarmed," I said.

He didn't speak. But I could hear the squeak of the bow bending.

"I'm not what you think."

Then the twang of release sounded, followed closely by the thump of wood sinking into the dirt less than a meter away.

I waved my arms in the sky. "Okay, maybe I am, but could we calm it down?" I threw the dandelion roots to the ground, to prove my good intentions. "I didn't mean to steal. I was hungry, is all. And I thought them only weeds."

Escape scenarios flowed through my mind like water over falls. Still kneeling, I put both hands behind my head, and said, "Those soldiers by the wreck would give you five, maybe six hundred standards for a find like me, delivered *alive*."

I could hear the man pulling back the bow again. I waited for the twang but it didn't come. Finally, he left the security of the rocks, bow drawn in front of him, and moved out of the shadows into the moonlight. He wore a cape, the hood covering his face with a grim-reaper-meets-black-hole pit of nothing.

"Don't move," he said, though the voice wasn't low or masculine. Either he was a kid, or the woodsman-reaper was a woman. "The next one's aimed at your heart."

Yep, *he* was definitely a *she*. "I believe you." I kept to my knees, my hands still on my head. I wasn't sure if she could see my face, as the moon was behind me, so I turned a bit to the left, revealing the tattoo on my right cheek.

She released the tension on the bow string, but kept the arrow nocked.

I thought about shouting, "I'm a Thinker!" but she had started the cloak-and-bow dance, so I followed her lead.

"Get up," she said. "Keep your hands behind your head."

With the awkwardness of a guy who'd fallen from the sky, crawled around a while, then kneeled for too long, I stood.

"Move towards the door." She indicated with her bow towards the rock-obscured opening.

My need to see her face grew. My data archives scanned random meetings, searching for a reference that might make sense of the woman. Her voice wasn't familiar, I was certain I had never heard it before, yet part of me knew it, knew her, knew my whole life had been building to this moment. Immersed in my data-space, my hands fell to my sides.

"Hands up!"

I jolted back to the moment and returned my now-shaking hands to the please-don't-kill-me position. Close now, her frame was discernable under the cape. She was my height, my build, and she smelled as though baths were rarer than straight fences in this part of the world.

After clearing my throat a couple of times, I found my voice. "If you don't mind me sayin', your fence sings of a Thinker's handiwork. Your husband?"

"Don't have one."

"Oh." More words would've filled the awkward gap, but I'm much better with calculations than I am with women. She moved aside so that I could pass her on my way to the door-hole. The moonlight found its way onto the tip of her nose. Her skin was as pale as the moon.

Still aiming at me, she said, "Keep moving."

A question lingered at the back of my throat but I didn't allow it to escape. "It's pretty damned dark in there. I don't suppose you brought an emitter?"

I took her silence as a "no." Shuffling between the rocks, I lost my balance and both hands rushed out of my neutral position to save my head from cracking open. "I was falling," I said, as an afterthought to keep her arrow out of my back.

"I'm watching you," she said. Her bow string squeaked in protest as she drew it back once more. For a moment, my mind reached out and plucked it like a violin. My archives chose a low G as the note that should vibrate along its desperate length. Before I continued into the total blackness in front of me, I took a final direction bearing.

I didn't like not being able to read her movements, but her breathing sounded easy, not the quick panting of fear. For now.

A tunnel led to the left, heading northwest. It was dug from the earth and braced with more wood of the same vintage as the fence. The floor sloped at a steep twenty degrees and the top was low, so I had to stoop as I scuffed along. With each step, dust stirred, filling my nose with earthen smells and my mouth with grit.

"How far?" I asked.

The bow string again. I'd never drawn one before, but a part of me wondered when it would snap.

The passage curved to the right, then left again, and I lost a bit of my directional certainty. A part of me needed to know my location, as though it could spell my fate. The more westerly a route, the deeper I moved into enemy territory.

We reached a branch and I stopped. She nudged my right shoulder with the arrow, so I took the right branch, relieved to be heading slightly more east. Thirty meters ahead, the tunnel opened into a room.

The overhead emitter glowed dim green. Wires snaked down the ceiling and met more wires on the far wall. A sideboard held a few dishes. On top sat a thermalater and below was a storage cupboard, for water I guessed. *All the comforts of home.*

"It's nice," I said.

"Kneel down."

I dropped back into position, my hands behind my head again. She released the bow and set it down in the dirt, well behind my reach. Next, she pulled first my left, then my right hand behind my back and tied them together. Neither of us spoke. With her knee, she knocked me face first into the dirt.

My jaw hit hard, hurting like hell, but I didn't hear the telltale snap of broken bones. "What was that for?"

"Your choices," she said.

Choices? As far as I could figure, every move since the airship had lost cohesion hadn't been chosen, more like thrust in my face like a sharp poker.

"You could've killed me back there. If you do me here, you'll be stuck dragging my body topside for burial."

"Who said I'd bury you?"

I looked down at the dirt. The greenish light made contrast tricky, but I could make out darker patches in the floor, blood stains maybe, bigger than what would leak out of a rabbit or a chicken.

She moved over to the sideboard. Her hood remained firmly down, hiding her face from mine. I wondered if she was ugly—scarred or savaged by some past indiscretion. Tapping the top of the thermalater, she said, "Can you fix this?"

"Got any tools?"

She opened the sideboard. A water purifier with a full tank took up most of the space. Tools had been tucked in around it, and some hung from the inside of the door.

"I need to walk over there."

Her head moved down, slightly, the smallest excuse for a nod I'd ever seen.

Standing was tricky without the use of my hands, but I managed it with a fraction of my dignity intact. "Take the cover off," I said.

Close enough to touch her, my curiosity peaked. The hood was so damned low and the cloth so thick that I'd never get a good look. As she popped the metal top off to reveal the machine's workings, a good stream of green light found its way into the dark-hood zone. For a second, I glimpsed her eyes reflecting the light back. Their intensity could've cut through me faster than one of her arrows.

She motioned with her head for me to focus on the thermalater. I leaned in closer, angling hard to each side to try and see past my own shadow into the gloomy innards. I opened a maintenance file in my mind and called up the schematic for a unit of similar size and power. A quick comparison to what I saw before me revealed the problem.

"There," I pointed with my nose.

She didn't move any closer.

"You see the striped wire leading down to that triangular component with five posts?"

"Step back," she said.

I gave her room to move in and check the workings.

"Yes."

"The wire's corroded. Probably not bringing enough current to the component, which is called the aggravator. Without enough juice, it can't get atoms busy enough to warm anything. You need to replace the wire."

"I've misplaced my spool of spare wire," she said. I could've done without the sarcasm, but she was the one with the weapon, and my hands weren't exactly in an offensive position.

"Take a length from up there." I pointed with my head at the ceiling. "The emitter could move a meter and still throw enough light around the room. And that'd give you two lengths of wire. One for the repair and one as backup."

She nodded.

"Have you got a knife to strip them?"

She pulled a knife from beneath her cape. A big butcher's kind of knife that would be awkward to use for close work.

"Got anything smaller?"

She shook her head. In my mind, I imagined the smile on her face, telling me she probably did have a smaller one, but she wanted to play.

"It'll do," I said. Sitting back, I bum-shuffled my way to the far side of the room while she worked. The bigger the distance between me and the knife, the closer my heart rate returned to normal. The bow wasn't far from her grasp. She worked the wire as though she'd been born an electrician. When she finished, she said, "You found it faster than I predicted."

I shrugged, too afraid to thank her for the compliment in case it wasn't one. Then the scenario unfolded for me. The thermalater had been a test. I'd been so busy trying to think my way out, I'd forgotten to pay attention to the moment.

With the unit fixed, she warmed a cup of water, sipped at it, and then turned her hooded face towards me.

"I miss coffee," she said.

"Don't we all?"

"You're an Atlanticer." Not a question.

If the uniform hadn't given me away, the symbols in my tattoo should've spelled it out for her: my family crest at the center, an old Boston name. My Thinker level swirled around it, and my battalion logo and rank had been burned onto the fringe. At the far right, two outstretched lines tapered to points—the only part of the design that my mother had chosen for me. On my first birthday, when my parents had sent me to be tested, I had scored off the standard charts. Enticed by the reward, they had decided right there in the facility to enlist me. Thinkers were rare, and one of high caliber would eliminate their debt and buy my sergeant father a promotion.

"The men in town would kill me for keeping your kind and collect the reward themselves. Convince me not to eat you."

"Well, ma'am, I helped you fix the thermalater."

"We both know I could've done that alone."

"I have a spare emitter in my pocket. A yellow one. It'd make your room twice as bright."

"Keep going."

I wasn't sure how much more I could reveal that she hadn't already figured out. Whatever game she was playing with me, I wasn't privy to the rules. Eating me wasn't a threat she'd carry through, only another attempt to unsettle me, keep my thoughts jumbled to slow me up. Whatever her ultimate goal, I had a feeling that I wouldn't be laughing at the punch line.

I swallowed, tasting more grit than saliva, and shuddered. Hours ago, I had been happy to hit the ground intact. Now I wondered if maybe I should've prayed for a hole in my chute.

Alternatives flipped by, each one ending with my death. The only variable seemed to be the amount of pain before the release. With nothing to lose, I threw my cards, hell, the whole damned deck, in front of me. "I'm a *high* Thinker. Designed for strategic plotting, navigation, and deployment. I carry more secrets than a brothel whore. With my reward you could upgrade your equipment and have enough standards left over for a half a side of cured pork."

She smirked. "With a high reward comes increased risk. A better chance I'd be murdered, not paid."

I saw my chance, then, like a tight opening big enough to squeeze through. "I could help you plan the handover, to ensure you get what's coming to you."

"I don't like the sound of that."

"Neither do I. But I'd just as soon not be eaten, if it's all the same to you."

"There're worse things than being eaten." Her voice turned the corner from hardened to bitter. Her life here—the cave, the well-planned fence, the sage grass—held twists of its own. Whatever the Pacificers had done to her, she wasn't loyal to them. My capture was personal. I should've slit my own throat instead of following her down the hole.

"What do you want?" I said.

"When the time is right."

⟶◦◦⟵ ⇐ — ⇒ ⟶◦◦⟵

Alone, my hands tied behind my back, I wondered when she would return. In the dim green light I had no sense of time. Hours could've passed; I certainly felt exhausted enough for it to be day, but tension and over thinking messes with my internal clock.

Though I'd been trained to compartmentalize, storing the most sensitive data below layers of operation manuals and navigational charts, I couldn't help but dwell on the accumulation of secrets I carried. The next strategic offensive, code name *Snowfall*, wasn't due to begin for another six days. With almost a week's notice, the Pacificers could easily ambush our battalions. We'd take huge losses, probably half the airship fleet. A dozen of my colleagues and I had spent three months on the strategy; choosing which waves to send on the primary mission, training the marines, waiting for the weather to be on our side.

She'd heated a bowl of stew in the thermalater and never retrieved it. The aroma of cooked roots and onions, mixed with a lamb-ish meat smell, filled the cave. My stomach growled loud enough to knock dust from the roof.

Saliva poured into my mouth from my glands. I hadn't eaten since the dandelions. By now, the stew would be tepid, but I could run the thermalater for another cycle.

Checking behind me, I stood and made my way to the unit. With my hands tied behind my back, I opened the door and stuck a finger in. Not too cold.

Nothing would have made me happier than to lick my finger, but that wasn't going to happen. She'd taken the knife, so I didn't have a way to cut my hands free. Instead, I grabbed the bowl, and then, with shaking legs, slowly kneeled down to set it on the dirt floor behind me.

In my haste to turn around, I stirred up a good-sized cloud of dust, most of which would end up in the stew. But with the kind of hunger spawning in my gut, anything would've tasted like heaven.

Leaning forward with my hands behind my back threw my center of gravity into a tailspin. I knew before it happened that I was going to face-plant into the stew, but it would taste great, so long as I didn't drown. When it splashed up my nose and into my eyes, I was glad that the contents had cooled.

"Want a spoon?" she said.

I should've turned around and looked at her, but I had committed to the food, and at that moment I was a rabid dog who'd chew off any hand that got between me and my meal.

"Greg!"

I spat out a precious mouthful of stew in shock. Gobs of vegetables and sauce stuck to my nose, my chin, and my cheeks. With the slow precision of a well-crafted plan, I turned around and faced her.

She still wore the cape and her face still hid in the shadow of the hood.

"How'd you know my name?"

She stepped closer, within reach. Pulling a rag from her pocket, she wiped away the mess on my tattooed cheek and pointed at the family crest, then my rank.

All along, I'd assumed the cave was her home. I shook my head, shocked that hunger had clouded my thoughts. Her facility must be beneath the hill I'd traversed only yesterday. *Was it yesterday?* Ten seconds of network access would be all the time she would have needed to search on my tattoo.

She stepped back and crossed her arms on her chest. "How are your wrists?"

"Sore."

From beneath her cape, she pulled the knife free of a leather holder. "Can I trust you, Greg?"

"Seems kind of unfair that you know my name and I don't know yours."

"As a high Thinker, you shouldn't ever contemplate fairness. Only precision, elegance, or logic."

"That's not how it works," I said.

Leaving my hands still pinned, she tucked the knife back into its holder. "Lying isn't the way to get what you need."

With that, she grabbed the near-empty bowl of stew and left me alone once more.

⊷⊷⊷ — ⊱⊷⊷

I had maneuvered myself closer to the wall and now leaned against it. I closed my eyes and drew my thoughts deep inside my mind, distancing myself from the pain in my wrists and the congealed stew up my nose.

Embracing data, I floated through my favorites—a list of the first one hundred prime numbers, the coordinates of every evac hospital in Atlantica, the height of every building in Boston. Each idea blanketed me, adding a buffer of comfort between the futility of my situation and the hope of rescue.

A trade was still a theoretical possibility. But she wouldn't dare bring anyone down to her cave. Nor would she reveal her cleverly hidden farm.

The trip for any such exchange would provide my only chance for escape. Whether the kind where I ran and hoped to find shelter, or the kind where I slit my own throat, had yet to be decided. But now I had the spores of a plan.

Decision brought comfort. For the first time in what must have been at least thirty-six hours, I found sleep.

⊷⊷⊷ — ⊱⊷⊷

I woke and had to piss so bad that I wet myself. The smell of the dirt and my own fluids brought me to full alertness. The room was quiet. If the woman was near, she was awfully still.

"Hello?"

She didn't answer.

In the dim green light of the emitter, I recognized her shape. She lay in the dirt, about as far from me as she could get in the room, and appeared to be sleeping.

Every muscle in my back, shoulders, wrists, legs, hell, *all* of me, ached. I needed to stand and walk around. Over to her. Pull back that hood and have a look at her face. I couldn't shake the haunting feeling that I knew her.

My mind flashed a thousand warnings. She would never sleep in my presence, especially when she had another place to go, to hide, to do whatever it was she did when she wasn't with me. But despite my misgivings I struggled to my feet. Ignoring every shred of common sense, I awkwardly made my way across the room. And as the danger volume made my head pound, I knelt on one knee beside her.

The cloak had been cinched tightly around her body, the hood drawn nearly closed, leaving a small opening for fresh air. Her chest lifted and fell with the long, slow breaths of sleep. If she still carried the knife, I might be able to fumble for it, but could I do so without waking her?

Instead, I turned so that my hands were positioned over the hood and craned my neck around to try and see my way to undoing the string holding it closed at her neck.

"Greg?"

Her voice made me jump. With my mouth was as dry as sand, I said, "Yeah?"

"Have you ever had a dog?"

The question threw me. I had expected her to scold me for touching her, or to pull out the knife and cut me. Deceit wasn't rewarded, so I followed along. "A shaggy one," I said. "Named *Sol.*"

"A male?"

My hands still waited, right above the string. "Sol was a bitch. The kind that never stops yipping, eats through everything that means something to you, and pisses in your bed."

She could've moved by now, sat up, grunted even. Instead, she lay in her prone position. Part of me believed she wanted me to undo the hood. She said, "How long did you keep her?"

"A few months, until the army deemed her gratuitous."

"Did you miss her?"

"I barely remembered her until you asked." My determination wouldn't last much longer. I bit my lip, grabbed a string, and pulled.

Her hands unfolded from beneath the cloak, the knife in her right. It moved in a slow, deliberate arc, and I braced myself for the pain of a thick hunk of metal sliding through skin, deep into my flesh.

Instead, she cut the bindings holding my wrists.

My arms flopped to my sides with an excruciating round of pain. I couldn't will them to move. Control wouldn't happen for a while yet. But I turned to face her and smiled.

"Thanks," I said.

She set down the knife like a line in the dirt between us. I stared at it then back at her. Without another word, she loosened the hood's string and pulled it down, revealing her face.

Nothing could have prepared me for the shock.

"Yes," she said. "It's real."

My thoughts tumbled, a flurry of questions, repercussions, and analyses until the room wouldn't stop spinning. I swallowed down the bile rising up my throat. After years of war, endless offensives, and then the fall from the sky, I should've simply accepted the reality. But Thinkers analyze. They make sense of the senseless. And what this woman had revealed to me was so incongruous, so unlikely, that my mind and body would not allow the truth of it to sink in.

"The airship," I said.

"I've been waiting a long time for the opportunity. The cost was worth the benefit."

"People died," I said. "The survivors were probably tortured. If they confessed our plans, you might've changed the course of the war."

"I didn't. There's no word of it on the network. This was about you, Greg. Nothing more."

"Thinkers never make a decision based on one parameter. But I don't need to explain that to you, do I?" My fingers graced her left cheek. Her tattoo had the family crest in the center, like mine. Her Thinker level swirled around it, with two more loops than I carried. The bare skin where her military designations should've been were so pristine, I had to touch them, again and again. Her level has higher than mine. How could she have hidden from recruiters her entire life?

She closed her eyes and I could almost hear the data connecting and re-forming. At the far left, two outstretched lines, identical to mine save for the tapers, reached out into the world. Her tapers ended in v-shaped forks. If I could pull my tattoo from my face and place it next to hers, my tips would fit precisely into her forks.

"I thought the marks were like snowflakes," I said. "Never this similar."

"Destiny lives in the tattoo's needle. No other pattern could ever find its way onto me."

"What do we do now?"

She rubbed at my wrists, bringing pain, but also the relief of blood circulation. "I had to be sure you were ready."

"You didn't answer my question."

"We run. North. I've spent years scouting safe stops and surveying trails. In five days, we can cross into the Northlands. Old Kanada. Neither side will look for us there."

She stood and picked up her bow which had been leaning against the wall near the tunnel. As she pulled back the string, testing the weight of her weapon, I saw her life as an operatic opus of choices: proximity to the border, high ground, along a logical flight path, the cave setup, the broken thermalater. All strategically placed like chess pieces, while she waited for the first white pawn to move.

"By tomorrow, they'll have finished with the airship," she said. "We can scavenge what we need from the wreckage. Can you walk?"

I shook my legs, one at a time, testing their workability. With a glance at her for permission, I staggered over to the side-board, dug out a glass, and slowly downed some water.

Another glassful.

After gasping with relief, I said, "Got any stew left?"

"In the kitchen. And clean clothes. The trip should loosen your muscles."

She reached out a hand and I took it. My thoughts felt fractured, disconnected. I'd gone from fugitive to prisoner to conspirator. "How long have I been down here?"

"Forty-one and a half hours, give or take six minutes."

I nodded. We moved into the tunnel. She pulled a portable blue emitter from her cloak and lit the way. I'd always hated the feel of blue light, as though it shouldn't count as light at all, more like an eerie glow that doesn't belong in the world.

She must've sensed my discomfort because she said, "They draw less power. Makes the batteries last."

I considered explaining to her that I understood the reason, and the feeling wasn't rational. But she knew.

"The facility had blue lights," she said. "Where they tested us. I despise the color, too. It makes me feel vulnerable."

And with her revelation, a compartment door blew outward in my mind. Its contents seeped across every aspect of the knowledge that built Greg. I'd buried every moment with her, from the warm, wet womb of our mother to the final grip of our chubby hands as they yanked her away from me.

"Alyssa?"

She nodded.

I closed my eyes and prayed for the strength to follow her north, to a place where we might find peace. My tattoo tingled at the tips. I opened my eyes to see her cheek lightly pressed against mine. I longed for a mirror, yet I knew the tapers had finally found each other.

⟶⟵⟶ — ⟵⟶⟵

Just as she'd said, the crash site appeared deserted. Most of the wreckage had been picked over. Alyssa's pack nestled on her back like an old lover. Mine simply made my shoulders ache.

I swallowed another mouthful of sage grass and chased it with a quarter liter of milk to coat my throat and gut, slowing the autonomic gag reflex enough to force down the grass. Alyssa said its chemical composition blocked my frontal synapses. My data stores would randomize then reconnect into patterns that distorted my archives of the airship. Otherwise the sight of it would trigger embedded beacons and call the good guys to extract my still-alive ass before the Pacificers found it.

Military my entire life—save for that first year—the instinct to regroup, to debrief, clung to me like dew on a leaf. Loyalty to the cause had never been negotiable, but the thought of a war-free zone with a cabin in the woods brought closure, and with it a level of comfort I'd never experienced before.

My twin.

I had blocked her existence for so long that acceptance fought against every neuron firing in my head.

"Hurry," she said. "We need to put some distance between us and the site."

I nodded. The gesture was easy, small, neutral. Hardly worth the attention of a mind overflowing with more important thoughts and decisions. But gestures can mean so much more, and this one, unbeknownst to me, would have been no exception, if not for the protection of her crop of vile weeds.

To distract me from puking another mouthful of the stuff, Alyssa shared her history. At the age of three, she had outsmarted facility security protocols. Alone, she fled Boston, making her way from culverts to abandoned sheds, hiding from the world while building her own place in it. Living off the grid meant no formal education, no military training, no family, no friends. She had constructed a hole in the world and waited for me to join her.

I spoke of my own life, my service, but it all seemed selfish and heinous compared to the purity of her choices. When I described my former platoon, giving life to the memories of my closest war mates, she said, "They'll come for you."

"But the grass—"

"It only blocks deliberate communication. They might have planted a deep initiative, just in case. To protect their investment."

"Is that all I am?"

"Not after I'm through."

⟶⟨⟩—⟨⟩⟶

Three hours and seventeen minutes later, give or take twelve seconds, a squad of Atlanticers caught up to us. We hid at first, but they outnumbered us twenty to one. We had discussed this inevitability, and dreaded our only course of action.

Alyssa buried herself and slowed her breathing to a near comatose state. I moved as far away from her as possible, and then snapped a twig so they'd find me.

As they cuffed my hands, I embraced a flow of data. It did little to block out my fear and guilt, but its solace was all that I had. I held it close to my heart, a buffer of hope while I braced myself for the long ride back.

⟶⟨⟩—⟨⟩⟶

I hadn't seen or heard from her in two years. I had buried her so deeply within my mind that I often wondered if I had simply dreamed her existence.

As the airship neared the front, we detoured north to avoid the enemy. The hit took us by surprise, so far from the main fighting. As the men and women around me prepared for the crash, I donned my gear and stepped out an emergency exit with an uneasy calm brought on by my constant diligence to check and recheck my gear.

I dropped from the airship like a rock, praying Alyssa would be waiting for me.

Suzanne Church "juggles her time between throwing her characters to the lions, teaching her sons how to define infinity, and working in direct sales. When cornered she becomes fiercely Canadian, making *Tesseracts* a perfect fit. Her short fiction has appeared in *Cicada* and *On Spec*, and in several anthologies including *Tesseracts Thirteen*."

Nights in White Linen

Daniel Sernine

Translated by Sheryl Curtis

It's a vision of marble or limestone, white under the moon: palaces or marble tombs, limestone cliffs, sand dunes, as white as shrouds in the night. And so many stars in the sky—it must be a vision of the past, in the desert. Weren't the greatest astronomers Egyptian and Arab?

There are steles, possibly a colonnade; long, shallow, empty basins, which must have once surrounded a courtyard or garden with water.

Far from the mosaics and arcades, an old dog wanders, gaunt, white with age. There's a wall, surrounding a city, a necropolis—blending into one another like a memory we dream about. Or the memory of a dream.

Then I wake, recalling only that it was night, but everything was white, ivory and bone powder.

⟶⊶⊷⊷ — ⊶⊷⊷⟵

Sometimes I manage to fall asleep almost as soon as I lie down—waiting 30 minutes or an hour for sleep, no more. But I wake in the middle of the night and that's when insomnia lies in wait for me. Too tired to read, too wide awake to settle back to sleep, a hollow in the pit of my stomach I don't want to fill.

Occasionally, insomnia has already settled in at the onset of the night. My desperation, then, is akin, I imagine, to that experienced by women when their husbands would slip between the sheets, men they didn't love but with whom they'd never the less spend two-thirds of their lives.

So I try to read as long as possible, magazines, newspapers, filled with the wars and massacres of the previous day. But my eyes weary and I have to turn out the lights. Yet, I still can't fall asleep. The images fill my mind, along with the memories, the thoughts. The syncopated flashing of the roof-lights, blue and red, like a raid on a shooting gallery, the fluorescent numbers on the police car doors, the crackle of the radio and the brief injunctions in a shocked quasi-silence.

And Xavier's white face behind the door window, a red blotch beneath his mouth as if he had been struck.

Once I thought I would come through this okay—the shock, the initial disbelief, a refusal all too quickly overcome by the evidence. For a while, I thought that was all there was, that it would pass.

There was no delayed reaction, only the slow upwelling of thoughts, of feelings, deploying like an army that takes weeks to take up its positions, a few hours at a time, every night. The things we said, the things we did, without knowing what turn events would take.

We'd known for some time that someone was dealing coke in the department. How long had we known? Impossible to say. Who had told us? Just as difficult to know. It would have been easy enough to ask, I suppose. And a short while later someone would have come up to me with what I needed. But I knew myself too well. I couldn't use or I'd be lost. There was no merit in my decision. It was the caution of fear.

We also knew about the pranks—there were more than in the previous years. I didn't know the victims. I supposed they weren't about to make a public complaint. Who found the scalp taken from a certain cadaver in their locker? Which professor found the index finger that had gone missing from another on his desk (apparently, at McGill, this was referred to as "giving him the finger"). The victims of these practical jokes didn't boast about it. Or possibly the department had dealt harshly with these tricks which were in poorer taste than usual.

I never thought that either Xavier or Geneviève was keeping company with pushers; I thought I knew them too well. Yet, I immediately suspected that Xavier was one of the pranksters—something in his tongue-in-cheek brand of humor, something in the tone of certain rejoinders, brought to mind a quartet of comedians from the 1960s (one of our profs had all their records).

The coke problem must have reached a peak for the dean to get worried enough to admit it. There was so much pressure on us all the time that the students needed something to keep up. That was a known fact. And everyone turned a blind eye up to a certain point. Apparently, the point of no return had been reached that year, or possibly the year before.

A conference was held on the problems of hard drugs. For third-year medical students! And on the resources available to health professionals who wanted to overcome their dependency. An anonymous, non-judicial program.

And we felt... I felt... that some of the people around me were being targeted: looks, allusions, a certain tension in the silences. Yes, it was serious and it was probably much more than just cocaine.

When did it all start? For Xavier and Geneviève, probably quite a long time ago. For me, I don't know. In my insomnia, it doesn't always start at the same time. It depends on the night. It didn't start with when I met Xavier, or Geneviève. They had already been in the background for an unknown amount of time, without me being able to recall a precise moment when we "met". No anecdote, no cute or touching story, like at the beginning of a movie. They were students, like I was, and they gradually stood out, taking on relief and depth, like other guys and chicks, as the weeks and then the months of the first year passed. It's not as if they were anonymous within the group. Far from it. I recall having noticed both of them, separately, for different reasons. Geneviève, because she seemed to be older than the average. She must have worked for several years, maybe as a nurse, before going back to school. I figured she was close to forty, but I readjusted this downward and gave her thirty—in any case, she was clearly more "adult," than the members of our group who were just out of Cégep.

Xavier too, I know this now, was older than the group average. But what was noticeable in his case was his small stature, which no doubt made him look younger. He reminded me of Roman Polanski, but with a Latino touch in the expressiveness of his face and the mobility of his eyes, not to mention his heavy five o'clock shadow.

So, when did it all start already?

The dissection team next to mine was desperate: their cadaver was unusable. They lost marks identifying anatomical structures since very few things were still in their rightful place in the obese mass that continued to decompose despite embalming and refrigeration between sessions. My neighbors were out of luck: instead of some good chap who died from a heart attack after deciding to donate his body to science, they had inherited an unclaimed body, some stiff from the morgue. There were cigarette burns on his torso, barbed wire lacerations on his belly, and several of his fingers were broken out of shape—surely the result of hanging out with the wrong crowd.

That day, we were supposed to open the skull. The teams at the other tables found their brains to be small pinkish masses, rubbery, too perfect to be real. But the head of that poor guy, which must have been used for batting practice, released a semi-liquid mass that overflowed onto the floor. One of the students uttered a string of swear words; another hurled her last meal.

Xavier and Geneviève were part of the scene, at the next dissection table, smiling at our colleague's colorful language.

So when did it all start, already? Possibly when I would run across Xavier in the hallways at med school, either alone or with Geneviève, late at night. Or when they would be walking down the road from the tower instead of taking the bus as we did when we went to the Tabasco Bar. When it was night.

Or maybe the whole thing started when I saw men talking with a worried looking dean in the reception area of his office, well after 5:00 p.m. then leaving, all looking like people who had failed to resolve a problem. Yet, judging by his face, it was the dean who shouldered the heaviest part of the burden. Maybe it all started then, when the problem had become so serious that the police sent in undercover investigators.

Of course, at the time, I had no idea they were police officers.

I recall one Friday, late afternoon. That week there had been no anatomy exam. The students were left to their own devices, without the usual pressure to keep them in line. The atmosphere was electric. It was hot in the old med school corridors; it smelled of formaldehyde. The most compulsive were thinking ahead to studying all weekend; the others focused on their usual Friday night drinking binge.

That evening, there was a group of us. Xavier and Geneviève were there. They didn't often mingle with the other students and occasionally seemed to have other cultural references, other memories, different tastes, like immigrants, like the elderly. We left the Tabasco Bar at about two in the morning; it was a typical autumn night—cool, yet not too cold. We crossed Decelles Avenue to walk up the long road to the tower. On our way, Charlebois took a small flashlight out of his car's glove compartment. When we were level with the Bronfman Library, we slipped behind the grove, climbed over the wire mesh fence and crossed into the cemetery. Xavier, who had waited until then, got out his coke and we all enjoyed some. I still didn't know if he was the supplier; but I did learn that night that he used.

Then we strolled about, our little group breaking up and then flowing back together, tracking one another by the sound of our laughter. At one point, Xavier and Geneviève took the lead; I was with Charlebois and his girlfriend, Luciane. Once again, a shadowy silhouette, black on dark, intrigued us. Charlebois turned on his flashlight. A man perched on all fours, on a long tombstone, posed like a beast. Shoulders hunched like those of a tiger, with a feline movement, he turned his head towards us, teeth bared in a grimace that distorted his entire face. Luciane screamed. Charlebois shouted, then swore. It was Xavier, and Geneviève's laughter brought his brief performance to an end.

But I thought I had seen something completely different. I'd seen a man crouched in the same position, but naked, head shaken vigorously, and a shroud draped limply over the tombstone.

Xavier climbed down from his perch, but a part of me was still somewhere else, the cemetery was a necropolis, the black earth and the naked trees replaced by bright sun and pale steles; winged lions with men's faces and curly beards, had replaced angels and archangels.

"Hey, Fabien, you coming or what?"

Everything returned to order, the streetlights on Côte-des-Neiges Road, the dome of Saint Joseph's Oratory. Xavier and Geneviève had already headed off. Luciane started talking about leaving the cemetery. In the time it took her to convince the two of us, Charlebois and me, the other pair had disappeared into the distance. We set about looking for them. We walked up and down the rows for a good thirty minutes. At one point, guided by my sense of smell, I took off on my own, yet I knew exactly where Luciane and her boyfriend were, behind me. I walked back to them some moments later and convinced them to leave without waiting for Geneviève and Xavier, who were old enough to go home on their own and were no doubt trying to spook us by hiding as they did. Perhaps they had already left, amused by the thought that we were still out looking for them as they were walking home.

Of course, the next day, Xavier and Geneviève said I had been right. Charlebois forgave them immediately, but Luciane remained cold and distant toward them following this nocturnal prank.

⸻

In the dissection room, the prof's staccato voice was familiar, but one day it rose an octave higher and I turned to look at the other end of the room. The man was beside himself, chewing out a big lump of a guy in a white lab coat. His colleagues appeared to be trying to disappear into the floor. The explanation passed from table to table, until it reached me. The team leader had decided it would be funny to remove the anatomy manual from the prof's lectern and replace it with another type of anatomical publication, open to the centerfold orgy. In the face of the old physician's anger, a girl from the next team over, who had started to weave garlands around her colleagues with a cadaver's intestines, hastily stuffed them more or less back in place.

The fact that this professor, usually so debonair, lost all patience with his students' tricks was an all too eloquent indication of the tension generated by the investigation into drugs at the med school. People had been questioned, minor seizures had been made, but they suspected a major ring involving hospital personnel as well.

Some students, who had chanced to overhear conversations or witness searches, wondered whether the tasteless pranks were also taking on a criminal turn. The janitors, the lab attendants, the night guards all knew more, but they must have been sworn to secrecy. It was only later, weeks or months later, that certain tidbits of information filtered out: cadavers had been dismembered—outside the dissection sessions—and their limbs had not been found. Another body, after having served for the anatomy course, had disappeared completely, its stained shroud stuffed in a recycling bin.

I turned to Xavier, a finger in his mouth, between his cheek and his gum, and knew he wasn't picking his teeth. He frowned and smiled at the same time as Charlebois gave him the latest news: a recently delivered body had disappeared from the morgue, the body of a murdered girl, a girl whose story might have touched us, vanished perhaps from Chicago or from Dallas, when she was a kid, who'd come to Montreal only to die a few years later from a pimp's needle. Charlebois looked shocked, and that was a sign of the wave of discomfort that had flowed over us. This was Charlebois after all, Charlebois who, at the beginning of the term had spent an evening demonstrating variations of the expression "to put your best foot forward," complete with the prop in hand.

I recall it clearly. Raymonde, who was with me, commented that people had to be pretty wound up to do something that disgusting and Xavier burst into hysterical laughter as if to prove her right.

I told myself then, that if Xavier wasn't more discrete, he would get caught by the narcs within a few days. Either a police officer or an informant had to have infiltrated the staff or the students, if the drug traffic was a serious as rumors said it was. What amazes me most, when I think back over it, was Xavier's temerity. He took unheard of chances. More and more, all the time. Either coke was something new for him and he was delving into it with a tragic frenzy, or he had been into it for a long time and using larger and larger amounts, throwing caution to the wind.

Like having an orgy in his mini-van in the middle of the university parking lot one evening, running the risk of alerting the campus guards. I was there, Geneviève was too, along with one or two other people. I was stoned, I would have liked to screw Geneviève, and she would have agreed, but I just couldn't. It's a bad memory. Lousy, even when I think back on it. She smelled bad and that was all it took, I just couldn't.

That and the fear, no doubt. There was enough coke in the mini-van to send each of us to prison for 25 years.

Towards the end, Xavier got out, despite a warning from Geneviève who suddenly grew angry—a murmured warning, an icy voice—an anger that immediately sobered me. But he got out anyway, with an urgent need to screw that apparently could not be satisfied with those in the mini-van.

I know it's stupid, but I hadn't realized that they— Geneviève and Xavier—were an item until then. That they were lovers, I mean.

Or that they had been. Obviously, things were not clear.

⇥⇤ — ⇥⇤

I started to be more cautious. Not avoiding them, not really, but avoiding their excesses. I did keep away from them at night, because that's when they seemed more... intense. Looking back, it seems to me now that, if a police officer had infiltrated our group, he could have arrested them for possession just by seeing the intensity in their faces, in their eyes.

I still don't understand exactly what triggered their happy-go-lucky attitude, the way in which they increasingly courted risk. For them, of course, it had been going on a long time. They must have been more cautious and discrete in the past, since they had never been caught. When I think back on it, it was almost suicidal, like the behavior of someone who knows he's condemned and wants to burn up before the end comes. That's it. They were burning up.

And I could have been burned as well.

⇥⊶← ⊸ — ⊳ →⊷⇤

I had my suspicions about what was coming when the med school morgue received a prostitute. Strangled, her face puffy. She was past her prime, but she offered a lot of flesh to her clients, tender yet firm.

Xavier knew when the shifts went on and off duty in the labs, and when the guards made their rounds. Now, I'm even convinced he knew about the police investigation underway, that he had identified the informer and knew when he was away. Obviously, running into someone in the corridors at that time of night was suspicious; it was so unusual. But it was just rare enough to make the risk acceptable.

He had coke on him. Yet, despite his feverishness, his hands weren't shaking. He could still make a line on the back of his hand, in the hollow of the thumb tendon, sniff it while walking and get to the door which was his destination.

Over the years, I suppose, he had acquired all sorts of skills. In any case, in his pocket, he had what he needed to overpower the lock. And, like me, he had eyes to see, so he knew the combination to open the door to the morgue.

I recall, I had a mental vision of a spectacular arrest, like on Miami Vice, with officers jumping out from all directions, weapons aimed, shouting "Freeze!", which would have been somewhat ironic for a suspect who was already totally stoned.

But nothing like that happened.

And I didn't at all expect what did.

⇥⊶← ⊸ — ⊳ →⊷⇤

Anyone can suffer from insomnia, I suppose, and much more than that.

Xavier opened a few drawers, in the half-light of the door window, until he found the woman, the prostitute. He unwrapped her white shroud. She had not been dissected yet, but had been opened for the autopsy and closed back up cursorily.

I don't know how he could have managed to get it up while looking at that meter-long scar. But one slit is as good as another, I suppose.

Since the sliding drawer could not have supported their combined weight, he placed her on the floor, as stiff as she was, with the shroud for a sheet and the cold tiles for a mattress. Then he removed his shoes, pants and briefs. He had probably decided, no doubt with reason, that if he were caught there was no point in hastily donning his clothes.

He had some difficulty spreading her thighs. Then he penetrated her, thrust in and out for a moment, while biting her on the neck, hard enough to stifle his cry. It was brief, like between two cats, and I thought—as I often have on other occasions—that people put a lot of energy into something that lasts such a little while.

When he pulled away, the perforation marks of his teeth were clearly visible between the woman's shoulder and her neck. I recalled how angry Geneviève had been with him another evening, another evening of lust.

Then, as he dressed, he said, in a matter-of-fact tone, "I'm counting on your discretion, Fabien."

Shivers ran up and down my back. I can feel them still, and I can hear his voice as he said those words: low, steady, as icy as an assassin.

I still have no idea when he had realized I was there. And how could he have known that I wouldn't denounce him, that I had not stationed myself there specifically to catch the person who was looting the morgue or that I had not followed him to witness a coke deal—after all, I could have been an informant; he had considered the possibility that an investigation was underway. But there was nothing like that. Just a face, filled with confidence—not calmness, not serenity, but something like the arrogance of a leader or an aristocrat.

He was right, or course, I didn't denounce him.

⋯⋙⋘ ⋯ ⋙⋘⋯

But I never hung out with them, either of them, after that—not even during the day, between classes. Anyway, they skipped classes, as they had always done, which didn't prevent them from getting excellent grades.

Things didn't end there. Not any more than my insomnia gave me a break. You can't stop events once they've been set in motion any more than you can force sleep to come.

The subsequent events, the memory of those events, are condensed into a few images, like the memory of a nightmare when you wake up.

There was coke on the corridor floor, not far from the morgue. I bent down and, waving my hand, blew it away. The silence was the same as every other night, the silence of an old building, the distant, confused murmur of the ventilation system, the buzz of equipment running on auto-pilot in the labs, or the hum of refrigeration in the morgue.

They had come—they—I knew it shortly after the fact: Geneviève and Xavier. The drawers were closed, there was no trace, no way for me to know a body was missing. Yet the odor was there. Only a dog could have picked it up, but it was perfectly identifiable for me as well. I followed the trail, already cooling.

I didn't know about the cubby-hole under the roof, at the top of a metal staircase I had never used before. A small corner of a linen sheet peaked out between the door and the frame.

They sensed that I was in front of the door, just as Xavier had known I had been there the other night. They opened the door to me, just as certain that I was alone. That instinct, those infallible senses, that's what had saved them all those years, all those centuries perhaps.

They were crouched down—the space was small. Like that night in the cemetery, they had dismembered the body, their mouths were full, at least Geneviève's was as she gorged on the liver. Xavier was sucking the plentiful marrow from a femur, mouth dripping with the juice that served to liquefy coagulated blood, to tenderize muscles, his lips drawn back to secrete it all the better.

In the red glow of the emergency light, their fangs shone, as did the shroud and their pale foreheads under black locks of hair.

"Well, don't just stand there," Xavier blurted out bluntly, almost aggressively.

⤙❖ ⫷ — ⫸ ❖⤚

The arrest, the police cruisers that rolled silently behind the building, roof-lights flashing... that was another night. Xavier—I can still see him—had traces of red around his mouth. Geneviève, had streaks of white dust on her black blouse.

That was their downfall.

They didn't do drugs in the past. The exhilaration had been enough for them, the intoxication of marauding nights, moonlight reflecting on marble tombstones, the fragrance of freshly dug earth, the dizzying fumes of the formaldehyde, which was no longer a poison for their species.

Geneviève enjoyed nothing better, she had once confided, than to rip the white satin lining from luxury caskets.

Their senses were infallible, night vision, hearing, smell, that instinct that enabled them to feel the presence of mortals within a radius of 1,000 feet, so that hunts and watches were in vain. And then there was that other talent, the ability to penetrate the minds of dogs and lull their alertness.

But the white dust froze their sense of smell and, above all, dulled their instinct. Otherwise, they could have gone on, for eons, moving from one medical school to another, periodically returning—under new identities—to that particularly well located medical school that stood next to a cemetery, to the University of Montreal.

Neither the police nor their dogs spotted me, but Xavier and Geneviève could see me clearly, standing behind a basement window, probably as white as they were. Geneviève's face was too swollen to reveal any expressions. But Xavier placed his index finger on his lips, not asking me for silence, of course, but promising me his own and, in his thoughts, I read not only "be discrete" but also "get away from here, far away."

Leave? Where could I go? It's the anguish of that question that no doubt keeps me from sleeping, that and the scenes of brutality, the billy club beating down on Geneviève as she leapt, her jaw shattered by the blow, Xavier's fierce shriek before boots kicked his belly, knocking the wind from him.

Where could I go?

⋘⋙

I've just woken. I didn't even realize that I had fallen asleep. Sleep came faster than it did yesterday, despite the hunger. Or perhaps as a result of it. I can still see the images of my dream, but they might just be a memory. Definitely a memory. I saw swarming stars in crystal-clear nights, lands of sand and rock under the full moon, pale as snow but still warm from the day's sun. I saw the shining domes and minarets of cities, the trembling of palms on white walls, villages of cubes stacked at the edges of wadis. I saw the angular framework of derricks in place of marble palaces, the endless double line of pipelines in place of caravans, but it is still the land of my ancestors. I saw the tiny, mismatched houses of the cemeteries, the sepulchres lining the hills, and I heard one lone sound, off in the distance, the barking of our lowly brothers.

Persia, Mesopotamia, Arabia. These lands are no longer as peaceful, but surely the jackals—and the hyenas—prosper there, feasting along churned up roads, and in ruined villages, in the shadow of wrecked tanks or around refugee camps.

I saw this in my dream and I woke, my chest tight. Sadness—no, nostalgia. Our ancestors, or so Geneviève claimed, had claws and fangs that were much sharper than ours. Above all, they had wings. Xavier, who was snorting at that moment, had swept her claim away with a burst of laughter, almost hysterical. Then, sounding like the narrator of some *film noir*, he uttered, "Ghouls, ghouls!" I don't know if what Geneviève asserted was true.

But in my dream, I was descending from the sky, as silent as a bird of prey, and by night I landed on the soil of my ancestors, dry between my talons or fingers, intoxicated already by the feast to which I had been invited, catching the scent of a mass grave off in the distance.

Tomorrow, I'm buying a one-way ticket to the Middle East.

Though less known to Canadian readers than some of his fellow Quebecois F&SF writers, **Daniel Sernine**'s career has spanned more than 30 years, with 37 books published. His works have repeatedly garnered prizes, including the *Grand prix de la science-fiction et du fantastique quebecois* in 1992 and 1996

The Machinery of Government

Matt Moore

In Paul's right ear, Eddie asked: "Next: Do you have your access codes?"

"I think so," Paul replied, moving into the front hall of the small townhouse he rented. Honestly, he had no idea where they were.

Outside, the siren was getting closer.

Three more notices scrolled up into his field of vision:

* MINISTER OF NATIONAL DEFENSE EDDIE LAZENBY ARRIVING AT GOVERNMENT OPERATIONS CENTER.

* PRIME MINISTER ANDREW RENAULT HAS BEEN ALERTED.

* LAND AND CELLULAR COMMUNICATIONS NETWORKS OVERLOADED; GOVERNMENT NETWORK REMAINS STABLE.

The upward movement of the red letters—a direction his inner ear told him was impossible while he turned to the right—made him motion-sick.

He shut his eyes, moaning, bile filling his mouth.

"Are you okay?" Eddie asked, sounding like he was next to Paul and not speaking through a device in Paul's ear. In the background, Paul heard a commotion of commands and responses, voices trying to get Eddie's attention.

"Yeah," Paul replied, tentatively opening his eyes. The messages had contracted and joined others in the upper right corner of his vision. Missed communications gathered in the lower right. "Just the heads-up display." He grabbed his briefcase from where it lay by the door.

Someone shouted Eddie's name as he spoke: "You'll get—*not now!*—you'll get used to it."

Paul sorted through the briefcase, wondering if he'd get used to the pain. Before now, he'd only worn the device for an hour during Question Period, his aides sending him talking points or statistics to deal with a question from the opposition. That limited exposure caused a dull ache behind his eyes. Now, the increased electrical signals the device was pumping into his occipital lobe, the vision center at the back of the brain, caused his head to throb. "Hope I didn't pack it in a bag that's on its way to Marcel's cottage with Laura."

Three more notices appeared:

* PUBLIC SAFETY MINISTER MARCEL CHARLEBOIS HAS BEEN ALERTED.

* ENEMY FORCES RE-GROUPING NEAR VARS.

* RUSSIAN, CHINESE AMBASSADORS DENY INVOLVEMENT OR KNOWLEDGE.

His eyes fought between focusing on the briefcase and the messages seeming to float two meters away yet superimposed over the leather case. Paul shut his right eye and the messages disappeared. Using his left, he kept searching.

He bit his lip. Not there. Maybe the laptop bag. "So much to keep track of."

"You get used to that, too."

He pulled open a Velcro flap to find the backs of two thick, black binders. "I feel so useless."

"Andy would not have picked you if that was true," Eddie said. In the background, someone screamed about "getting some fucking air support."

Not for the first time, Paul wondered if his skin color had more to do with his promotion than his abilities. Having a young, black man from the prairies in cabinet helped silence critics who claimed his party was the domain of old white men from the coast.

He pushed the idea away. Now wasn't the time for those thoughts.

He pulled the two binders apart to find the thin blue binder containing his security codes pressed between them. "Got it." Paul opened his right eye to see:

* SPEAKING POINTS: "SENSLESSS AGGRESSION," "DISRUPTION OF PEACEFUL CO-EXISTENCE"

* AVOID: "INVASION / INVADERS / ATTACK"

"Last item: is Laura still there?" Eddie asked.

"She left about an hour ago." Paul returned to the living room. The siren sounded like it was somewhere in his neighborhood. "Said she couldn't wait to get down by the water." The muted television showed a view down Highway 417 to the east of the city. Just at the edge of the camera's range, indistinct shapes moved, sending up plumes of blue-gray smoke. "Wanted to enjoy this great weather."

They'd both been looking forward to the long weekend. His first two weeks as cabinet minister had been spent getting hammered in Question Period and attending endless meetings scheduled by his chief of staff. In both venues, he parroted the talking points sent down from the Prime Minister's Office— deflect attacks, stay on message, defend the government's agenda. Nothing about using his own discretion. Nothing about the government's response to the first foreign army to invade Canada since the Fenian Raids. He felt like a cog—messages from the PMO made him spin and he, in turn, spun others.

So this weekend, he and Laura were going to a cottage in the Gatineau Hills owned by Paul's other mentor, Marcel Charlebois, the current minister of public safety, to review the government's agenda. Until an hour ago, the front lines had been stable for months so the Prime Minister—"Andy" to his friends and caucus members not out to replace him—had given them the okay to get out of the city. Just a quick, last-minute meeting with his chief of staff on The Hill and Paul would have been on his way.

An emergency notice 45 minutes ago had changed everything.

"That's the best place for her," Eddie said. "*One more second!* Marcel's at his cottage now. We can evac her with him if it comes to that."

The kitchen phone rang. Pain pulsed in time with its simulated bell sound. Paul shut his right eye. The caller ID showed: Laura—Cell. "Eddie, it's Laura on the house phone."

"Go ahead and take it. I need to figure out what's happening here. Tell Laura to stay at the cottage. GPS shows your security escort is almost there. Let me know when you're on your way."

"I will." The connection clicked off. Paul hit the "GO" button on the handset and pressed it to his left ear. "Sweetie, have you—"

"Thank God!" she exclaimed. "I've been trying to reach you." Sirens shrilled in the background, nearly drowning her words.

"What's happened?" Paul asked. "Are you at Marcel's cottage? Has something happened there?"

"No, I'm downtown. Paul, what's happening? The streets are jammed. People are running. I can't get on the Web."

"Why are you still downtown?"

"Paul, what the hell is happening!" Her shriek an ice pick through his brain.

Paul grit his teeth, taking a moment to let the pain fade so he could speak to her calmly. "It's—" Paul stopped himself. How much of what he knew had been released to the public? Best to go with what the news had said: "Enemy forces broke through our lines an hour ago."

A pause. "They're coming here?" Terrified.

The siren right outside.

"We don't know." His temples throbbed in time with his racing heartbeat. "Can you get to your car? Can you still get to—" He paused, picking his words, not knowing if the enemy could be monitoring phone lines—"where you were going?"

"No." Near tears. "Streets are jammed, Paul. Accidents. I'm headed for The Hill, hoping you'd be at your meeting."

Tires screeched. He turned, right eye popping open. Messages—shifting and scrolling—filled his vision. Beyond them, an RCMP cruiser skidded to a stop out front. Pangs of nausea beat in time with its pulsing lights. Paul turned away just as the messages re-arranged themselves into a tighter pattern. His stomach flipped and he clamped his teeth and eyes shut—

"Paul, say something!"

Paul yanked the strap off. He had a moment to feel the tension of the fabric slide free from the back of his head before pain sliced through his skull, the consequence of not shutting down the interface. He leaned on the kitchen counter. Fighting to keep pain from his voice: "Sweetie, can you get home? There's a Mountie here to get me someplace safe. I can wait for you." The comm-piece in his right ear chirped, announcing a new call. Paul pulled it out.

"I'll have to walk," she replied. "Traffic isn't moving."

A horn blared. Paul looked up to see a constable next to his cruiser, dressed in dark blue fatigues with a flak jacket covering his barrel chest, waving for a passing car to slow down as it rounded a curve. It sped past, moving faster than was safe for the narrow streets. Paul moved to the front door. "That'll take—" He didn't know the city well enough to do more than guess, "—an hour or so, but I'll be here."

"I wanted to get you a present for making it to cabinet," she said. Tears now. "And something for Marcel and Eddie for taking you under their wing." She sobbed.

"Sweetie, shhh." Paul opened the front door, letting in a cacophony of sirens and car horns and revving engines. He waved to the constable. "Find an RCMP officer and tell him who—" The floor trembled and the phone roared static. Paul held it from his ear. When he put it back, he heard screams. "Laura?!"

"Oh my God! Paul—I think it was The Hill!"

Two steps and Paul stood before the television. "Are you okay?" he asked. The screen had split into two images. On the left, peace protestors on Parliament Hill—half of them with green, white and black armbands in a show of solidarity— scattered from a still-smoking crater. *Suicide bomber*, Paul thought, but the image on the right showed the view from the highway. The distant shapes shuddered and belched tongues of fire and black smoke.

"I'm okay." People screamed in the background, grunts and curses of a crowd fighting itself. "What was—" The house shook again. Laura screamed.

The television image panned over in time to show a corner of Parliament's West Block explode. Its green copper roof collapsed in a cloud of fire and smoking debris.

On his hip, Paul's PDA vibrated.

The constable—his name tag read Tessier—appeared in the doorway joining the living room and front hall, nearly filling it. Orange-tinted goggles hid his eyes. He motioned to the front door.

Paul shook his head. "Laura—" The line was dead.

"Minister," Tessier said, "we need to get you out of here."

Paul dialed Laura's number. "Just a second." An automated message told him all circuits were busy. Incisors dug into his lower lip.

"Now, sir."

The house shuddered. Glasses clicked in the kitchen cabinets. The bass-note *boom* of a distant explosion hit them a moment later.

"My wife is stuck downtown and trying to get here. We have to wait for her."

"Where downtown?"

"Rideau Centre."

"She won't make it."

Ice formed around Paul's heart. He fought back memories of hospital rooms, of helplessness, of his wife wasting away. "Can you send a car for her? Get her out of there?"

"My orders don't include her."

"An hour. I just need one hour. That's how long it would take her to get here, right?"

"Sir, I'm not going to debate this. You need to come with me—"

"No." Paul turned his back and moved into the kitchen. He wondered how far Tessier's authority extended—could he remove Paul by force—but the constable stepped into the hallway, speaking into his radio.

Paul let out a breath. She had come to Ottawa to be with him. Despite his travel and some late nights—and being 100 km from the front—she wanted to spend as much time with him as she could in this cramped, rented townhouse rather than be back home, safe but alone. Getting into cabinet meant more late nights, sometimes not getting home until midnight, and being gone by 6:30 the next morning. Since they'd first met, co-workers at Regina City Hall, she liked to be in bed by 10 P. M. But no matter the time he got home, he found her on the couch—sometimes awake, but usually not. He'd gently rouse her and she always had a smile and hug. Never a sour face, never a rash word, no matter the hour. She'd been a rock—the one thing he could rely on.

Every day—every moment with her—was a gift. Five years ago, they'd learned it was cancer growing in her belly, not the baby they'd hoped for. Her ability to have children was removed with the cancer, but the doctors only gave her a fifteen percent chance of lasting two years. It's aggressive, the doctors had said. It comes back.

But here she was—healthy and active. No sign of—

Another explosion, close enough to feel its *crack-boom.* Something upstairs shattered as it hit the floor.

A deep, animal instinct twisted in Paul's gut, screaming for him to run. If they do to Ottawa what they did to Moncton—

But how could he leave? Why should *he* get to go? He was nobody special—a well-spoken policy junkie who'd mastered the non-answer reply of deflection. The only difference between him and a dozen others was that he was black and young...though after the last two weeks, 35 didn't feel so young.

And the only reason there was a spot to fill was the opposition had dug up some dirt on Eddie's predecessor at National Defense—tapes of a conversation where she suggested Canada's foreign policies were to blame for the invasion. She'd been forced to resign and the ensuing cabinet shuffle left a junior cabinet minister spot vacant. A few words from Eddie and Marcel netted Paul the job. If not for that, he'd be another backbencher, hunkered down and waiting—

Brakes shrieked. A car horn—

Metal and glass screamed, twisted, shattered. The living room window like a movie screen: a car spinning, somersaulting left to right, debris flying, striking the house.

Tessier from the front hall: "Shit!" The front door banged open and Paul raced to it, the stink of burnt rubber hitting him halfway there.

He stopped on his small porch, bits of glass and plastic crunching under his feet. Engines revved, horns blared. Two more *booms* shook the air.

Tessier pounded down the street through chunks of metal and plastic toward the gnarled, smoking remains of a car resting on its roof.

In the street in front of Paul, tire tracks snaked in an S-shape. What had happened clicked into place: the car had taken the curve too fast, swerved to avoid the cruiser and rolled.

Over the cacophony of a city descending into panic, someone shouted "Paul!" Across the street, his neighbor Sarah, still in black running gear from her morning jog, descended from her porch and crossed the street. Waiting for her, Paul noticed others peering from doorways.

"The news said they're coming," she said, stopping at the bottom of his steps, a finger looping itself in her long blond hair. "They're shelling downtown and they're coming."

Before he'd pulled off the interface, enemy forces had been stationary. In the last few minutes they might have continued their push, but he had no way of knowing. Confirming what she said could make her panic. Denying it could cause false hope. Political instinct told him to deflect: "Sarah, you should get back inside."

Down the street, Tessier got on all fours and looked into the overturned car, one of its wheels still spinning. Half a kilometer past, a three-car accident blocked the intersection into the major avenue, causing a line-up of cars.

Paul had a moment to wonder how the hell Laura could make it home through what was happening when a voice yelled: "We fighting back?" An older man came down the sidewalk from the opposite direction, leaning on his cane. Paul recognized him—tall, thin, olive skinned—but didn't know his name. "We finally gonna kick their butts or what?"

"You should—" Others were coming. Down the sidewalk, across the street—a dozen or so converging on him. Paul realized that standing on his porch, the cruiser with its lights still flashing and others gathered around, might look like he was giving some kind of speech.

"Yeah!" a teen girl—Asian, decked out in a black hoodie and jeans—shouted. "We ain't taking no more shit from them! We'll fuckin' kick their asses if they come down our block!"

Paul held up his hands. "Please, you should—"

A helicopter buzzed overhead, low and fast.

"Everyone get back in your homes!" Tessier boomed. Heads turned to watch the constable come back up the street.

"The driver—" Paul began.

"Dead," Tessier replied, stopping at the trunk of his cruiser. To the crowd: "Get back inside. It isn't safe out here."

"*He's* out here," someone shouted. "He's in cabinet now, right? If we weren't going to kick some ass, he'd be gone, right?"

Tightening the chin strap of a helmet he'd taken from the trunk, Tessier said: "If I have to say it again, I'm putting people in cuffs." He removed a submachine gun, loaded it and slung it over his shoulder.

Despite Tessier's words, more drifted toward Paul, their faces and body language showing curiosity, even hope.

"Talk to us, Paul!" a familiar voice shouted. Paul scanned the crowd: Emily, Laura's best friend in Ottawa even though twenty years separated the two women. She'd eaten at their table many times and he'd helped her with chores since her husband Edwin had passed away three years—

Tessier leapt up the steps and leaned close to Paul. "It's time to *go*, Minister."

"Then find my wife and tell me she's safe," Paul replied.

Another voice: "Hey, the bombs have stopped."

Sarah, fist gripping a lock of hair: "They're coming!"

The older man: "Uh-uh. We pounded 'em flat!"

Emily again: "Tell us what's going on, Paul!"

A good question. "Look, I'm not—" *in a position to comment* was not something to say. Just deflect. "Go back inside. Please." He turned and went back into the house, Tessier following.

"Minister—" Tessier began, shutting the door.

"No." Paul moved into the kitchen. The smell of breakfast— an onion and pepper omelet, sausages, coffee—they'd made together that morning still hung on the air. Not even three hours ago. They'd been laughing, flirting, looking forward to the weekend, glad to have a small cabin to themselves—

"You a hard-ass?"

Paul didn't answer. He imagined Laura pushing through panicked crowds, fighting to remember which streets—

"'Cause times like this," Tessier continued, "hard-asses are the ones who get stuff done. Unless they got their heads shoved up there."

Paul turned, but Tessier had his back to him, talking into his radio.

He couldn't get more than a flat silence from the phone. His PDA regretted to inform him all lines were busy.

Another helicopter thrummed overhead.

Only ten minutes had passed. If she ran, it would still take another half-hour for her to get here. And what if she figured the RCMP had already taken him and she'd sought shelter?

Could he get that information?

Watching the crowd out front—shifting, waiting, motioning toward the house—Paul slid the comm-piece into his right ear, shivering at how deep the cold, custom-made shape went. A rainbow of colors reflected from the neural interface device where it fit against the back of his skull. He pulled its flexible, inch-wide strap over his head and fitted it into position. Biting his lip, he activated the neural connection. For an instant he felt like he was falling, then words and diagrams filled his vision. Pain beat in his temples. Messages told him four ministers were not accounted for, and two were likely killed when the West Block had been hit. Multicolor shapes moved across a map of the eastern edge of the city, following and crossing dotted and solid lines.

Accessing his directory, he scanned for Marcel's direct line. As minister of public safety, Marcel had oversight of the RCMP. If Tessier wouldn't budge on getting help to Laura, Marcel—

The PDA shrilled and INCOMING COMM—MIN NAT DEF flashed before him. "I'm here, Eddie."

An automated voice said: "Please hold for Minister—" The line clicked and Eddie said: "Paul?"

"I'm here."

"That's a problem. GPS shows you and the constable still at your place. What is the hold up?"

"I'm waiting for Laura." Movement made him turn. He forget to shut his right eye, but the nausea didn't strike as hard. Eddie was right: he was getting used to it.

"I don't understand."

Outside, two of his neighbors squared off—pointing, leaning in, gesticulating madly. "Laura stopped downtown. She's trying to make it home on foot."

"From where?"

All the shapes on the right side of the map suddenly became red. "Rideau Centre." Shapes on the left side blinked white, then disappeared.

"Paul," Eddie said, "come on. That over an hour's walk on a good day. You don't have time to wait."

Outside, the shorter of the two neighbors took a swing.

"You want me to leave her?"

In the background, someone yelled "Red status!" Eddie replied: "Oh Christ!" To Paul: "I want you to do your job."

"I can't leave her here."

Others pulled the two neighbors apart. Sarah held her hands out in a "Please stop!" gesture.

"Can you reach her?"

"No, the phone—"

The crowd was taking sides. Now several were confronting others.

"Then get out of there. Laura's in the system. If she's found—*give me a second!*—she'll be protected."

Pain gathered in a hard knob at the front of Paul's head. "That's not good enough."

"*I already signed that!* Good Christ, Paul!"

"Eddie, you know what we went through. I always said she'd come first. Just an hour." He'd resigned his seat when it looked like the end. When she recovered, he'd sworn that no matter what, he'd be there for her. He'd made sure Marcel and Eddie understood that when they talked about recommending him for cabinet. For Eddie to go back on that—

"You are a cabinet minister. There are—"

The television showed a bouncing image from the back of a vehicle, the highway pouring out behind it. In the distance, blurry gray/green shapes pursued, their flags green, white and black smudges.

"Barely two weeks in a junior—"

The crowd scuffled with itself. The older, olive-skinned man fell from the melee. The black-clad girl had a fistful of Sarah's hair, pulling her away.

"You listen to me!" Eddie interrupted. "Get this through your head: You are in cabinet. You *cannot* put this country at risk over one woman. I don't care if she's your wife! Thirty-nine million—"

"Then I resign."

"Bullshit!"

Eddie's exclamation a bolt of pain. Paul dug his teeth into his lower lip, literally biting back the curses he wanted to hurl. Eddie's wife was in Vancouver, over three thousand kilometers away from the front. Who was he to tell him to leave? "Then what do I do, Eddie?"

"You do whatever I tell—" A high-pitched whine replaced Eddie's voice.

The house shivered, glasses clinking in the cupboard.

The PDA's screen showed it was still operating, but more than that Paul couldn't glean from the complex read out.

Eddie's voice—"range of their artillery!"—blasted in his right ear.

"Eddie?"

The crowd, more than twenty now, moved and thrashed like an insane beast. Peacemakers pulled combatants apart only to be sucked into another conflict. Paul had an instant to wonder why Tessier wasn't out there when Eddie's voice returned:

"—hit!" Screaming. "Paul?" In terror. "Good Christ, we're taking fire." In agony. "We're—"

Silence.

Past the shapes, maps and text Paul hadn't been aware he'd been scanning, the image of the highway flipped, then changed to static. A terrified anchor appeared a second later.

> * GOVERNMENT OPERATIONS CENTER HIT
>   BY ENEMY ARTILLERY—DO NOT APPROACH!

appeared at the center of his vision. Next,

> * ENEMY ARMOR ADVANCING WEST ON
>   HIGHWAY 417.

Laura...

Still in the hall, Tessier said, "Roger that," then appeared in the living room. "Last chance, Minister. If you're going to stay here, fine, but I'm to escort Minister Charlebois."

> * DEFENSE MINISTER LAZENBY, INT'L
>   TRADE MINISTER GRANGE FEARED KILLED.

> * HIGHWAYS 417/416 WEST OF CITY AT
>   STANDSTILL.

"Marcel... is coming—?"

"Helicopter. One's inbound. Now or never."

Outside, his neighbors had reached a momentary state of calm. Some were bleeding, others panting, all of them waiting. Waiting for him to do something. "What about them? Are there plans—?"

"Probably not," Tessier replied. "But if our boys can hit back hard, there's no need to evacuate."

"My wife—"

"I checked. If she's found, she'll be evacuated."

"But she hasn't been—"

"Maybe. I don't know. Lot of pieces moving right now."

> * ARMOR UNITS RE-GROUPING TO ENGAGE
>   ENEMY IN ORLEANS.

> * BREAK-OUT ATTACK TO SOUTH POSSIBLE.

Paul hoped Laura would understand. And forgive him. "I'm coming. Let me leave a note."

"Make it a short one." Tessier spoke into his radio while Paul grabbed a pen and the pad they used for shopping lists. He found he could focus on the paper despite the heads-up display superimposed over it.

Laura—
I have been evacuated out of the city. If you've made it home,
contact

He moved into the hall, grabbed the blue binder and transcribed the names and numbers of everyone who could put her in contact with him. He continued:

I will be in touch as soon as I can. You are the best gift I could ever hope for and ever need.
Love Paul

"I'm ready."

Tessier nodded and unslung the submachine gun. "Stay close." He opened the front door, letting in the noise, and moved down the steps, barrel lowered.

"Paul, what's happening?" someone shouted.

"Move away from the car!" Tessier roared. He turned to Paul. "Let's go."

Paul, standing at the top of the porch steps, looked into the faces of his neighbors—scared, confused, angry. Lost.

Between them and him, messages informed him Canadian units were taking heavy losses.

Smoke and exhaust fumes and burnt rubber assaulted his nose.

"Are you leaving?" someone asked.

Emily: "Tell us what's going on."

Smoke blotted the sky. Horns, sirens, the roar of traffic came from all directions. Sounds of the battle drifted from the east.

"Everyone keep back!" Tessier yelled. To Paul: "Minister—"

"One more second," Paul said. Tapping his PDA, the heads-up display blinked out. To the crowd he said, "Listen, I know you're scared. I'm scared. Laura, my wife, is out there some place. I don't know where. But standing out here isn't going to do you any good."

"But where are you going?" someone asked.

A question he could answer honestly, "I don't know."

Another voice asked, "They're coming, right?"

"You should get back inside. Listen to the TV or radio for what to do."

"But you're leaving, right?" Angry.

Someone else yelled out, "Take me with you!"

The black-clad girl: "Yeah, get us the fuck outta here! Get busses or some shit down here—"

A pair of helicopters, skimming the rooftops, buzzed overhead.

Tessier turned to Paul, his patience gone.

"The TV and radio can tell—" Paul began.

Sarah, both hands buried in her hair: "They're going to kill us, Paul! Like Moncton!"

Paul thought of what Eddie might say if he was there—pulling no punches, wasting no words. Not deflecting but being a leader. Paul ignored the realization that Eddie was probably dead. "Stay inside. Our troops are going to be moving through, so don't be out here in their way. This isn't going to be like Moncton. We got caught by surprise. We know who we're fighting now. I'm in that fight. But I can't fight from here on Ridgeline Crescent. I need to organize the counterattack. I need to get the Americans off their 'neutral' butts and in the fight. And I need to make sure we can get supplies to people who need it when the fight is over. Do you want me to stay here and hold your hand and tell you what to do? Or go kick some ass?" No one answered, but a few clapped. It made Paul feel ill.

He descended the steps.

"Make a hole," Tessier commanded, leading Paul to the cruiser. As Paul got in, he let out a breath he hadn't realized he'd been holding.

Tessier pulled the car in a U-turn and raced down the street, dodging around the smoldering wreck. More people stood out on their lawns, watching. Waiting. The car jerked to the right onto the sidewalk, Tessier hitting the siren as they passed a line of cars waiting to get into the intersection at the end of the street, then turned right onto a side street that ended in a cul-de-sac where a Griffon helicopter waited, bright lights pulsing, rotors kicking up a cloud of grit. Getting out of the car, Paul saw a second chopper above them, circling a few meters above the rooftops. This one had weapons pylons mounted to its sides, gunners in the open doors.

Paul got out of the car and ran for the helicopter, Tessier behind him. A door in its side opened, revealing Marcel—face pale, terrified—Caroline and their two daughters, all in the weekend wear of shorts and T-shirts. A serviceman helped Paul aboard and into a seat next to Marcel. Tessier slid in next to him, his large bulk squeezing Paul against his mentor. The serviceman shut the door, helped Paul strap in and passed him a headset. Paul removed the comm-piece and put the headset on.

"Laura never made it, Paul," Marcel said. "Is she..."

"I don't know." Paul grabbed the edge of his seat as the helicopter lifted off. Inertia pushed him down. "Can you find her? Tell RCMP—"

Marcel shook his head reached for his wife's hand. "Mon dieu. I don't know what is happening." Eyes wide, he stared out the window, lower lip trembling. "I cannot... cannot..." His wife patted Marcel's hand. His daughters clung to each other.

Rooftops fell away, the city spread out below them. Almost out of sight, on the horizon, distant specs raced toward each other. Larger specs circled in the air. Explosions erupted in and above the suburban neighborhood that had become a battlefield.

Laura...

She'd be on the chopper if she hadn't stopped for him. She'd be safe. He saw her getting home, finding Emily there, telling her he'd left. The ground would be trembling by then as the enemy closed—

Paul shoved the image from his mind. Guilt and fear twisted in his guts, but he reactivated the heads-up display. Five ministers were confirmed dead and the PMO was making new assignments. Paul had work to do.

Outside, silhouettes of fighter planes raced across the sky and disappeared behind a cloud.

By day, **Matt Moore** is a mild-mannered online communication specialist with the federal government. By night, he is a science fiction and horror writer with work in *On Spec*, *The Drabblecast*, the anthologies *Tesseracts Thirteen* and *Night Terrors*, and an eBook from Damnation Books. By later at night, he is the marketing director for ChiZine Publications, a small Canadian publisher.

Grandmother's Babies

Jonathan Saville

It's amazing how simple things can become complicated when you don't listen. I had been in for an eye exam and needed a prescription change. I thought the lady making the arrangements said the lenses would be made elsewhere and that she would phone me when they were ready. The part I apparently missed was that I was supposed to bring the old pair in first. Anyway, days passed and when I phoned to check out what was happening I finally got it straight and agreed to bring them in at the beginning of the next week.

The day I brought my glasses in was one of the first nice days of spring after a brutal winter that seemed to have no end. After struggling to find a parking spot in the crowded mall parking lot, I was enjoying the short walk to the entrance in the sunshine. Approaching the doors I noticed a new white Jeep picking up passengers. There were two older, Asian men in the front seats that were gesturing and laughing. They looked rather out of place in the monstrous, jacked up Jeep. They also seemed oblivious to the plump lady who was attempting to get into the vehicle without letting go of her parcels and handbag. It was pretty clear that she was not going to make it without some help, and since I was in no hurry and the sun was warm I offered my assistance.

"Can I help you grandmother?" I asked as I approached. I'm not sure why I added "grandmother," it just seemed right.

She whipped around to face me with a speed that belied her apparent age. Initially she seemed quite stern, almost angry, but her countenance softened and she handed me her armload of bags.

"Thank you kind stranger," she said. "This new car is too high for an old lady like me to climb into, and my husband is too busy entertaining his friend to help." She was still struggling, so I offered my free hand and together we raised her into the seat.

"Do you make a habit of helping strangers?" she asked as I started handing in the bags I was holding.

"Not really," I replied. "This was likely a combination of your need, a warm day, and my good mood. Are you settled in there okay?"

"I'm fine, but I have a question," she answered. "Why did you call me 'grandmother?'"

"I thought it would be a sign of respect," I said hopefully.

"It is something I have wished to be for so long I forget when the longing began," she said, looking wistfully into the distance over my shoulder. "I have many relations, but no children of my own. My niece, Shazan, has offered to bear children for me to call my grandkids, but, until today, I had not found a man to be the father. Now I believe I have." She was looking right at me.

"Grandmother, you can't be serious," I stammered. "You don't know me from Adam. I'm married and I don't think my wife would like the idea of me making babies with your niece."

"Do you have any children?" she continued as if I hadn't spoken.

"I have four sons," I replied. "But that doesn't matter because after the last one I had a vasectomy that has held for twenty years."

"I have relatives and friends in all sorts of medical fields," she answered smugly. "They would find a way around that."

Now I was getting frustrated. Start by helping an old lady and wind up shooting live ammo instead of blanks at her niece. I just didn't want to go down that road. "I'm not interested in doing anything that would change me," I stated in my most firm voice and I turned to walk away.

"At least tell me your name," she called after me.

"Thomas Eberle," I answered over my shoulder as I turned for one last look. "And I don't want any more children." The two in the front seat were still sharing a good story and apparently paying no attention to our conversation. I headed for the mall doors.

That night, after supper, I told Vicki about my experience with the "grandmother."

"Don't get your hopes up Romeo," she kidded, "the niece is probably forty years old and two hundred pounds. Besides, you'll have to go to all the trouble of finding yourself another wife if you get that operation reversed. I'm looking forward to some travel and fun time not some diaper changing time.

⟶⟶❖⟵⚜ — ⚜ ❖⟶⟵

After several days the visions of Asian grandchildren were fading fast when my cell phone rang.

"Good morning, Thomas Eberle," I answered cheerfully.

A female responded, "Well good morning Thomas, aren't you the sunshine of my day. This is Grandmother."

It took a second for me to realize who was on the other end and another second to quell the temptation to hang up. "Grandmother?" I questioned, "how did you get my cell number? I suppose you have relatives working with the phone company?"

"Oh Thomas, don't be paranoid," she laughed. "Cell numbers are as easy to find as land lines if you know where to look. Now, do you have a few minutes to talk? I have some exciting news to share."

Thinking I was going to be sorry for not ending this conversation right away I gave a mental sigh before asking, "What news Grandmother?"

"My uncle, a surgeon and fertility specialist at the university hospital, tells me there is a procedure that is completely safe and reversible and only takes three days to complete. They insert a temporary collector to gather the sperm your body is still producing. After enough has been collected the device is removed and you are back where you started. He likened it to drawing sap from a maple tree by driving a metal spile into the trunk. When the sap quits running, you remove the spile and the tree heals itself. Does that make sense?"

The analogy brought back the memory of large kettles of maple sap boiling away on its journey to becoming maple syrup. My family had tapped trees every spring that I could remember. However, sperm was not sap. "Grandmother—" I began, exasperated.

"And," she ignored me, "I'll pay you one million dollars to have the procedure done and one million more for each child that comes from the sperm we gather. And you'll drive home from the hospital in an AMG Mercedes CL65, black on black; it's already on its way to Edmonton."

She paused to let her offer sink in. I knew I would be hard pressed to say no, so I did the only thing a man can do when he's cornered; I passed the problem off to my wife. "I'll have to talk with Vicki," I explained humbly, "and I'm not at all sure that she will be excited."

"You are too pessimistic Thomas," she replied, "I'm sure she will be thrilled to retire from that stressful job she struggles with."

Who was this woman? I wondered, *and how did she know so many buttons to press?*

"You seem to know a great deal about us Grandmother," I said warily. "I don't even know your name or how to get in touch with you."

"My real name would not be easy for your English tongue," she laughed, "so I go by Iris Chen. My husband's name is Norman and you can reach us at 888-888-8888. My uncle has an opening for this coming Friday afternoon that would likely see you going home Sunday evening. I'll expect to hear from you tonight."

"Yes, Grandmother," I sighed, "tonight." I wondered as I hung up how Vicki would react.

⭄⭅ ⧲ — ⧲ ⭆⭃

I waited nervously all day for Vicki to come home and got very little accomplished. Grandmother sure knew what levers to pull. The car was one of my dream cars and the money, with what we already had, would mean we could both quit work and live out our days quite comfortably. And that was if there was just one child. I suspected Grandmother would not stop at one. But Vicki was the practical one, she would think of possible legal responsibilities and procedural complications well beyond what I would consider reasonable.

The hours dragged by. At four-thirty, having completed all of a page and a half of the system documentation I was supposed to have finished for Monday, I went upstairs and started making supper. I enjoy cooking, experimenting actually. Sometimes it works, sometimes not, but it's always interesting. My mom couldn't boil water, but all her kids are pretty good in the kitchen. Her story now is that she helped us become good cooks because she was so bad.

It was going on six by the time Vicki came strolling into the kitchen with a handful of junk mail fliers and a few bills.

"Hey beautiful," I said kissing her on the cheek, "how was your day?"

"Hot tub tonight," was all she said. That typically meant there was some venting to be done but she needed to get comfortable first.

"Like some wine?" I asked.

"Sure, but not your Italian stuff. Do we have any Merlot?"

"I think so. I'll bring it up." I headed for the bar and soon returned with two glasses of red wine.

I decided I couldn't wait through supper to bring up Grandmother's proposition so I started in after the first sip of wine. "The grandmother called today," I began.

"Your old Chinese lady friend?" asked Vicki seeming a bit startled. "How'd she get our number?"

"Don't know," I replied. "She called my cell. She had an intriguing offer."

"I'll bet," Vicki said sarcastically. "You know how I feel about you getting potent again."

"I wouldn't, not the way she described it," I answered hurriedly. I felt I needed to get everything out quickly before she could pick apart the pieces. "I would go to the university hospital Friday afternoon and a surgeon from the fertility clinic would insert a kind of collector in me and they would collect sperm for a couple of days. My body still makes it, it just never goes anywhere 'cause the tubes are cut. When they're done, the collector is removed and I'm the same as before I went in. She said it was like taping a maple tree."

"Very poetic," replied an unconvinced Vicki. "And what do we get from this, a gallon of syrup?"

"Actually no. We get one million plus an AMG Mercedes for me to go through the procedure," I answered as calmly as I could. "Then we would get another million for each child that's born from my donation."

Vicki straightened in her chair and gave me an unreadable look. "You've called and told her yes, right?" she asked.

"No I haven't," I said. "I wasn't sure how you'd feel about it, or if it's moral to do something like this."

"Moral?" she almost yelled, "you want to talk about moral, we'll talk about what that bitch in public relations pulled on me today! Call her! Call her now!"

I guess I spent all day worrying for nothing. I thought to myself. I went to the phone and dialed the Chinese lucky number. "Grandmother," I said when the phone picked up, "you have a deal. When and where on Friday?"

"Norman will pick you up at your house, be ready to leave by three. He will deliver you to the fertility clinic. Your appointment is with Dr. Charmin Yu. You can tell Vicki that she can visit Saturday morning any time after ten. If everything goes as planned, you will be driving home in your new Mercedes sometime after supper on Sunday. Any questions?"

"No," I replied. "I'll be ready Friday afternoon."

"Good," she said. "I'll see you in the hospital at some point. I want you and my niece to meet. Have a pleasant evening." She hung up.

"Well, we're all set. I go in Friday, come back Sunday evening and you can actually visit starting Saturday morning," I smiled at Vicki.

"I may be too busy shopping to visit," she snickered. "Now I really need a tub. We'll have supper later."

—◄◄ ▄ — ▄► ►—

Norman arrived promptly at three on Friday to drive me to the hospital. He seemed a rather jovial chap, chatty and cracking jokes. His driving skills were definitely oriental but we managed to get to the fertility clinic in one piece. He wished me good luck as I left the car.

The receptionist, obviously used to handling delicate subjects, asked for the name of the specialist I was to see today. "Dr. Yu," I answered.

"You'll have to be a bit more specific," she said, "there are five of them working in this unit."

"Dr. Charmin Yu. Sorry, I didn't know it was such a popular name," I mumbled apologetically.

"Please have a seat Mr. Eberle," she pointed to a waiting area. "Dr. Yu's nurse will be out to collect you shortly."

The rest of the evening is a bit of a blur. I don't do well with drugs that knock you out, so other than the fact that the nurse was rather pretty and the doctor rather fat, my story is vague. I remember coming out of the fog around seven but it was past nine by the time I managed to lift myself up on one elbow and take a drink of water. One of the nurses came to take my pulse and pressure and see if I was okay. I lied and said I was, but I had this pinching feeling between my legs that was uncomfortable. Fortunately she read my mind, lifted my sheets and maneuvred something under there and the pinching ceased.

I was about to see if there was a hockey game on the TV when Grandmother entered the room trailed by one of the most gorgeous women I'd ever seen. She was an Asian beauty— perfect skin, long black hair down to her waist, everything in the right proportion. "Thomas, I hope you are well," Grandmother began. "This is my niece Shazan."

I raised myself to one elbow and said, "Your grandmother is a liar Shazan. She told me you were a 'pretty girl,' but you're a beautiful woman."

The rising color of her blush was all the thanks I needed.

"Don't be flirting where you cannot proceed," warned Grandmother. "What would Vicki say if she heard you talking like that?"

"She'd probably agree with me," I responded. "But you're right; I am a happily married man."

She handed me a cashier's check for one million dollars. "I suspect you'll be more happily married once she sees that check," chuckled Grandmother. "I have something, a family piece, that I would like you to have Thomas. I gave a matching pendant to Shazan. It's jade, but the piece in the middle is so fine it is almost transparent. You would honor me if you would wear it; it's a little piece of me that I can give to the two of you for making me so happy."

"Thank you Grandmother," I said as she slipped the fine gold chain over my head, "it is very pretty; in a masculine sort of way."

Grandmother laughed, "You men need a bit of the Yin to counteract all your Yang. Now I'm going to find Dr. Yu to make sure everything is going well. You two get to know one another." With that she left to find the good doctor.

"Is there any pain?" Shazan asked when the door had closed.

"There was some discomfort, but the nurse fixed that. Now it's just getting used to lying on my back for a couple of days. I'm a stomach sleeper so I'll have to make some adjustments."

Shazan approached the bed and surprised me by lifting the covers. She reached in and touched me softly, with the predictable result. Holding my erection firmly in her hand she whispered, "When I am in the pain of my labor I will think of the joy we should have had making this baby and I will be content." She kissed my forehead and retreated just as the door opened and Grandmother reappeared.

"All is well?" she asked.

We both nodded. I wasn't sure but I suspect Grandmother noticed the rise in the bed sheets. She said nothing however but came closer to the bed. "Norman will bring the car for you Sunday evening. His friend will give him a ride home so you can return directly to Vicki. I cannot tell you how thankful I am that you agreed to do this for me Thomas. I'm sure there will be a beautiful child as a result. When it arrives would you like to visit?"

That caught me by surprise. I had suspected that she would not want anything to do with me after she had collected what she needed. "Yes," I stammered. "Yes, I believe I would like to see what an Asian Eberle would look like; especially with such a beautiful mother."

"We will call you when the time is right then," said Grandmother. "Until then Thomas, I would appreciate it if you honor our privacy."

"I trust you Grandmother. I'll wait for your call."

Then they left. Leaving a poor male to contemplate things that would never be.

Sunday afternoon Dr. Yu came in beaming from ear to ear. "You good maple tree," he said. "We have many sperm. You can go home knowing you have lived up to your side of the bargain. We'll take out the collector now, then you rest a few hours and Norman will come for you."

Sure enough, about six thirty that evening I was wheeling my way home in one of the sweetest rides a man could ever hope to enjoy. Black on black with just enough chrome to look awesome. Not to mention 0 to 100 in 4.4 seconds; the kind of acceleration that can give you whiplash. I had given Vicki the check when she came to visit Saturday morning. She'd called since then but had work to catch up on so hadn't been by to visit. The check had gone into our account and we almost immediately received a call from one of the investment branch people wanting to lavish their support on us. When the second check came, we promised ourselves that we would both quietly retire and enjoy some world travel time.

I'll have to admit the next nine months seemed to take forever. Men don't do patient well, that's why God lets women get pregnant and men hand out cigars. Even though I didn't really think of the up-coming birth as a member of the family, in a way I did. It was an odd double standard—it was and it wasn't mine.

The phone call came during that quiet week between Christmas and New Year's. Shazan had delivered beautiful, healthy twins! A boy and a girl. Grandmother named them Adam and Eve, her first grandchildren. And Norman came around almost as soon as I had hung up the phone with another cashier's check; this one for two million dollars.

"Well stud, you did good," smiled Vicki as she looked at the check.

"Thank you, but I think I need some more practice," I replied as I put my arm around her waist and headed for the bedroom.

A few days later I got a call on my cell from Shazan. "Thomas, it's Shazan. Can you talk?"

"I learned that a long time ago," I joked. "I hear you have the most beautiful twins in the universe."

"Oh Thomas, they are. I know I would think so regardless, but they are perfect. And you are their father Thomas; we should be a family, together."

Red alert! This is not a path to be taken. "Shazan," I said, trying to keep my voice as neutral as possible, "Grandmother would be devastated if you took those children from her. I'm not sure but I suspect she would hunt us down even if we ran to the ends of the earth, and the result would not be pretty. Not to mention what Vicki would do with what was left."

"Thomas, the children need you as their father," she cried into the phone.

"It cannot be Shazan," I tried to reason with her. "Grandmother paid me to do her a service. I don't know your part but I suspect you were looked after too. I can't do what you want, I cannot betray the trust my wife and Grandmother have placed in me. I cannot."

"Goodbye Thomas," she said and the phone went dead.

I tried calling Grandmother but it went to voice mail. "It's Thomas, Grandmother," I said, "I just got a call from Shazan. I think you might want to check on her and the babies, just to be sure everything is al right. Bye."

⊷⇐⊲ — ⊳⇒⊶

Time rolled quietly onward. It was summer; Vicki and I had joined a golf club and were enjoying playing almost every day. We had just returned from the club one evening when the house phone rang.

"Good evening, Thomas Eberle," I answered.

"Thomas, it's so good to hear your voice. It's Shazan."

Like I needed to be told who it was! "Shazan," I said, "how are the babies and Grandmother?"

"We are all doing wonderfully," she replied. "Grandmother is planning a summer party and was wondering if you would like to come?"

"Absolutely," I said, "when is the day?"

"Two weeks this coming Saturday, can you make it?"

I cupped my hand over the phone. "Two weeks Saturday can we make a party at Grandmother's?" I asked my social convener.

After a few seconds she replied, "You can, but I'll be on a seminar in Florida."

"Too bad for you," I said to Vicki. Back in the receiver I replied, "That will be great for me, but bad for Vicki, she's on course. Will you take just me?"

"You are always welcome in Grandmother's house Thomas; of course we will take just you. Tell Vicki we're sorry she can't make it."

"Can I bring anything?" I asked.

"Grandmother would be offended if you brought anything but yourself and an appetite. I'll give you the address, write it down and don't lose it," Shazan laughingly replied. "See you then."

Saturday eventually arrived. I had picked up two little stuffed animals for the twins, and then I drove my beautiful Mercedes over to the address Shazan had given me. When I arrived something didn't feel right. I expected more cars, more people, more something. I was on a quiet residential street in a good, but not great part of town, and it looked like I was the first to arrive. I checked the car clock, it was after eight. *Maybe grandmother's guests are late arrivers,* I thought as I parked the car and headed for the house.

I rang the bell and Shazan was quick to answer. "I'm very glad you could come," she said with a smile that lit up the room. "The twins have been so good today, it's like they knew this was going to be a special night. And you brought them puppies! How adorable, let's see if they know how to play with them."

"They'll likely try to chew the heads off," I suggested, "everything our boys touched at this age went into their mouth."

She gave the soft puppies to the kids and I was right. Straight into the mouth they went. "Well, it's nice to know some things are still predictable," I said. "Where's Grandmother and Norman and the rest of the party?"

"Just a minute," she called back as she started down a hallway, "I just need to check something."

I sat on the floor between the twins. I had to admit they were two of the cutest kids on the planet as they gummed their new puppy dogs. We played peek-a-boo for a bit and then I had the sense there was someone behind me. It was Shazan, and what she was wearing was not the type of robe a mother of twins entertaining a married man should be wearing. There was precious little left to my imagination as I stood up and turned to look at her.

"This is the twins' six month birthday," she started quietly, taking a step towards me, "and I wanted them to be with their father. I wanted to be with their father too. Why can't we be together, even if it's just for today, would that be so bad?"

She wrapped her arms around my waist. *No, it wouldn't be so bad*, I thought, *in fact I suspect it would be great—until tomorrow. Until Grandmother and Vicki and my boys found out I was just talk and no substance.*

I reached down and held her arms and gently pushed her away. "I can't do what you want Shazan," I said quietly. "I can't ruin the trust Vicki and Grandmother have in me. The cost of being with you, no matter how sweet, is just too high for me to pay. I care for you Shazan, but like a sister. And I love the twins, but like an uncle. I have my own life to live; you need to find one for yourself."

I didn't trust myself even to give her a kiss on the forehead so I turned and walked to the door. It seemed that just as I went to turn the knob, the door flew open and four young men burst into the room. The first two pinned me against the wall, while the last one in took in the scene quickly and then ignored me. "Well, Shazan," he leered at her, "you never got that sexy stuff on for me. Who the hell is this joker and why does it look like he's about to leave?"

"Get out of here Jerred," she yelled. "If Grandmother finds you here you will be in trouble." She moved to the children and picked up Eve.

"The old witch must be out of town or your lover boy wouldn't be here," he jeered. He beat Shazan to Adam and scooped him up off the floor and pretended to toss him to one of the other punks.

"Don't!" she screamed at him. Immediately both babies began to cry.

"Close the bloody door," he ordered the one that wasn't holding me. "We don't want to involve the neighbors in this."

"Now Mr. Fast Car," he continued as he walked over to me, cradling Adam like a football, "that's some sweet wheels you have out there. Who the hell are you to deserve such a peep show? We don't care much for rich, white men taking advantage of our women."

"I don't care much for you threatening her and the twins," I said without thinking.

Jerred turned and gave Adam to the one who closed the door and then spun to face me. Shazan must have know what was about to happen as she cried out just as he pulled back and let me have a round house punch to the face. I barely had time to realize what was going to happen and brace myself against the wall when a flash of light filled the room and Jerred crumpled to the floor.

"What'd you do to him?" the one holding Adam yelled. He dropped Adam and charged at me, looking to drive me through the wall. Once again the light flashed and the punk fell at my feet with a thud. But this time I figured out what it was. The jade pendant that Grandmother had given me in the hospital was protecting me. When it saw a threat, it some how neutralized it. I wasn't sure if the effect would be permanent or not but I was sure happy to have the help.

Now the two that had me pinned to the wall were undecided what to do. Without Jerred to give the orders they were rather like sheep without a goat. Shazan seemed to have come to the same conclusion. "Let him go, you morons, or you'll be next!," she yelled at them.

That was all the help I needed. As they focused on her I pushed away from them, grabbed the necklace and pointed the jade pendant at them. There were two almost simultaneous flashes of light and the pair went down like I had hit them with a sledge hammer.

I picked up Adam who had stopped crying and seemed to be observing the action with some interest. I ran over to Shazan and cradled her in my arms as best I could while holding Adam. For a brief moment I just wanted to stay there holding them and forget the rest of the world existed. Finally I broke away and gave Adam to Shazan. I went over to Jerred to see what condition he was in. When I knelt over him to check for a pulse I couldn't believe how cold he felt, almost like ice. I couldn't find a pulse, but then again I couldn't stand to touch him for very long either. The other three were the same, like they had been fast frozen.

"Do you have any idea what happened here?" I asked her.

"Grandmother's protection," she mumbled quietly. "There are some things Thomas that are beyond our comprehension, and perhaps that's just as well. I must leave now or Grandmother will surely end my existence."

I was stunned. "You think Grandmother would kill you because these losers are frozen?"

"No. But she would find out eventually that I wanted to leave with you and the twins. For that she would have no sympathy and no mercy. I would be gone in a puff of smoke or flash of light or some such end; just like these poor souls." She knelt down and cradled a baby in each arm. "You do make beautiful babies Thomas," she sighed. "I will miss them."

"But where will you go? Won't Grandmother find you? How will you keep yourself?" I had many questions and no answers.

"Grandmother cannot find me if I don't wish it," she replied enigmatically. "You need to look after the twins until she comes for them. I must leave tonight. Your use of the pendant will surely have aroused some curiosity in the guardians."

"How will you travel?" I asked.

"I'll take Jerred's car; no one will be looking for it. We just need to check that there aren't any drugs in the trunk. After we parted company I heard he started dealing."

I started to turn Jerred's pockets out, looking for his keys and found a wad of bills that would choke a horse. Eventually we had keys to a very nice Celica and over a hundred thousand in cash. "If they're not dealing," I said, "they've been very lucky at the casino."

"Will you check out the car for me while I pack?" she asked.

"Sure, be back in a bit." I left with the keys. The car was clean. Evidently Jerred kept better care of it than most anything else in his life. I backed it into the driveway and went inside.

I was playing on the floor with the twins when she reappeared with her bags. "You know, I really don't have to leave immediately," she said sliding on to the floor beside me and hugging my neck.

"Shazan, I'm just a man. If you keep this up we will make love, no man I know could resist you for long. I'm asking a favor, if you care for me at all, take the car and the money and start over somewhere our paths won't cross again. I'm not sure I could say goodbye to you twice."

She gave me one long kiss and I thought I was a goner, but then she got up, picked up her bags and left. I didn't get up to see her out. I held the twins and listened as the Celica fired up and headed down the road to somewhere.

Since I thought that Vicki might call, I decided I had better take the twins to my house for the night. In the morning I would try to get in touch with Grandmother. I figured I owed Shazan at least a half day head start. I started gathering all the baby paraphernalia together and had a twenty year flashback of doing the same for our boys. Boy was I glad we were through that phase of our lives.

Vicki did call. We chatted a bit about her conference, but I didn't mention the events of my day. I was too tired to answer all the questions that would come up. After we said goodnight I put the babies in their car seats on the floor in my bedroom, managed to get my clothes off and fell soundly asleep.

⇒⊱⊰ — ⊱⊰⇐

I woke the next morning to the quiet murmuring of the twins. They weren't crying; it was almost like they were talking to each other. I got up and did the usual change, feed, play routine with Adam and Eve. As much as I was glad to be past the baby stage in our lives, I did enjoy my morning with them. Finally I got around to calling Grandmother; boy did I get an earful.

I never did find out exactly when Grandmother knew the twins were not with Shazan, but she walked up one side of me and down the other for not calling the moment I had taken her babies. She had been frantic with worry over what might have happened to them and I was responsible. Eventually the ranting changed to chastisement and then to the questions that I was not looking forward to answering.

"Where is Shazan?" she demanded to know. "How could she have left her babies? What had I done to make her run away from such a comfortable home?"

"Have you been to Shazan's?" I was finally able to ask.

"No, I've only called. If she was there she would answer my call," came the curt rebuff.

"Well let's meet at her house in half an hour," I suggested. "I'll bring the twins. There's something you need to see there."

"Why can't you bring them here?" Grandmother's question was more like a veiled command.

"You need to see what's at Shazan's with your own eyes," I replied. "Half an hour, can you be there?"

"Yes, yes, I'll get Norman to drive me. But I hope it's worth the trouble," she answered grumpily.

I hung up and went to get Adam and Eve ready to travel. I wondered idly if Grandmother would have the patience to look after her two young charges, she would definitely need it.

I was just pulling into Shazan's driveway when Norman rolled up in his Jeep. He had told me once, when he drove me to the hospital, that he wanted to take the Jeep off-road and see what it could do. I doubted that that would ever happen; he had enough trouble navigating on pavement.

I got out and went over to open Grandmother's door. "The kids are sleeping," I said. "I don't think we'll be long here so I'll leave them in the car."

"What is so important for me to see that you had to drag of my comfortable house to see?" she demanded.

"You need to see for yourself," I said noncommittally. "I didn't believe it when I saw it so it's hard for me to explain."

We entered the house together. Norman had decided to have a smoke outside and watch over the twins. Nothing had changed from the night before. The four "frozen" bodies were still as they had been left, lying of the floor of the living room.

"Who did this?" Grandmother asked with her head cocked questioningly at me.

"I'm not sure exactly," I answered. "For the first two no one did anything. Each one had tried to hurt me, and there was a flash of light, and you can see for yourself what happened. Then I figured out it was the pendant you gave me that was flashing, and I just pointed it at the other two and they got frozen as well."

"Really? They did nothing to you but the pendant took them anyway?" Grandmother seemed unsure that I was re-membering correctly.

"Actually, they were more interested in Shazan at the mo-ment, but they weren't really doing anything."

"There were no others?" asked Grandmother.

"None that we saw," I answered.

"Where is Shazan?" Grandmother's question had a sharp edge to it.

"I don't know," I said. "She drove off after the last two got frozen."

"Just like that, with no explanation," Grandmother seemed to be passing from wonder to disbelief.

I tried to think of a plausible story that didn't involve Shazan's attempted seduction and I hit on using Jerred. "She was afraid you'd find out Jerred was back in her life and punish her some how. She seemed frightened of what you might do, so she left the children with me and ran."

"Stupid girl," said Grandmother giving me an appraising look; something like a Grandmother lie detector. She seemed to buy my story, for now at least.

"Get in your car and follow us," she commanded. "We're going to my house to follow this some more." I noticed she locked the door as we left.

We eventually arrived at a huge house, mansion really, in an older, but still upscale part of town. Norman signaled for me to park by the front door as he put his car in the garage. I had finished getting the twins' car seats unhooked and was waiting when Grandmother opened the front door.

"Come in," she smiled. "The nurses will get the children."

Sure enough, two ladies dressed in white uniforms came out as I went in. Each one took a car seat and one grabbed the bag I had been using to cart around the requisite twenty kilos of baby supplies. They whisked past me again in the entry and disappeared up the winding oak stairway to the second floor.

"Norman is waiting for us in the study," she said.

I followed her through several large rooms and into a spacious but cozy study. There were a number of overstuffed chairs, a pool table of mammoth proportions, a bar and a beautiful teak desk and hutch that looked to be hundreds of years old.

"You'll have a scotch," Norman stated more than asked.

"With some ice if you have some," I replied. I wondered again how these two seemed to know so much about me.

"Give me your pendant," Grandmother ordered, "I wish to try a test on it."

I slipped the necklace over my head and handed it to her. She took it to the hutch and placed it in what looked like a large silver bowl inlaid with emeralds and jade. Immediately the inside walls glowed with a smoky light. "Come here," she said.

When I got close to the bowl I could see vague shapes sliding around in the bowl. I counted four distinct ghosts.

"Here are Jerred and his friends," she explained, "trapped in the ghost world of the jade. As long as they remain here, their earthly bodies will remain frozen, waiting for their spirit's return."

"I really don't believe in magic and spells," I told her. "Surely there's another explanation."

"Thomas, I see you can be as stubbornly western as you are kind and honorable. Please sit down and enjoy your drink, I have a story to tell you that will be hard for you to believe, but I swear every word is the truth."

I took the drink from Norman and sat in one of the lounge chairs. Norman took the one next to mine while Grandmother sat across from me on the sofa.

"My mother went by many names," she began, "Lady of Mt. Tai, Heavenly Jade Maiden and Primordial Lady of the Emerald Cloud were a few of them. She was, and is, perfected as a heavenly immortal."

I looked from her to Norman to see if either one of them was secretly smiling at the joke that was obviously being played. Both looked as sober as a Mennonite minister on Sunday morning.

Grandmother continued, "To a Doaist, honor for the elders and ancestors is expected of a child, to disobey is one of the worst sins a son or daughter could commit. As was usual for the Chinese, my mother had arranged a marriage for me to a deity I had never met. However, before the time I was to be wed, I met Norman and fell in love. He was abbot of the Jade Spring Temple and the most kind, humorous and loving person I had ever met. We managed to keep our affair secret until I became pregnant. My mother was outraged, I think more by the embarrassment than any real sense that I had done something wrong. She took my baby when I delivered and I never got to see it, I don't even know if it was a boy or a girl. She cast Norman and I out from our kind and placed a horrible curse on us. She vowed that neither of us could conceive a child and, worse, that we could never make love to one another again."

She sat silently with her head bowed for a while. I glanced at Norman and he was wiping a tear from his eye.

"Because of this we have learned to value simple displays of affection, holding a door open, a smile first thing in the morning, the gift of a flower, all the little ways a spirit can be lifted up." Grandmother looked at me and said, "That's why, when you helped me into the car at the mall it meant so much to me. That's why I bullied Shazan into having your babies. Yes I made her do it, but I think she likes you anyway. She left to get out from under my control but it will be temporary, she is bound to me by birth and I will find her when I need her again. I think we can give him the keys Norman."

"If we give him the keys we had better give him the number too," he replied.

"I suppose," she said walking back to the desk. She took a wooden box out of one of the drawers and a business card from the jade and silver card holder. "In this box are keys to the fifty-two houses we have for visitors, the card has the number to call to arrange for a private jet. There will be no cost to you and no need to call us to arrange a visit to any of these places; they are available to you anytime."

"Grandmother, I don't know what to say or how to thank you," I stammered.

"Those babies upstairs are all the thanks we need Thomas," she answered quietly. "Now if you'll excuse us we're going to start becoming the parents we never could be. Let yourself out when you've finished your drink."

She came over and kissed me on the forehead and then took Norman by the hand and the two of them headed out to be parents for the first time in a thousand years.

Jonathan Saville is the pen-name of the author who holds a Master's in Mathematics and has bounced between teaching and working in the computer field since 1970. For the last twelve years he has been a self-employed computer consultant working in the Edmonton, Alberta, area. He is married (for twenty-four years this time) with four boys ranging in age from 36 to 18. His wife is a C.A. who is currently consulting to the provincial government. This story is his first attempt at producing something other than a lecture, a client presentation, or system documentation.

Basements

David Nickle

Mr. Nu was in the basement of his small workman's house on Larchmount when our firm's team came for him. At first they thought he was barricaded down there—possibly sitting on a cache of weapons, or explosives, or biological agents. Possibly, on something worse.

They had swept the two above-ground floors and found nothing there—almost literally.

This by itself, put the team on guard—even without the incriminating weight of our firm's considerable file on him, the paucity of personal effects in Mr. Nu's dwelling was suggestive of a life led to a particular end, of a particularly quiet march...to a *particular* end.

The basement was only accessible by one staircase off the kitchen. Marisse, the team leader, was confident that he would not flee. But that was not a comfort, either. If Mr. Nu were of a desperate frame of mind—if he were under instructions to avoid capture at all cost—being cornered in the basement with no exit but one, might lead to acts similarly desperate.

These were thoughts upon which Marisse did not wish to dwell.

Later, before an ad-hoc panel of her superiors in the Peel Room at the Marriot, she faced questioning; "Why did you not send a team to the basement immediately? Why did you search the remainder of the house, when the infrared imaging indicated with some certainty that Mr. Nu was not in the kitchen or the bedroom or the upstairs bath?"

Marisse had no satisfactory answers. She grew quiet, almost sullen. On the hotel notepad, she doodled images of cubes, stacked upon one another in such a way as to make it impossible to tell whether the boxes were stacked like a giant pyramid, or a precarious overhang of packing crates. Benoit demanded that she respond as a professional, and she mumbled something softly, then leaned toward the microphone in the middle of the table, reached across and turned it away from her, and to Benoit. "You respond," she said, and Benoit became angry enough that I had to intervene.

"Marisse completed the mission," I said, sliding the note pad from Marisse and underneath my laptop." Don't forget that, Bennie."

I caught her eye for a moment, attempting to draw out some connection and put her at ease; we had known each other for many years at that point, and sometimes confided in one another on matters personal and professional. But not tonight.

Tonight, nothing.

⊷⊶⊷ ⊷ ⊷⊶⊷

The apprehension, when it came, occurred without serious incident. This much we confirmed during the meetings at the Marriot. Marisse, her team, did complete the mission. No one was injured, not agent, nor civilian, nor the target: Mr. Nu.

Mr. Nu arrived at Sandhurst Circle with just the clothing he wore: a dark brown T-shirt, a pair of greenish cotton briefs and low white socks made from a material designed to transmit perspiration during exercise.

He had been there only a month when I attended the Marriot; a month and a day, when I made my way up the highway to Sandhurst itself. To see Mr. Nu's new home.

⊷⊶⊷ ⊷ ⊷⊶⊷

Twenty-three square kilometers, and Sandhurst in the middle of it—specifically, at the municipal address of #12 Sandhurst Circle.

Seven hundred and fifty square meters on the main floor and second. Granite counter-top in the kitchen, and in the three baths, except the master bedroom's ensuite which was a deep pink marble. Dark hardwood floors throughout, matching the beveled trim around doors and other openings. It was, as the brochure stated, ducal.

The yard, now, *that* was incomplete. A swimming pool, defined by stakes and string in tamped-down topsoil, waiting for the builder to come and finish the job with landscaping and excavation.

The basement, although considerable, was not mentioned in the real estate listing for the home when the subdivision was, briefly, on the market. Before the developer went bankrupt, and his assets were spread among an ad-hoc group of companies and funds that together formed something more useful.

Before we moved in.

"That's where we keep the cells," said Stephan as he sipped the espresso he'd made in the identical granite-countered kitchen in #42 Cathedral Crescent. There we sat, waiting for the driver to take me to Sandhurst. Stephan took the time to bring me up to date. I ran my finger along the lip of the counter-top.

"There are seven altogether," Stephan said as he set down the tiny cup. "Seven cells. An interrogation room. Laundry room. Three piece bath. "Stephan allowed himself a smile. "Italian tile. Etruscan fixtures."

Mr. Nu's basement on Larchmount was no comparison. *That* one *was* small, barely six feet of clearance, the floor made of uneven concrete sloping to a drain in the middle. Light from bare bulbs, two of them, either end of the long space. Under one bulb, the canvas lawn chair, where the team found Mr. Nu. One pale thigh crossed over the other, hands folded over brown-shirted belly as Marisse and team finally— finally!—crept down the stairs, their laser sights tracing jitter- ing nonsense script across his wide chest.

"Some of us were thinking slate," Stephan's smile faltered and his eyes strayed to the French doors, beyond which sub- terranean sprinkler systems flicked water across the newly laid sod of #42. "But really, for a three-piece it was overkill. And the tile we chose—two kinds—big octagonal pieces, the color of cream, and the palest blue in square...you know, to fill the spaces."

I didn't interrupt him as he continued, outlining the pat- tern on the counter-top with his fingertip. I had not known Stephan for as long as Marisse; he was relatively new to the firm. I had, indeed, only met Stephan once before, at a con- ference in Las Vegas wherein he and I shared a panel discuss- ing covert logistics opportunities. I think we had impressed one another but that was as far as it went. I was even more at a loss here than I was with Marisse. So I waited for Stephan to exhaust his renovation stories, refill his espresso cup, and fall silent, staring into the foaming murk, before saying it, as gently as I could:

"There is no driver, is there?"

He looked at me, naked apology in his eye, "I'm sorry, sir. You're on your own."

⭑⭑⭑⭓ — ⭓⭑⭑⭑

It should not have been a long walk, but it took more than an hour to cross the distance between Cathedral and Sandhurst. The subdivision was constructed at the crest of a gentle hill, foundations sunk in land that had until very recently anchored nothing more than rows of corn. It was the highest farm in the area, between a low marsh to the north of it—and the city and the river it sat on, to the south. Standing amid those corn-stalks, how intoxicating it must have been, to turn and everywhere, see the world beneath you.

The walk was quiet. Most of the houses we kept in the compound were vacant, but not perpetually. When we acquired the real estate, we determined that maintaining a population equivalent to one-tenth of the subdivision's population capacity was adequate both to our cover, and to staffing needs. And so our sub-contracted staff moved about—from one structure to another, clearing driveways and cutting grass, paying taxes. Keeping up appearances.

It was a hollow facade, and could not be anything else, given the limitations of our contractors... hard men... hard women.

Comparing it to Larchmount, now: a straight street, and short, with tight-packed houses with front porches, but no driveways, cars jam the curb, even at eleven in the morning. From dawn, elderly men sit on porches in their plaid shirts and baseball hats, having seen it all, still watching; pleased young mothers with baby carriages make their way down to the coffee shop at the bottom of the street. On such a street, in such a house as his, Mr. Nu might hide forever, ensconced in his basement beneath his light bulb, wearing his brown T-shirt and greenish shorts, his socks...

...of a fabric, to carry perspiration, from flesh.

⭑⭑⭑⭓ — ⭓⭑⭑⭑

The subdivision surrounding #12 Sandhurst was intended for wealthy families with good credit. So even the smallest home is overly-large, more dramatic than practical, and the houses grow as they reach the center. Number 12 Sandhurst, near that center, is of course, one of the largest. Sheathed in limestone or something like it, the building presses against the lot's edge. It has a square tower at one end that resembles a clock tower. Although no higher than its neighbors, the elevation of the ground on which it was built grants it a subtle dominance.

It might be approached from two directions—but from either, doing so is an ascent.

It must have been a warm day, because I was perspiring heavily. Itching, too; Sandhurst Circle was the last portion of the subdivision scheduled to be finished, and the collapsing banking industry—the sudden extinction of wealthy families with good credit—did not wait for the developer to complete the landscaping.

So the hot breeze blew clay dust up in miniature sandstorms, eddies that swept across the front walk and driveway, frosting the tall, dark windows gray. The dust coated my throat and stung at my eyes. I approached the front door. It ought to have opened—#12 Sandhurst is equipped with well-hidden cameras and security with access to face- and gait-recognition software, and I was in the database. But it was left to me, to shift the door-knocker aside and enter the access key. The double oak doors swung inward, and I stepped inside, into the front hall.

The room climbed two storeys, with the sweep of a staircase following a curved wall upstairs. The only light came from the tall windows behind me, and somewhere within, I heard the pulsating whine of a vacuum cleaner.

How near was it? I couldn't tell at first. While I had some idea of the layout of #12 Sandhurst, I had not studied the floor plans in great detail. Whatever the trouble with Stephan and the driver, I was expecting that I would arrive here and be greeted by the duty officer, then ushered through the appropriate hallways and staircases. Not standing alone, attempting to triangulate the location of a housekeeper, while work waited to be done.

There were five exits from this space, counting the stairs and the door that I had come in: two on either side of me, and another in an archway beneath the stairs itself. Pale, dust-colored light hinted from all of them. As the vacuum cleaner shifted from pile to board, some of that light flickered—as though the cleaner passed before a window—then seemed to pulse brighter—as if perhaps that cleaner drew back a curtain. The banister from the staircase cast a sharp shadow at one point, the wall behind it glowing a dusky orange. The light of the setting sun? Perhaps. The shadow moved as I watched, growing and climbing to touch the ceiling before fading again. It was as though time were accelerating, and I was left behind, here in this dark vestibule, watching it Doppler ahead.

I blinked, and my eyes stung ferociously, so I blinked again.

In front of me stood a tall man, hair close-cropped in the Marine style. He wore an olive-green T-shirt that showcased a powerful physique—black trousers that tucked into high military boots. His fists were clenched at his side; jaw clenched too, with tendons swelling and subsiding up and down his neck. His eyes were wide. Brimming with tears.

And again, I blinked.

Behind him, on the staircase, was an upright vacuum cleaner, a dozen steps up, abandoned—the power cord descending taut from the dark of the second floor, like a single, black marionette string. At the very end of its reach.

Once more: the blink. With a grandiose leisure now, as though the passage of time had slowed and was readying itself to stop here, in the infinite silence of the instant between heartbeats.

I didn't let it. I took a shuddering breath and shouted, and so did he, and then we both screamed, yowled like animals, into the dark chambers of #12 Sandhurst Circle.

And it was only then I turned from him and fled out the front door, into the deepening night.

→∞← ⊰ — ⊱ ♦ →∞←

His name was Scott Neeson, and the haircut did not lie. He was a former U.S. Marine Sergeant, recruited after three tours in Iraq. He was living at CnMqmNc84 Twilling Row, and there he would stay until he could finish building a vast wooden deck with an installed hot tub and a covered grill-house.

He came over with a twelve-pack of beer and a pair of sirloins, the day after I settled into #37 Ridgeway. So named because the houses scattered along the northern edge, their yards edging on a drop that looked down on woodlots and farmlands in the old marsh. A ridge-way. In moving in to #37, I had inherited an immense barbecue grill, five burners on the grill itself, with a small gas range attached. Neeson, sporting a pale blue Hawaiian shirt and long brown cargo shorts, came around the back of the house in the late afternoon, set down the clinking case of beer and fired the beast up.

"You're joining us?" he said, bending to pull bottles from the case. He handed me one.

"Something like that," I twisted the bottleneck and set the cap down on the deck railing.

"Good. We can use good people here. And it's a nice place."

"Is it?"

"It is. Nice big houses, and the money's good when you don't have to pay for them. Nobody bothers you." Neeson turned to the grill, examined the dial. "Pretty light lifting, is what. You come from the Service?"

"You think I'm a Marine?"

"I thought you were a Marine, I'd have said the corps. But service isn't the word I was looking for, either." He snapped his fingers as he spoke.

"You're thinking about Company?"

He nodded. I shook my head.

"Does that even mean anything?" he asked. "You saying no?"

I smiled. "If I told you, I'd have to kill you." And although that is what I always said, and that is what most of us always said when we could not think of a proper joke, Neeson laughed as though he'd just heard it.

"But you're from up the chain," he said, turning serious, "aren't you?"

"I am."

"You came here to check out what was happening with..."

"Nu."

"With him." Neeson lifted the grill and peered into the dark, hot space. "We met in Sandhurst, you and I."

"We did."

He let the grill cover down.

"And now, you're moving in."

I took a long pull of my beer. It was a dark-colored ale from a local brewery. I thought I might remember the brand, for later.

"Word gets around," I said. "I'm moving in."

"That's some inquisition you must be planning. How long do you think?"

I sipped my beer. Stephan had told me I could have Ridgeway as long as I needed it, so long as I kept up the lawn and did the same for four other houses near mine. By the book, I would rotate out of it after a month. But that could be extended, he explained, if I were engaged in some special project, one that only I could properly finish—like Neeson's deck.

Neeson leaned back against the railing, crossed his arms. "So you have any questions? Figured I'd come here, save you another trip out."

"In."

"Yeah. It is 'in' from here, isn't it?"

We looked at each other for a moment. In the sunlight, Neeson's face took on a harder quality than it had in the shadowy foyer of Sandhurst. No tears, that was one thing. But the late afternoon tempered him in other ways. Lines at the corners of his eyes, a droop in the corner of his mouth, flesh beneath his eyes folded like lava-flow. It made him a hard statue that the years had eroded as much as they ever would. He was a man who knew about car batteries and pliers.

"What have you learned?" I asked.

Neeson opened the top again, and the heat hit us like the wind. He nodded, lifted the sirloins from their wrapping, and draped them over the grill, causing a ferocious sizzling and a cloud of smoke.

"Better get a spray-bottle," said Neeson. "There'll be flare-ups, and we don't want to turn this fine meat to shoe-leather."

I found a tall plastic spray bottle beside the sink, filled it with tap water, and hurried back. Sure enough, he was right—fat from the steaks had dripped down to the steel plates that stood in for the rocks you'd find in older models, and it was burning furiously. We sprayed and sprayed, but the flames never quite went out.

⟶⟵ ⟶ ⟵⟶

The subdivision is fairly remote from major shopping districts. The nearest is a 40-minute drive through farm country, past corn-fields and finally across a great, near-empty parking lot, to the massive building supply store that had once been a continent spanning chain.

The road is never very busy, but it is a particularly pleasant drive on a Sunday, in the dark green mini-van from Ridgeway's garage. It is a drive that I have done more than once—gathering paint and lumber and exotic power tools that were not already in the well-equipped workshop in Ridgeway's basement.

Some days, I recognized my neighbors in the aisles: Scott Neeson on more than one occasion, hauling sheets of plywood as big as flags and bags of concrete on orange-painted dollies; Stephan and Lynette, a slender South-Asian woman some years older than he, looking speculatively at kitchen cabinetry; Luis, a small and swarthy man with black hair to his shoulders, a thin and patchy beard and an unstoppably cheerful grin, who one Sunday afternoon admitted to me that he was flirting with the idea of building a sauna, but mostly shopped for floor lamps and fine art prints. "There are so many *rooms*," he explained.

One day, I met Benoit there.

"It has been months," he said. We were loitering in the aisle for drop ceilings.

"I know. I'm sorry."

"Sorry," Benoit snorted. "I hear that you have taken a house there. You are doing—what?"

"It's a complex enterprise. I cannot complete it in a day."

"Months," he repeated and glared up at me. Benoit was a head shorter than I, and heavy in the gut. If he was higher on the chain than I, it was not by much—and although I don't think he was much lower, either, I have taken it as a matter of pride that he has never had the capacity to intimidate me. But when our gazes broke, it was I, not he, who looked away.

"I haven't reported much, I know," I said.

"You haven't reported at all. We received word of your arrival from the superintendent. But from you? Nothing."

Benoit led us to the end of the aisle as a couple pushing a big orange cart appeared at the other.

"What is your impression of Mr. Nu?" he asked. "From the meetings you have no doubt had by now?"

I didn't answer, and Benoit nodded.

"No meeting, hmm?"

We rounded the end of the tandem, and stepped into an aisle filled with exterior siding materials, and window frames. Benoit smiled gently.

"You think that I will be shocked now, and angry, don't you?"

"You would have the right."

He shrugged. "I, the right. Do you know that there was a time that I actually feared you? Now—*you* tell *me* I have the right to be angry with you. I wonder: is it because I have become so much more impressive?"

"I'm not afraid of you," I said, and he nodded knowingly.

"Marisse," he said. "What was your impression of her, after our interview at the Marriot?"

"You have my report—"

"I do," he said. "Now tell me. Do you still think that she suffers from a 'simple dissociative disorder resulting from mission-related trauma?'"

"That's what I wrote?"

"It is," Benoit looked down. "Two weeks ago, she killed herself. Shot herself through the eye with a semi-automatic pistol. Her customary sidearm. You'll forgive me if I cannot summon the precise make—"

"A Glock," I said. "Lately. She also had a Desert Eagle."

"Not the Desert Eagle. Absurd. No. The Glock. Yes. She was the fourth member of the team that assailed Larchmount to attempt suicide; the second to succeed."

I put my hand on the shelving and leaned hard. It had been built for siding and window frames and, on the other side, ceiling tiles, and it didn't so much as quaver.

"Her family?"

"Grieving, I imagine. I have not had opportunity to inquire in detail. We are concerned now with the examination of other links in the chain."

We hurried from window frames and siding, and moved into gardening supplies. There, Benoit expounded on the fate of the transfer team, whose leader had simply vanished three weeks before; on the firm's government contact, a small former FBI woman named Lester, who had spent ten minutes with Mr. Nu, the two of them on either side of a glass barrier. Suddenly and inexplicably replaced by an older man, because, the firm's intelligence indicated, she had gouged her eyes out and attempted to disembowel herself with an X-acto knife during a debriefing.

And then, the matter of Sandhurst, and the changes that had wrought themselves there.

"You have noticed," said Benoit, "or perhaps you have not, that we have suspended prisoner intake at Sandhurst these past few months. We are making other arrangements."

I had not.

"You must have also noticed," said Benoit, "that in spite of your obvious failure to resolve matters, we have not taken steps to replace, or indeed even supervise you."

That, I had.

"Don't worry. I am not doing so now. You can continue where you are—as long as you wish—to do what you wish. You will be compensated. You may leave. Or stay. You may also, of course, do the thing you came to do. But I will remind you, my friend..."

And we made it through gardening supplies, and stood by the tall glass doors that were wide enough to haul a houseframe through, and Benoit extended his hand.

"...Marisse shot herself in the eye."

And with that, he turned and stepped into the brilliant Sunday afternoon sunlight. And that was the last that I ever saw or heard of Benoit.

One evening not long after, Scott Neeson stopped by Ridgeway. No beer this time. He came with a single bottle of red wine. It had no label and he bashfully admitted that was because he had made it himself, using a kit he'd obtained from the winemaking outlet next to the building supply store. He suspected that it might not be adequate. I suggested we try it and see.

We took it to the back deck and sat beside the barbecue, now hidden by a form-fitted cover I'd found in the garage. Scott drew a breath at the view of the woodlot, orange and red over a carpet of pale yellow and dark brown leaves that had fallen the past week, all set alight as the sun set over the rooftop of #37.

I poured the wine, and sat beside him. He didn't speak for a long time, and I didn't prompt him. He finished his wine. I poured him another and topped up my own. As the light faded, so did the hard lines of his face, the slack flesh beneath his eyes. The shadow of #37 Ridgeway erased years. I watched them vanish, one by one, until finally he was ready.

"I used to know what to do," he said, in a voice that trembled, looking me with eyes that were wide, and wet. "I used to be sure."

I put my hand on his arm.

"Not now, though," he said. "Now, I have no fucking idea whether I'm coming, or going."

We spent time deciding which of the houses to inhabit next. Scott had not put all the touches on Twilling Row's elaborate rear deck; the plumbing and electrics for the hot tub installation were barely roughed-in, and the covering for the grill area was up but needed shingling. We talked about remaining there; the winter would not treat the unstained decking kindly, and he'd done so much work already, it seemed a shame to abandon it now. But he insisted he didn't care anymore. He wanted to be away. So we tried a few nights at Ridgeway, and that worked well enough, at first. We slept curled together on the king-sized bed in the cavernous master bedroom; took turns cooking and clearing dishes in the bright kitchen; in the sitting room, we watched the classic western and noir and science fiction films that were shelved under the entertainment console.

But that didn't last either. I woke up on more than one occasion suddenly shivering, alone in the bed, to find Scott, standing by the open bedroom window, naked, arms wrapped tight around himself as he looked north, up the gentle slope, to Sandhurst, and wept. Or once, finally, in the bathroom, looking blankly at the open medicine cabinet—filled with razors and sleep-aid medications—hands on either side of the sink, muscles in his forearms tensing, as though he were readying himself to leap into it. That night, I went to him, put my arms on his shoulders, and gently, drew him back to the bed—thinking all the while of Marisse, and the bullet that Benoit said she had put through her eye.

And so in the end, with Stephan's help, we found a new house: a genuinely new one this time, near the southern part of the subdivision—#60 Wyatt End. So new the drywall in the family room was still unpainted. The basement bathroom was only roughed in.

No one had lived there since the firm moved in. It was a blank slate.

At Christmas, we had a party there. I invited Stephan and Lynette and some others I'd met over the months; and Scott invited some of the others who worked with him—the Sandhurst Crew, they called themselves. They all brought bottles, and threw them in with Scott's batch of home-brewed wine, and we carried on through the night.

I had too much to drink, I have to admit. Stephan and Scott had to help me up to bed. Early Christmas Day awakened by stale wine in my gut and off-key caroling a floor below, I found myself standing naked by the window, looking through thin snowfall to the few, dim lights in the city many kilometers to the south.

Thinking of Larchmount.

→⊷←⊰ — ⊱→⊷←

Children. That's what was missing.

Larchmount was the kind of street that was lousy with them: infants and toddlers and teenagers, sullen and giddy and beautiful and awkward; fat moms and dads, going to work and coming home again, where they chased diaper-clad little fatties from room to room, catching sleep in precious moments until they did it again. If Mr. Nu sat next door, in a chair beneath a light bulb in a house nearly empty...well, the people of Larchmount had other things to bother about.

There were no children on Wyatt, or Cathedral, or Twilling or any of the others here. Nothing came from Stephan's friendship with Lynette—nor, obviously, Scott's and mine—nor any of the other half-dozen couples who'd coalesced around Sandhurst over the days... the months...

The years.

⟶⟶⟵⟵ ⟶ ⟵⟵⟶⟶

Even without children, we got fat.

It happens. All you have to do is sit still for long enough. And that is what we did. Trips to the building supply store grew less frequent—a combination of its diminishing stocks, and our own waning interest, the growing complacency of our house-pride. Power wasn't reliable enough to keep watching DVDs, but we enjoyed reading. Anything to sit still.

It's not always a bad thing, being fat. The roundness of it smoothed Scott's skin, took the worry from his eyes, the knowledge from his mouth. Combined with his less and less frequent visits to Sandhurst, it allowed a measure of innocence to return, or perhaps just emerge. He smiled so easily, and I envied him. I was the ugly fat man, a furtive gray toad that couldn't even meet its own eye in the bathroom mirror.

But I don't blame the fat.

⟶⟶⟵⟵ ⟶ ⟵⟵⟶⟶

We kept having parties. Smaller parties, but more of them.

Smaller, because of the subdivision's shrinking complement. Early on, it was simple departures. The medical station in #4 Battleford Avenue lost a surgeon; Linguistics in #52 Burling Street lost their Russian and Farsi specialist—a serious blow, that one; and at least two cleaners.

The flow was finally stemmed when Stephan announced that the firm had established a covert perimeter around the subdivision. He went in to no further detail about what that perimeter entailed, but enough understood the implied threat, to need no further encouragement to stay put.

Yet still, we diminished. There were some suicides, three of them among Scott's former team-mates at Sandhurst. Some didn't die, but locked themselves in their houses and refused to communicate or co-operate when Stephan sent in rescue and medical teams. They remained in flesh, but truly, were no longer present in the subdivision.

Smaller parties. But far more frequent.

Never properly sodded, our yard was soon taken over by tall wildflowers and thistles, vines that could tear flesh. So we limited our celebrations to the concrete-tiled back deck, where perhaps a dozen of us would sit on resin chairs, heads tilted back to look up at the froth of stars that gathered into prominence over the ever diminishing glow from the city, a hundred more stars each year than the last. We would drink Scott's wine and talk and stare at outer space.

Enough wine in me at some of these and I would bring myself to wonder, would tilt my head from the Heavens down, to the top of the subdivision's hill, and Sandhurst.

One night, helping Scott up to our bed, I posed a question:

"Who is looking out for Mr. Nu now? Is he even still alive?"

"Nu." Scott lowered himself to his bed, and let out a long, labored sigh. We were both drunk; drunk, fat old men. "You asked me a question, a long time ago."

"Okay."

"When we first met, and the time after."

"The time after. In my yard. With that beer."

"And steaks. 'What did I learn?' you asked me."

"And what did you learn?"

He looked at me in the dim candle light of our bedroom, my happy old fat man.

"When you go into a dude's house—make sure you're invited," he said. "Make sure the dude knows you're coming, and is cool with it, and has taken the steps. Steps not to show himself. And if he's in the basement—" and in his slurry, drunk, *innocent* voice, Scott whispered:

"Leave him be."

What did you learn?

The question doesn't come easily. I don't think it can come easily.

When I can't sleep, I take out Marisse's notepad, and look at that doodle she did, in the meeting room in the Marriot, in her last debrief—a stack of cubes, either made sturdy like a pyramid, or impossible, precarious, boxes stacked on ceilings. Ball point perspective makes both true. Both a lie.

And both a lousy answer to the question: why would you search every room but the one you knew that Mr. Nu was in? Lousy answers, but as it happened, the only answer forthcoming.

Not everybody puts a bullet through their eye but everybody dies.

Stephan's Lynette, for instance. Dead. Cancer, started in her left breast. Undiagnosed. Spread all over. And so. Dead.

Stephan took it hard. The two had been together for decades when it came, and as Stephan told me: "There's no one now, forever." He was right, and I gave him a long hug—although silently, I thought (perhaps unkindly) he ought to have prepared himself, she was so much older than he. But I didn't argue when he announced he wanted to turn the faux Tudor mansion on Wellington Way into a mausoleum, for "the beloved departed"—Stephan's code for those who died not from suicide or escape attempts, but simply in the course of things. So we worked to seal off some rooms in the basement as crypts. And into the first of those, we bore Lynette—her boney cadaver wrapped in 600-thread sheets from an upstairs linen closet—and by the light of a dozen candles, listened to Stephan as he sang her praises, and wept, and said a prayer. Then Luis, who'd volunteered, stayed downstairs with trowel and cement and bricked in the crypt.

Stephan could have expected to bury Lynette. Burying Scott, now...

Yes. Scott Neeson. Heart attack. Too fat. Too drunk, maybe. So a massive coronary, while I snored beside him. And yes.

Dead.

I took it hard too. But who would have thought? I'm a fat old man. Fatter, older, and I never was a Marine, and I never was strong. Scott should have been burying me. But there he lay, eyes wide and wet and empty in the morning light. Soon to be the second resident of the crypt, the catacombs, beneath Wellington Way.

⇢►◄ ◁ — ▷ ►◄⇠

I could leave. I could stay. I could do the thing that I came to do.

I put on my parka, a pair of boots. I fished around in back of the china cabinet until I found the latch, and opened it, and from there pulled out the little Russian automatic pistol that Scott favored, and a clip of ammunition. The kitchen, where I found an LED wind-up flashlight. Then I went upstairs one more time, to look at Scott, make sure I wasn't tricking myself with ball point perspective, then left as fast as I could to the front door, and into the street.

It was tough going. A week ago there'd been a heavy snow-fall, and then it had been cold since, so the road was rutted and icy. And uphill, around and around, in a gentle and exhausting slope. It took me until the noon hour to reach Sandhurst Circle.

I nearly turned back. The whole street was choked with high drifts of snow, rising in places to the tops of first-storey windows. There was, simply, no path to or from #12. I couldn't see how I could make it to the front doors, which were buried in snow up to the handles. But I thought, *I could do the thing that I came to do.* And, *there's no one now. Forever.*

I pushed through the snow, nearly fell as I climbed over and through the drift to the door. Pulled aside the knocker, and spent some time recalling the access code before entering it. The doors swung inward, and the snow fell inside along with me.

There: the same vestibule. Dark, but for what light filtered in through snow-covered windows.

No one was vacuuming. The house was icy cold. But there was a sound of running water. A burst pipe? That's what I thought, too.

I might have stood there again, for hours, guessing at where the sound came from, losing myself in the rhythm of this place. I might have just fled. But finally, I was done with guessing; done with fleeing, just so far. My thumb found the switch on the flashlight, and soon the three blue LEDs cast a circle on the floor ahead of me. I thought only a minute about looking upstairs first—and thought about Marisse—and decided not to. And so I stepped through an archway, wallpaper peeling from it in wide strips. From there, I passed through a high living room, floor-boards creaking underfoot. At one time, this room had been used for conferences; there was a long table in here, and at one end a projector with a bay for a laptop computer. Chairs everywhere.

"Mr. Nu," I shouted. "What are you up to?"

The water—perhaps just a tap left on, in one of the bathrooms? No. I passed into a wide, short hallway, and through the archway beyond, where one might expect a kitchen, but over the decades I had become savvy to the architecture of the subdivision, and didn't get my hopes up.

"You have associates," I said, "isn't that so? Tell me who they are, and we'll give you back your clothes."

I was right. The next room had a sunken floor, high shelves on every wall but one, and where the floor dropped, a big metal fireplace, open at every side. That fourth wall: tall windows of leaded glass. Mostly snow-covered now, so what light came in was a creamy gray. Some of the shelves had books on them.

"No one's coming for you," I said, in a threatening tone. "I'm your only hope. Now tell me: What are you up to, Mr. Nu?"

Not a tap, not a broken main. The water sounded nearer now, and more elemental. It made me think to times long ago, sitting on rocks on a hot summer day, by rapids, mist making my breath cool.

"Our operative—never mind what her name was, you don't need to know that—she shot herself in the eye. Dead. Why did you make her do that?"

Next to this room, was the kitchen. A fine kitchen, but not the finest in the subdivision. I reached into my parka's pocket, and pulled out Scott's gun. I stood there for I don't know how long. Then I lifted it high, flipped the safety off and shot the refrigerator.

"You think I put that bullet in my eye? You are wrong, Mr. Nu. That was your friend. He wouldn't talk to us. Now he's dead too."

Beside the refrigerator—a doorway. Not as grand as the others, but why should it be? It only led down to the basement. I put Scott's gun down a moment on the butcher block, gave the flashlight another cranking and opened the door.

"Why do I want to go upstairs right now, Mr. Nu, not down? Is it you?" I asked, as I shone the light down the long flight of metal stairs. The light caught rust like moss growing on the edges where the paint had scraped away, a rime of frost that coated the banister. The beam hung ahead of me in thick, icy mist. The sound of running water turned into a racket; it was close by now. It sounded like a river.

The stairway was long—so long it switched back on itself once and then bent out at 90 degrees for the last five steps. Slow going, too; the mist and the frost made the metal treacherous for a young man. Fat old men carrying guns and flashlights had to take particular care. I passed the time asking more questions. Some were questions I'd come to ask: more about Marisse and her team, and as it followed the things that might have happened to the transport team, and to the firm's government liaison. And more that had occurred to me in the months and years that followed: What of Scott? Of me? Of the world? What have you done, Mr. Nu, Mr. Nothing, Mr. Null—to cause us all to so badly recede? Is it you, now you and your *associates*, that walk the world you persuaded us all to so easily abandon?

Why us? Why not Larchmount?

I stood alone, finally, in the basement of #12 Sandhurst, playing the flashlight beam across the wet, icy stone—looking for some sign of the interrogation room; the three-piece bath, with the Italian tile that had so pleased Stephan. Were there any remains of the seven cells in this cavern? Would Mr. Nu somehow still be in one of them? Alive? After so long?

There was nothing that I could see. The place was all ice and rock, flickering in dim reflected light.

I took care as I moved along, but it was no good. I slipped, and pinwheeled, and landed hard on my behind. Nothing was broken, but in the fuss of it all, I let go of the light and the gun. I listened to them both, skittering down rocks as might lead to a fast-moving stream on a summer's afternoon. There was a splash, and then another.

A stream. Was that what had happened here? An underground stream, an aquifer, broken through the thin layer of concrete that the bankrupt builder had spread over the ground, and flooded the basement, over years perhaps corroded the foundations; swept away the neat, leveled chamber here, the seven cells and the interrogation room and the three-piece bath... leaving only this cavern?

This cavern, where a man might sit, under a single lightbulb, on a canvas lawn chair, in a brown T-shirt, pale green underpants and socks of a material that drew moisture away from flesh. Looking with a hollow, knowing eye at another: this one an old man, fat, blind, freezing cold, looking for purchase on the slippery stone...

→••←◦◃ — ▹◦→••←

...finding some, finally, on a ledge of concrete, just inches above the icy, flowing earth-water. I might have stood; there seemed enough space. But I tucked my feet close under my knees instead, stayed low, because I knew, if I stood up, I would turn, and try and scramble away, flailing in the dark until I found the base of the stairs. Then, I would haul myself up those stairs, fast as I could, and run. Flee.

I wrapped my arms around my knees, and looked, and checked against the data from his file, some of which (not all) I had committed to memory. Might he have lost weight over time? It didn't seem so. He was if anything a little chubby. His dark hair seemed long for the style he'd cut it in, but it was hard to say whether that was a result of inattentive incarceration. His clothing seemed fresh, though. And he was clean-shaven.

He leaned forward in his chair—looking straight at me, frowning, as if deciding whether to say anything; whether after all these years, this time, he had any answers for me. Whether he'd thought of any questions, for that matter.

Then, both hands on his knees, he stood. His head came near the 200-watt bulb that dangled over his chair, and he shifted from the hot brilliance, of a kind that had not come to light the night at Sandhurst in decades.

And he looked down—down at me—and yanked his briefs from the crack in his behind, adjusted the waist-band so it cradled his gut. Fattened on stillness.

Head still bent under the low beams of Larchmount, he eyed me once more.

No. No questions worth asking, of one such as I.

And with that, Mr. Nu made his way to the narrow wooden stairway and climbed, to the kitchen at Larchmount. To the world, which he now inhabited; which he had, in his agreeable solitude there, spared. Which I had abandoned.

Mr. Nu reached the top. He stopped there an instant, as though considering one more time, then flipped a switch, and so. The bright yellow light vanished. Larchmount, forever gone.

In its place, nothing.

Toronto writer **David Nickle** has had stories published in *The Year's Best Fantasy and Horror, Cemetery Dance, Northern Frights*, and six previous *Tesseracts* anthologies, among other places. His short story collection, *Monstrous Affections* was published in 2009. He is also the author of *The Claus Effect* with Karl Schroeder.

Random Access Memory

Michael Lorenson

Max smiled his way past the first sasquatch posing as security at the door and submitted himself to a frisking and subsequent weapon and coat check. All he had under his long coat tonight was the black knife. He wouldn't need it here, but he hated giving it away, even temporarily. "Take care of my baby," he said to the girl behind the counter. "Just last week the other girl thought she lost it and I had to kill her. True story."

The girl rolled her eyes as she took the blade. "The other girl was me, Max. I dyed my hair, and I don't feel very dead."

"Bonnie?" Max examined her face more closely. "Why blue?"

"Why not blue?" She shrugged her shoulders, then kissed her fingertips and brushed Max's cheek. "Go play, your stuff is safe. Rocco's inside already."

He eyed the small arena and silently ordered his hardware to give him a basic readout. There were six participants seated around a round table at the center of the lowered floor, with one referee walking a circle around them. Nine bookies stood idle in the aisles between the three-hundred-and-eighty-one spectators filling the seats. The hardware also pinpointed Rocco, thin as the leg of a spider, sitting in the third row with an empty seat to his left.

"Sorry I'm late," said Max as he occupied the seat beside Rocco. "Did I miss much?"

"Round two. Just added a drowning. No losers yet."

"Icy. Do you think our boy will pay up tonight?"

Rocco pursed his thin lips, sighed through his nose, and paused for a long moment. "One way 'r'nother," he said.

Max shook his head and turned his attention to the game being played at the table. "Well thank you. That was very inspiring."

⋯⋯⋯

Chad trembled in his seat as the referee pushed the gun along the tabletop and left it in front of him beside the shot glass full of vodka. "Hurry up, let's move," the ref said. "Ten seconds until forfeit. Ten..."

Chad stared at the gun and was surprised to see his own quivering right hand reach out, unbidden, to wrap around the weapon's rubberized grip. His left hand found the vodka.

"Eight..."

Only a one-in-three chance of biting it, he thought. *You made it through one round, how bad could it possibly be?*

"Six..."

God help me.

Chad downed the vodka and grimaced as its oily bitterness hit the back of his throat. Sweat beaded his forehead and his clothing adhered to his damp body. He chose to blame the perspiration on second-rate alcohol.

It won't be that bad, and you can't leave here without the money.

"Four..."

He closed his eyes, lifted the gun and pressed the flat barrel up to his right temple. It felt cool against his wet skin, but the subdermal implants there came alive with a pleasant warmth.

Chad heard some voices from the assembled crowd begin chanting.

"Die, die, die!" The words washed over him like a tsunami and threatened to wash away his resolve.

"Two..."

God help me!

"One..."

Chad pulled the trigger.

⋯⋯⋯

"He's still in," said Max. "Who started this round anyways?"

"Chad's third. Three shots left."

The referee gave the gun's cylinder a spin. It whirred for a bit before settling into position with a click, and the sealed casing made it impossible to tell whether the chamber was loaded or not. He placed the gun in front of player four and started a ten-count. This one must have been braver than Chad, because he downed his drink and fired the gun into his temple before the ref could finish saying the number eight.

The gun hissed as the mem-slug discharged. The player convulsed and slumped forward in his chair, his face slamming onto the tabletop. His arm fell limp at his side though his hand still clutched the gun, and blood slowly pooled from beneath his face.

"Damn," said Max as the crowd around him cheered. "He's going to feel that in the morning."

"Bullet," said Rocco. "Best way. Fast, painless."

Max snorted. "Painless, my ass. His nose is broken, and if he's poor enough to be here, then he's too poor to pay a doc to fix it. Plus he's the first one out, so he doesn't even get paid."

Rocco grunted his accord. "Still the best way."

The referee pried the unconscious man's fingers away from the gun and motioned with his free hand. Two large men appeared and dragged the player out of the arena, each gripping one of the man's arms. The ref reached into his pocket and pulled out a box, from which he selected another slug.

"Animal mauling added!" The referee's voice echoed off the walls, filling the small arena. "Round three!" He pulled a six-sided die out of a pocket and rolled it onto the tabletop. "Player three starts, place your bets!"

The crowd around Max and Rocco surged to its feet; individuals shouted bets to the bookies who struggled to keep up with them.

"Betting?" Rocco asked. Max's hardware enhanced the sound of Rocco's voice, bringing it out amidst the noise of the crowd.

"Not yet," he replied. "I like to wait until at least two people are out. There's less of a payout but it gives me a chance to get into the game."

"One minute remaining!" The referee shouted, pacing around the table as a pair of naked women wiped the blood away and refilled the players' glasses. He turned the gun over in his hands and spun the cylinder before placing it on the table in front of Chad.

⸻ ❦ ⸻

Chad dropped the gun down on the table with a clatter, as though it might still discharge and affect him if he held it for too long.

Fucking mauled by fucking animals! These fucking people are fucking crazy. Where do they even get these fucking memories?

He had survived the third round unscathed, and he stared at the empty glass on the table, willing it to be full again. The referee came over and randomized the slugs before sliding the gun past the now-empty seat and over to the next player on Chad's left. Player Five waited until the count reached two and fired empty as well.

The referee randomized the slugs again and passed the gun along.

Player Six's eyes were closed and he groped for both the gun and the glass, the latter of which was filled with a dark amber liquid. It looked to Chad like whiskey with a splash of tar. The man drank it and grimaced. He snapped the barrel of the gun to his temple and squeezed the trigger as the ref counted four.

The gun hissed and the player collapsed, thrashing to the floor. His screams echoed off the metal walls as he writhed and were lost as some people in the crowd rose cheering to their feet, pumping their fists in the air. One of the man's legs lashed out and sent his abandoned chair tumbling across the ground and into the first row of spectators.

The referee picked up the gun and set it on the table. His brow furrowed as the man on the floor stopped screaming for a second, and then launched into another thrashing fit. Player Six clawed at his own skin, his legs and arms struck out against invisible attackers.

The assembled crowd grew silent as it became evident that something was wrong. The thrashing slowed as the man ran out of energy, but his terrified eyes remained open and staring. The referee's expression slipped from puzzled to disgusted, and he spat as he signaled for the clean-up crew to come take the man away.

Chad forced his lungs to take in air, willed himself to shift in his seat to prove to himself that he wasn't nailed to his chair. He was relieved when Player Five asked the question that he was too numb to say. "What the fuck is that?"

"That," the ref replied, "is what happens when we post our minimum system requirements and people don't pay attention. Obviously his substandard gear can't handle the memory properly. It looks like it's looped." He prodded the body on the floor with his boot and snorted in disgust.

Five stared for a few moments as the ref reloaded the gun. "Looped? You mean the scene didn't end? So he's—"

"Being eaten alive," interrupted the ref. "Yes. Over, and over, without the cut-scene. I think that one was alligators."

"You're just going to leave him like that? How long is he going to be looped for?"

"What do you care? If he's lucky, the hardware will hang and reboot on its own, usually within an hour. A cy-med can reset him if someone takes him there. Otherwise, who knows?"

Five stood up. "That's bullshit, I'm out." He left the arena under a hail of boos and thrown garbage.

The ref shrugged and placed the gun on the table, then rolled his dice.

"Fire added! Round four! Player two starts, place your bets!"

⇒∞⋖⋘ — ⊱ ⋗∞⇐

Max stood from his seat. The crowd of spectators parted before the shadow of his physical presence and cleared a path to the nearest bookie. He smiled at those with the courage to look him in the eyes.

"One thou on three to die in round four," he said to the bookie.

"That'll double your money. Wager on the method?"

"No."

The bookie entered Max's bet and moved on to the next bettor.

Rocco waited until Max took his seat to ask, "Why bet against? Don't we want him to win?"

"We do," said Max. "If he loses, then I double my money and my wife doesn't kill me for gambling because no money's been lost. If he wins, then he gets money, which means we get money, which means my wife doesn't kill me for gambling because no money's been lost."

"Wife's not scary," Rocco monotoned. "Met her."

Max chuckled. "You wouldn't understand. She's nice to other people. Wives are different than regular girls, Rocco. Whores treat you good as long as the money's good; marks... well, marks are supposed to complain. But a wife? She'll stab you to death in your sleep, and for nothing more than you tracked mud or blood in the house, or you gambled away a couple of bucks."

The ref closed the bidding for the round, and slid the gun over in front of the second player.

"Hey, Rocco. If you had a choice, would you pick fire or water?"

"Neither."

Max punched Rocco in the arm. "You can't pick 'neither,' you have to pick one. Would you rather burn or drown to death?"

Rocco sat in silence, appearing to contemplate the question. "Neither," he said. "Always got m'gun."

Max sighed. "Fuck you, Rocco. You're no fun at all."

Player Two didn't appear to Max to care about what had happened the previous round. That, or he had more confidence in his gear. He fired the gun into his temple without touching his drink. When nothing happened, the ref spun the barrel of the gun and placed it in front of Chad.

Chad shook as he picked up the gun. He scanned the faces in the arena as the referee counted down. His eyes stopped and fixed on Max and Rocco.

Max couldn't help himself. He smiled and gave Chad an encouraging nod, pointing two fingers of his right hand at his own temple for emphasis. The ref counted four.

"Don't tell me he's going to forfeit now," said Max. "He's made it to the final three, that's a guaranteed payout if he pulls the trigger. What does he have to lose?"

Rocco faced Max and arched a single eyebrow.

"Well, besides that, I mean."

Chad downed his vodka as the ref counted one, and he pulled the trigger. A second of silence followed the trigger pull and relief quickly washed away the grimace on his face.

Then the gun hissed.

⤜◈◆ ⊰ — ⊱ ◆◈⤛

Chad opened his eyes at the sound of the gun firing and saw the faces of the reacting crowd. Some of them looked jubilant, some looked crushed, many looked indifferent. All of them seemed to be in slow-motion. He opened his mouth to scream when the roar of the crowd gave way to the roar of water.

He was standing on a surfboard, flying down the face of a wave which was at least sixty feet high. A cramp in one leg made him compensate forward and to the left, but the movement overbalanced him and the surfboard shot out from under his feet. He gasped as he belly-flopped into the water and lost most of his air.

Countless tons of water crashed over him. The thunder of the wave was instantly muffled as he was borne under the surface, and the force of the water drove him down into the depths. His chest compressed under the pressure of the water above, but he had been spun around several times and no longer knew which way was up.

He was disoriented, sore, and terrified. He curled into a ball, felt a force pulling at him and went with it, trusting buoyancy to tell him which way the surface was. His ribs and lungs hurt from the pressure, his cramped leg hindered his swim towards the surface, and every molecule in his body screamed for air. A slight exhalation sent bubbles streaming to the surface, and his mouth filled with water. The taste of saltwater was revolting.

God help me. Chad heard the thought echo from two places at once. One voice was his own, the other a stranger's.

The pressure of the water intensified, each pulse of his heart resonated through his body. The pain in his muscles flared and his eyes felt as though they would burst from their sockets even as his vision faded and the light diminished. Chad's hardware fed oblivion into his synapses, and his brain mercifully obeyed.

Chad awoke to the sensation of a floor being dragged across his face, and when he opened his eyes he saw only concrete. He vomited and the resulting splash coated his face, neck, and shoulders. His vomit smelled like failure and cheap vodka.

Pressure, darkness, spiraling.

Hands released Chad's legs and the leaden extremities thudded to the floor.

"Goddamn fucking asshole drownings!" The voice came from above him. Chad started to turn his head towards the sound but the sudden motion made him dizzy and forced him to close his eyes.

"Drowners always puke. Why can't they stick with bullets an' shit? Cleaner that way. Now I got some on my leg!"

"Because they pay us good money and they figure we may as well keep busy mopping up puke?"

Chad counted two voices. He waited for his head to stop spinning, then wished it hadn't because the vertigo was replaced by a pounding, as though his head were being used as a kettle drum. He rolled over onto his back to see a pair of blurry faces. Wet vomit seeped into his hair from the floor below. "W'd'fg," he said.

The act of speaking dislodged something in Chad's throat, which tickled his esophagus, which made him roll over to heave again. He lay sideways with his cheek in a pool of his own warm vomit. The kettle drum beat fortissimo now.

The crest of a wave washed through his vision, obscuring the two faces which came back into focus as the wave receded. One of the faces was moving its lips. Chad's ears heard the sound through the phantom rush of water, but it took a few moments before his brain parsed it into something he could understand. "You drowned."

The face waited a few seconds before continuing. "You lost. Now stop puking on my floor and get out!"

"Lost," Chad whispered. Vivid flashes of images from someone else's memory crowded his vision.

Azure sky and cotton ball clouds. Aquamarine and shaving foam waves. Indigo-black.

Pressure.

Black.

"I made it to the final three." Chad heard the voice, and afterwards realized that it had been he who had spoken. "I get something for that."

"Yeah, yeah," said the second face. A hand appeared in Chad's vision, and it held a credit chip. "Here's your two-fifty." The body attached to the first face opened a door which led into an alley, and motioned for Chad to leave.

Chad stared at the chip in his hand. "I need more than that. There was supposed to be ten thousand."

"You want ten grand?" Face One called to him from where he continued to hold the door open. "Make it to the end next time."

"You don't understand," Chad pleaded. Face Two slipped his hands into yellow rubber gloves. "I need more. You have to help me, I'm in serious trouble."

The two faces looked at each other. While Face One held the door open, Face Two leaned in close to Chad and hauled him to his feet by his shirt. "I get paid to lug bodies around. I get paid to hand out cash. I even, apparently, get paid to mop up puke. I *do not* get paid to help you, and I do not get paid to give a shit about your problems."

Face Two launched Chad through the open door and into a pile of garbage leaning against the opposite wall of the alley. The men disappeared from Chad's view as the door closed.

There was the audible click of a locking mechanism, and Chad sat alone in his pile of garbage.

Chad bolted to his feet at the sound of a nearby whimper, and immediately regretted the sudden motion. He followed the sound and found the second loser, *Mr. Animal Mauling*, lying under a bag of refuse. The man's eyes were open and staring at nothing; he whimpered and trembled, and a sheen of sweat covered his visible skin of his hands, neck and face. Someone had taken his shoes.

The sight of the wet body reminded Chad of swimming in the ocean—reminded him of falling and splashing, of sinking below the surface.

Another noise intruded upon the memory of drowning. Chad was surprised to find himself on his knees. He looked toward the new sound to see Max and Rocco at the far end of the alley, walking towards him. Chad climbed to his feet and ran in the opposite direction. The alcohol and the drowning skewed his vision and sense of balance, and he had to push himself off the walls several times to stay upright. He exited the alleyway onto a dim, unoccupied street. At a distant intersection he spotted a red and blue booth and ran for it.

A viewscreen came alive as he crossed the threshold, and the face of a pretty, blonde woman in a police uniform filled the bright rectangle. "Bowers Corporation New York Police Department, please identify yourself using the station to your right."

Chad pressed his thumb onto a small square and stared into a retinal scanner; red lines flashed across his eyes and thumb.

"Hello, Chad Oliver. You are not a priority customer. Please come back during normal business hours for assistance."

"I can't wait! Someone's after me, they're going to kill me!"

"It is three thirty-five a.m. Only priority customers with an off-hours support contract are eligible for assistance at this time. Please come back during our normal business hours, Monday through Saturday, from eight a.m. until eight p.m."

Chad pounded the screen in front of him with a fist. "I said I can't wait! They're really going to kill me, I need police now!"

"If you require immediate assistance and would like to become a priority customer, please choose the contract that best suits your needs, and select the payment option below. Take advantage of our current special; purchase three months of priority service, and receive a fourth month absolutely free."

Chad glanced at the payment options, none of which were affordable with a two fifty chip. Tears streamed down Chad's cheeks. He tasted the salty wetness when one drop reached his lips. The tears tasted like seawater. Chad shook his head before the memory could crush him again. When his eyes opened, the screen had gone black.

"Need help?"

Chad yelped and whirled at the unexpected voice, and the sudden motion brought the percussionist back. Max and Rocco blocked the booth's only exit.

"C'mon, Chad," said Max. "Come with us, let's work something out."

Chad thrust out the hand with the credit chip. "Take it, it's all I have."

Rocco took the chip and scanned it. "Two fifty," he said.

Max put an arm around Chad's shoulder and guided him out of the booth. "Well, two fifty is a start. Do you remember how much you owe the boss?"

"Twenty thousand," said Chad.

"Twenty thousand," Max agreed. "Good stuff, that gun didn't fry *all* your brains. And tonight was the last chance to pay it all back. So what can we do about the rest?"

Chad whimpered. "I have nothing left. The business went under and the bank took everything. I don't even have a home anymore."

"Don't worry about that," said Max. "We've got a place where you can spend the night. But word on the street is that your business went under because you got caught cheating with illegal hardware. I know the boss helped hook you up, but getting caught was stupid."

"Hardware." Chad stopped walking. "I can sell the hardware. I'll go to a doc first thing and have it taken out."

"Chad," Max continued walking, and pulled Chad with him. "You don't have any money. There's no doctor around here that's going to work on you if you can't pay him."

"I know," said Chad. "I'll figure something out. I just need time to get back on my feet."

Max nodded in agreement. "That sounds reasonable to me," he said, guiding Chad into an alleyway. "What do you think, Rocco?"

Rocco grunted and swiped a keycard into the pad of a nearby door.

"My problem with that, though," said Max, "is that my boss really isn't a very reasonable kind of guy."

Stars went nova in Chad's vision as Max drove a knee into his groin. His lungs emptied, his intestines cramped, and Chad cupped himself as he fell to the ground in the fetal position. Chad could only gasp as Max dragged him through the open door and into a small room.

Max pulled a pressure syringe from the handle of his knife and pressed it against Chad's neck. There was a hiss of air and a coolness spread from Chad's neck through his body. He was paralyzed, but could still feel the burning in his insufficient lungs, the fire in his groin, and the invisible fist which clamped his internal organs. Max sat Chad on the floor with his back against a wall.

"Now," said Max. "Let's do some math."

Rocco grabbed two chairs from around a small table. He slid one seat over to Max, and fell into the other one.

"You owe the boss twenty thousand," Max tapped his right index finger onto his left pinkie, as though going through a gro-cery list. "You gave me two-fifty tonight, which leaves us with... pretty much twenty thousand."

Rocco fished into a pocket for something, but Chad couldn't turn to see what it was.

"You have hardware," continued Max, counting out one more finger. "That can be sold for probably ten or twelve, but you don't have the cash to pay a doc. Well, this is your lucky night, Chad. Rocco and I have some ideas that will let you pay off your debt."

Max lay the point of his knife on the bridge of Chad's nose. It looked to Chad to be nano-edged. "You see this knife? It's the sharpest one you'll ever see. I got into an argument once with a friend who said his knife was sharper, so we pulled them both out. His blade snapped when he dropped it onto the table, almost like it had seen my knife and committed suicide, just out of shame and inferiority. True story!"

Chad's mind screamed, and begged for mercy, and ran for the door. His body sat silent, sweating, and still on the floor in front of Max with the knife in front of his eyes.

"Anyways, back to the issue at hand. I know some basic anatomy, so I'll do the op for you—pro bono. But the other eight to ten thousand, that's going to be a problem; the boss doesn't like to take losses." Max tossed the knife from hand to hand as he spoke. "We bet you have some other hardware that we can make use of, so we're going to clean you out. And Rocco had another idea, too."

Chad's vision went dark as a blindfold was placed over his eyes. The tightness of the fabric constricting around his head alleviated the pounding, as though muting the drum.

"You inspired us tonight, Chad. We bet the arena would pay top dollar for a memory of someone being autopsied, that being the sort of thing that usually only happens *after* the fact."

Chad felt something being slipped between the fabric of the blindfold and his temple, felt his implants warm with activity as he was being recorded.

Felt everything as Max got to work.

Michael Lorenson was born and raised in Montreal where he still resides with his wife, two sons, and cat. He recently rediscovered a love for writing after an extremely long hiatus. "Random Access Memory" is his first submission and publication but he is looking forward to many more years of letting his imagination carry him where it will.

Nightward

John Park

From a nest in the scaffolding, an avian shrieked and dived through shafts of low golden sun and plunged into the stream. Where it struck, the water leapt like flame. Sparks flew, but the splash was lost under the sounds of construction—the bellows of digging machines, the hammering of riveters. The water continued to churn, and when it rippled smoothly again, the transformation was complete and a black serpentine creature undulated out of sight among ooze and weed.

The man named Korliss, who had disturbed the creature's nest, jerked to a stop as his hands crunched the twigs and dried bones. He had been climbing by feel. His eyes were screwed tight but tears had leaked over his cheeks. His jaw was quivering; his body trembled with strain. Convulsively he swept away the nest, felt for the next foothold and climbed again.

At the top, he groped forward until his foot found empty air. Then he stepped back, straightened his spine, lifted his head, and looked. Before him, the land flowed sunward. The stream wound into a stand of trees, reappeared and then lost itself among dusky scrubland. Cloud shadows slid towards the horizon, to where the earth turned brown, and beyond, to where it began to bake. And there, over a band of iron-gray cloud, floating free of the black-toothed horizon, higher than he had ever seen it, huge, crimson-veined and hypnotic, was the sun.

Korliss' eyes filled. His mouth gaped and sobbed. He reached towards the sun, stepped forward, and fell.

⊷⊷⊰—⊱⊶⊶

"You're alive."

The sun.

Heat on the brow, bright red through the eyelids. Look now, look, look. Eyes filled, arms spread wide to embrace, mouth gaping to scream, to swallow down the glory of light.

"Can you hear me?"

At last—to let go. To plummet with eyes still full—with light-choked lungs and light-filled eyes, with mouth straining a scream of light—down into an abyss of glory.

"You all right?" Someone was talking. "Looks like your cloak saved you. That's a long way to fall."

He opened his eyes. His head throbbed; his limbs felt wrenched out of shape. A man's face swam into focus. Beyond it were thin streaming clouds in a cobalt blue sky, then, as his gaze shifted, the skeletons of new buildings. Lower down were hulking, grimy-yellow machines and the glassy shimmer of cutting beams. A team of centrosaurids with horn-stumps capped in brass hauled a wainload of timber. Their snorting was drowned by the roars of machinery.

"You all right?" the man repeated. "Know where you are? What's your name?"

"Name." He groped through a mental darkness, and found nothing. Further off, between two of the syncrete shells, the dusty air blazed with long, low beams of sunlight. His hand felt under his cloak, opened an identipak, found a name.

"Korliss," he said hoarsely. "Yes, Korliss." His hands shook and his cheeks were wet.

"Aye, but do you *remember?*"

"I know the name, now I've found it." Korliss pushed himself up on one elbow, then gasped with pain. He clenched his teeth and waited for his head to stop pounding. The centrosaurids were passing through the sunlight. Their leathery hides gleamed; brass fittings blazed. The dust the creatures stirred up might have been the entrance to a heaven or a hell. "What was I doing?"

"You were up there. They should keep people off. That cloak shocksilk? Don't see it much these days. But it broke your fall all right."

"How did I get here?"

"Same as the rest of us. You climbed up there to see the sun. You don't remember that either?"

"The sun." Korliss realized he knew about the sun. You could stare at it until you starved, and hardly sense it had moved. For a little time in the history of this world, humans would live in the sunlight, would watch the almost invisibly slow setting draw the shadows out longer and begin to chill the air, until the time came to abandon all they had built, to pull down, move onward. The sun drew all life towards it.

Behind him lay the city, stretching itself out like a caterpillar after the slow retreating sun. It left its husks behind it, among the shadows, where the air cooled, and the sky dimmed towards the icy mysteries of nightside.

"See," said the other, "you're standing up. I thought you'd be dead when I saw you fall."

"Yes. I suppose." The sun filled his eyes again. For a moment he remembered an ache. Then he turned away. "Can you help me? I don't know—I still don't know—who I am, where I belong."

"You got an address in there?"

"Right, of course. Thank you." Korliss started to reach for his identipak again. "I'm sorry—your name...?"

"Call me Seth," the man said with a eager smile.

As Korliss turned to shake hands, a flicker of gold caught his eye. He broke away. "The river?"

He ran to the bank, then plunged in to his knees, splashing water over his face, scooping double handfuls up to his mouth. Streaming, he stared at the water flashing beneath the sun. Then he turned upriver, to where the bulk of the city rose up like a bank of solid mist. The river snaked out from it, its source lost beyond the intricacies of towers and bridges, the shadows and mysteries that led nightward.

"I've got to go back."

Korliss waded out of the water. Slowly, then more certainly, he began walking along the bank, beside a stand of trees, watching the ripples flow towards him. He heard Seth's hurrying footsteps on the gravel behind him.

"Go back to the city," Seth said. "Yes. They come out here, they see it, they stare at it. And then, then—it just gets so hard to leave. Some try to go on sunward. Bones out there, I've heard. But mostly there doesn't seem to be any reason to go back. So you just stay."

"But not many come or stay?" Korliss said, waiting for him to catch up.

"I suppose not, when you think how many back in the city never feel it. Funny though, sometimes you hear of a sphig or a griff going sun-happy. Seen one or two myself, heading out alone."

He broke off and gestured Korliss to keep quiet.

They were approaching a clearing. A gray stone sculpture stood on a plinth; below it were cages with serrated bars, a cruciform scaffold, and a parked car, its wings gleaming like scythes.

Korliss approached and looked up at the sculpture. Silhouetted against the sky it threw its shadow across him. It was a gryphon crucified. He felt a chill.

"Orlando's cross, the vigilantes call it," said Seth. "You remember it?" He was standing beside Korliss, talking quickly. Watching Korliss' expression he went on, "I say leave the shifters be, as long as they're not hurting—" Suddenly he beckoned Korliss away.

Voices were approaching.

Through the trees came a group of men carrying something in a net slung from a pole. Korliss crouched behind a clump of bushes and watched as the men went to the scaffold.

Out of the net was dragged a gryphon, evidently stunned. A pulley was set up and the gryphon was hauled onto the scaffold. The shadow of its head fell almost at Korliss' feet. The creature began to struggle, but by then its limbs had been pinioned to the arms of the cross. Its beak opened and a harsh cry belled into the air.

Suddenly its captors began to shout. The creature was changing, it wings shrinking. One of the men drew a blade and triggered it, adjusting the setting so that the shimmering blue beam was twice his height. Teasingly he brought it to the gryphon's body. The creature began to shriek, again and again.

Korliss had seen this before. Where? He had stood and watched, listened and watched, too terrified to intervene—

He burst from the undergrowth, wrenched the blade from the man's hand, threw him aside. Shouts rang in his ears. He shortened the blade and slashed, slashed again as the crucifix toppled, and ended the gryphon's agony. Then he was running towards the car. Seth was already there, the vigilante's identipak in his hand. He unlocked the door and flung it open as Korliss reached him.

"Can you fly this?" Seth yelled. "Then go! They're coming for us!"

Korliss' hands flickered over switchpads and buttons he could not have named, and took manual control. The car lifted and banked out over the river, then fled upstream as projectiles whipped past its wings.

Out of sight of the clearing, he climbed again. Sunlight streamed over his shoulder and flung his shadow onto the nose of the car. To either side, the horizon was a serrated line of dark mountains. Nearer were fields and pastures speckled with livestock. And ahead, as far as he could see, the city stretched towards the shadowed horizon.

Below him, towers cast shadows across highways, parks, industrial spheres, squared blocks of commerce. He found a great gray snake like a twisted spine to the whole city. Carts and wains, groundcars, equines and teams of centrosaurids speckled it like parasites. The name suddenly bloomed in his mind. "*Heliodos.*"

"Aye," said Seth, "the Sunroad."

"I remember!" Korliss cried. Immediately another memory rose, of riding behind a dappled equine on a cartload of tubers, and squinting in awe at a glimpse of the sun between the white towers. "I remember!"

"I am required to remind you," said the car, "that once airborne, I charge full tariff whether or not you specify a destination."

He had come here seeking the sun. But from where?

"I am required to advise you to select a destination."

Korliss looked at Seth, who shrugged.

"Here," Korliss fed the address from his identipak into the car's reader.

⊷∙❖ ❧ — ☙ ❖∙⊶

The car landed on the flat roof of a building half-shaded by a newer tower, and the two got out.

The door to apartment seventeen opened and Korliss stepped into a mystery. The rooms were dim and stark. Korliss could see nothing of himself in any of them. Seth had slipped away.

"Back already? You've been there, seen it?" asked a voice in the doorway. A thin, graying man was standing in a stiff half-crouch, his head pivoting back and forth like an avian's. His eyes were blank white globes. "Of course you've seen it," he said with a faint smile. "Of course. Can tell just by looking at you."

While Korliss groped for a memory, the man took a step into the room. "Like all the others," he said.

"This was my room?" Korliss asked.

"Still is. Paid up. I thought you'd be back."

"How long was I here?"

"Just a few days," the man said, then nodded. "So that's where you're burned."

"I don't know what you mean."

"Aching for the sun, to get to where there's nothing between them and it. Some just climb a tower. Climb it and stay there, staring. Till their eyes are scabs..." For an instant the man's expression made Korliss flinch. Then his sardonic manner returned "Others—they have to keep going after it, trying to hunt it down. Some just stare, and it burns them out right then. Like the old story—you get too close and you burn and fall. I've seen them. All kinds. They come through here and they go on, and some of them come back, but, sure enough, they're all burned somewhere, inside or out; they're falling. I've watched 'em all fall. More every year."

"You can't have watched them," Korliss snapped. "You're blind."

"So I am. Doesn't mean I can't see what's happening. Some of them can't bear to leave it. And here's a place they can stay, quiet, among people who understand. Always a cheap room here for the burned and falling."

No, Korliss thought. *That's not me.*

"Why did you think I'd be back?"

"I know the type. And besides, why else would you have saved all this?"

The man felt across the wall, slapped twice, and a panel popped loose. He pulled it away and gestured at a stack of gold-edged cards inside. His blank eyes had gazed past Korliss' shoulder the whole time.

"You could check that it's all still there. But since you don't remember it anyway, you'll have to trust me, won't you?"

Korliss stood speechless.

"So now you don't know whether to break my neck for searching your room or thank me for finding your money for you. Isn't life interesting? In a minute you'll be asking me where you came from."

"You know?"

"Ha! Of course!" The man half-turned, spreading his arms. "Out of... Out of... "

"Stop clowning around and say it!"

"Out of the womb, like the rest of us. Out of the dark and into the light!"

"Are you going to tell me?"

"I have! I've told you all I know, more than you ever told me."

"Why don't you get out of my room and let me think."

Korliss listened to the man's footsteps retreating; then he examined the pile of currency. Gold cards. It must have taken years to accumulate so many. Where had he earned them? His identipak told him nothing. He began to search the room. In a closet lay a pile of clothing. Korliss spread it on the floor. There was a stained blue-gray tunic with an emblem embossed on the lapels: a crimson fountain and a golden caged gryphon. He inhaled sharply, then sat down and closed his eyes. A picture began to form.

After a few minutes, Korliss left the room and made for the stairs.

He found Seth in a vacant room, sitting on a wooden bench staring at a small canifel curled up at his feet. "Had one of these once," he said when he noticed Korliss. "When I was a kid. Named it Stalker. Brings back memories."

"Not to me," said Korliss. "I've got to go now. Are you coming?"

"Yes, you see, I haven't been in a place like this for half my life, it feels like. Just let me look around a bit. I'll be with you in a minute."

Korliss sighed and sat down. Seth bent and picked up the canifel. It opened its eyes, showed a pink tongue as it yawned, and licked his hand. Korliss got up and paced the corridor. When he looked in the room, Seth had lain back on the bench and was dozing with the pet on his lap.

Korliss hesitated then shook his head; he slipped a handful of cards into Seth's hand and went to the car.

"Follow the Heliodos," he told it. "Nightward."

⚬⟨ ⟩⟨ ⟩⟨ ⟩⚬

The shadows had grown longer, and darker. Ahead of him, lanterns on carts and groundcars made stretches of the Heliodos sparkle as though the snake had been sprinkled with gold dust.

To the north was a field ablossom with glowing tents, clusters of lights, some spinning or tumbling into the air like jeweled insects. The open spaces were furry with crowds. He put the car into a wide circle about it, hoping for a prickle of recognition.

Finally he turned away and the field slipped past his wingtip and vanished among blocks and canyons and low hills with slums and ruined towers in their shadows.

Halfway to the horizon a squat gray factory sent clouds of dark smoke into the sky before they bent sunward. Korliss watched it slide above his wingtip and vanish behind him.

He was approaching one of the wetlands, a steel-gray marsh stippled by reeds. Walls of dark trees and slab-sided buildings threw gray shadows across it, and only the far edge glittered where it caught the sun.

Beyond was a grove of trees and another cleared space. A crowd was milling in front of a circular tent and a group of low structures. From the center of the field a pyrotechnic burst upward, unfurling into a crimson rose that drooped back towards the earth. A red fountain.

Korliss was suddenly short of breath. His palms were sweating. He urged the car lower, staring at the field, at a line of square shapes, at a row of cages.

"Land."

Ahead was a mass of gray shrub and tall trees. The trunks were in shadow but leaves on the upper branches shimmered golden.

"I have exceeded my allowable range," said the car. "Under my license agreement, once I set you down I must return immediately to my franchise zone."

"Land!"

The car touched down at the edge of the field and opened its canopy. The vehicle was in the air by the time he had gone ten paces.

At the far side of the clearing, in front of a stand of red-leaved quercids, a crowd was gathering around three gilded carriages lit by flaring torches. Korliss worked his way around the edge of the clearing towards them. Halfway there, he saw that the carriages formed the wings for a wooden apron stage backed by red velure curtains.

He had paused beside the row of cages. They held chimaeras and gryphons. Serpentine, he suddenly knew, the creatures would have slipped through the bars, but they had been held in their current forms for too long to change back. (*Had someone told him that? Who?*) Standing amidst a litter of stones and empty drinking bulbs thrown by the crowds, the creatures stared over his head with wide, knowing eyes.

He realized he was quivering with tension.

One of the gryphons lowered its head toward him. Breath hissed through its nostrils. The creature's eyes were bile green, with horizontal black slits for pupils. A nictating membrane slid across and back. The eyes gazed at him.

Korliss saw wings and legs shrinking to nothing, feathers and fur smoothing into silvery scales, the beak blurring into fanged jaws—and he could not tell if he was imagining or remembering.

Then he saw his own hands dumping a bucket of meat scraps into the feeding trough at the back of the cage. He had a clear vision of the wings spreading and the creature soaring towards the clouds. *No more than a speck of gold ahead in the purple sky as the maglev crossed the ravine.*

Korliss shivered. The gryphon raised its head again and backed away, one unblinking eye still turned to him. He could hear breath rumble in its throat.

Behind him, from the stage, came the sound of the evening bell, distorted by a worn amplifier. As the crowd moved towards it, Korliss' hand reached out and entered the code that unlocked the gryphon's cage. Then he worked his way into the crowd, waiting for the theater.

After two strokes of the bell, municipal police in dark uniforms appeared at the far edge of the clearing and began moving forward. After twelve strokes, the curtains swept open. In center-stage, under a blue spotlight, stood a silver-clad giant. He raised his arms to the crowd and began to intone in a sonorous voice. "Friends, I bring you the tale of star-strider Orlando, guardian of the Firstfall Bridge, the terror of tyrants, the freer of the oppressed, banisher of the form-twisters, that you yourselves—"

The voice fell silent. Two dark uniforms had vanished behind the stage. Korliss thought he could hear raised voices. Then the blue spot went out and in place of the giant was a white-haired man in sagging trousers and a patched gray jacket. Some of the audience started to laugh.

Korliss edged around the back of the crowd. It had been stupid to open the cage. The gryphon might no longer be able to fly. It could be hurt; people in the crowd could be hurt. But his hand had moved and he had not questioned the impulse.

One of the police stepped onto the stage. His voice, too, was amplified. "This is an unsanctioned performance," he began.

Korliss bent his knees and shoulders a little and joined a knot of people heading towards a row of vehicles.

From the cages came gasps and stifled screams.

"A ride sir?" a shrewd-faced young woman sitting in a light trap called to him. "Half fare for the first hour?" She twisted the reins of her gray equine in her hands. "I was supposed to take old Jovinian—the Prologue—out for his ale and back before his final curtain speech. The cops'll put him out on the streets again in a week or so, but I don't think he'll be needing me today. But you look as though you might."

"I do?" He walked around to examine the equine, which snorted and lifted its head away from his hand.

The woman leaned down and triggered the lanterns. "You've had a nasty knock on the head in the last couple of days. And you're avoiding the cops. Perhaps you've got something to do with what those people over there are shouting about. Now you're putting old Cinerius between you and them."

"Am I?" He swung himself up beside her. "I'm going nightward." Over her shoulder he thought he glimpsed a bronze shape fleeing into the woods, and he relaxed into the seat. "Take the Heliodos and I'll tell you more when we're on the way."

⸺⊹⋰⋰ ⸺ ⋱⋱⊹⸺

"A car would be cheaper to run," Hippolita remarked as they joined the nightward traffic. "But it's hard to get them repaired nowadays, and equines have more prestige with the customers here."

"You're right," Korliss said after a moment. "I don't live in these parts. You have nothing to fear from me, but I'm not sure why you assumed that."

"If you're avoiding the law here, it's no worse than a coin toss whether I'd be on your side anyway. In any case, I can look after myself."

The equine worked up to a brisk trot that Hippolita assured Korliss it could keep up for most of a day.

He held out a gold-edged card. "As far as this will buy."

She looked quickly at him as they rattled over cracks, into the shadows of giant redwoods.

"For that you could sleep at a place I know. Half a day from here."

Behind them the sun was eclipsed by the distant towers, leaving a blaze of orange and violet in the sky. Dark buildings appeared beside the road. Floating blue globes cast harsh light on intersections. At the crest of a rise, a tree stretched a leafless limb across half the road. Only the bare upper branches were gilded by sunlight.

"That branch was still green..." he murmured, and shivered.

"Leaf borers," she nodded to herself and added, "So you have been here before."

Yes, thought Korliss. But some time when he had been much, much younger...

After the tree, the road descended again. Ahead of them a long straight path sank into shadow. As the sunset vanished behind them, Hippolita engaged the brake gently, so that Cinerius would not be pushed into a canter, and said, "Let me tell you a story."

The clopping hooves drew them deeper into the shade.

⟞⟞❖ — ❖⟜⟜

"Once upon a time," she said, "a poor family lived by a river. They had lived there for more generations than anyone could count—ever since, it was said, the sun had shone down full on their home. They had tilled their garden plot, sold vegetables, repaired furniture for rusty metal coins, and remained poor. But now the sun was almost set. The air was cold, and fuel expensive. Their garden grew only hard tubers. Worst of all, was the dark.

"There were two children, their parents and their grandfather. The father tried to find work repairing groundcars, but usually he had to settle for straightening bent cart axles or repairing sonic blades. Sometimes he drank too much or used the wire for hours at a time. The mother had built control units for videos, but now she spent most of her time caring for her own father, who was almost blind.

"The elder daughter had glamour, and though she might have made a living as a herbiculturalist she spent time and effort on her appearance and manners, and became affianced to the son of the local landgrave.

"And the younger daughter: what shall we say about her? She was jealous, of course, and tried to hide it. She felt she was the talented one in the family. She was the one who had scored best on the education programs, the one who had the ideas for solving their problems with their old groundcar. She was also the one least happy in the old dark house by the river. She knew her ancestors had lived where it was light, and she craved the light. She would lie awake in her bed to listen to the river and imagine it carrying her towards the sun."

Hippolita shook the reins as the trap rattled over a wooden bridge. They had left the Heliodos for a less-traveled artery. Ahead, a hunched black shape was plucking at something beside the road. As they approached, it snarled from reddened jaws, then twisted into a shadow that scurried up a tree and vanished.

"Sphynx," said Hippolita. "They're common around here. I was afraid it might attack Cinerius. People used to say they came in across the ravine. But the bridge has been down for years now, and they're still around."

Korliss glanced into the woods as they passed the place where the creature had vanished. Nothing stirred.

"I'm hungry," he said. "Do you think... ?"

"A good courier is always prepared," she told him. "There's a place up here we can stop."

In a fenced-off glade, she unmounted the carriage lamps and spread a cloth on the grass. From a basket she produced bread, milk, cheese, fruit, and a bottle of wine.

After a while Korliss realized she was watching him. She was sitting back, one eyebrow raised.

"I carry half a bale of hay as well, if you want more," she said. "When did you last eat?"

He couldn't remember. "I've been busy," he said, and looked at the empty basket. "I'm sorry."

"Don't worry about that. But we should get going now. Help me pack up and then open the gate for us."

As Cinerius drew the trap beyond the fence, Korliss closed the gate and then swung himself up beside Hippolita.

"You didn't seem concerned about sphynxes in there, but that fence wasn't much of a barrier."

"It's enough," she said. "They don't like the spikes. And besides, they prefer to attack from ambush. Otherwise they're usually only dangerous if they think you're after their food."

"You said people hadn't expected them to keep coming because the bridge was down. Which bridge was that?"

"The rail bridge. Everyone thought they came out of night-side—but obviously not. The line runs next to the Heliodos, but that ends at the ravine now, too. The rail bridge lasted longer, but a maglev train lost lift on it at top speed and they never re-built it. The other side is mostly ice, from what I've heard. Too cold for sphynxes, though people say you can see some sort of tracks in the snow still. Is that what you wanted to know?"

Korliss nodded. "I think I remember the maglev bridge. When I was young. I think I saw a gryphon from it." They made their way back to the main road. "Sphynxes, gryphons—everyone hates them," he said. "Whether they kill or not."

"Perhaps because they change shape, and you can't be sure what you're facing. Perhaps because they were here first and we're squeezing them out. Guilt..." Hippolita frowned and eased her grip on the reins. "I think I should finish my story."

⋘─⊱⋗

"One day," she said, "the younger daughter asked her sister how she hoped to live with a man as rich as her betrothed, and her sister told her the family secret, passed on only to the eldest child. The family over the years had hoarded savings in a metal box hidden in the brickwork of the riverbank. The savings were for emergencies or special occasions, to be replenished immediately afterwards, and her father had promised her a wedding and a dowry from them.

"She must have said something sympathetic to her sister, but when she was alone, she brooded, and she hated.

"The younger sister knew she could make use of that money; she had the talent to create a career for herself away from that dark cul-de-sac. A day later she found the hoard and fled with it.

"It was quite easy to find her way to the new towers, where the sun shone on her. Soon she would be successful and send the money she had taken, and more, back to her family. She too met a man, a rich man, who promised to marry her and sponsor her career in the theater. But she found that her money did not buy as much as she expected or last as long. And when it was gone, her benefactor had vanished too."

⋘─⊱⋗

They shared a long silence, while Hippolita's trap rattled on into the dusk. Overhead the sky was a deep luminous blue. Two stars gleamed, and dark streamers of cloud flowed towards the sun.

Finally they crossed steel tracks in the road, then entered a rutted side-street.

On either side loomed low dark buildings with tall windows. Only a few were lighted. Korliss looked at them, waiting for another prickle of memory, and felt nothing.

"This is a place I come and stay sometimes," Hippolita said. "It's not a good neighborhood now and no one wants to buy. Half the houses around here are empty."

They rolled to a stop as the bells chimed for evening. The echoes rolled over them and faded into the dusk. She stabled Cinerius at the side of the house, in a low barn that also held a stub-winged car with its nacelle open and its drive shrouded under canvas. Then she took out an antique brass key and went to insert it in the front door.

Korliss heard the movement before he saw it, and without thinking threw her aside. She cursed, and the key clinked on the step. His blade was just out when the black shape dropping from the roof smashed him to the ground.

Sprawling, he clenched his fist, and the blade thrummed. There was a howl, and clawed feet pranced back from his face.

A shot slapped his ears, and the creature spun away.

Korliss pushed himself to one knee, the outthrust blade shimmering. A sphynx lay on the path, half feline, half simian. Shot through the chest, it hissed between curved fangs as its body changed and it died.

Hippolita shone a lamp up at the roof, her pistol steady in her other hand. "That was careless of me," she whispered harshly. "I'm sorry." She lowered the light, put the pistol away and came to him. "Are you hurt? I was stupid not to check. *Stupid.*" Her voice trembled.

"Bruised. Shaken a bit," he said, getting up slowly and feeling his shoulders. "It's all right. I should have stayed back and speared it with the long beam as it fell. Only..."

She looked at him and then at the place where he had fallen, where her key lay by the doorstep.

"Come in," she murmured. "Let me look at your bruises."

She lit a candle and led him through the house, lighting candles, lanterns, globes, on every wall she passed, in every niche and corner.

He stopped.

"What's the matter?" asked Hippolita.

"I can hear water."

"Yes," she said softly, "it's under the street. They built over it long ago."

"Ah," he whispered. "Of course."

Their gazes locked. Then both looked away.

"I don't think you finished your story," Korliss said after a pause. "How long did the girl stay there in the sunlight?"

Hippolita lifted a hand in a warding-off gesture, cut short. "You're right. I didn't finish. She steeled herself to return and beg forgiveness, and made her way back to her home by the river. The journey took weeks this time. When she arrived, the house was empty. Later she learned her sister had fallen ill the day after she had left. Perhaps it was shock, perhaps something else. But there was not enough money to pay for proper care. They had sold their tools, their minimind, even some of their clothes, and it was not enough. Her sister had recovered physically but her mind was destroyed. Her betrothed had offered to care for her, but now her father refused anything he could not earn.

"They were unable to feed themselves; so they were taken to the House of Sharing, where they feed you but take your organs after you die, and when she tried to trace them, their records had ended months earlier.

"So now," Hippolita finished, "she sits by the river and sometimes thinks about sunlight. And she wishes to be with her family."

She peered at him quickly, then looked down at her hands.

"That's a sad story," he said at last. "Could it have another ending? Will the girl join her family? Or will she learn that the river has nothing to say to her?"

"Perhaps she'll learn to behave as though she no longer hears the river," said Hippolita, "but inside she will still want to join them."

Now she was facing him, her eyes wide and unblinking in the candlelight.

Korliss looked at her and could not speak.

She took his hand. "I did say there's only one bed, didn't I?"

He nodded his head. "Yes."

"We can share a bath first," she said softly, and rose. "But there's a price. Everyone who stays here has to tell me something about himself, something secret, something that has shaped him and that he wouldn't tell a stranger."

"Like your story?"

"Yes. Now you know: I'm a monster with a human face."

"Don't say that!" He stopped and drew her to him. "I don't care about that. But the price—can it wait until morning?"

"All right," she whispered, and pressed her cheek into the base of his neck. "'Til morning."

⊶⊷⊶

Later, he lay on his back and listened to the insistent murmur of the buried river. Her tears had dried on chest. He tried to imagine himself in a class of children watching the instructor. Tried to imagine parents, a home, with sunlight on the roof tiles. A job, or half a life in the penal mines—anything but the emptiness inside him. He pictured a creature leaping from an opened cage and struggling to remember flight. He was shivering again. Hippolita gave a low moan and rolled away in her sleep, then put her arm across his chest. Her breathing calmed, merged with the whispers of the underground stream.

The candle burned to a stub and went out. The hollow inside Korliss ached. And the water whispered.

When he was sure she slept, Korliss slipped her arm from him and gathered his clothes. Dressed, he went to the door, then paused. After a moment he came back and slipped a handful of the gold-edged cards under her pillow and smoothed her hair over it.

⊶⊷⊶

As the morning bells chimed, he was striding through narrow, dim streets. A star shone between high pinkish gray clouds. Their reflections scudded sunward across the lightless windows of second-floor rooms. An old man in shirtsleeves glanced down as Korliss passed, then went back to gazing over the rooftops that hid the sun.

He headed towards where the Heliodos must be.

On a main road, a line of wagons creaked through a rutted intersection, hauled by baluchithers and centrosaurids. A group of children scampered across between two of them, while four laden provisioners waited and quietly cursed. A police floater turned from a sidestreet, its fans whining in a cloud of dust and litter. Without thinking, Korliss took two running steps to a wain loaded with water barrels, swung himself up and clung to its hidden side. When the floater passed, he stayed on.

Towers rose further than he could see and a deep incessant thunder filled the air. He moved through a twilight of purple globes and smoky lanterns.

Down a cross-street he glimpsed the front of a wide, rounded building faced with transparent panes, many cracked or replaced with faded brown canvas. It tingled with familiarity. He dropped from the wain and strode towards the arched entrance of the building.

Inside, he hurried up rusted metal steps that once had moved, and fed gold cards into a machine that passed him through a barrier. Then he boarded a maglev train that would take him nightward.

⊷⊶⊷ ⊷ ⊷⊷⊷

The air was icy. It stung his cheeks as he left the maglev terminus. Behind him he heard the sparse crowd boarding the train for its return journey. He did not look back. Over the dark streets, a dead stretch of magrail continued nightward. He jogged beneath it, remembering an elongated fleck of bronze soaring between two clouds.

The street ended in a wooden fence. Korliss climbed over, followed a faint path and peered up at where the bridge had once launched itself in a clean arch across the ravine, and now stopped short in a stump of torn metal.

Straining his eyes, he made out the other side of the ravine, and the stub of the bridge jutting towards him, looking no more than a handful of crumpled wires.

The wind from the nightside pulled at his cloak, called in his ears.

Below him, a couple of black cables curved towards the other side. Power and communication links. He wondered if any were still active. Almost at his feet the ground dropped away: stone and earth streaked with ice and patches of snow. And only darkness beneath.

It would be insane to go on.

From the sky above the far side of the ravine, a faint auroral flicker showed snow-covered hills like a world of cloud.

He caught a rocky ledge with one hand to swing him over, and dropped.

He fell for two seconds, and hit rolling. The shocksilk cloak took most of the impact, but he was barely able to save himself on the two-meter lip of the cable housing. He peered back up the cliff, allowing himself one minute to get his breath.

Then he gulped air into his chest, rolled and lunged for the cable.

He hit and slid, grabbed, and squirmed beneath it, clinging with arms and legs. The cable was as thick as his body, and he managed to worm his way on top of it. That was better: he could put his weight on the cable and rest. But now he could see how the cable was angled down, how it curved and rose and shrank to nothing in the dark, and how it swayed, slowly and inexorably, back and forth, against the pattern of grays and blacks on the far wall. The wind ran cold hands over him, slapped him playfully on the back. Knowing it would be a mistake, he peered down.

A gray ribbon of ice snaked below. On either side of it ranged black skeletons of trees taller than those beside the Heliodos; the dead growth-points at their tops glimmered below him like pale stars.

He shut his eyes and crawled.

What was he doing? What ran hidden through the depths of his mind?

Stars in a black sky, with the dayside a thin red glow along the horizon.

Absurd. Insane.

The cable writhed beneath him in the wind. He shut down his mind and crawled.

The cold clamped icy palms about his body, began to squeeze. He felt his flesh becoming thin and brittle, and could not tell if the cable was still under his hands, or he had slipped and was falling through kilometers of emptiness.

Perhaps he was flying, swimming through the air. Perhaps his shoulder blades had sprouted pinions, his forearms were fletched with filigreed horn. Or was he chest-deep in snow, heaving himself through it with forelimbs like white-furred sweeps?

His sight returned with the clarity of a dream. And in the dream, his hands were human hands. They gripped the cable, reached forward, gripped again. Beyond them a crumpled metal structure jutted towards him.

An age later, he dropped from the cable to the floor of a tunnel, crawled to an access shaft and climbed a rickety ladder to the open air. He began running nightward.

He passed places he knew: a bridge over a frozen stream (whose crimson-edged waves had lapped the central pillar), the skeleton of a dome, where leafless black boughs leaned over an ice-choked fountain. In obedience to the dream, he turned to the right and lengthened his stride.

Once, an arachnocryoid sprang from the shadows, and his senses were so dulled it was almost on him before he struck it. He severed two of its legs, then pierced its thorax, which hissed and flared blue as the alcohol in its blood ignited. He kept the shimmering blade before him as he ran on.

And finally he came to an icy slope he knew he must climb. All the way up, his feet skidded on ice; the wind cuffed him, tore the breath from his throat. But at the top, with his lungs full of a fire that smoked from his mouth, he could see, through a river of cloud and a pulsating aurora, the stars of nightside.

He pressed against the side of a tor, and a slab shifted, opening a cleft that he slipped through. The darkness was welcoming. He descended into it down steep uneven, familiar steps. The lap of running water sounded, grew louder. Home, he thought: he was coming home. A formless blue glow softened the darkness. The very rock walls offered him light. Soon now.

Finally, in the dimness something stirred.

A ponderous, white-furred creature faced him, bearing a complex metal shield. "Wait," she said.

"I am—"

"I know you. Wait."

Memories began to well up in him.

"I've come back to see my family, my parents. Let me go to them." A more recent memory suddenly made his heart pound, and he stammered. "Are they still—? Are they well?"

"They pray you have lost your obsessions with the sun and its creatures."

Korliss let his breath pour out. "Please take me to them."

"There is movement in this sector," said the guardian. "Have you betrayed us?"

"No," he shook his head wildly. "No one cares enough to follow me this far." He reached towards her. "I've come back. I want to come in now."

"Wait," she stared at him wide-eyed for a count of five. "I am required to ask if you are ready to return permanently."

"I have seen the sun."

"That is not an answer."

"I lived among them, lived as one of them. I let innocent creatures be crucified in front of me because I dare not reveal myself. Because I wanted the sun. But then I tried to atone, I— let me in."

"You must answer clearly: do you want to return permanently?"

"Where else—where can I go? Take me back."

"In that form, the cold will kill you," said the guardian finally. "We will admit you, in your proper shape."

Korliss gasped and fell to his knees. "Thank you. Yes. Yes, of course." He bowed his head and breathed deeply until his pulse was steady again, then closed his eyes. He waited for his limbs to thicken, his jaw to swell, his back to bow, and gray hair to mat his body. He tried to will his mind to clear.

He did not change.

He moaned and reached toward her.

"Either you have lived with them too long," said the guardian, "or some experience has fixed you in this form. Or fundamentally you do not wish to return. We will try to maintain contact and support you, but if you return here often you will threaten our secrecy. I am sorry, but I must return to aestivation soon."

Korliss stumbled forward. "Help me! Take me back!"

The guardian stood and raised her shield. Knowing what would happen, Korliss triggered his blade and swung.

A flash hurled him against the wall. Steam swirled about the guardian, who was unmarked. The blade was dead in Korliss' hand.

Shivering he backed to the stairs and climbed to the waste of snow. He snarled and flung the blackened hilt into the shadows, then sank to his knees and put his head in his hands.

"A cheat!" he whispered. "Everything. All of it."

He slumped sideways and drew his knees to his chest.

The cold sank icy teeth into the joints and extremities of the body he wore. The body hurt, forced him to his feet. Made him walk.

He wished he had not destroyed the blade. But it would not matter much longer. If not the nightside creatures, then the cold. He had gone without food and sleep, and he would obtain release soon enough. After a while, he found he was following his own tracks, and his mouth twitched at the irony.

The tracks passed the frozen fountain, but he did not. His knees buckled. He lay down in the lee of the stone plinth and pulled his cloak about him and did not care what found him in the dark.

He thought he would dream of clinging to threads stretched over black abysses, but instead he drifted in a darkness filled with the rush of water, and once he watched a face, picked out by a single light, drown in a river of tears.

Later, he thought that he heard the water roaring through subterranean tunnels, that he was falling towards it, and he was caught by surprise when his cloak was jerked away.

Hippolita flung half a dozen gold cards at his chest. "That's all I had left after I fixed the car," she snapped. "You can have them back." Behind her, a small stub-winged car stood on a steaming patch of roadway. "Gold cards weren't what I asked for," she said, her jaw quivering. The aurora shimmered above her head. "Korliss, you owe me a story."

He stared at her, at the car, at nothing.

From far away, across the ravine, the bells of the city tolled through the icy air, bringing morning. He looked at the fountain and imagined it as it was meant to be, the water leaping from its underground courses high into the long, golden light. "Yes," he said finally, and reached for her hand. "I do."

John Park was born in England and moved to Vancouver as a graduate student in chemical physics at the University of British Columbia; while there he published his first story professionally and attended the Clarion Writers Workshop. He now lives in Ottawa, where he has worked at the National Research Council in Ottawa and as a partner in a scientific consulting firm. His fiction and poetry have appeared in a number of North America publications, including several issues of *Tesseracts*, as well as in French and German translations. "Nightward" originally appeared in the anthology *Tranversions* (2000) edited by Marcel Gagné and Sally Tomasevic.

Hydden

Catherine MacLeod

I toss the core of Luke's apple out for the blackbirds, and, bent over as I most always am these days, don't see the Hydes until I sit on the doorstep.

There are five of them, twenty feet away, standing in the long grass between the house and the stony beach. They're dark, silent, silken-furred, horribly human. I don't want to look at them, but do—it seems only polite to acknowledge the angels of my death. I was hoping for another day, but they always know. They're never wrong.

I spread my fingers over my swollen stomach and feel the rippling, like small waves ahead of the tide. I might have another hour.

Luke didn't come down this morning. Maybe he finally wised up and got scared. Maybe his father found out he's been sneaking out to see me. Either way, it's about time. I don't want him here for this.

I don't want to be here for this.

He brought me food yesterday. He'd polished the apple until it glowed. He shrugged away my thanks and said it was no big deal. But it was; you can go hungry here in the birth house. Meals are provided by your loved ones, if you have any left— and if they can stand to be near you. I know that by helping me Luke was rebelling against his father; and no doubt there was some morbid curiosity over my pregnancy. But it was also an act of compassion. There are no small kindnesses anymore.

(Three acts of generosity: Susan Bennett gave me her lasagna recipe; Winnie Martell gave me a drive home when my car broke down; Calvin Zanberger gave me his name.)

The sea is calm this morning, a chilly blue-green. The wind is sharp; you can smell winter coming. It's beautiful here, but the location wasn't chosen for the view. The house was built past the edge of town so the Hydes wouldn't come near the other dwellings. My husband, Cal, wondered if anyone remembered that, in olden times, women in labor were sent away to protect their village from the demons that hovered around them. Then he went and helped them shingle the roof.

The walls are scrubbed after every birth, but you can still see where the blood spattered. The stain by the door looks like a tern. The one over the window resembles a downy woodpecker. The one on the ceiling makes me wonder why the blood sprayed that high.

I'm sure all the women before me played this game. There's not much else to do, and not much in the way of comfort: no point making things nice when they'll only be ruined. I have a bed, a blanket, and a surprisingly comfortable wooden chair.

And I have birdsong. The familiar *zeet!* of a junco finding food is exactly what I need right now. I would live longer just for that. But no one survives childbirth anymore. Hydes can't even be taken by caesarian—they grow so fast, and move so much, it's almost impossible to make an incision without cutting the baby. And we do *not* want to do that. Learned that the hard way.

Babies aren't killed at birth anymore. The first few, yes, but now the adult Hydes come for them. They've come for mine, and I can't help thinking of the stain on the ceiling.

What *does* that look like?

⤐ ❖ ⇥ — ⇤ ❖ ⤏

"Name three birds in the backyard without looking."

I listened for a moment. "Black-capped chickadee." I could picture the little guy, fat and sassy, picking up sunflower seeds. A familiar sliding whistle cut into his song. "Cedar waxwing."

"And?"

A single sweet, stuttering note. "A robin!"

We had our own tradition: when we saw the first robin of spring, we made plans to go hiking. We'd done it in snow and rain, and the most glorious sunshine. We had no way of knowing it would be our last hike.

In my heart I still curse that stupid bird.

Cal tolerated my quirks with good humor, from bird-watching and graceless yoga to my fondness for making lists. I always had a to-do list; it made me feel as if I was on top of the work. I never was, really, but I enjoyed the illusion. Back when we started dating, he invented a game called *Three Things*, in which he requested a list out of the blue. In twenty years he never ran out of questions.

"Three things you like," he said.

"James Taylor singing *"Mexico,"* wasabi ice cream, the soundtrack from *Jude."*

"Three things on the top shelf of the fridge."

"Skim milk, raisin bread, the leftover minestrone."

"Three things about me."

(You have the most beautiful hands that have ever touched me. I'm addicted to the scent of your skin. The way you say my name still makes me shiver.)

"You snore when you sleep on your back, you think Benny Goodman is God, you don't like Mondays."

And evolution didn't change his mind. September 10, 2029, was a Monday—the first day all laboring women gave birth to Hydes. The first was a cause for horror—the arrival of a dark little humanoid with leathery skin and its eyes already open. And teeth. Many. The father shrieked at the loss of his wife, and, I'm sure, silently cursed her ancestry.

But it was just once, they must have thought: the kind of genetic hiccup that only happens once in a horrific while.

The second Hyde was born fifteen minutes later, in Paster County, three thousand miles away. The third was born the same moment, in the Australian outback.

Of course, *born* isn't exactly the right word. Birth didn't used to do that much damage.

"What do you know," Cal said, "the conspiracy theorists were finally right."

They were. Those births couldn't have been a surprise to everyone. The Hydes' differences may not be apparent during an ultrasound, but amniocentesis must have shown a few abnormalities. Not every pregnant woman had pre-natal treatment, and there must have been some abortions before the Hydes put a stop to them, but still, medics talk among themselves. Somebody saw this coming.

Rumors flew. New theories flourished. Survivalists loaded up and headed for their camps in the mountains, not the brightest thing they could've done. It was too late for survival. Some geographical oddity caused it, people said. Aliens were forcibly mating with our women. A bio-hacker's genetics experiment had gone terribly wrong. And that old standby, something in the water.

Eventually we learned the truth. Most of us would've been happier with aliens.

Extensive tests were done on a dead infant. We paid dearly for that one death, but we learned what we needed to know.

The Hydes are human. They're stronger, and able to stand extreme temperatures, an improved if less attractive model, but still...the DNA had too many human markers to be anything else. We were evolving. We were *becoming*.

I forget who quipped that they were the Hyde to our Jekyll, but the name stuck.

I do remember Cal turning off yet another news report and asking, "What will the world be like, if this is what we have to become to survive?"

⊷⊱⊰ — ⊱⊰⊶

There was candy in Luke's last pillowcase. He must've found his mother's secret stash— Susan Bennett had the worst sweet tooth of any woman I've ever known, including me. *(My three favorite chocolates: mint, mocha cream, hazelnut truffle.)*

I found Luke sitting on my back doorstep one morning, reading a paperback, glancing around furtively as if smoking his first cigarette. I was town librarian until recently, and it tickled me to see a kid with his nose in a book. Reading is pretty much considered a waste of time now; and Luke's father, Neil, always thought so anyway. That would've been especially hard on his son. Along with the short-story collections Luke checked out, there were a fair number of how-to books. He wanted to be a writer, and I, like a good confessor, said nothing.

"Hello, Luke."

He looked up, startled, his gaze fastening on my baby bump. "Um...hello, Mrs. Zanberger."

I said, "It's okay, I'm only a couple of months along. And you can call me Reann."

I had maybe six months left. I was looking for red-winged blackbirds.

"It's good to see you, Luke. I don't get much company." I sat on the step beside him, glad we were at the back of the house where we wouldn't be seen—he could get in big trouble for hanging out with a time bomb like me.

"What are you reading?"

He showed me the cover. *"Repairman Jack."*

"Ah. I haven't read that one." It said volumes about him. Like all boys his age, he dreamed of being a hero. But what a role model! "A mysterious jack-of-all-trades who fixes impossible situations. It's a nice thought, isn't it? I don't think there's a way to fix this one, though."

He sighed, "Yeah. As if."

My laughter surprised both of us. "As if. I haven't heard *that* one for a while."

"What?"

"I miss listening to you guys in the library. I liked all the new expressions. You know, *'as if.'* And *'not.'*—that was a good one."

He grinned, "I thought you were supposed to be mad at us for mangling the language."

"No, that was just the English teachers." It felt good to smile again. "I always liked the way you broke down whole paragraphs into a few words. It wasn't poetry, but it was efficient. Although I didn't much care for *'Waddup.'*"

He snorted, "Don't blame you."

"Who else do you like?" I said, tapping the book. It was one of the few non-abrasive questions I could think of.

He shrugged, still a little shy; probably not used to talking to women. Just at the age where he liked girls but wasn't sure what to do about it. Not that you can do much about it at all anymore. The facts of life have changed drastically. These days the rules of sex can be summed up in one word: Don't.

"I miss your mother," I said.

"Yeah, me, too."

She'd died in labor, one of the first. His father wouldn't talk about it, just buried himself deeper in his work. Neil's a truck driver, one of the heroes of the modern world. He leaves Luke alone for long periods of time. Not much peace to be had for a boy in that house.

In another time my friendship with Luke would've been inappropriate, even suspicious. In this one, friendships have fewer, and newer, protocols. Maybe Susan would have been happy her son came to me.

"I thought you'd be at work, " Luke said. "I didn't mean to trespass."

"No harm done. I'm through at the library now. I make people uncomfortable." He nodded. "And, really, it doesn't matter if they bring the books back anymore."

So many things come under the heading of "It doesn't matter anymore."

"What other writers do you like?"

He talked about Ray Bradbury and Neil Gaiman. I talked about Alice Hoffman and Robert Frost. I don't remember the last time I heard of a new book being published. We have so little time left, we'll never finish the books that are already here. Though I'm sure there are still books being written by hand in secret corners. Most of them will never be read, but there are still those of us who need to put words on paper.

I said. "I'll be right back," I gave him my copy of Sean Stewart's *Perfect Circle,* and watched his face light up.

"Do you have morning sickness?" he asked suddenly. It's in bad taste to mention pregnancy these days. It's akin to asking a death row inmate, "When do you hang?" But I didn't mind. We're all on death row now, and who else was there to tell him? I was willing to bet Neil never talked to him about his mother.

"I have nausea. But, frankly, I don't know how much is pregnancy and how much is fear."

"Do you think it's...bad?"

A distant scream was his answer. He reached for me, unthinking, a child seeking reassurance from the grownup. I had none to offer, but held his hand anyway.

"Who?" he whispered, as if speaking aloud could bring the Hydes down on us.

"Winnie Martell. They took her down to the birth house last night."

The screams were louder, and lasted longer, than I would've thought possible. Then they ended suddenly, and the evening was soft and quiet again. I thought of asking Luke to stay so he wouldn't have to go home to an empty house, and I could feel someone else disturbing the air in mine.

But he was already gone, clutching his new book like armor. I rose to go inside, and made a small clatter as I kicked something. He'd left his novel behind. He hadn't forgotten it, not a boy who loves books so much.

I made tea and read, and got through the night. It was a kindness, the first of many.

⊷≺≼ — ≽≻⊷

There's one basic theory of evolution, but many assumptions. My favorite is the one that says you see it coming.

Not.

Pigeons hatch already fearing hawks, which they've never seen. The warning is in their DNA. Ours is warning us to adapt *now.* What do we already know that we haven't told ourselves?

(Three things we know about the Hydes: they're suited to thinner air and colder climes; they have excellent night vision; they're obsessive about protecting their young. Three things we can infer from this: the world to come will be cold, dark, and more dangerous.)

That first year, a lot of pregnant women committed suicide. It was an act of well-founded fear. Then it was a very bad idea. The Hydes started coming back. Not mature, not quite full-grown, but big enough to cripple anyone who fought them. We saw it on TV like everyone else: a dozen of them showing up in Seattle, holding vigil on Alma Dechesne's lawn as she went into labor, demonstrating an unsuspected bond with the unborn. They stood quietly, obviously waiting for their child.

They didn't get it. In an act of malicious bravado, Alma's husband killed the baby. He didn't live long enough to regret it. Neither did the neighbors on either side of him. We saw that on TV, too, and learned from it. Best just to give them their young; the birth mothers wouldn't be around to raise them anyway.

I turned off the newscast, my hands shaking. "It's like those old war movies where the guy beside you gets shot if you make trouble."

Another quirk Cal put up with: endless film references. He took me to the movies every weekend, our Saturday night date. I loved scarfing hot popcorn and watching the latest thriller. But there haven't been any new films since the Hydes showed up. Entertainment isn't a huge priority anymore. I miss hearing new songs on the radio, but at least no one has to listen to the sobbed details of some pop diva's traumatic pregnancy. There are no more divas, and traumatic is the only kind there is.

There's no school, either—no point in learning history when you're about to join it—and I wondered sometimes what Luke did in that big house by himself. "You don't read all the time, right? Do you like movies, too? Susan said your dad bought a lot of DVDs."

I had Luke figured for a chop-socky fan, until he looked away, blushing, and I guessed he'd been into someone's porn collection. I doubt anyone would scold him for watching it, though. These days porn is the only really safe sex there is.

There are no math classes, but the numbers aren't hard to tally—the current-model human is obsolete.

We are dinosaurs.

Cal asked me once, "What was the first bird called?"

"Archaeopteryx. I don't know if I pronounced that right."

He leafed through my bird book idly, pausing for the more colorful photos. His dark hair was silvered at the temples. His dark eyes turned silver when the moonlight hit them just right. He'd spent the morning playing clarinet along with *Glenn Miller's Greatest Hits,* and finished his practice with the usual comment, "That's a good note to go out on."

He said, "What do you think of the theory that birds evolved from dinosaurs?"

"Or lizards?"

"Whatever."

I shrugged. "It says their scales evolved into feathers when they started leaping from tree to tree looking for food."

"Do you believe it?"

"There's no fossil evidence to support it."

"But do you believe it?" he prompted.

"I'd like to," I admitted. "It's a lovely thought."

"Adapt or die," Cal mused. "That's quite a spectacular adaptation."

"Not as spectacular as the Hydes. Evolution is supposed to take a lot more time."

"Maybe we don't have much left."

He didn't.

I replay his death in my head every so often. Not that I want to, but sometimes it's just there. Twenty years together and we parted with no fond words or loving gestures. But he died for me, and how much more could I want?

I could want him back. I could want that much.

If he'd had his way, we'd have gone camping, but I could never see why we should sleep on the ground when we had a comfortable bed at home. Hiking seemed a reasonable compromise. On our last morning, heading up the mountain, he said, "I'm sorry."

"For what?" I was admiring the view across the gorge, listening with only one ear.

"There's something I haven't told you." The other ear perked up. We rarely kept secrets. "We have more money than you think. But I waited too long to use it."

"I don't understand."

"I was saving to take you someplace for our anniversary. Paris would have been nice."

"Ah." Money was worthless, and travel more difficult. "You romantic, you. I don't mind, dear. Really."

He didn't look convinced. I wound my arms around his neck, determined to persuade him, and stepped back, taking him with me. Through a scruffy pile of windfall. Into the Hyde standing behind it.

Maybe nothing would've happened if the three of us hadn't been startled. But I screamed; Cal made a move to protect me; the Hyde made one to protect itself. As it leapt, Cal opened his arms, snaring it. The Hyde's momentum knocked him backward, taking them both into the gorge.

I stopped shrieking when my voice became a croak. And even knowing Hydes rarely travel alone, I waited a desperate hour to see if Cal might climb out. The logical part of my brain, the tiny part that was still functioning, didn't believe he would.

But Robin Hood and Indiana Jones survived terrible falls. My heroes always came back.

Except one.

⟶⟶❦ ⟶ ❧❦⟵⟵

The police came to the house. There were questions, but not many. Their hearts weren't in the job. Every day there are fewer humans and more Hydes, and no one polices them. It's possible a lot of murders are blamed on them.

But the Inspector was obliged to ask if my husband's death was one more.

By the time I told my story I'd had good reason to reflect on some of the nights in our comfortable bed. *(Three things I remember: the pleasant rumble of Cal's voice; the taste of the curve of his right shoulder; his fingers ghosting over my face.)*

No method of birth control is perfect, and I'd thought I was too old. *Not.*

I said, "I'm pregnant."

The conversation stopped. Notebooks closed. "I see." He seemed to search for words. *Take care* would be meaningless. *Good luck* would be cruel. He settled for, "Good day, then." Yes, that was still reasonably safe. I wasn't his problem anymore. This thing in my belly calling to the Hydes made me their concern. Guilty or not, I'd been handed a death sentence.

I watched them leave, as glad to see them go as they were to be gone. A wild dove folded its wings on the lawn, a movement like a man cutting a deck of cards with one hand. I could never do that. Cal could. I waited for tears but none came. Not that I didn't mourn, but there was just so damned much *to* mourn I didn't know where to start.

I blew a few notes on his clarinet, but they didn't sound like music, and I put it away.

—••◄◄ ◄▄ — ▄► ►►••—

(Three ways I never wanted to die: drowning; choking; bleeding.)

I thought about going up the mountain and ending it in the ravine, but the Hydes strike back for that, too. You don't just choose the means of your own death anymore. I don't want to do that to my neighbors.

And I don't want to do it to Luke. Healthy and handsome, one of the last recognizably human children, he might live long enough to find out what's going to trip the next ice age. Poor him. This morning I looked up at the sky, wondering if another meteor was spinning toward us, but only saw a string of geese.

I stopped listening to the news. Every day is a slow news day now. Work and money still matter, but not enough to kill ourselves over; not when so many things are waiting to do it for us. There are still wars, because we haven't quite outgrown our stupidity, but nothing major—why fight over what you won't be here to use? And soon those of us left to fight will be too old to bother. Silencing the radio was a comfort. I didn't miss the conjecture; I didn't need the predictions. I knew my future: I could see the birth house from my back door.

But I can't see my house from here.

Luke always told me the latest anyway. Yesterday he said the Hydes are going further up the mountains, into the thinner air. We can imagine why, but not ask. They don't communicate with us; except for killing us, which gets their point across perfectly. Maybe they think we have nothing to say worth listening to. I reminded Luke that we couldn't track them at first, back when we still enjoyed the illusion of security. Newborns, the ones that weren't killed, seemed to disappear if you took your eyes off them. I picture them straggling toward the mountains, like baby turtles heading for the sea. Sightings were rare. No one wanted to go searching, and thermal scanners only work if you have an idea where to look.

"Where could they possibly be?" I asked Cal.

He said, "Maybe they're Hydden."

I biffed a cushion at his head.

Luke put a book in yesterday's pillowcase, too, a collection of Shakespeare's sonnets. I hope the cleaners leave it for the next woman. It would be a great kindness, better than trying to make a design out of that smudge on the ceiling. To me it looks like something getting ready to fly.

We're not dying out. We're growing wings.

Cal flew.

I should be easy for them to scrub up. My water just broke. It's going to happen here on the steps, and already the pain is fierce.

There's something in the water.

There are nine thousand species of birds on Earth. I've seen a hundred; I remember their voices. I hear the sharp *eep!* of a piping plover, an endangered species that will outlast us; and the rasp of crows, birds that are almost impossible to kill off. I hear the sweet warble of a chickadee, a bird who thrives in cold weather and doesn't care who he sings to. He was always my favorite.

It's a good note to go out on.

Three things about **Catherine MacLeod**: she's pleased and proud to be making her third appearance in the *Tesseracts* series; she's always been a list-maker; chickadees really are her favourite.

The Pickup

Leah Silverman

There's a dead girl lying on her side in the mud.

"I wonder if anyone tried to find her," Mithune says, looking down. He has to shout so the rest of them can hear him over the rain. He sniffs, wipes his nose and grimaces. Water is sluicing off the peak of his cap and it's so wet by now that there's no point in keeping it, but Mithune always wears the full required uniform; it's just who he is.

"Probably not," Bramin says. She crouches next to the dead girl, shining her flashlight beam along the cold, gray skin of her face. The girl is all curled up, mouth and blank eyes wide open like she died screaming. "Looks like she's been here for awhile." Bramin's just thankful all the rain's keeping the smell down.

Behind Mithune, Kole giggles. Bramin swings her flashlight around in time to see Kole spit a gob of something onto the wet ground. It looks dark as the mud, which means he's bleeding again.

"You okay back there, Kole?" Bramin asks him. Then, "Hey, Kole, you hear me?" because he's not answering. Kole just stares, like he can't figure out what she's saying.

Mithune nudges Kole in the shoulder with the end of his rifle, jerks his chin in Bramin's direction, scattering water. "Captain's talking to you, Lupyi," he says. "You need to say something."

"Use his name," Bramin snaps. 'Lupyi' is some kind of slang for baby dogs where Mithune comes from. It was funny before but now it's just pissing her off, though she can't say why.

"Sorry, ma'am," Mithune mutters. He nudges Kole again but with his hand this time. That's a risk, so he's probably doing it to show Bramin that he means the apology. "Come on, Ben," he says. His voice is kind, despite having to force it over the rain. He points at Bramin. "The Captain asked you if you're alright."

It's not like Bramin even needs an answer now, but Kole tilts his head a little, then grins. "I'm great, thank you, ma'am," he says, with the exaggerated care of someone who's really drunk or drugged, and it might be cute if Kole were actually either of those. Then he laughs again, and a bit of blood dribbles down his chin, then gets washed away by the rain.

Bramin turns away from him without answering. It's not like Kole cares anymore.

Mithune's come up next to her and kneels beside the body. His knees sink into the mud as he lifts his flashlight, shining it over the corpse. "I don't know if it's the same thing," he says, glancing back at Kole, "but there's no way we'd be able to see blood in all this."

Bramin grunts in agreement. She glances at Kole as well, but he's just standing there with his face tilted up to the on-slaught of water. She wonders if he'll let himself drown; if he's so far gone he'd do that. The Major was probably right, and they should have shot the kid by now. Better for everyone.

Coward, Bramin thinks, but she isn't sure if she means the Major or herself.

"We can still fix him," Mithune says like he pulled the thought from her head. "He's not even hurting yet, right? When the pickup comes—"

"Where do you think she was running from?" Bramin asks, ignoring him. She lifts her head and looks in the direction the girl most likely came from, but all she can see is the black shape of trees and more rain.

"There's probably a village over there," Mithune says. He pulls himself back to his feet with a sigh, then gives Bramin a crooked, resigned smile. His teeth are very bright against the smooth black of his skin. "Flatfoot express, right?"

"Right." Bramin nods and accepts Mithune's hand. She looks at the girl again. It'd be the decent thing, to bury her, but none of them have the right equipment even if they could dig a grave in this rain. "We might be able to borrow a vehicle, at least. Move a little faster."

Mithune sniffs again. "They could've chased her out," he says. His eyes are on Kole, who's smiling vacantly, white as milk in the beam from Mithune's flashlight. There's blood com-ing out his nose, turning to light pink in the rain.

"They might've been trying to help her," Bramin says. "Come on." She jerks her chin in what she hopes is the direction of the village, if there even is one. Right now she'd give just about anything for a roof over her head and something warm to drink.

Mithune glances at Kole one more time, but he moves obediently past Bramin, gun ready. Bramin takes a breath and walks the few steps to Kole, who hasn't moved. "Hey," she says. She puts her hand on the back of his neck, rubbing the cold skin. She knows that's a bad idea—people as sick as Kole is right now have been known to bite, or worse—but Kole just blinks slowly and turns his head towards her.

"Captain?" he says. He sounds confused. "Where are we?"

"Glencaran," Bramin says. She moves her hand to his wrist, tugs a little. This isn't the first time she's told him. "Come on. Mithune's waiting for us."

"Okay," Kole says. He starts following obediently, doesn't try to pull his arm back. He looks around, like he might be alert for once. Bramin tries not to hope too much. "Glencaran," he says, like he's never heard the name before. "I'm cold."

"We're all cold," Bramin says. She starts walking a little faster. Kole keeps up with her. She can see Mithune's light, shining steadily up ahead, cutting a slash of yellow through the rain.

"Where's our drop?" Kole asks, looking around like he might see it.

"We crashed, remember?" Bramin tells him. "We're heading to the pickup site."

"Oh," Kole says. Bramin hears him spit. "I don't feel so good."

Bramin stops dead, whips around. "Does your head hurt?"

Kole shakes his head. "No."

"Good," Bramin says. She lets out a slow breath, then slides her hand down Kole's wrist until her fingers are wrapped around his palm. "You'll be fine," she says. She starts walking again.

"Okay," Kole says, like all he needs is to take her word for it. Bramin grips his hand more tightly, but he doesn't hold hers. She moves her hand back to his wrist so he won't slip away.

"Where's the Major?" Kole asks.

Bramin grits her teeth, hard enough to make her jaw ache. "She's dead," she says.

Kole doesn't speak for awhile, and Bramin wonders if he's trying to remember that, or if he's just faded again. She doesn't look at him to find out.

"You killed her," Kole says.

"Yes I did."

"Okay," Kole says.

"We're here," Mithune calls from up ahead, and Bramin walks faster to catch up to him, dragging Kole with her. Mithune sees that she's got her hand clamped around Kole's wrist, but he doesn't comment on it. Instead he kicks a loose stone, rolling it through the mud with his foot.

Bramin lets go of Kole so she can hold her gun in both hands again. "Hello?" she shouts, loud as she can to be heard over the rain. "HELLO?" She tries it again in the three other languages she knows, but each time no one answers.

"No one came after her," Mithune says.

Bramin looks where his light is pointing and sees the first of the bodies. A man this time, old enough to be the girl's father. He's in white, and it's easy to see the blood stains on his shoulders and chest, too set in the fabric to be washed away by the rain. The heel of his hand is stuffed in his mouth, covered with bite marks. His eyes reflect their flashlight beams like glass.

"There're three over there, too," Mithune says, voice so quiet it's hard to hear him.

Bramin nods. One of the corpses has long rents in her face from her fingernails. Some are curled up like the girl was; another has fistfuls of hair in his clenched hands. Their mouths are all gaping, eyes wide with fear and pain. One died sitting against a wall, protected from the rain by an awning. There's blood all down the front of her dress, a thick congealed mass of it under her mouth and nose and eyes. The wall has blood on it too.

"We're not going to get any help here," Mithune says, as if it needs saying.

"No, we're not," Bramin says. She shifts her pack, then wipes water uselessly off her forehead. "We have to keep going."

Mithune doesn't move. "Maybe we should check inside some of the buildings, get some supplies."

"No," Bramin answers with a quick shake of her head. "It's probably all contaminated. This might be the vector, for all we know."

Mithune looks at Kole. They're already contaminated and they both know it, but Mithune doesn't argue.

Bramin checks her compass, nods to herself when the red dot is still blinking securely to the southwest. "The pickup's this way," she points and starts walking again. "Make sure Kole keeps up."

She hears laughter behind her, knows it's not Mithune's. She doesn't look back.

⋙⊰ ⊱ ⋘

"Hey, you hear that?" Mithune says suddenly, startling her. Bramin had fallen into a kind of stupor made up of aching cold and the endless walking.

"What?" she snaps, nastier than she meant to, but Mithune is grinning so widely Bramin sucks in a breath, half-expecting blood to come dripping out his mouth.

"It's the ship!" Mithune shouts. "Listen! It's the ship!"

Bramin does listen, and realizes she can hear the faint beeping from her compass. She yanks it off her protective vest and shuts off the magnet, then stares at the small screen, shaking her head to keep the rain out of her eyes.

"Got that right," Bramin says, grinning herself now. She uses the hand with the compass in it to point. "That way, through the clearing."

"Hallelujah!" Mithune throws his head back, arms out wide. Bramin laughs.

She slaps Mithune on the shoulder, then starts walking faster, clenching her hand in Kole's collar so he'll stay with them. He won't walk in a straight line anymore, not unless someone's got their hand on him, and he's stopped talking.

"You're going to be okay," she tells him. "Not long now, almost there." He stumbles after her, boots squelching in the wet dirt.

Bramin's still smiling as she drags Kole into the clearing, but there's no ship. Nothing's there but a rambler, sunk up to its axels in the mud. It's off, and she thinks maybe it shorted out in the rain, but it lights up as soon as the three of them come close to it.

"The ship is late, that's all," Mithune says. He's looking at the sky like he might see it through the clouds and the night's darkness. He turns towards Bramin. "We didn't get our signal up right away, did we? So maybe...maybe they're a few hours out, still."

Bramin doesn't reply. The compass wouldn't have shown the pickup if there hadn't been a ship. The rambler has to be a drop-off, which means the pickup came and left again.

"Keep watch on Kole," she says, and lets go of him, walking to the rambler.

The neck swivels as she gets nearer, so she can see the robot's readout screen. It flickers on.

"This is Captain Marlee, of *Rescue Seven*," the face in the recording says. Bramin's never heard of her, but there are hundreds of Rescue-class pickups in the fleet. The woman in the recording is as dark as Mithune, silver streaks in her hair. She looks really, really sorry. "We answered your call for pickup, but couldn't do more than make landfall to leave the rambler and some supplies. Fleet orders."

"Fleet orders," Mithune repeats behind her, like he doesn't know what the words mean. "Fleet orders? What—?"

Bramin shushes him. On the screen Captain Marlee starts talking again. "We have reason to believe this world has been contaminated, and as such have been expressly forbidden from landing personnel for any length of time. Or picking up any teams.

"I'm sorry," Marlee says. "God be with you."

And the recording shuts off, just like that. Bramin can see her reflection on the black screen, the fear in her own eyes.

"But, they have a cure for it," Mithune says. "They've had a cure for at least a year now, right? That's what the info drops said." He looks at Bramin, eyes begging, like whatever she could tell him would make any kind of difference. "They're just leaving us here?"

"Looks like it," Bramin says, rain hissing over her voice. She doesn't move.

"They have a cure for it!" Mithune shouts. He snatches his cap off his head, throws it on the ground, then kicks at the rambler. "You fuckers!" he yells. "You fuckers! You said you had a cure!"

He twists around to look at Bramin, eyes big and white in her flashlight beam. "What are we going to do now?" he asks her. "What are we going to do?" Then, "Captain!" Angry, when she doesn't answer him.

"Get the supplies," Bramin orders. "We'll put a tent up, get out of the damned rain, at least."

Mithune stares at her for a long moment. "Yes, ma'am," he says finally.

Bramin watches him work, sliding open the panels on the rambler, pulling the rainproof bundles out and dropping them into the mud. At least he's calm.

She thinks of the Major, holding the gun on Kole. And Kole, standing there shaking, tears running down his face mixing with his blood and the rain. He'd still been clear enough then to know what was going to happen.

He's going to die anyway. The Major had said, voice shaking like her hands. *We're all going to die anyway.*

Bramin adjusts her grip on her gun, lifts it. Kole is where Mithune left him. He's sitting in the mud like a baby, knees drawn up. He's rocking back and forth with his arms wrapped around his head, keening in pain. Blood's running from his nose and mouth and his staring, unseeing eyes.

Bramin shoots him. He slumps over, dead before he hits the ground.

Mithune's head jerks up over top of the rambler. He stares at her.

"It's okay," Bramin says. She wipes her face, her eyes, but there's no blood on her fingers. Not yet. "Get back to work."

Mithune doesn't move. "Kole?" he asks, like he doesn't already know.

"Here," Bramin says. "I'll help you." And she walks around the rambler and takes a package from his unresisting hands.

Leah Silverman saw *Star Wars* at the age of five, and knew immediately afterwards that she wanted to create universes the way George Lucas did. She became a writer, and had her first story published in the *Tesseracts 3* anthology when she was eighteen. Since then she has been published in *On Spec*, *Challenging Destiny Magazine*, *Parsec Magazine*, and textbooks for fiction and language arts in Canada. In the inauspicious year of 2001, she moved to Texas for her beloved husband's job. She now lives and writes in College Station, where she also raises her wonderful son, negotiates daily with three cats, and is still trying to get used to the high temperatures.

Flight of Passage

Jon Martin Watts

"Hello Liz... [crackle]... Jack here. I'm at the site."

"Copy, Jack. How does it look?"

"I'm about a hundred meters away. I can see the broken gear and the piece of wing a few hundred meters back that we imaged from orbit. The crew compartment looks fairly intact."

"Okay, can you take a look inside and report?"

"Stand by."

"Ah, Jack. While you're getting over to the ship we've got an update on the disposition of the survivors."

"Descendants you mean, Liz."

"Yeah, descendants."

"It's hard to believe Kathy and her crew came down here more than a century ago. I'm still taking care of her cat."

"Sorry, Jack. I know you two were close."

"That was two years ago... for me at least. What were you going to say about the locals?"

"Okay, this one comes from the anthropology section. They've been snooping as best they can from up here and they just don't see how these people are able to survive at the rate of acquisition of resources they've been observing."

"You think they're up to something we haven't noticed so far?"

"We know they are. Two days ago they began setting out what look like several small aircraft on the hilltop, south of the hamlet."

"Aircraft?"

"Yeah. We know they can't have real functional airplanes. They don't have the materials or the technology to build engines. Anthropology are saying it might be some sort of cargo cult-type of behavior."

"Huh?"

"It's like a religion. They build an airport complete with fake planes in the belief that passing air travelers will land and bring them goods."

"What passing travelers?"

"Yeah, I know. There aren't any, so they couldn't have figured that for themselves. But the buzz is that maybe the crew taught their kids to do this to attract our attention, which means..."

"They might have figured out we're here."

"Be careful, Jack. We want you to avoid contact until you've found out as much as possible at the crash site."

"It'll be okay. I bet no one comes to this side of the mountains much. It's all desert. No resources here."

"But the ship is there. Maybe they know that's where we would head first."

"I bet you this new activity has nothing to do with us. Keep watching those planes. I think you'll find they fly just fine."

"Jack?"

⟶⟵ ⊰ — ⊱ ⟶⟵

Julia wandered to the very edge of the village and looked down over the plain below. The first week of griffin season was nearly over and still no hunt had been launched. In the calm air streamers of smoke rose straight up from a few of the huts as early risers stoked up their stoves. The rain, which had fallen thinly all night from a dense, low overcast, formed small rivulets that ran over the valley side at her feet. More than a kayem below her, the terrain was shrouded in a heavy, ground-hugging fog. Only the greatest trees, more than one hundred ems tall, pushed their crowns through the mist, like verdant little islands in a milky lake. In the mist below, griffins crooned their haunting contact calls as they flew blind and unseen on their migration route. There would be no hunt today. Julia plodded back to the hunters' lodge.

A few hunters were up and huddled in front of the communal stove, nursing mugs of steaming pepper root tea. A few were tinkering with bits of hunting tackle. Others swung, hung over and listless, in their hammocks. When hunters can't hunt, they drink. For six nights the hooch had flowed as the frustrated hunters boasted, fought, and told unlikely tales of their exploits. Now both food and hooch were in short supply. The hunters were bored. A few looked up as Julia entered. She shook her head.

"Ten tenths at three hundred ems, rain, and a thick fog below." She gave an apologetic shrug.

Julia looked forward to her first hunt, but feared it too. Each time the sky looked as though it might clear, she began to feel a flutter of apprehension begin in her belly. With bad weather apparently set in for the day, she relaxed a bit, sharing the languor of the older hunters. Most of the men and women of the Family shared a common set of features and coloring. Standouts were rare and regarded as somewhat precious. Julia wasn't one of them. Children of similar ages could be hard to tell apart unless you knew them well. Members of the Family felt their individuality keenly, and adults wore distinctive facial brands and tattoos. Julia still wore the anonymous look of unaltered youth. She had already designed a face for her adult self, but wouldn't be allowed to apply it until she participated in a successful hunt.

She looked to the corner of the lodge where Pak, her assigned hunting partner squatted. Pak, the harpooner, was a quiet, wiry little woman. She was old for a hunter, perhaps three times Julia's own age. She had had no children, and was now almost certainly too old. Julia wondered how it would be to hunt with her. Old Jared, the teacher, said Pak was good, perhaps the best of her generation. That was exactly why Jared put Pak and Julia, an untried novice, together for her first season. Pak was knapping a flinty cobble, her mind and body intent on the task. Her left hand had only a thumb and forefinger. The rest had been lost to a half dead griffin in a moment of adolescent carelessness, long before Julia was born. Pak turned the flint around and around in her hands, looking for the minutest hint of a flaw, trying to visualize its internal fracture planes. Then she would take up the hammer stone and strike a precise blow. Most times all she got was a sharp "clack" and maybe a tiny splinter of stone. Then she would grunt quietly, as though in surprise at her failure, and turn the rock some more. Once in several attempts she knocked off a good flake, with a fine sharp edge. Then she picked it up without expression and tucked it into the little leather pouch hanging from her belt. Such flakes were Pak's skinning tools. She seemed to sense Julia's gaze, for she looked up from her work.

"Don't fret little one." She wiped her nose with the back of her hand. "Stick with me and you won't stay a virgin for long." She threw back her head and cackled. Julia felt her face redden.

The ribald talk in the lodge often did that to her, and she hated it. Some of the other hunters chuckled quietly at Pak's joke. Jared handed Julia a mug of tea and pushed her closer to the stove.

⊶⊷⟨—⟦ — ⟧—⟩⊶⊷

"Ah, Jack. Liz here. How did you make out in the ship? Over."

"Well there are no bodies. All three of them made it out okay. The main turbine is trashed. There are some organic remains, like bones, inside it. It looks like the engine ingested some flying animal. The cabin has been gutted as far as usable equipment and supplies go. The main power panel is smashed, which explains why there was no Mayday. They activated the emergency beacon, as we already know, and left. That's about all I can tell you."

"No personal notes, messages, anything like that?"

"No. Did you know she was pregnant?"

"No. I didn't know that, Jack. I'm sorry."

"Long time ago, I guess... What's going on at the village?"

"It's hard to say. There's a heavy overcast, and rain. Infrared and radar imaging shows that no large objects, like the supposed aircraft, have moved and the people are still concentrated within the dwellings for the most part."

"I guess they are holed up waiting for a break in the weather."

"I guess so."

⊶⊷⟨—⟦ — ⟧—⟩⊶⊷

Julia thought back to the last season, when she learned to fly a skysail, but was still too inexperienced to hunt. Before her first flight, old Jared had lectured her for an entire exhausting week. They sat together in Jared's hut day and night, drinking pepper tea and smoking shredded baccy roots to stay awake. Jared's philosophy was that lessons learned while suffering would stay with the pupil forever. Julia had sat in the craft while a group of sturdy hunters offered it up to the wind and she felt it twitch and twist as she worked the controls. Ultimately however, there was no better test than to catapult the student into the air and let her fly or crash.

The wind was good. It blew steadily up the launching slope at a near perfect angle. Julia sat in the cockpit, her bowels churning. More than surviving the flight itself she hoped to hold her sphincter tight. If she died, Julia wanted to be remembered as a *woman* who had gone to her death without shitting herself. Jared and the hunters tied a couple of spare chutes and a large boulder into the front seat, to replace the weight of the absent harpooner.

As he fastened the leather straps that held Julia fast to her seat, Jared jabbered into her ear. "Don't let the nose get too high. Set the brakes half out on approach. Then you can go long or short. Hold off until she mushes onto the ground." Julia recognized elements of the speech. It was the wisdom of Kathleen, given to all young pilots, in order that they might survive to be old pilots.

About eight old lags heaved the skysail onto the greased wooden launching deck and hooked on a cable. They all backed off except for Jared who held the craft level by one wingtip. Julia extended two fingers and waved them back and forth. At the edge of the cliff, thirty ems away, where the launch deck ended, a hunter pulled a rope and threw herself flat on the ground. The skysail began to scrape forward on its wooden skid, pulled by the net full of rocks descending from the cliff top. Julia worked stick and rudder furiously as she was hauled rapidly forward and hurled into space, directly into the wind. She flew out for a few seconds and then turned back, trying to cruise alongside the hill adjacent to the cliff, hoping to pick up some of the rising air that ran like a buoyant river along the slope. The air lifted her up and gave her hope. As she stayed aloft for a few seconds, a minute, a few minutes, she felt the gods at her back, buoying her up, willing her to succeed. Her goal was simple: gain enough height from the hill to get in a position to land without killing herself or destroying the skysail. Julia worked the skysail back and forth above the slope, making sweeping turns at each end and trying to strike an efficient balance between skidding and slipping through the air. Either one would cause her to lose height and earn her the scorn of the experienced hunting pilots. In the steady updraft, each beat took her higher, until the launch site receded and the hunters resembled small bustling insects.

As her confidence grew, it outstripped her ability to concentrate upon the task. Her turns became ragged as she was exhausted by the effort of controlling the craft. She began to consider getting on the ground a matter of urgency, lest her ability to fly dissolve before she accomplished the most important part of her flight. Julia popped the airbrakes and descended steeply toward the hilltop directly at the throng of watching pilots. At the last moment, fearing she might kill someone, she heeled the skysail over on a wingtip and cartwheeled through a mass of bushes, shedding strips of griffin wing membrane and pieces of airframe in her wake. Old Jared had a rule for this situation too: you break it, you fix it. That winter, Julia learned how to pare tree branches into wing ribs using a stone tipped adze.

⇒▸●❮ ❄ ─── ❄ ❯●◂⇐

"Liz, are you there?"

"Go ahead Jack."

"I found graves."

"Okay..."

"There are bodies buried under rock cairns, two of them, not far from the ship. I don't know how I missed them before."

"Who?"

"Bryan Carver and Yves Pelletier. Names and dates are inscribed on flat rocks. Carver died on the day of the crash, Pelletier a day later."

"Oh God, Jack. Do you realize what that means?"

"I can't think about anything else."

⇒▸●❮ ❄ ─── ❄ ❯●◂⇐

The next morning dawned bright and clear, with a steady breeze. Before long, little puffs of cumulus cloud were spreading together into the long parallel streams Jared called "cloud streets." A ragged group had assembled at the head of the launching deck from which they would depart. Julia squirmed to the front of the group the better to be a part of the event. The hunters were dressed in warm skins and mufflers of hand spun chute fabric, to keep out the chill winds aloft. The nervous chatter dried up and they stood waiting as Miles, Captain of the Family, shuffled up to bless the hunt and to read, as he always did, a passage from the Log of Kathleen.

Ancient and stooped as he was, he had a sense of occasion, and had dressed himself in the garb of the ancestors. Julia had seen the old man's performance many times, but never before from the perspective of one who was to be part of the hunt. It was a comforting tradition. The costume Miles wore was quite unlike the skins of the hunters. His body garment was of an orange hue, like a flame. Most of his head was enclosed by a gleaming red gourd-like hat decorated with a motif of jagged blue-white lightning bolts. His eyes were covered by a curved sheet of a bright, smooth substance that reflected an image of the semicircle of standing hunters. His face covering resembled the black snout of some strange animal, with a flexible proboscis that hung down to his waist and swung as he walked. He carried the Log in a leather bag slung over his shoulder.

A couple of the hunters helped him lower his frail frame to the ground, where he sat cross-legged. With a snap he detached the snout thing first at one side and then at the other and laid it reverently before him. Then he pushed up the silvery face covering until it rested on top of his headdress. He regarded the hunters with piercing blue eyes, as though deciding whether they were worthy to hear the venerated text. The hunters sat silently, respectfully, as Miles drew the precious book from its bag and opened it with great care at the very last page.

"This is the wisdom of the first person on this world," he said. "She was my grandfather's great grandmother, and her name was Kathleen. I did not know her, but my grandfather did. She was the leader and only survivor of the people who fell upon the world from the deep ocean of the sky. She was not able to return to her home among the stars. Instead she founded our village and became the mother of every one of us. She was a pilot, as many of you are. But she flew farther, higher and faster than any of us. She flew between worlds.

"She possessed much knowledge within her head, and she resolved to write down all that she knew that might help us, her descendants, to survive. She crafted this Log and recorded her ancient skills, so that we might profit from them. Before she died, she taught her grandchildren to build the first skysails, from the boughs of the forest and the skins of animals. They used them at first to scout for game in the valley and later to hunt the griffins, as you will do today." He pointed at the leather bound tome of rough parchment before him. "This is the Log of Kathleen the Pilot, my great great great grandmother." He took a deep breath and then began to declaim the wisdom of Kathleen. Though the book was open in front of him, he did not read from it, rather he recited from memory the precious words of his ancestor.

Julia hardly listened. She was too excited and nervous about the upcoming hunt. She was a pilot, like Kathleen was. Not a space traveler, but a skin, bone and branch skysail pilot. Her mind raced ahead, full of pitch angles, glide ratios, turn rates and pursuit tactics. She felt for the pulse in her neck, aware that her wheels were spinning crazily. She took a few slow breaths and forced herself to listen to the end of Miles' recitation, the last words Kathleen recorded in the Log.

"One day my people may come. Do not fear them. They are only people, like me and like you. Remember, this is your world. Until then, my children, happy hunting."

⊷⟨⟨ — ⟩⟩⟩⊶

"Jack here. Liz, I keep going over in my mind, what Kathy must have gone through. The choices she must have had to make."

"I know, Jack. I've been thinking about it too. If she only had herself to worry about, she could have lived out her life alone and died alone. But the baby—obviously it was a boy, she couldn't make that choice for him."

"Actually she was having twins. A boy and a girl."

"So that just complicates the question of who begat whom. It doesn't change the fact that she's the ancestor of them all."

"So am I. Liz."

"I know."

"I guess she had good genes."

"I guess you do too."

⊷⟨⟨ — ⟩⟩⟩⊶

From above the griffin was easy to see, as a dark silhouette against the background of scrubby bush and baked clay soil. In flight, the forelimbs with their deadly talons were held in front, to grasp and slash at prey, while the shorter, stouter walking limbs folded back, streamlining the creature. It soared in a dusty column of rising air, delicate wing membranes outstretched, climbing toward them. Julia leaned forward, slapped Pak on the shoulder and pointed. Pak turned and nodded, grinning. Through her goggles Julia could see that Pak's eyes were bright with anticipation and, perhaps, a trace of amusement. Pak tapped the side of her head in a silent gesture that meant "I know." Pak was testing her, she realized. She had already spotted the target and wanted to see how long it would be before Julia saw it too. Pak began to unsling her harpoon from the side of the cockpit.

Julia pushed the stick forward. They were momentarily weightless as they pitched into a steep dive toward the oblivious prey. She knew what she should do: build up speed as they swooped down below the target, and pull up hard into a steep climbing turn, to present Pak with a clear shot at the vulnerable belly. Judging distance when the target is below you is difficult though. Even seasoned pilots don't always get it right. Julia was way off. She undershot the griffin as it turned in a left-handed spiral. Finally the creature noticed her and turned tighter into its circle, denying them a shot. Julia rolled to follow the turn. The griffin turned tighter. Way tighter. Banked hard over, the inexperienced Julia hauled full up elevator to tighten her own turn and discovered something she had never been taught. Most young pilots believe stalling is caused by a lack of speed.

Wrong.

Stalls are caused by excessive angle of attack.

Julia and Pak experienced a split second of bone jarring vibration as the turbulent airflow breaking away from the wing passed over the tail. And then it happened. The nose dropped with a sickening lurch. At the same time the skysail rolled violently to the inside of the turn and was caught in a sudden and vicious autorotation. The ground spun ahead of them, growing larger by the second, as Julia, instinctively, but quite wrongly, pulled the stick hard into her stomach with all the strength she could muster.

--- ❖ --- ❖ ---

"Jack, you were right!"

"Huh?"

"The planes are going up. They're flying them around in circles, gaining height."

"Figures. Kathy used to be a sailplane pilot. What do you think they're going to do?"

"Well a bunch of those big shite-hawk things are winging along the valley. It looks like a migration. Maybe they're trying to scare them away."

"Keep watching, Liz. I'm pretty much done here. It's time for me to make contact."

--- ❖ --- ❖ ---

In the seat in front of Julia, Pak was loosening the straps that held her in place, pulling her drogue from its pouch. She was getting ready to jump. Julia forced herself to push her foot firmly against the yaw bar to slow the spin, relaxed her death grip on the pitch and roll stick and eased it forwards. At once the stalled wing began to fly again. They were in a steep dive. The rush of wind against her face told the young flier the skysail was close to the speed at which it could come apart. Gently she eased out of the dive. Treetops shot by in a blur, only just beneath the craft. She pulled back as hard as she dared, trading speed for height, getting heavy in her seat, zooming upwards until the tell-tale buffeting of chaotic air over the tail told her there was no more momentum to be had without stalling again. She pushed the craft over into a shallow glide. They were barely a quarter kayem above the ground and the startled griffin was nowhere in sight. Pak waved the folded drogue above her head. The gesture meant "look how close you came to making me jump, you moron." She stuffed it back into her belt pouch. Julia knew they were too low for bailing. It was up to her to keep them in the air.

She closed her eyes for a moment and breathed deeply, trying to relax. She juggled with the pitch angle until Pak's ears were level with the horizon in front of her. The screaming of wind settled to a steady whoosh as the skysail slowed to what she hoped was the speed at which it would achieve its flattest glide. She made a wide turn to the left, toward home. Remembering all that she had been taught, she balanced her bank angle with just a little rudder and elevator. The small piece of yarn on the mica windshield blew straight up, showing she wasn't wasting height by slipping or skidding. She knew there were but two or three minutes to find some lift or else they would face a hazardous landing amid the scrub below. The sky that had seemed to be bubbling with columns of rising air only moments before, now looked ominous. Julia had managed to find herself under a big dirty gray mass of cloud amid an otherwise perfect hunting sky. In the distance, skysails wheeled among griffins, in bright sunlight under fluffy white cumulus. All around her was overcast. That meant the supply of thermal lift could very soon stop.

Suddenly she felt the skysail pitch down a little, giving a jolt to her stomach. She had flown into a patch of sinking air and was rapidly losing the little margin of height that remained to her. After a split second of panic and against all instinct, learning triumphed. She pushed the stick forward, urging the skysail to fly faster through the downdraft to conserve her height as best she could. After a moment, Julia felt the craft wander into a gentle roll to the left. At once she pushed the stick firmly the other way, forcing the right wing down and into a clockwise turn. She hardly dared breathe as the skysail entered a pocket of turbulent air. After two or three turns she felt they were just maintaining their altitude. She flew straight for a couple of seconds and then banked hard over into a steep right turn. And she caught it! Her stomach lurched as the skysail entered a swiftly rising thermal. She held the steep turn, even as the thermal tried to throw them out. The turbulent air rocked and shook the puny glider, until Julia began to feel nauseous, but she rode the rising air with determination. Pak waved her arms over her head and gave a great ululating yell like a victorious hunter. The ground below them receded to a more comfortable distance. They rose until the cloud base threatened to engulf them, as they flew through wisps and streamers of vapor. Pak pointed out to their right and Julia saw the landing field atop the valley side in brilliant sunshine two or three kayems away. She rolled out, lowered the nose and headed directly for home.

By the time the skysail had slid to a dusty halt on the ground, she was exhausted. The craft dropped one wing onto the dirt and rested there at an angle. Julia sat breathing heavily, her mind in a daze. Pak unstrapped herself and jumped out, turning to face her, clenched fists resting on her hips. Julia began to mumble an apology. The older woman spat a brown wad of chewed *capra* root onto the ground and grinned at her, baring blackened broken teeth. Then she leaned into the cockpit and kissed Julia hard, laughing into her astonished open mouth.

"But I nearly killed us!"

"But you didn't."

"I undershot the target. You didn't even get to cast your harpoon. The others are out hunting and we are right back here with nothing!"

"It doesn't matter."

"My first hunt and no kill!"

"Hey, you brought us home alive. That means we can hunt again tomorrow."

Pak leaned over and threatened to kiss her again. She laughed as Julia recoiled in confusion. Pak slapped her firmly, and yet playfully, on the back of the head and ran off toward the village.

Julia sat alone in the skysail for a long time, watching griffins and hunters whirling in the far distance. A chute blossomed as a harpooner descended to tackle a downed prey. Plumes of smoke were beginning to rise from distant signal fires, marking kill sites for the villagers, who would trek out to help the harpooners butcher and bring home the meat. Presently she heard light footfalls behind her. An orange clad figure crept under the high wing of the skysail and alongside the cockpit.

It must be old Miles, come to taunt her for her failure. She turned her head.

It wasn't Miles, though the man wore the same type of clothes and a red gourd upon his head. He looked a little like Miles, but younger, and although he was certainly an adult, his face had no tattoos. He knelt beside the skysail and placed a hand on the edge of the cockpit. The man looked at her silently for a long moment. His eyes were wet with tears.

"My name is Jack," the man said. "You look a lot like a girl I used to know. Her name was Kathleen."

Jon Martin Watts lives on a very small farm near Saskatoon with a wife and son, two dogs, eight cats, a few sheep, and a llama. He has a PhD in applied animal behaviour and a MSc in biological anthropology. Jon is a member of the Saskatoon Critical Mass writers group. His short fiction has appeared in *On Spec*. He is also a fraction of the pseudonymous author "Alexis Ayrth," who recently published her first novel, *Dragon Calms the Fire*.

Vermilion Dreams
The Complete Works
of Bram Jameson

Claude Lalumière

1. Pirates to Nowhere (1961)

In *Pirates to Nowhere*, a group of seven plunderers invade Venera, seeking its lucrative stores of vermilion, the euphoria-inducing spice manufactured from a plant that reputedly grows nowhere but in the soil of Vermilion Gardens, an inner borough of the archipelagean city-state. The vermilion plant has never been successfully smuggled out of Venera.

No outsider knows, exactly, how to locate Vermilion Gardens, never mind how to recognize the plant or even find the building (or buildings) where the precious stores are kept. One of the pirates, a Canadian named Bram Jameson, who may or may not be the same person as the book's author, boasts of having been in Venera as a child. The captain is counting on Jameson's memory to guide them all to riches.

To the pirates' surprise, no one opposes them; in fact, at first, Venera appears deserted. The would-be thieves almost immediately lose their way in the unfamiliar streets of Venera, their poorly laid plans in shambles. The five men who comprise the rest of the crew blame both the captain and Jameson for this failure. The ensuing mutiny causes Jameson to be separated from his fellow criminals. He tries in vain to retrace his steps, to find the harbor where their ship set anchor. But, as he navigates the streets of Venera, his sense of direction fails him. He loses himself in this alien cityscape, so unlike any other metropolis on Earth and so unlike his memories of it. He loses sight of the sea and cannot locate any of the aquatic vias that so famously serve as Venera's main thoroughfares. Instead, he is caught in a maze of claustrophobic, cobblestone streets that zigzag through the geometrically confusing architecture of

Venera. Often, he can barely see the sky through the overhanging maze of passageways, balconies, arches, bridges, and vegetation. For days on end, the vegetation grows so dense that he comes to forget that he is in a city at all, believing himself lost in a labyrinthine primeval forest. Eventually, albeit temporarily, the jungle becomes more recognizably urban, although the bizarre geometry confuses his sense of logic and, even, of self. Throughout his journey, Jameson encounters visionaries, prophets, lunatics, sadomasochists, holy whores, defective automata, and deformed doppelgangers of his former crewmates.

Time ceases to have any meaning for Jameson. Eventually, he wends his way into a garden. Cubist paintings hang from trees. The paintings are all different, but each of them is a stylized, distorted closeup of someone's face, perhaps his own. Each in turn, the cubist heads spring to life, asking Jameson a series of surrealist riddles too arcane for Jameson to answer.

He ventures deeper into the garden. A path leads him to the edge of a whirlpool made of light. The book ends mid-sentence as the hero descends into the luminous whirlpool.

2. The Great Disasters (1964)

Starting in 1965, the U. S. paperback house Full Deck Books planned to release Bram Jameson's gargantuan opus *The Great Disasters* as a series of four slim mass-market paperbacks. They published the first three as *A World of Ice*, *A World of Fire*, and *The Great Flood*—and had advertised the fourth, *The New World*. However, assaulted by lawsuits claiming that most of their line consisted of pirated editions, including sometimes furtively reprinting other publishers' books by simply changing titles and names of authors, Full Deck Books ceased operations before the series' final installment could hit bookshops. Presumably, the shady U. S. publisher never actually acquired the rights to *The Great Disasters* from Jameson or Vermilion Press, which, aside from that one aberration, remains the sole source of the author's books.

The original one-volume edition of *The Great Disasters* sports a cover illustration by the renowned Jake Kurtz, the prolific New York cartoonist who created comics classics such as *The Internationalist*, *The Preservers*, *The Last Boy*, *Dinosaurs on the Moon*, *Destroyer of Worlds*, and many others. The cover is split in four quarters, with a title box in the middle. Each vignette illustrates, respectively, one of the book's four sections.

The expression "The Great Disasters" usually refers to the apocalyptic hysteria of 1961, when worldwide civilization—capitalist, communist, and preindustrial—was convinced its end was imminent, first by ice, then by fire, and finally by water. Although people who were alive at the time claim to remember the mini Ice Age, the scorching droughts, and the great floods that successively afflicted the entire world, and certainly newspaper headlines and magazine covers from that era confirm these memories, current scientific studies point to the whole thing being a hoax—or a strange, shared fever dream—as no quantifiable evidence of any of these phenomena remains. Perhaps worldwide anxiety in that tense Cold War era had reached such a pitch that humanity collectively imagined these primal disasters as a way to cope with the looming threat of nuclear war and the consequent destruction of civilization?

Indeed, *The Great Disasters* concerns itself with this epochal moment in world history. This time around, Jameson is not a pirate but an aviator who made his fortune as a vermilion merchant and now zips around the world at the helm of his solar-powered jet in search of adventure. The book is separated into four sections: Ice, Fire, Water, and the baffling conclusion, The New World.

At the start of Ice, our intrepid adventurer witnesses a clandestine bomb test in the arctic. There is no violent explosion as such, but concentric waves of energy emanate from ground zero, forcing the aviator to crash his airplane in the snow. The damage to the aircraft is minor. While Jameson repairs his jet, a group of five scientists surrounds him, and, at gunpoint, they take him prisoner.

The scientists mean to lead him to their headquarters, but they lose their way in the arctic desert (the astute reader will notice a recurring theme). They explain to Jameson that their bomb test has inadvertently set in motion a rapid ice age and that within a few months the entire planet will be covered in ice, possibly ending all life. Soon, they forget their weapons and begin treating Jameson as one of their own. Jameson himself forgets his own past, his identity, and the group increasingly behaves like a hive mind.

The hive mind eventually reaches the rogue scientists' arctic lair. For the next ten or so pages, the action is described in a series of geometric tableaux, dense with allegory and challenging to decipher. Gradually, this virtuoso narration segues into a more conventional style, with Jameson, triumphant and individuality regained, flying his aircraft over a retreating ice age.

Both Fire and Water follow a plot structure similar to that of Ice, each time with Jameson the aviator accidentally encountering a quintet of scientists responsible for the disaster, and each time seeing him involved, always in a similarly allegorical fashion, in saving the world from its latest armageddon. Could these adventures detail the true, secret history of that apocalyptic year? Perhaps—although part four, The New World, veers off into obvious fantasy.

The New World, which is itself longer than the three other sections combined, opens with Jameson flying over the receding floodwaters, providing clear continuity from the previous section, Water. Jameson spots an unfamiliar land formation and directs his plane toward it. Reaching his destination, Jameson wonders if he has discovered a new continent. Unfamiliar cityscapes appear in the distance. Intrigued by this mystery, Jameson lands his plane in a field and sets off on foot. In this strange land, Jameson encounters tribes, settlements, villages, and even cities populated by humanoid animals, but the species do not intermingle, save for trade or war.

The various animal species all possess the power of speech, and, even more startling, they all speak a recognizable human language: English, French, Italian, Japanese, German, Arabic, etc. (In the text, all the foreign dialogue is rendered in the original language, with no translation.)

But Jameson soon discovers that he has lost his own ability to speak. He can now vocalize nothing more than grunts and moans. Typically, he has lost his bearings and can no longer locate his airplane.

He sees few other humans; like him, none of them can speak. They are slaves to the most privileged animals. The dominant animals recognize that Jameson is different from their servants; invariably, the animals treat him as a guest.

This long section is marked by Jameson's predilection for repetition. Every encounter unfolds in a similar manner: as dawn breaks, Jameson wanders into the territory of a new species; he meets a guide who escorts him; Jameson is witness to activities and conflicts whose nature he barely understands; as night falls, he is invited to a ceremony; there, before Jameson's eyes, a human slave is ritually slaughtered—although the specifics of the ritual differs from species to species, even the herbivorous animals perform this act for Jameson's benefit—and the meat is offered to him. Always, he refuses to eat the human flesh; he is then cast out. He wanders until he encounters the next group.

Eventually, in a city of cats, the ritual is preceded by the intake of vermilion. When the meat is offered to him, the intoxicated Jameson enthusiastically agrees to consume the flesh before him. The sacred food is delicious. Once Jameson has chewed and swallowed, the mayor of the cat city says, "Now, speak your name."

The novel ends with the hero saying, "My name is Bram Jameson."

3. Why I Want to Love (1969)

Why I Want to Love is a difficult, experimental book. Here, the author eschews such writerly conventions as chapters, paragraph breaks, sentences, and punctuation. For the entirety of its four hundred and seventy-five pages, *Why I Want to Love* consists of one uninterrupted string of words. Set entirely in Venera, this book, unlike Jameson's first two releases, is narrated in the first person, although, paradoxically, the protagonist and narrator is never explicitly identified as Jameson and remains nameless—at least in the text itself. The introduction by Lee Williams, who also appears as a character in the narrative, namechecks Jameson as the narrator and claims that Jameson's text is the real, accurate, and uncensored record of life in Venera, circa 1967. Jameson's text is vague on personal details, but the Williams intro mentions Jameson's Venera mansion, with its throngs of naked, young, beautiful sycophants, both male and female, as eager to sample Jameson's stores of vermilion as they were willing to give their bodies to whoever desired them.

In the 1950s, Williams was better known as the international gun-toting costumed vigilante Interzone. After the tragic death of his wife and crimefighting partner, the archer Arrowsnake, he reportedly retired to Venera, although this has never been officially confirmed. *Why I Want to Love* is the only document authenticating this rumor.

This is the first time a Jameson book is explicitly touted as nonfiction, but that claim is suspect. For one thing, despite the well-documented sexual openness of the late 1960s, especially in Venera, legendarily notorious for its history of unbridled promiscuity, the story—a nonstop hedonistic display of sexual excess, perversity, and depravity described in bluntly explicit anatomical detail—stretches credibility. For another, it's hard to believe in the parade of celebrities the three protagonists (the narrator; the now homosexual Williams; and a shockingly teen-age Tito Bronze, who already displays the enthusiasm for spanking female derrières that made his later films so scandal-ous) encounter on their orgiastic odyssey: Ronald Reagan, Jacqueline Kennedy Onassis, Richard Nixon, Doris Day, Sophia Loren, Audrey Hepburn, Orson Welles, Ringo Starr, Jayne Mansfield, Fred MacMurray, Federico Fellini, Nico, Anita Ekberg, Anouk Aimée, Ursula Andress, Serge Gainsbourg, Brigitte Bardot, Pablo Picasso, Diana Rigg...

Perhaps Jameson (and Williams) really do remember the events as described, regardless of what actually occurred. Both the Williams intro and the Jameson text mention that the three protagonists were at the time constantly under the influence of vermilion, in a state of perpetual imaginative euphoria that would certainly lend itself to hallucinatory experiences. As some studies have shown (see, for example, Jasmine Cockney's 1974 counterculture bestseller, *The Vermilion Fix*, published by Albion Pulp Press), it is possible, although not definitely proven, that prolonged communal consumption of vermilion can produce shared hallucinations. And if that is the case, then *Why I Want to Love* might be simultaneously memoir and fiction.

4. Motorcrash (1974)

Few remember Venera's brief and disastrous attempt to join the car culture of the twentieth century. Renowned for being a pedestrian haven, the archipelagean city-state has never re-peated the experiment.

Motorcrash is Jameson's personal account of those events, which had transpired the year before. The book's first-person narrative has the ring of authenticity—especially given what is on the public record regarding the period in question. More tragic and affecting than anything to that date in Jameson's eclectic bibliography, *Motorcrash* opens with Jameson driving on the newly constructed elevated highways of Venera, his recent bride, Kara Hunger, in the passenger seat.

At the end of the first chapter, which otherwise describes the view of Venera from these new roads, their car collides with another automobile. In the aftermath, both Jameson and Hunger, having suffered only minor bruising, find themselves sexually aroused; every aspect of the process—the collision; the exchange of insurance information with the other driver; going to the garage for repairs—only increases the couple's sexual tension.

As the repairs cannot be finished that day, their car is kept overnight at the garage. Jameson and Hunger are compelled to break into the garage at night and have sex on the backseat of their damaged automobile, tearing their clothes and drawing blood from each other in the process. Jameson admires the various bodily fluids smearing the interior of his new but already well-worn vehicle.

Afterward, they are accosted outside the garage by Raphael Marcus, the driver who collided with them earlier, and thus begins their journey through the underground world of motorcrashers, a cult worshipping the automobile as the trigger for the next phase in human evolution and the motorcrash as the ultimate form of prayer, the most intense form of communion with the divine force driving human existence.

Jameson and Marcus become inseparable: Jameson refuses to buy into Marcus' messianic ravings but warms to the madman because of the intensity of their conversations on the effects of the automobile on human consciousness; Marcus, for his part, cannot resist trying to convert this fervent nonbeliever. The sexual tension between the two men is thick.

Although Jameson is never convinced by Marcus' techno-mysticism, he nevertheless gives himself up totally to car culture. His automobile allows him the most satisfying expression of his sexuality. Jameson's text fetishistically describes automobiles, sexualizing every aspect of car culture: likening maintenance to prolonged, devoted foreplay; conversations with other drivers to public displays of mutual masturbation; visits to the garage for minor repairs to breast-augmentation mammoplasty; driving to marital relations; hitchhiking to prostitution; car-pooling to orgies; automobile parts to erogenous zones of the human body; and, most dramatically, car crashes to primal, uninhibited animal sex.

The plot comes to focus on a sort of eroticized duel between Marcus and Jameson, each of them espousing different, although not mutually incompatible, visions of automobile worship. Caught in the middle of this conflict of machismo and techno-theology is Jameson's wife, who finds herself drawn both to Marcus' cult and to Marcus himself. The motorcrasher messiah welcomes her conversion but rejects her sexual advances.

Eventually, Jameson and Marcus consummate their rivalry in a brutal act of automobile sex: that chapter is written in virtuoso style, the multiple perspectives colliding violently. Meanwhile,

Kara, with unbridled religious fervor, engages in a series of reckless car crashes, until her transcendent death-wish is finally realized.

The book itself ends with Jameson learning of Kara's death. In the real world, following a rash of traffic accidents, Venera dismantled its highways and permanently banned automobiles. The first car in Venera had ignited its engine on 1 March 1973, and the autoroutes closed forever on 1 December of the same year.

5. Icarus Unlimited (1978)

Once again, Jameson is in the cockpit of his solar-powered airplane, previously seen in *The Great Disasters*. He snorts a line of vermilion, revs up the plane's engine, and takes off from Venera; thus begins *Icarus Unlimited*.

It is never stated when, exactly, the book takes place, but presumably the events follow closely on the heels of those related in *Motorcrash*. Grief-stricken over the death of his wife, Jameson decides to leave Venera behind and fly aimlessly around the world, to wherever the sky and the winds will take him.

The entirety of *Icarus Unlimited* takes place inside the cockpit of Jameson's airplane; in fact, the whole narrative is set in his mind. Jameson's fifth book is a philosophical, stream-of-consciousness meditation on flight, travel, identity, war, mortality, love, sex, masculinity, friendship, and violence, peppered with breathtaking and often surreal descriptions of the view from Jameson's cockpit.

By the book's final pages, the vistas Jameson describes are unrecognizable as Earthly, the meditations following an increasingly inscrutable logic. *Icarus Unlimited* does not conclude so much as simply stop.

6. Skyscraper (1981)

Skyscraper is another rare instance of a Jameson book cover sporting the work of a recognizable artist, this time paperback legend Obama Savage, well-known for his heroic and evocative covers of men's adventure novels. The cover depicts a muscular man in a ripped shirt standing with his fists clenched (presumably the iteration of Jameson described in the novel); behind him a skyscraper burns. The colors are rich, the intense gaze of the protagonist mesmerizing, the attention to minute detail captivating.

Is *Skyscraper* another descent into pure fantasy? In the heart of Venera, Jameson, now described as a chiseled, hyper-competent übermensch adventurer of near-limitless resources, inhabits the top five floors of the Venera World Trade Center, a phallic, modernist spire piercing the lush, sensuous shapes of the Veneran skyline. (There was indeed a skyscraper, the only one ever, built in Venera in 1978; it burned down in 1980.)

Joining him is a team of five assistants: the hirsute and muscular biochemist Hank Priest; the dapper lawyer and fencing champion Teddy Cauchon; the ruggedly handsome engineer and retired boxer J.R. "Junior" Fox; the sinuously athletic daredevil and inventor Bobby Long; the bespectacled archeologist and linguist Billy Poderski.

Each chapter describes a densely detailed, fast-paced adventure, each with its own lurid, sensationalistic title: "The Hydra of a Thousand Heads," "The Menace of the Meteor Men," "Treasure Hunt at the North Pole," "Werewolves by Night," "Oasis of the Lost," "The Monster-Master," "Land of Terrors," "The Mysticals," "City of Phantoms." Each adventure follows a strict formula: one of Jameson's aides bursts into the group's headquarters accompanied by a person in dire straits; the problem is stated to the group, minus Jameson; Jameson then appears, having heard everything on his security system, and accepts the case; the group then goes into action, taking off aboard their "solar jet gyro" from the launch pad on the roof of the skyscraper; they encounter the menace and defeat it after exactly two of them face near-death challenges.

Only the final chapter, "The Fall of the Tower," breaks the formula. Returning from an adventure (the otherwise unreported but perhaps aptly named "The Case of the Vanishing Pulpsters"), the adventurers find their headquarters invaded by a group of men in perfectly cut striped gray business suits. With alarming efficiency, the intruders dismantle Jameson's headquarters. The intruders ignore all questions put to them and, whenever one of Jameson's band tries to grab one, the man in the business suit manages to evade his would-be assailant's grasp with snake-like suppleness.

When the power goes out, Jameson and his crew reluctantly descend into the lower floors to investigate. They find the skyscraper's inhabitants transformed, the office workers' clothes in tatters, revealing the flabby bodies beneath. The offices have become atavistic temples; desks are now altars where living human flesh is sacrificed to unknown gods. Amid the screams of the sacrificial victims, the skyscraper people chant in a cacophony of alien tongues that even linguist Billy Poderski cannot begin to decipher. One by one, the members of Jameson's team forget who they are. Jameson struggles to keep the group together, fighting to keep his sense of identity.

The fires from the sacrificial mounds spread to the walls. As the skyscraper burns around him, Jameson takes out his knife and peels off strips of his skin, feeding it to his companions.

7. Hello Venera (1984)

In 1982, Mike Walters, the self-appointed American "Theme Park Emperor," finally unveiled his secret European project, built on an artificial archipelago in the Mediterranean: Vermilion World, which he claimed was "a near-exact replica of Venera, its facades, its streets, its mysteries." Being a privately held corporation, WalterWorlds Unlimited never disclosed the cost of developing and constructing this immense luxury attraction. Day passes went for US$1,000, not including transportation, food, or anything besides entrance to the theme park. Hotel stays began at US$2,000 a head per night on top of the entrance fee; vacation rentals started at US$25,000 per week for studio apartments and went as high as US$3,000,000 per week for the most upscale villas, with support-staff fees not included. Within a week of the announcement, the park was already fully booked for the next three months.

With this project, the entrepreneur threatened to lift the veil that surrounded the mysteries of Venera. As Walters had leased French territorial waters for this endeavor, the Veneran government tried and failed to get from the French courts a quick injunction to force Vermilion World to close its doors until the matter could be settled, in or out of court. However, while the firm of Hawk, Murdock, Spencer, and Associates was still figuring out its next move on behalf of Venera, a disaster befell Vermilion World that rendered further legal action moot. The precise details of the incident never reached the press, beyond the fact that, following a number of explosions of such large magnitude they could be heard and seen everywhere along the French Riviera, the theme park sank into the sea.

In *Hello Venera*, Jameson proposes an unlikely but thrillingly recounted scenario explaining these events. Jameson is now an agent of the Vermilion Eye, Venera's secret organization of international operatives, i.e., its super-spy agency. Assigned the Vermilion World case, code-named Hello Venera, Jameson gains access to the theme park as a paying guest, with false papers that identify him as Jimmy Flamingo, an American expat living in London.

In short order, Jameson confronts Walters, portrayed here as a madman whose world-domination scheme involves replicating the greatest cities on Earth as theme parks and then destroying the cities themselves, with agents provocateurs arranging for the blame to be shouldered by so-called "terrorist" groups.

Jameson fights Walters' giant automata, escapes elaborate traps, and finally physically battles Walters after having dispatched hundreds of his goons through a combination of unbelievable luck and even more unlikely prowess. The mad developer falls to his death in a vat of boiling chemicals, setting off a series of explosions that ultimately destroys the theme park, and with it Walters' megalomaniacal scheme.

To save himself from the conflagration, Jameson snorts a specially prepared vermilion concentrate, chants a mantra, and jumps one month forward into time. Finding himself adrift in the Mediterranean, he swims briefly until a submarine sporting the Vermilion Eye logo on its hull surfaces and takes him aboard.

Mike Walters has not been heard from since the Vermilion World catastrophe. His body has never been recovered, but he is presumed dead. A popular conspiracy theory propounds that Walters is being kept alive in suspended animation in a secret laboratory owned by WalterWorlds Unlimited.

8. Empire of the Self (1987)
At age thirty, in 1984, Veneran filmmaker, pornographer, and iconoclast Tito Bronze was only beginning to have his work recognized. His every movement was not yet subject to the minute scrutiny that would begin in 1989, when his fame and notoriety hit the stratosphere with the scandalous Cannes premiere of his first feature-length film, *In primo luogo, esamino il culo*.

It is then possible that he embarked on an ill-fated film project with Bram Jameson in 1984, namely *Empire of the Self*, the story of Jameson's childhood travails in Nazi-occupied Venera.

The main thrust of the book of the same name is a behind-the-scenes look at the disaster-afflicted production of what could have been Bronze's first feature. On-set lethal accidents, bankrupt investors, legal entanglements about ownership and authorship of the screenplay, personal betrayals, petty pranks, sabotage by persons unknown, incendiary love affairs, the producer threatening to replace Bronze with a commercial Hollywood director...what didn't happen to this film project? Ultimately, much of the footage was lost—stolen, misplaced, maliciously destroyed?—and the film cancelled. Interspersed dreamlike into this narrative are Jameson's memories of life in Venera, circa 1941-45.

Here, Jameson reveals that his father was a Canadian botanist on contract in Venera when the Germans invaded with no warning. The young Bram's parents were captured and sent to a POW camp in Germany, but their son eluded the Nazis and spent the next four years with no permanent residence, acquiring through necessity a knack for hiding in plain sight and living as a ghost in the besieged city-state. He moved with ease between the resistance and the German invaders, secretly befriending people on either side, other times playing pranks on whomever his fancy or opportunity dictated. Trickster, freedom fighter, collaborator, traitor, thief, squatter, saboteur, informant, spy...the young boy was all of these. After the end of the war, Bram was reunited with his mother and father in northern Manitoba, Canada.

Despite Tito Bronze's celebrity, this aborted collaboration with Jameson has never been reported on outside of this book. Bronze was explicitly named as a character in three Jameson books (see also *Why I Want to Love*, above, and *Millennium Nights*, below), yet Bronze has never publicly mentioned Jameson, let alone the long friendship described in these books.

Bram Jameson: hoax? pseudonym? reality? The enigma persists.

9. Nostalgia of Futures Past (1991)

If Venera ever considered operating its own space program, it's a well-kept secret. Yet, that is the premise of Jameson's *Nostalgia of Futures Past*, which finds Jameson one of six astronauts awaiting the final countdown for the launch of Venera's first rocket, *The Nostalgia*, en route to orbit Venus. Much like in *Icarus Unlimited*, Jameson never leaves the vehicle within the time frame of the narrative.

Whether or not the space program is factual, the majority of *Nostalgia of Futures Past* is unquestionably fiction. For the bulk of the book, while Jameson waits for the ship to blast off, he daydreams about the future. He imagines his voyage taking much longer than the projected seven-year mission. He skips over any speculation about the mission itself, and instead his thoughts linger on what will happen once he and his crewmates return to Earth.

They find the Terran population in a state of lethargy. Fossil-fuel reserves have dried up. Entertainment conglomerates have all gone bankrupt. Governments have all been dissolved. Pandemics have wiped out hundreds of millions of people. Shopping malls have become post-capitalist ghost towns. In the face of civilization's collapse, instead of chaos, there is merely resignation. Even Jameson's beloved Venera seems to have withered, its former luster turned drab, its gardens of vermilion plant overrun with weeds.

Whenever Jameson attempts to communicate with anyone, there is no conversation, no connection. Although they speak in turn, his interlocutors talk in dull tones as though responding to another conversation entirely, lost in the dreariness of their arid inner lives. Jameson's emotional outbursts are ignored by those around him. Even his former crewmates are eventually infected by this generalized apathy.

Jameson yearns for escape. He decides to return to space. With the help of his solar-powered airplane, he embarks on a worldwide tour of space centers, now all deserted and derelict. He hopes to find one functional ship to take him back into space. But every vehicle he finds is rusted and in complete dis-repair. Besides, there is no fuel left anywhere.

Returning to Venera, he resolves to push his solar-powered airplane beyond its limits and fly it into space—an escape into his own imagination...

As he prepares to take off, the real world interrupts his rev-erie with the shriek of a loud siren. In his headphones, he hears the phrase "Launch aborted" repeated again and again. Thus ends the book.

10. The Voices of Creation:
The Complete Short Fiction of
Bram Jameson (2000)

The Voices of Creation: The Complete Short Fiction of Bram Jameson displays a heretofore unrevealed aspect of Jameson's writing: Venera is never mentioned, the protagonists never bear the author's name, and, for once, there is no doubt that we are dealing completely with fiction.

All culled from obscure, defunct periodicals such as *Brave New Fictions*, *Gambit's Fantastic Quarterly*, *The Pringle Zone*, *Research and Story*, *Innerspace Argonaut*, and *Pulp Wave*, these 101 stories highlight Jameson as science-fiction writer, a genre his book-length works often flirt with. Here we find space voyages, mad scientists, adventures to microscopic universes, utopias and dystopias, apocalyptic disasters, bizarre mutations, lost civilizations, and time travel. The earliest story, "Prime Bell," dates from 1956, and the last, "The Obscure Planet," from 1997.

Vividly imaginative, composed with elegance and economy, characterized by a careful attention to unusual and troubling images, possessing arresting psychological depth, these stories linger disquietingly in the mind.

11. Millennium Nights (2002)

Millennium Nights, a return of sorts to the epic scale of 1964's *The Great Disasters*, is split into three self-contained sections: Vermilion Beach, The Velvet Bronzemine, and Supermall.

At the start of the first section, an aging yet still vigorous Jameson and his girlfriend, Victoria Shepherd, a private detective, arrive at the eponymous Vermilion Beach, a new gated community for the ultra-rich located on one of Venera's outer islands. They have bought a unit there, as a vacation home. The climate is especially clement, and the beach is stunningly beautiful. Also, the open sky provides a calming change from the dense urban settings of either central Venera (Jameson's home) or downtown London (Shepherd's home). The resort community is a boon to Venera's economy. Jameson jokes to Victoria that the elite, egocentric colonists have no idea that the "gate" is mostly there to keep *them* out of Venera itself, while the city-state gorges on their money.

The couple is soon befriended by the resort's administrator, Colin Harper, a charismatic figure who sees in Vermilion Beach the key to humanity's future, the template for life in the 21st century and beyond. In his utopian dream, everyone will live in ever-increasing isolation from the distractions of both society and the natural world. This isolation will accelerate the evolution of human consciousness as everyone will eventually achieve full self-knowledge. A skilled rhetorician, Harper deftly evades Jameson's pert socialist objections ("What about the serving staff?" etc.). Jameson finds Harper's elitist fabulations ridiculous, even offensive, but cannot deny the man's aggressive charm.

Attentive readers will notice that Harper is a similar figure to that of Raphael Marcus in *Motorcrash*, albeit more refined and subtle in character.

There is a death announced on the couple's second morning there. But the deceased was elderly, and a natural passing is assumed. In the coming weeks, the deaths pile up, and eventually Harper hires Shepherd to look into the case.

Victoria's personality undergoes a progressive change in the course of her investigation. She becomes increasingly apathetic, parroting Harper's rhetoric in listless tones, accepting each new murder as inevitable, even necessary.

Soon, she is permanently entrenched in her beach chair, shielded from the sun by a parasol. When Jameson prods her on the progress of the investigation, she claims that she is solving this case in a manner appropriate to the facts: by submerging herself in her own mind. She ignores Jameson's scoffs and concerns.

Jameson takes up the case, but, whenever he attempts to question anyone, Harper is there, subtly but surely blocking Jameson's investigation.

The death toll keeps increasing. Every day, someone dies. Yet, no one leaves. Jameson decides to grab Victoria and escape before Vermilion Beach becomes fatal for either of them. But he can't find her. Finally, he confronts Harper, who admits that Shepherd now lives with him; he even lets Jameson see her, but she refuses to leave. "Why should I?" she says. "I think I'm finally understanding this place. I'm understanding myself. It's the same thing." Heartbroken and enraged, Jameson seeks to escape Vermilion Beach, but the ferry service has been shut down. At the pier, he steals a sailboat and leaves the doomed resort behind.

The abrupt closure of Venera's short-lived Vermilion Beach resort community, amid rumors of mass suicide, was mentioned in the news in 2000. London private investigator Victoria Shepherd was listed among the deceased at Vermilion Beach.

The second part of *Millennium Nights* occurs over one night, during Tito Bronze's notorious Millennium Bacchanal, held at his Venera mansion, the Velvet Bronzemine. But the orgy that ensues is not of the expected sexual kind.

Early on in the evening the internationally bestselling thriller writer Magus Amore gathers a number of party guests into a circle at the center of the Bronzemine's banquet hall, inviting them to participate in a rebirthing rite to welcome the new millennium. He strips, revealing that his tall, thin, scarecrow-like body is covered in tattoos of sigils and lizards. He speaks a few ritual phrases in a language that sounds inhuman. Then, in English, he invites his audience to shed their own clothes, and most of them do.

Amore chants, and his tattoos glow. The assembled partygoers gawk at the writer-priest, enraptured by this strange spectacle. Luminous, ethereal snakes ripple out of Amore's body. The snakes converge on another of the guests: Bram Jameson. They orbit around him, ever more rapidly, creating the illusion of an iridescent whirlpool. Throughout all this, an odd serenity spreads through Jameson and through the rest of Amore's congregation. Jameson remains calm even when some of the snakes bind him and others slither into his body via his facial orifices. As the binding serpents drop away, Jameson starts to tear at his own flesh: emerging from inside his own decaying body is a rejuvenated version of himself in the prime of adulthood. Soon, all of his old body has been shed. The viscous gore of his discarded self covers the new skin of the reborn Jameson.

Amore gestures theatrically toward another mesmerized congregant, but then a look of panic etches itself on the writer's face. He convulses uncontrollably; his eyes become vacant. Dreadful monsters emerge from Amore's shimmering body. Soon the mansion is overrun with these beasts, who slaughter not only each other but also anyone within their reach. Only the reborn Jameson laughs through it all; bare-handed he rips apart every monster in his path, eating their otherworldly flesh, their gore mingling with his own on his naked flesh. But there are too many beasts for this lone man to deal with; and, anyway, he seems unconcerned, even amused, by the carnage around him. More monsters pour out of Amore by the second.

Meanwhile, Bronze wonders if he should shoot and kill Amore, but he worries it might make matters worse. Instead, not really knowing what else to do and miraculously sidestepping the barrage of deadly supernatural creatures, he blows several grams' worth of vermilion up Amore's nose. There's a blinding flash of light, and then all goes quiet. Reality has been restored. Only the rejuvenated Jameson and the strewn, dismembered corpses of most of Bronze's guests remain as evidence of the weirdness that occurred. As for Amore, his mind is all but wiped clean, either by his own spell or by the vermilion overdose, or perhaps by the combination of both. (In 2000 Magus Amore dropped from public view amid rumors of insanity just as his latest, and last, thriller, *The Best Americans*, hit the international bestseller lists.)

Supermall was the name of the luxury "retail sanctuary" financed by an international development consortium, set to open for the Christmas shopping rush of 2001. It was built on an artificial island just outside of Venera's territorial waters. The Veneran government was not happy at this intrusion, but all their efforts to halt construction failed. Supermall's inauguration attracted thousands of shoppers, but it was shut down on the very day it opened, with no further comment from the consortium, which disbanded soon after.

According to part three of *Millennium Nights*, Jameson was among the patrons on Supermall's opening day. In this section, the text fetishistically deploys brand names and lingers voyeuristically on detailed descriptions of designer fashions and other luxury consumer products.

At noon an alarm sounds, and a loudspeaker announcement proclaims that Supermall has been locked down. The director of the mall, Marilyn Danvers, has been found dead in her office, and security wants to question all three thousand people at Supermall in relation to the presumed murder. But, although no one is allowed to leave, no investigation is instigated.

After several days, Jameson confronts Rex Danvers, the head of security. Danvers makes a show of listening to Jameson's concerns: already, there have been instances of looting and outbreaks of minor violence among the imprisoned shoppers. But Danvers appears unworried. When Jameson inquires whether he was related to the deceased director, the security chief answers, "Yes, she was my wife..."

As the weeks roll on in the artificially controlled environment of Supermall, time loses meaning. Danvers' megalomania becomes increasingly overt, as he encourages tribal rivalries among the shoppers, whose devotion to consumer goods lead them to create new rituals, to forge alliances based on allegiances to popular consumer brands. The abandoned stores become the temples of this new atavism. Wars break out between the faithful of different branded sects.

Again, Jameson confronts Danvers, who answers, "But people adore consumer goods. I'm allowing them to live out their passions to the fullest, to accept their true religion..."

Jameson is grabbed by a group of Danvers' men. They are five in number, and they match the descriptions of the pirates from Jameson's first book, of the quintets of scientists from the first three sections of *The Great Disasters*, of the five men in Jameson's *Skyscraper* team, and of the astronauts in *Nostalgia of Futures Past*. Are these all the same men? Similarly, the captain from *Pirates to Nowhere*, Raphael Marcus from *Motorcrash*, the villains in various *Skyscraper* adventures, Mike Walters from *Hello Venera*, the meddling producer from *Empire of the Self*, Colin Harper from Vermilion Beach, and Danvers all appear to be different iterations of the same character. And what of Jameson's repeated motifs, such as getting lost, cannibalism, atavistic rituals, vehicles, escape, capitalist development projects, vermilion, and Venera itself? What of the books that stray from his typical scenario? Which are more factual, and which are more fictional? Can these enigmas be solved, to reveal the primal Jamesonian ur-story hiding behind these bizarre phantasmagorias, to understand the life of this author? What is Jameson, if he indeed exists, struggling to reveal or trying to conceal?

Back to *Millennium Nights*: in a Supermall office, the captured Jameson is tortured by Danvers and his men. When they release him, Jameson's perceptions are altered. The meaning of Supermall and its inhabitants is reduced to their geometrical shapes. Within these shapes lies the path to his escape. His mind engages in arcane calculations as he wanders through increasingly abstract landscapes... until he finds himself in a whirlpool of light. He steps out of the whirlpool and into a garden. Readers will recognize it as the same garden previously encountered in Jameson's first book, *Pirates to Nowhere*.

Jameson reaches out toward a vine, snaps off a leaf, and smells it. His gaze returns to the luminous whirlpool as he starts to chew on the leaf. The end.

12. The Terminal Dream (2010)

From the back cover of *The Terminal Dream*: "Bram Jameson (1930-2009) was one of the twentieth century's most significant writers. This revelatory memoir spans the entirety of Jameson's remarkable life: his birth in Canada; his childhood in Nazi-occupied Venera; his young adulthood in Manitoba and England; his first-hand testimony to the great, sweeping changes of the twentieth century; his involvement with many of the most mysterious and emblematic events of the last century; and his meetings with some of the world's most provocative figures. With incisive precision, Jameson recalls the experiences that would fundamentally shape his writing, while simultaneously providing a lucid perspective on the latter decades of the twentieth century. *The Terminal Dream* is the captivating and definitive account of the uncommon life of an extraordinary human being." Thus I learned of the death of this enigmatic author.

The Terminal Dream is a handsome volume, the cover featuring a grainy black-and-white photograph of a very young boy, certainly Jameson, playing in the snow (presumably in northern Manitoba, before his family moved to Venera). The image evokes palpable nostalgia. Is Jameson's oeuvre a strange coded yearning for a return to that state of innocence, an attempt to map out a surreal or mythic path that might lead to his personal nirvana?

I have carefully read and reread *The Terminal Dream* many times. I treasure it with deep affection, even reverence. That it has engaged my imagination more profoundly than anything else I have ever encountered is a risible understatement. But... it has yet to help me finally discern truth from fiction in the author's baffling body of work, or regarding his mysterious life. Every one of *The Terminal Dream*'s pages is written in a cipher that has so far resisted all my efforts at decryption, no matter how much vermilion I consume...

Sometimes, I think the drug allows me to see a whirlpool of light. But when I reach for it the illusion is always shattered.

Claude Lalumière is the author of the story collection *Objects of Worship* (2009). *T14* marks his third *Tesseracts* appearance, having had stories in *T9* and *T11*; in addition, he edited the Aurora Award-finalist *Tesseracts Twelve: New Novellas of Canadian Fantastic Fiction*. With Rupert Bottenberg, Claude is the co-creator of Lost Myths (lostmyths.net).

Near the Ends of Things

THREE POEMS

by Michelle Barker

Fire

If my life were set on fire
and I could stand aside
to watch it burn
I'd toss in sickness
dark winter mornings
harsh words over breakfast
and breakfast
which often burns anyway
I'd burn loneliness
and nightmares
and, for your sake,
the monsters that live upstairs
to my years in high school
I'd add gasoline
stand back at the burst of flame
give a silent cheer
I'd burn all the things
I didn't do
I'd burn bridges
and not stand
forlornly at one end
mourning lost passages
I'd add headaches
and in-grown toenails to the flames
nights spent tossing and turning
would give off an acrid
burnt-hair smell

which I wouldn't mind
regrets would melt
like plastic dolls' heads
long eyes oozing
into frowning mouths
until they looked ridiculous and mushy
which they were all along
but you—
you I would tuck into my pocket
you I would hold
like the memory of a good dream
I keep wanting
to have again.

⟶⟵⟵ ⟵⟶ — ⟶⟵ ⟶⟶⟵⟶

Onwards and Upwards

dying is this journey they make you take, only you don't know where you're going and you're not allowed suitcases and the pilot is blind and the dog that comes with you won't tell you what's going on, only it seems happy enough sitting there panting with its long sly snout-smile

and you get on this conveyor with a line of people all headed in the same direction like one of those walking sidewalks they have at the airport only this one is going up and everyone is walking with such a purpose except you so you stop someone and ask them, where are we going? and they look at you like, don't you know?

and you feel as if you're in the wrong movie or maybe you spent the last five years in a closet because someone hasn't filled you in, you've come to the conference with the wrong files, and you'd like to complain only no one around here seems to be in charge and you're not quite sure what you'd complain about

and everything is moving onward and upward and the pilot is laughing and the dog is laughing and the people around you are laughing and it sweeps you up in its embrace, all this laughter and movement

and you don't understand it but it doesn't matter because suddenly you feel lucky and you catch yourself because you want to say, lucky to be alive, but that's not it—

that's not it at all.

⟶⟵⟵ ⟵⟶ — ⟶⟵ ⟶⟶⟵⟶

The Door

Say death is just a door
that opens onto the next place
only it's locked
and the guard stands there
impassive
unarmed, but for an impressive moustache
expecting that you already know
how to get through
since this is something
you were supposed to figure out
in your lifetime.
You had years, after all.
What is your excuse
for arriving here
without the secret code?
How could you have wasted
all that time?
Everyone hopes the guard
will have mercy
and whisper the password to them
on the sly
until they see
he has no mouth.

Michelle Barker recently moved from Quebec to the Okanagan
region of B.C. Her poetry has appeared in such magazines as
Descant, *Room of One's Own*, *The Antigonish Review*, *The Mitre*,
Carte Blanche, *Cahoots*, *Cicada*, and *Taproot IV*. In 2002 she received
a National Magazine Award for personal journalism. Last year
her short fiction (fantasy) won honours at the Surrey
International Writers' Conference. Presently she is finishing work
on a young adult fantasy novel.

Ghosts, Monsters, Superheros and Scientists

EIGHT POEMS
by David Clink

The Monster at our Door

Monster
Monster and the woman
The monster at our door: the global threat of avian flu
Monster by moonlight
Monster/beauty: building the body of love
The monster from earth's end
Monster from out of time
The monster in the machine: magic, medicine, and the
    marvelous in the time of the scientific revolution
Monster of God: the man-eating predator in the jungles of
    history and the mind
The monster that ate Hollywood
The monster that is history: history, violence, and fictional
    writing in twentieth-century China
Monster: the autobiography of an L.A. gang member
The monstered self: narratives of death and performance in
    Latin American fiction
Monsters
Monsters and grotesques in medieval manuscripts
Monsters and other lovers
The Monsters emerge
Monsters with iron teeth.

⇥⟡—⟡⇤

The Monster Home

The monster home, when it was just a child, was found abandoned at the door of the Church of St. Francis. It smelled as if it were a part of the rain, had the taste of a withered old dog, and was rough as a wire brush growling in the January wind. Father Lachine said, "Grabbing it by the scruff of the neck was like embracing courage, listening to the color of urine."

I visited the home, and daydreamed that I entered all the rooms at once, and Nicky, who was born without a jaw, lit a candle in the drawing room. The covered furniture was stoic in those times of uncertainty. The unhappy caterpillars landscaped the backyard. Paint cans covered memories and recalled the time a wounded wolf came this way to rest its weary eyelids. The candlestick watched Nicholas and three other generations crawl back into the ground, as the houses on the hills bent under their own weight like tombstones.

A Ghost in the Window

The ghost
A ghost at noon
The ghost at the table: a novel
The ghost dance of 1889 among the Pai Indians of North-
    western Arizona
Ghost hunters: William James and the search for scientific
    proof of life after death
The ghost in the atom: a discussion of the mysteries of
    quantum physics
The ghost in the house: real mothers talk about maternal
    depression, raising children, and how they cope
A ghost in the window
The ghost of Peg-Leg Peter, and other stories of old New
    York
The Ghost or The woman wears the breeches. A comedy
    written in the year MDCXL
Ghost plane: the true story of the CIA torture program
The ghost talks
The ghost walks
The ghost writer
The ghostly lover

Ghosts at my back
Ghosts before breakfast
The ghosts call you poor
Ghosts from the nursery: tracing the roots of violence
Ghosts have warm hands: a memoir of the Great War 1916-1919
Ghosts in photographs: the extraordinary story of spirit photography
Ghosts of Rwanda
Ghosts of slavery: a literary archaeology of black women's lives
Ghosts returning
The ghosts that haunt me.

The Mad Scientist's Shopping List for Hosting a Barbecue

time machine, sauerkraut, Dijon, disembodied brains
Acme^{tm} mind scanner, hotdogs, hamburgers, buns, dials
tomatoes, olives, carrots, bread, butter, beakers, mayonnaise
pterodactyl food, potatoes, tin foil, corn, ketchup, relish
briquettes, lighter fluid, flame thrower, matches
mechanical man, salad, salad dressing, croutons
lightning rod, jumper cables, neck bolts
cooler for beer, pop, various organs
pie, Cool Whip, antigravity suit, shrimp ring, steak, steak sauce
Van de Graaff generator, cheese, crackers
paper plates, napkins, plastic cutlery and cups, more dials
Acme^{tm} death ray, three bags of ice

Collecting Bird Farts for Dummies

First you need a bottle with a lid, and quick hands. Next, place the open end of the bottle near the bird's bum, and collect the fart; then put the lid on quickly. Finally, label the contents: the name of the bird (Ptarmigan, Long-tailed Tit, Little Green Bee-eater); the date and time. Do not be concerned about the dignity of the bird. The bird will soon forget, its brain is so small that it can barely remember its own name, let alone the early worm it had for breakfast. Birds have no historical memory, otherwise they'd celebrate the anniversary of the first bird to stop being a dinosaur. People may think you're peculiar, collecting bird farts, but just tell them, "There are people who like red doors." And that should shut them up for a while.

Catman

The first superhero
was Catman.
He was half-cat, half-man.
Leaping tall sofas
in a single pounce
and spitting atomic furballs,
he fought crime
when he wasn't licking
himself or sleeping.
They built a Cat Signal
for when they needed help,
shone it against the clouds
hoping Catman would see it
and come to their aid.
It was ignored.

At the Temporal Café

At the Temporal Café each table has a sunset view, and time stands still for you at that particular point of evening when skylarks drink in the last remnants of sunshine, and your food arrives before you order it, before you have a chance to send it back.

At the Temporal Café you can revisit the past, so you can hang out with friends you haven't seen in years, parents who're passed away, relive days of triumph, when it was all up to you and you came through.

You can experience again that kiss that lingered on.

At the Temporal Café you can introduce your new boy-friend or girlfriend to people no longer around, and they'll say, "She seems a bit tall", or, "He talks a lot, don't ya think?" but they'll like your new friend, nonetheless, and be happy for you.

At the Temporal Café there is no closure, just the promise of one, and as you leave, the people you met there fade into ghosts.

Alien Spaceship

I stepped onto an alien spaceship,
the smooth surfaces, the walls
seeming never to end,
glowing like fireflies.
I stepped onto an alien spaceship,
the signs in an unfamiliar language
next to images that could mean
food, quantum reactor, or toilet.
I stepped onto an alien spaceship,
found a window in one wall
and saw thousands like me,
terrified, looking for a way out.

David Livingstone Clink is the board president of the Rowers Pub Reading Series in Toronto and the webmaster of poetrymachine.com. His poetry has appeared in *Chiaroscuro*, *The Dalhousie Review*, *The Fiddlehead*, *Grain Magazine*, *The Literary Review of Canada*, and in the anthologies *I.V. Lounge Nights*, *The 2008 Rhysling Anthology*, *Imagination in Action*, and *Distant Early Warnings*. He has appeared three times in *Analog*, twice in *Asimov's*, and twice in *On Spec*. He was co-publisher, along with Myna Wallin, of Believe Your Own Press, and the author of five poetry chapbooks. His poem, "Falling" was nominated for two awards: the Rhysling Award and the Aurora Award. His poem, "Copyright Notice 2525" placed second in the 2007 Asimov's Reader's Poll. His first book of poetry, *Eating Fruit Out of Season* was published by Tightrope Books in 2008. His second book of poetry, *Monster*, a collection of dark, strange, surreal and unusual poetry, will be published by Tightrope Books in the Fall of 2010.

Beautiful with Want

NINE POEMS

by Sandra Kasturi

Rampion

A young girl is like nothing
so much as a lettuce;
new, mouthwateringly crisp.

Your skin, so pale it's almost green—
that's why Mother has locked you up,
so suns and sons can do no damage.

Her hands wind in your hair
each morning up the tower,
its vertical path pointing heavenward.

She reads you fairy tales in one incessant moan
of strange vowel combinations. She never translates them.
And then she is gone.

You are left alone again
with the weight of your hair
a security blanket, a shroud.

One night you pry open the cupboard
where her indecipherable books are kept.
You don't even know what writing is.

But there are images in strange colors of beings
with straight bodies like yours, unseamed faces.

You touch your oval cheek. Imagine
it is mirrored on the page.

Her rage at your betrayal is a thing of legend, of myth.
She is the towering fury, shredding every story
into pieces smaller than your fingernails.

Then she's leaping out the window
at the end of your braid, the weight of her
nearly breaking your neck.

Later, you lay fragments of fairy tales on your skin,
paler than the pages. Water runs from your eyes
and your chest winds as tight as Swiss clockwork.

You take your sharpest tool, a soft gold dinner fork
to your hair, but the white-blonde strands just coil
about your feet like fat, malcontented serpents.

One night, after weeks of giddy solitude,
down to your last sup and last cup—
a new voice at the base of the tower.

It is a being like you, but larger, its skin darker,
the sounds it makes, deeper. He climbs up your hair,
just like Mother. His touch, you learn later, rougher.

He watches you and speaks. Strange noises, his voice hard
with consonants. You listen for her voice,
but it is gone from your head.

You put your hand over his open mouth,
feel the ignition of warm breath on your palm.
Your hand moves from his mouth to the iron at his belt.

The knife is sharp and cuts your finger with joy.
You draw a curl from your temple
across its edge, pallor floating free to the floor.

You run to the window. Weightless.

Invisible Train

The steam train chuffs through the night,
ghosting over rails made gleaming
by the alien light of distant stars,
the moon's round paleness.

The specters of cattle low in the rattling cars,
their sounds too faint to be heard
by anyone except perhaps other spirits,
passengers of cars crashed long ago.

Ghosts can no longer have collisions—
their interactions in this world
fraught with molecular dissonance,
they loiter at crossroads, railway crossings.

Unseen hands pick up invisible hymnals
in the chilly churches that dot the towns
along train lines clitter-clattering
their way over the turning world.

The steam train pauses in each place,
rests its length as ethereal passengers
embark and disembark: cattle and coal,
children, soldiers back from emptied wars;

Undelivered packages in faded paper,
fading even further into spectral antiquity,
steamer trunks filled with bodies or books,
husbands, wives, parakeets and prams—

All traveling anywhere and nowhere,
stopping to sing in ghostly choirs,
grazing on grass long gone into the otherworld,
resending lost telegrams, rekindling ashes.

The infinite train hums on its rails,
clings to the earth, carrying with it
the longing dead, their yearning eyes—
a silvered rotoscope flash, unseen, gone.

Moon & Muchness

My moonsicle sour-candy-pocked moon!
I have licked and loved you to a dim luster,
the hollow-smooth swell of an orchestral bassoon,
a worthy glow that can only be mustered
by the administrations of my spectral
tongue. Let us lap up the song-elevated
spheres!—the phases and phrases of their kestrel
migrations, the meandering paths of crenellated
stars. Let us tower and fall to crumbled-
cake battlements, forge to life from god-dusted bellows,
and spoon-feed the sun in all his pie-humbled
runcible wit—let us be beam-struck bedfellows.
We can swallow the universe in its entirety,
its star-spackled, moon-freckled boundless absurdity.

Big Bee Story

I have a bee in my shoe, its buzzing
erratically loud down by my heel,
its plush body increasingly fuzzing
against my sock, its yellow-striped keel
clearly unmoored, or perhaps lost at sea,
a sort of dirigibly-fat, apian
ghost ship, damned for whatever sins bees
commit, a veritable Flying Dutchman,
a bumbleship, doomed to sail far from hive
and home, mysteriously pulled into orbit
around my ankle, where it now thrives
in its existence, its bee-busy gambit,
just as our planets elliptically do—
perhaps the sun grows weary of us, too.

The Medusa Quintet

(i)

Was I daydreaming by the seaside
when the gods gave my sisters everything,
gave them the gift of forever?

I know you worried, mother.
That night you pressed my face into warm clay.
"It's a life mask," you said. We hang it
on the wall next to the Blue Willow plates
from your grandmother. I notice you leave
room to hang something else. Me.
My death mask. One or the other.

My sisters snicker behind
their perfect immortal hands.

(ii)

It's Tuesday
and I've angered the goddess.

She tears me in two
and stitches me back up.
The new me, hair writhing
and a face to stop a bus.

My sisters say I don't look any different.
They go back to their mirrors.

(iii)

I'm not allowed out after the unfortunate
incident with the neighbors.

There's mother again, afraid for my life,
our lives. If only I could be married off
to some handicapped princeling,
someone safe. Poor blind Oedipus.
He would have been perfect.

(iv)

News has arrived from the Oracle.
A hero with winged feet en route,
his face bright as a sword.

The sisters are aghast, can't believe
anyone would have me.

But in my own stories,
I'm the desired one, the youngest princess,
the one who breaks the spell, stops
the wolf, saves everyone.

(v)

Mother readies my dowry;
the snakes braid themselves
into an elaborate headdress.
I am beautiful with want.

A Curse for Alice

To bed, to bed with your beautiful head,
the small of your back, the fall of your hair;
let the lull of the stars and the lead
foot of sleep, iron the creases in your fair-
weather face, your twirling carnival heart.
The stars! The stars, big and Van Gogh round,
spinning like teacups at the Queen of Tarts
Ball, where cards and angels are thrown to the ground.
Let even your swords fall or be swallowed
by themselves, if sword-swallowers remain
unavailable. Let your candle-tallowed
fortunes go to smoke in spiraling refrain.
Off with your head, off with your beautiful beauty,
your darling-drained, echoing, star-hollowed empty.

Wild Boars in Berlin

Thousands of wild, tusked ancestors of domestic pigs
have discovered the charms of urban living in
Germany's capital city. Some humans are happy
to coexist, while others see the boars as a pest
that should be eliminated.
"In Berlin's Boar War, Some Side With the Hogs,"
by Marcus Walker, Wall Street Journal, 12/16/2008

     dapplesides whiskersnout wild in the flower
shop five fat little boarlets running rampant
through the hybrid teas Double Delight
and fragrant Floribunda Sexy Rexy
     scattering pink petals as sows squeal
bristleback daddyboars grunt toughguy
tones lumbering lost into Alexanderplatz
grinding up garden laburnum and laurel
     tabloids telling of pigs needing police
protection against lean hunters licensed
to target flank and hock into sniperscope
stalemate against enviropig enthusiasts
     tusked ancestor of Babe Wilbur Hen-Wen
sheepshifters spelling champions oracular
prognosticators famous literary personages
in pigform
     overshadowed now by vigorous
tiptapping of unruly hooves on pavement
Circe-called four-footed wriggling
rooting reversing that natural order
of pigs vs. people
     freeing fenced farm
brethren of bacon porkchop hambone fears
in an untamed unashamed riotous rout
through the streaming streets
     of ballyhooed boar-ridden Berlin.

Bluebeard's Grandmother

If you must marry at all, my dear,
marry the handsome, the honey-tongued,
the man of wealth, of dead-bolted
double-locked rooms; marry the tiger,
the wolf in the suitor-suit, the giver
of unblemished keys, of pearlescent
pure eggs into your hands,
so clean, so pretty! Don't you worry,
my dear. My grandson will put red
onto those cheeks.

Talking with the Dead

There is no answer, no solace from the dead;
Your teeming anguish is nothing to them
But the roar and roil of earthly dreads
That carry the memory-ticks of blame,
The bombs of rage and need. The dead deny
These arrows, deflect them back toward you;
Pale presences that refuse your outcries,
Your farewells, turn away from every new
Gash their visitations open up. But hush
Yourself to bed—lay down between the sheets
Of your thready sorrow; let the tireless push
And pulse of sleep wash you clear of such defeats.
Though the dead may still not answer you in dreams,
Their manifest will be naught but sighs and seems.

Sandra Kasturi is an award-winning writer, publisher and
editor. She is the poetry editor of *ChiZine* and co-publisher of
ChiZine Publications. Sandra's work has appeared in numerous
magazines and anthologies, including many of the *Tesseracts*
volumes. She is a founding member of the infamous Algonquin
Square Table poetry workshop as well as part of the MUSE
Cooperative. She managed to snag an introduction from Neil
Gaiman for her first full-length poetry collection, *The Animal
Bridegroom* (2007). Sandra is currently working on two novels:
Medusa Gorgon, Lady Detective, and a steampunk epic.

One Nation Under Gods

Jerome Stueart

On every channel, the nightly news tracked Lady Liberty as she walked whisper soft across America, in case you wanted to see her yourself. She didn't always walk through Kentucky. She tried to cover every state of the country in a year. So if you were poor or tired or the huddled masses, you could look up from the street and see her gray body passing overhead, see her torch light up your face and find yourself taken up in her skirts as she passed. It was the best thing for the poor, they said.

My family would gather on the porch with our binoculars when she passed once a year. We couldn't stay outside to see her pass directly overhead; looking up, letting the light fall on you—that would pull you in, so you had to be hidden. But she was beautiful to see on the horizon—sometimes just her crown, moving like a slow train across the land. Then later, we would see her head with her torch held low below the horizon, blazing in a constant stream of orange, combing the streets.

Her feet never crushed anything, her skirts never tossed cars or knocked down buildings, she just walked and searched, looking and looking like a mother for her children, and then— I saw this on TV—she disappeared at the first morning's light and appeared back on her base on Liberty Island. I think she was my favorite of the gods, maybe because she was consistent and regular, and the rest of them we didn't see up close and personal. And we knew, whatever happened to our family that Lady Liberty could take care of us, though nobody really knew what life was like once you were taken up.

"Are you sure people don't get killed?" Celia asked.

She didn't know History very well, and this was the biggest problem in her life.

And now it was our problem too.

⇥⟜⟝ ⟝ ⟞⟜⇥

We didn't understand how Celia could grow up and hear all the stories of the gods and not remember them. Mom and Dad wouldn't let us have dessert without first telling a story from the big leather-covered *One Nation Under Gods*. Dad read them in a voice he saved for stories that "would possibly save your life." I loved all our stories, even though a few of them—like stories about the brothers, Strike and Patriot—would make my dad get a crack in his voice, and some—like the Union and Revolution story—well, he just couldn't read them all the way through. He had a soft spot for Union, always thought he'd been betrayed when Revolution left him for someone in France. "She'd sleep with anyone who asked," he said sometimes, and then catch himself, and tell us not to mock the gods, ever. You never knew who might be listening.

Well, it wasn't Celia. Celia sat staring ahead, thinking about things I didn't know. She wasn't really hearing the stories when she watched Dad tell them. It wasn't a problem until she started failing the eighth grade.

⊶⊷ ⊰ ⊱ — ⊱ ⊰ ⊶⊷

Until the eighth grade, she'd passed History with a D, just skating by, not even able to fill out the Families of Gods Charts. She couldn't name all their first generation children—she almost always missed Independence, though I thought he was the easiest to remember, since he never got married. It was just charts and the simple stories until eighth grade and then you had to really know how the gods worked with Americans to shape our country—so many more events than I had to learn in the sixth grade. In eighth grade, you have what happened when Revolution left, the Declaration of Independence, the Constitution—which you have to know by *heart*—and the names of all the Presidents and all the Reginas.

At the end of Eighth Grade you had to pass the Test to see if you got into high school or whether you would serve the country as a Pizza Hut or a Piggly Wiggly, or something useful.

These are the "transformed" people I personally knew: Mike, a bridge who'd been a good soccer player; Donny, a 7-11 that once let me borrow his bike, and the Drive-In Theater on Bronson Street who was this beautiful girl who loved to watch movies with Celia. She became a Drive-In last year. I knew their families had tried hard to get them to pass the Test, but when they didn't, they got changed.

"Aren't you afraid?" I asked Celia.

"Afraid of becoming something else? No," she said. "I'm more afraid of not becoming anything, Danny."

She had her Preference List already filled out. Every kid had to make one before they took the Test, but Celia had been thinking of hers for a while.

"I want to be a Cloth Store," she said. "We don't have any good ones in town, really. I think if Mom ran the shop, we'd have more money coming in. And other people who make quilts would have a decent place to find material. I've actually planned pretty good for this."

"But why not just study harder?"

She looked at me, squinting. "You don't think I have been? It's hard. I don't know how to put it all together. I'm not going to make it." She started to cry, then she looked out the window until she stopped it—she could make an angry face that would freeze all the tears. She showed me her list. "I'm thinking practically."

Some kids put down on their Preference List that they wanted to become missiles, but only the really poor kids got to be missiles. I don't think it was fair but Mom and Dad told us that missiles didn't last long. And restaurants allowed parents to keep their kids around longer, even if they were ovens and tables and salad bars. I thought being a Triton 2 missile would have been much cooler—shoot yourself over the ocean and land in someone's back yard and explode.

"What's the point of being a missile?" Celia asked me.

She didn't understand the glory of exploding. Every real boy wanted to blow something up. I showed her by falling backwards onto her bed and told her that she was really lame. Her stuffed tigers and bears fell on my face.

She sat down beside me on her bed.

Her room was quieter than mine.

I didn't want her to be a Cloth Store, so I threw a stuffed bear at her face.

⇥⇠◃▱ — ▱▹⇢⇤

In the summer, we would bus downtown together to the library or to the movies, or to the pool, and we would sometimes eat in the old-fashioned soda shop, My Little Girl, that used to be Courtney Simmons. "Her cherry phosphates taste the best," Celia would say. And maybe they did, but I think it was because we'd known Courtney. Not that well—but when you know someone, and they get changed, it makes you attached to the place. I think the Chamber of Commerce knew this.

I only remembered that Courtney had been in love a lot, with every boy, whether he knew or not, and she used to hang out at the mall. She liked to watch people. Now she was a pretty popular soda shop, only one street from Main. My Little Girl had bright red walls and white tiled floors, and we sat on the silver stools and talked to Courtney's dad, Al. He believed Courtney still talked to him.

"She chooses the songs on the jukebox," he'd say to everyone. "And if you listen, she'll have a song for you."

It was true that sometimes the jukebox did not pick the songs you picked out when you put your fifty cents in. And sometimes, when it was on random, she often went back to Mr. Mister, *Take these broken wings, and learn to fly again and learn to live so free*.

When she first was changed, the jukebox was stocked with fifties music. But she refused to play the songs from the fifties, and her dad, figuring out that she might prefer the eighties and nineties songs, stocked it full of her music. "She plays it all day long now."

My sister would look at me sometimes, and then look at the embossed ceiling, "So, see, she's still here. She's turned the place into her. It sounds like her."

She said that to make me feel better. Like I wouldn't miss her if she were a cloth store.

"I think if you asked her, she'd rather be human," I said.

She looked at me, "You say that like she had a choice."

Oh there were choices. Most of them were illegal. You heard about them all the time at school. There were ways to escape, car pools, safe houses, train cars that had secret doors. Sometimes, if you were rich, you could afford the "summer trip to Europe," they called it. You just never came back. Maybe you became European. Parents were in on it. They would risk never seeing their kid again to keep him from being changed.

But it was a risk. There were stories of kids being caught too. Trains being boarded by Truants. Kids going to jail. Being changed into other things: dumpsters, public restrooms, city buses, sewage plants.

"Yuck," the kids in my class would say. "That's cruel!" And they would laugh.

But it made us learn. It made us study. It made us scared. And now, it made me scared for Celia.

Mom and Dad were trying to play this legal. They hired a recent graduate as a tutor, someone with a serious reputation, who had references for bringing many eighth graders through the Test.

Holly stood over six-foot tall and stooped when she talked to people. She had red hair but dressed like a business executive. "You have to think of it like friends you know. History is just the story of different people you know. Like your mom or your dad or any of your friends. You have friends?"

"I have friends. I'm not weird."

Actually, Celia was kind of a loner. She read craft books. She knew some science. She spent weeknights sewing. She made beautiful things—mostly quilts. But she didn't exactly make friends. She considered what other eighth graders did boring and irrelevant. It didn't help, either, that Mom and Dad moved us a lot. We lived in Missouri, in Kansas, and in Illinois. Dad was a furniture maker. Mostly dining room tables and chairs. We had a small house, but a very nice kitchen table.

Holly and Celia sat at this table, going over Holly's notecards.

"These are your new best friends," Holly said, spreading them out.

I loved Holly's cards. She had pictures of the gods that I'd never seen published. I wanted my own set. I was hoping that she'd leave them when she fixed Celia up, but I figured these might be the "magic" that transformed slower kids into geniuses. So, fat chance that I'd be pinning that smiling Patriot card on my wall.

Holly talked about the gods as if they were just like us. "Guess what I saw Independence doing yesterday?" which at first, sounded like sacrilege to me. She talked about them as if she'd seen them buying clothes at Sears. "He was talking to a bunch of guys in a tavern—that's a bar. And he was talking about breaking away from England! I thought I would just die," she slapped her hand on the table. She seemed so caught up in it. As if it were happening to her, as if these were her memories. "He bought them all dinner and it came to $17.76. Remember that. The bill was $17.76."

I wanted to eat dinner with Independence. I wanted them to come on the soccer field with me. Or chase me through the park. I wanted them to talk to mostly. I sat and listened to Holly, wishing that her stories were true. "And then Patriot told me a secret," she said. Oh, *gods* I wanted to know his secrets.

Celia must not have because she forgot them just as soon as Holly left.

"It's like I've gone to a party and everyone has introduced themselves," she told me, picking up a quilt she was making, showing fleet foxes darting into a cornfield. "I can't remember what anyone said. I'm getting them all mixed up."

Lessons with Holly lasted only two months. After that, it was as if everyone in the family knew a history that would be written on those cards—a history Celia was writing even then.

⇢➤◆ ⊰ — ⊱ ➤◆⇠

The President of the Chamber of Commerce came and spoke one day at School Assembly, and he had a map of the city up on a screen. Everyone got to attend—from the sixth through the eighth grades. He showed the eighth graders all the best pieces of business real estate, which could go to anyone at a huge discount if they chose them now. He talked about what the city needed, how students could help the city grow by investing in the future. He wasn't as much counting on them failing, he said, as much as offering them the best of the available options.

Did you want to be a park? They'd put your picture up in brass.

Did anyone consider a trolley system? An interpretative center?

"Businesses are not the only thing you can be. Non-profits also benefit our city; beautification shouldn't be overlooked. Even your own school needs repair," he said smiling, opening his arms wide, as if to draw them all in.

"Paducah Chamber of Commerce welcomes you. To us, you are never a failure."

⇢➤◆ ⊰ — ⊱ ➤◆⇠

In desperation, we tried new things for Celia. Mom and I made a giant chart on her bedroom wall where we put up butcher paper until it covered the blue-sky wallpaper. She took down all her pictures, working ahead of us pulling out the nails while Mom and I put the paper up with sticky tacky. Then we just started charting a timeline. I drew the long black line around the room and she put all the historical events on top and all the god events on the bottom of the timeline so Celia could see how they were related. "Because god stories happen while history is going on. That's what makes America different," she said. Celia took notes sitting on her bed while Mom lectured and I drew key words Mom and Dad had already written down.

When that was finished, we drew pictures of all the gods based on the pictures in the encyclopedia, and some I saw off of Holly's cards. Mom said there wouldn't be any part of the Test to identify pictures, but that the images were for Celia. She could remember them better if they were pictures. "She zones when people are talking," I told Mom in front of Celia.

"I don't zone," she said. "I'm thinking."

"You're not thinking about gods," I said.

"I think about the gods a lot. I just don't think about their entire life stories. I don't know why we're tested on this. I mean, history is what happened, but it isn't what's going on now. What does knowing that Congress was turned into a bunch of monkeys for a day really have to do with my life?"

Mom stopped writing. She was writing on Lewis and Clark. "Honey," she turned to Celia. "Congress was turned into monkeys because they filibustered for three weeks—the country nearly shut down. They got turned into monkeys as Democracy's punishment on them, and they learned about being more bipartisan, about working together. The gods change you so you learn." She kneeled down beside Celia. "If you don't pass this test, you'll be changed just like Congress—except you won't get changed back at the end of the day. Whether or not you like what you have to learn, this is the way it works. We get to make some of the rules, and that's more than anyone else has ever gotten to do with their gods. The least we can do is learn history."

"Why can't we make a rule that middle schoolers don't have to become buildings and things when they don't pass a silly test? Why can't we save the lives of children?"

You could tell this was as hard on Mom as it was Celia. Her eyes got red around the edges. "I'm trying to save the life of a child, Child. What exactly are *you* doing?"

Mom walked Celia around the room and showed her all of America's history. Then Mom started talking about one part of history and Celia had to run over and point to where it was on the timeline. It wasn't hard—Mom had written in all the stories, but it made Celia have to know about where the story happened to get there before Mom finished telling the story.

"The gods created the City of Friends and Walt Whitman becomes our first Friends ambassador." Celia ran over to the spot on the wall just before the turn of the 20th Century.

"The gods help the Founding Fathers write the Constitution and the Great Promise." Celia ran to the end of the timeline, but

I pointed the other way, and she changed direction and stood in front of 1789.

"When Watergate happened, this was the first time that an entire Administration flew into the air above the capitol to meet the gods in the Special Court." Celia ran to the end of the 1960s.

"Revolution leaves Union, walks across the Atlantic and marries Fraternité. The French Revolution begins." Celia ran back to the 1800s and scanned the wall. Oh, back farther than the Louisiana Purchase, I thought. Way before Manifest was born and pushed us all westward with the Energizing Fire. "The French Revolution," Mom hinted, "was right after our revolution."

Celia walked to the 1780s again and stood in front of the "Day Revolution Left."

We placed the cards with the pictures of the gods on the floor.

"Pick up the picture of the God who Defends the Country." Celia picked up Patriot. Good.

"Pick up the picture of the God who is America's offense." Often known as the Offensive God, I thought. Celia knew these easy. She picked up Strike's picture.

"Pick up their brother, the one who protects us from ourselves." She looked around the pictures. I was sitting on her bed watching, because Mom said this would be great training for me, and because I wanted to help Celia win, and I saw something different.

Celia had all the gods at her feet. Arranged around her, they just stared up at Celia and I thought, wow, Celia is like a god looking down on the gods. Her blonde hair was pulled back in a pony tail and every time she bent down to pick up a god, she got more excited, as if she knew she was close. She picked up Freedom because he protects us from ourselves. And Freedom's wife, Liberty, the gift France gave us to thank us for Revolution, was the next card, and then one by one, Celia picked up every god in her hand like a giant book and held it close to her and screamed for joy.

But that wasn't it. Then she had to place all their names on a Family chart Mom papered across the Dining Room. It was just like the Test, she said. "You're going to have to know who married whom and which children they had."

The toughest was Union because he kept changing not only his gender but had a lot of partners, some of them were kidnapped or forced. Mom just put five blanks up next to his name, but I already remembered two more.

Mom and I made up songs for Celia too. We put American History to music, singing about the Constitution, the Great Depression, the Emancipation Proclamation—and we did it to The Beatles.

It's a dirty story about a dirty man and his cheating wife never understands, and it's based on a story by a man named Lear, and I need a job 'cause I'm living in the Great Depression! Great Depression!

Listen. Do you want to know the secret? It's about the Civil War, whoa, oh, oh. Closer. Let me whisper in your ear. Several reasons are so clear, whoa, oh, oh.

Celia listened to them all night long on an endless loop on her CD player. I heard them when I turned out the lights in my room. Sometimes my voice, sometimes mom's, about this war, about famous people, about parts of our history everyone thinks is important—first inventions, first discoveries, first people who did this or that.

Mom says I'm going to know seventh grade history before I get through the sixth grade. Sometimes she says this around Celia. Not on purpose.

⊷⊶ ⊷ ⊶⊷

All night long I dreamed about Presidents walking around in my room. They pulled up a chair and told me about their accomplishments, and I was interviewing them to see if I should let them into my clubhouse.

"With Emancipation's help, I wrote the law that would free the slaves," President Lincoln said.

I asked him, "Is this *enough* to get into our clubhouse?"

"I lived in a very cool cabin," he said, and so I let him in.

I remember the Wright Brothers were in my room with their noisy propellers. "Do you want a ride?" they asked. And I thought, heck yeah, they would definitely be in my clubhouse.

Lewis and Clark came out of my closet, just opened up the door and Sacajawea led them towards my bed. Clark must have already passed through our hometown Paducah, Kentucky, because he was already a dog. Chief Paduke had asked the Great Spirit to stop them from moving Paduke off his land, and this was the Great Spirit's answer. Clark was a golden retriever with a really whiny voice.

He jumped up on the bed with me and licked my face and I wrestled him until he promised me sailing rights up the Mississippi. "Okay, you can come into the clubhouse too."

Lincoln, Orville, Wilbur, Lewis and Clark led me to stand at Celia's door and we listened to their stories coming through the door.

"Those stories—they're about us," they said.

But I could only hear the names Democracy, America, Independence, Freedom. We didn't have many stories where the gods weren't doing something.

"We were great!" they said. I wondered if they were deluded.

We all sat down by Celia's door and listened to them and when I woke up I was alone and I walked back into my room and got into my bed, and Clark wasn't there either, and I wished I had him back most of all—a talking dog would have been nice. I was really jealous of Merriwether Lewis. We had a rottweiler named Toby in the backyard. He didn't say a thing.

Celia woke up in the morning and couldn't recall anything, no matter how much Mom and Dad quizzed her. At one point they considered she might be doing this on purpose. They cut her allowance. They cut out desserts.

"You're not trying," Mom would say, trying not to scream. "You're not *dumb*. I know that."

And all Celia could say, "I'm not dumb. I'm not dumb."

"Celia, honey," and she would kneel, and wipe Celia's tears back, roughly, "this is your *life*."

⸺⸺

One Saturday, in March, when the Test was two weeks away, the Regina Proximas, our local representative, came to visit our family. I answered the door when she knocked her staff on it, a staff with the giant Twister Face on it. Every Regina had the same staff but the Regina Primoris had one whose faces swiveled from the Conservative to the Moderate to the Liberal faces depending on the ruling of the gods. While she was in our house I kept thinking the marble faces would turn—turn and look at me—but hers didn't.

"Mr. And Mrs. Woodhouse, I'm here to see about Celia."

All the Reginas wear flowing robes of the same green Lady Liberty is made of. So sometimes it's easy to think that Liberty is walking around in the daytime if they come by, but normally the Reginas stay at the Courthouse, helping turn the criminals into other things, or sometimes just making them disappear.

This one was old like my grandmother but thin and walked like a President.

Her mountain lion came through the door too. She walked through our house looking for a place to curl up. Celia placed a pillow on the floor and the mountain lion laid down peacefully. To tell you the truth, I liked the mountain lion most of all. I watched her lick her paws.

"You may pet Sybil, and you may sit near her if she lets you."

I walked towards this great cat, scared and brave at the same time. "Hello, Sybil." I had my palm out, trying to make friends with her, but I kept my eyes on *her* eyes and those teeth.

Sybil looked at me and shook her head, so I went to sit back on the couch with Mom and Dad.

The Regina talked with Celia. Celia looked tall sitting in the chair.

"I've come to talk to you, Celia, about the Test that's coming up." She talked formally, as if it were difficult to talk to Celia, instead of a room full of people. She glanced down at a small notebook in her hand. "With your current grade in History, no doubt you know how important to your *very life* this test is. Scores in Paducah have been very worrisome as of late. We had forty-seven students fail the Test last year, as you know. Paducah was way below the national average for a city our size."

Here she closed her eyes, and maybe the whole city was on her mind. I wondered if she were thinking, too, about Mike, the bridge. I was.

"The test is nothing to be taken lightly. The Chamber of Commerce would have you believe that you are doing the city a favor, but let me tell you as your Regina, that one new business does not equal a human life. I do not know as a household," and here she looked at me and Mom and Dad, "where you stand on your obedience and worship to the gods. That is not my place to decide; I am merely the representation of the gods in Paducah, and your representation at the Temple services. I am a go-between. And in times like these, I feel the need more than ever to be a go-between," and she turned back to Celia. "I cannot change the law. I can only encourage you to follow the law in so far as you want to remain human." She looked at all of us one at a time. "In so far as you remain human, you have the benefits of the law. So, therefore, do everything, *everything* in your power to remain human. In this way I serve you best, Celia." She picked up the cup of tea Mom had served her and sipped. "The question then falls to you: will you do everything in your power to help me?"

Celia nodded. "Yes," she said. "I've done my best to learn History, Regina."

And here the Regina smiled, nodding.

Celia looked at her hands, thinking. "But what if—what if a person doesn't have the ability, the natural ability, to remember facts?" She looked at the Regina now. "Would that person remain a person?"

The Regina breathed in. Sybil stirred on the pillow.

"As you know, individuals who were considered unable to pass the test were removed from schools in the first grade. Everyone left in school after that is considered of at least average intelligence, and therefore responsible under the law for the Test."

Celia nodded. "But, some people are capable of doing many things, and they are still of at least average intelligence, but they can't recite facts. They get stories mixed up. Shouldn't there be a program in place for students who are smart in other areas but not so good with History?"

The Regina placed her cup on the table. "Tell me, child, what *areas* are you smart in?"

We stopped for a moment, our heartbeats in rhythm.

Celia stood up and walked to our family quilt hanging on the wall opposite the couch. It was me and Celia flying in the sky above Mom and Dad. Everyone's arms were up, as if our parents had thrown us into the air so we could fly. I was wearing an orange T-shirt, but I don't really own one. Celia said it balanced out the colors. It could cover a whole bed, but instead it covered our whole wall.

"I made this," Celia said. "I designed the pattern, I found the cloth, I sewed it together myself."

The Regina stood up, her robes rustling, her eyes never leaving the quilt. She walked towards it and rubbed her hands across it. "Yes," she nodded. "Yes, this is very nice work, Celia." But she said nothing else.

Celia asked, "May I bring something here to show you?"

The Regina said, "I will follow you."

We all stood up. We were beginning to hope.

Celia led us into my parents' room. She smoothed out the quilt on their bed. It was my mom and dad and their bodies were long and they were wrapped around each other, my dad's whole body was like a quilt around my mom. And they looked at each other on the quilt like they were in love.

"And this one, too?" the Regina asked, walking to the edge of the bed.

Celia nodded. "Touch it," she said.

The Regina touched it. "That's," she paused. "I've never felt cloth that soft. It's cotton, isn't it?"

"It's revived cotton, rubbed three times, and I do it by hand, because I don't like the material you find in the stores." She pointed to the rendition of our mother's hair. "I dye my own cloth. You won't see that red in a store. It's the exact color of my mother's hair."

The Regina turned around and looked at my mom, as if she were just making sure.

"If you hold it up to her, they'll match perfectly," Celia said, "and I matched this knowing it would be washed."

She led us into my room, where I think the Regina was very impressed with me. She looked at all the pictures I had on the wall—all the posters of the gods saving us. I was kind of em- barrassed, to tell you the truth—like I was showing up my sis- ter, but Celia walked us in here. Not me.

On my bed was the best of Celia's quilts: Patriot standing beside me as we protected Our Country. His hand was on my shoulder, his other hand snapped a set of arrows. My hand gripped an olive branch. My foot stood on a soccer ball. The gods of other countries quivered and were blinded by our mag- nificence on the border around the quilt.

After a long pause, the Regina said, "Very dramatic."

"I know," I beamed.

Finally we went to Celia's room where she showed the Regina the sewing machine.

"It's a very nice sewing machine," the Regina said.

"I bought it myself with money I made from babysitting." She turned to the Regina. "I worked hard to learn how to make these quilts. But I can't memorize facts. I can't. I've tried and we've all tried. And I think there should be another way to honor the talents of kids who can't take tests. And a way to save their lives, Regina."

The Regina looked very carefully at Celia, and around the room where we had run the butcher paper around the walls, where all the stories of the gods were, and I thought she was go- ing to say that Celia didn't have to take the test. Dad held Mom as if they believed it too. Belief was the strongest thing in the world. If we didn't believe in the gods, they would disappear, which was why the Great Spirit wasn't as powerful anymore and Bison didn't ride the prairies with his herd nowadays. It was our one power, I knew it, and I thought if we believed hard enough that Celia would be spared, that she would be spared, so I believed. I prayed to Patriot and Democracy and Freedom and Justice. Even though the Reginas are there for us to pray for us, I still put my two cents in when I heard how Celia tried to convince the Regina. I'd never heard of a Regina ever stopping a student from taking the Test, especially one who was failing History. Maybe Science, 'cause not everyone's good in science, but History was different.

The Regina took Celia's hand and she led her to the wall where all of American Time divided up in front of them. "Celia, why do we learn about history? Why is it important?"

Celia didn't answer right away. "It's important to know the stories."

"*Why* is it important, Celia?"

Celia looked towards the window and I could see what she did with her face. She turned back to the Regina. "We have to know what happened to know who we are now."

The Regina paused. "That's part of it. What else?"

Celia stared at the wall and I wished all the people in history could have told her the secret of History, underneath the black lines of charts, in between the names, because sometimes I didn't know either. I just knew how to make the charts.

The Regina breathed in and said, "They want you to remember who they are."

"But I know who they are," Celia said. "They're the gods. Everyone knows them."

"You know *of* them, Celia. But you have to know what they have done for more than two hundred years. It's important that everyone who grows up in the country knows the history of the way things have been run, everyone down to the baker, the police officer, the garbage collector, even the quilters. All those people have one thing in common: they know their history, their gods, and this makes them careful, smart, and they don't get into trouble. People who don't know their history might hurt an entire city—," she stopped. "Did you ever hear about the levees of Caruthersville, Missouri?"

Celia shook her head.

"There was a man there. He was running for mayor. He campaigned on a platform of innovation and independence.

He wanted to overthrow the gods, especially the gods of the Mississippi—which ruled his city and the surrounding land. The Mississippi heard this, and overran its banks, crushed the levees, flooded the town, and the gods had to step in and make things right. They turned everyone who voted for that man into a flood wall. They lay toe to head around the city, like great statues on their sides, holding back the Mississippi, lest she get upset again.

"As he promised, he protects the city from her," the Regina said, with only a hint of irony in her voice. "But so do all the people he convinced. People who didn't respect the gods—both those gods who live with them and those who protect them. If people don't know their History, they threaten everyone around them."

Celia nodded. "But the river—the river was really at fault, wasn't she?"

The Regina's face hardened. "Do you know why the Regency was created, Celia?"

She was quick. "To serve mankind and to serve the gods."

"Yes, but even more to save people from their own igno-rance." She became resolved and tired, her eyes looking upwards, as if she'd just played hours on the soccer field and someone asked her to walk to the car. "Someone must help each person know and understand the laws and those that govern them. That's why we are here, the Regency, from the Regina Primoris—may the gods listen to her—to every Regina under her responsibility, including me. I have to help people know History, the law, the way to work with the godhead." She traced her fingers along America's timeline. "These are the gods, this *collection* of events, the *scenes*, the *moments* all strung together—because you can't define them any other way. They are beyond our comprehension, except through their deeds. If I didn't know America, could I tell you what she might say if your parents tried to disobey her, if they tried to hide you."

I looked at Mom and Dad. They would never try and skirt the law, I knew. Dad carved the names of the gods in all his tables.

Mom put her face against Dad's shoulder.

The Regina continued, "I know her because I know what she's done in the past. Even the best craftsperson can wander into trouble if they don't know their history. We want the gods to care about us—each one of us in this land of thirty million people. To do that we have to show that we care about them."

"I care about them, but I don't know the dates of their...their *deeds*." Celia flung her arms out. "I want them to care about me, too."

The Regina squinted and her mouth got firm. "You want them to care about *you*. Celia, what are you doing for them? They ask only that we know them. That we respect and love them. They've already done so much. You live in a country where the gods sacrificed ultimate power to share it with the people they should have ruled absolutely. Yet you don't want to know who they are and what they did." She blinked with effort. "When was your brother born?"

Celia looked at me. "June third—but that's not the same—"

"It should be. These are their lives. We honor them by remembering their histories and our history is intertwined with theirs."

"I'm doing my best....can't they honor my *best*?" Celia looked around the room. "What if I did a set of quilts to honor the gods—quilts of their stories? Wouldn't that be enough?"

That was a *great* idea, I thought.

The Regina looked as if she were thinking about it. She suddenly pulled Celia close to her, hugged her and looked down over her back. "The test is the test. It is standardized across the country for *every* child. Not all the quilts in the world can help you pass that test. I can't help you pass that test. I'm confident, though, that the study you have done will propel you forward into the future."

Sybil loped into the room, her tail swishing opposite of her head as she looked back and forth at everyone. She came walking straight towards me. She put her face close to mine and smelled the breath coming out of my nose. She said to me, *And you will walk bravely into that new world fearing no one.*

⋙⋘ — ⋙⋘

Later that night, in my dreams, every Regina Primoris in history crowded into my room. They all had the same green gowns, the same staffs and they looked at my posters of gods and my postcard collection of Liberty as she passed through different cities (Liberty ducking under the St. Louis Arch was my favorite.) They went through my bookshelves reading my book titles aloud: *Strike Goes to Afghanistan, Theodore Roosevelt and the Capture of the Philippines, How the Gods Appreciate You, Field Guide to the Kentucky Gods of Rivers and Streams.* Two of them played with my action figures, flying Strike through the air on a stretch of fire, making Patriot grow into a giant. I counted 26 of them.

I sat up and went to the first one. It was Regina Primoris Riessen from the Eisenhower years. I remembered her nose and her tiny glasses. I said to her, "You don't need to come in here. You need to be in Celia's room. Come with me."

I took them all into the hallway and I tried to open Celia's door. The knob turned but the door didn't come open. The Reginas lined up single file in the hallway, waiting for me to get the door open. I turned and pushed and Celia's door. It didn't have a lock. Why was it locked? It couldn't have a lock. It *couldn't* be locked.

And it opened. I waved all the Reginas from all of history into Celia's room. And I saw General Lee and General Grant riding from the bathroom on horseback and I guided them into Celia's room. I did this with anyone I could. "She needs you more than I do. Talk to her."

But Celia kept on sleeping and we could hear the CD singing about Reginas, *She believes you, yeah, yeah, yeah, Represents you, yeah, yeah, yeah, Understands you, yeah yeah yeah. You say she's human too, and that's the way to be-e-e...*

But the people did nothing.

"Tell her who you are!" I yelled at them. "Make her remember you."

They looked at me like I was crazy. They wandered around her room looking for themselves in the timeline. And when they couldn't find their names, they marked it with their fingers, a blue mark for every human being missing from the story of history. Soon they were busy making the timeline blue.

"Get into her head! Please." And I said please again and again, though they never responded. I woke up next to the door of my closet. I'd never made it into Celia's room. It was dark outside, and I knew it wasn't even midnight. I got up and walked to Celia's room. I turned the knob and the door opened.

Celia had her arms around a big tiger, but with just the moonlight from the window, it looked like a little Sybil. I walked to her bed softly, trying not to wake her. I looked down at her face like I was looking down at something I borrowed and really didn't want to give back, something like stars that are gone in the morning.

I kissed her on the forehead, praying, "Take everything I know."

⟶⟿⟨⟩⟷

On the way back to my room, when I was in-between, still in the dark hallway, I heard Mom and Dad talking from their room. Their voices came from the wall, from the family photographs. They must have been in bed.

"I don't want to do this," Mom said. "Look what happened to Jeffrey."

Jeffrey was our cousin. His parents had sent him north when he wasn't going to pass the tests. Sometimes parents did that. We never saw him again. Nobody knew if he'd been caught or just escaped. That was a couple of years ago. Were they thinking of sending Celia away?

"Aunt Berry will tell her where she needs to go next. She'll be fine," I heard Dad say. "When I talked with her, she said she knew people along the way."

I felt the hallway grow blacker and the light behind me from my room pull back under my feet like a tide. I would lose Celia either way—whether through the gods, or my parents.

⇥⇥⇤ ⇥ ⇥ ⇥⇥⇥⇥

In my room the gods stared at me from the walls. I was frightened of them. Would they turn Celia into a cloth store? They didn't even know her. They stood around me like a bunch of bullies on the playground, with their hands on their hips, staring down at me.

I stuck my hand underneath the corner of a poster and lifted it and pulled down the poster. *I can do that. I can take down your poster*, I thought. I took down the other posters, too, one after the other. And after the third one I was ripping them down. I ripped Independence to shreds. I couldn't stop myself. I plucked the postcards of Lady Liberty off the wall. I threw them on the floor. I threw my action figures into the closet. I took off my Patriot bedsheets, the Patriot quilt, and I bundled them in a pile at the foot of my bed. I didn't want to sleep on them or see them right now.

I pulled out the quilt Celia made me a long time ago from the closet where it stayed folded. It had me holding our new puppy Toby. I pulled this quilt over my whole body. Her work was all around me, soft, dark, holding me.

I hated myself for praying to Patriot. *Please put all my education in Celia's head. All the stupid facts about you, all the stupid things you did. Give them to Celia so she can stay human with us. Please, please, please.* I prayed like I was choking, and my stomach got all churned up. I pushed the bed against the wall. I hated them all. *Please, America, save my sister...* the gods were all I *had*.

A scrap of Patriot's face was just under the quilt. How sure of himself he looked. When the Blitzkrieg had attacked, he'd risen like a fortress, spread open his arms like a shield around us all. I'd seen the footage from the warplanes. He'd become four hundred stories tall, inflated by all the belief of an entire nation. The German planes were like wasps to him, zapping against a buglamp. I remember his face—there was a moment where he turned his face away from the explosions against his cheek. He gritted his teeth and stood there.

He had courage.

I took the scrap that held his face and I shoved it in my pocket.

I jumped up, ran to my closet and grabbed my backpack and stuffed clothes in it.

⟶⟨ ⟩ — ⟨ ⟩⟵

In Celia's room, I turned off the CD player, and the music stopped. I leaned over Celia and gently woke her. "We're running away," I whispered.

"What?" she said. "No. I can do it, Danny. I can pass the Test."

She saw I didn't believe her. I didn't want to hide that from her.

"No, really. I think I can. I mean, it all came to me. I think all the music has been helping." And she noticed the player was off. "I thought I turned that on."

"Celia." What could I say? "Celia, what if you fail? There's only one try. They don't let you leave the school till the Test is graded." I remember all the students packed into the gym, playing games, waiting, trying not to think about the test, or what might happen.

"I'm telling you, I can do it," she said firmly, sitting up in bed. "You aren't even going to let me try." She flipped back the covers, stood up, crossed the room, and turned on her desk lamp. "Well, you're not going to stop me."

She used to guide me through the woods like that. She didn't slow down. She remembered all the trails—every one of them. She knew where the raccoon tracks would be on the banks of the creek. She would know where to go.

"Celia, remember the creek last summer?" Behind our house, behind all the other houses was a forest and a creek that we played around. It had some narrow places and some wide ones. She wouldn't let me jump the wide one.

"You were going to break your—," she stopped. "That's not the same." She flipped randomly through history, her fingers darting in and out of the Civil War. "You don't believe in me at all. You don't believe I could ever, *ever* pass the Test," her voice broke.

"I don't believe in the Test, Celia. They don't know who you are. I always believed in you."

I opened her dresser drawers and gave her a knapsack, and I made sure she saw my eyes. "You know how to get us to Aunt Berry's."

"I can't leave Mom and Dad."

"Mom and Dad have already called Aunt Berry. They're going to send you away tomorrow. I'll never see you again. Jeffrey never came back," I stopped, tried to look away like she did, to pull all my tears back in. But I wasn't smart enough for that. "This is the only way—I can think of. We'll be together."

At least she wouldn't be lost like Jeffrey—she wouldn't be alone. I would be there. I would know if she got somewhere safe. We would go north to Canada. I heard there were frost giants at the borders who stood toe to toe, but I was more worried about getting out of Kentucky.

"You can do this, Celia. You're smart. You know the woods. You know all the paths, the ways, even in the dark. You can guide us to Aunt Berry's house. She'll tell Mom and Dad where we are. She knows ways to get us out. She helped Jeffrey. She'll help us. Celia, I don't want to be alone."

She stared into the dark room for a moment, past the parts the lamp could reach.

Finally she said, "I can do this. I can make it to Aunt Berry's house. I know which streets to go down, which paths I can cut through. We'll have Aunt Berry call Mom and Dad from there." She looked at me. "Don't worry, Danny."

I remembered what Sybil the mountain lion had said to me. "I'm not afraid," I whispered to Celia.

I helped her put things in the knapsack, and she grabbed her own quilt, one that was dark and full of children swatting at quilted stars, and some needle and thread and some yarn and other cloth—"Just in case," she said—and we left through the backyard, where the moonlight trickled across our feet in the grass. I wondered where Lady Liberty was, which state she was in tonight. I asked Celia.

"Oh, maybe she's in Kentucky," she said, looking around. She nearly stopped walking, and she smiled. "She'll save us, Danny. Pray that she walks by."

I looked around the backyards we were crossing and the fields on the edge of town and I looked across the two rivers and I hoped she didn't find us. I hoped no god did. I hoped we found ourselves with people, real people, somewhere. I was scared of seeing the lamp of Lady Liberty at any moment crest a hill, her ghost like body rise up like a cloud. I knew that if she came for us, I would hold Celia back, even if Celia looked up to be saved.

Jerome Stueart lived most of his life in the United States, the son of a Baptist minister. After spending three years in the Yukon Territory, he moved there as a landed immigrant in 2007. His work has appeared in *Fantasy*, *Strange Horizons*, *On Spec*, *Redivider*, *Metazen*, two other *Tesseracts* anthologies, and the *Evolve* anthology. He's also a regular contributor to *Yukon: North of Ordinary*, the Air North in-flight magazine, and *What's Up Yukon?*, an arts and living paper. He lives in Whitehorse, teaching writing and keeping an eye out for bears.

The Transformed Man

Robert J. Sawyer

Space, The Final Frontier...

I used to be called Robin. But when I was ten I discovered my legal name was Robert, so I switched. I was tired of getting invitations to join girls' skating teams.

Back then, Mississauga was farmland. Now I live in a high-rise there. But you can still see one farm out my window; the guy refuses to sell.

We science-fiction writers talk a lot about the *singularity*, a coming moment during which the rate of technological progress will asymptotically approach infinity, and—*whoosh!*—plain old human beings will be left far behind. Charles Stross, a writer I know, calls this "the Rapture of the nerds." Charlie has recently started shaving his head.

On an early episode of *Star Trek: The Next Generation*, guest star Stanley Kamel was supposed to say the word "asymptotically," but he'd never heard of it, so he said "asymptomatically" instead. He died recently of a heart attack; he'd had no previous signs of heart disease.

My favorite movie is *2001: A Space Odyssey*. Arthur C. Clarke died recently, too. He lived long enough to see the actual 2001 come and go with none of the miracles he portrayed becoming reality.

My editor claims science-fiction writers should never put dates in their books. "The future has a way of catching up with you," he says. He has a Ph.D. in comparative medieval literature—so he should know.

Battlestar Galactica used to be camp; now it's serious. Ditto, *Batman*.

The Presidency of the United States used to be serious. Now it's camp.

They remade *Planet of the Apes*. They shouldn't have.

Computers, The Ultimate Tools...

I did a talk recently in Second Life. My name in that virtual world is S.F. Writer. I have hair there.

SFWRITER is also my license plate, but I don't drive. When I talk about the plate, I say, "Oh, the car vanity!" People younger than me don't get the pun.

My Canada includes Quebec—but its license plates no longer call it *La belle province*. I can't remember what they say now.

I went to the Yukon in the summer of 2007, on a writing retreat at Pierre Berton's old house. It had been renovated the previous winter by the Designer Guys. They put diaphanous curtains on the windows. Dawson City gets 21 hours of daylight in the summer, but the Designer Guys hadn't thought about that.

I got to see the Northern Lights. The aurora changes moment by moment.

Biotech, The Last Challenge...

My father sold his vacation home last year. He'd had it since 1974. It was time, he said.

I'd lost my virginity there.

When I turned 40, I had a vasectomy. The Ontario Health Insurance Plan will pay for your vasectomy, and pay to have it reversed, and pay to give you another vasectomy. But they won't pay to have *that* one reversed, because, you know, that'd be frivolous.

I've had all my amalgam fillings replaced. What were they thinking, putting mercury in people's mouths?

I got my degree in Radio and Television Arts in 1982. I can edit audiotape with a razor blade.

When I went to Ryerson, it was called Ryerson Polytechnical Institute. Then it became Ryerson Polytechnic University. Now it's Ryerson University. But people still call it Rye High.

After I graduated, Ryerson hired me to help teach TV production. My salary was $14,400 a year. Even then, it wasn't much.

Six million dollars used to be a lot of money, though. You could buy a cyborg with it. But the bionic woman didn't cost *quite* six million. After all, said her boss, her parts were smaller. He always called her "babe."

I cringe when women today refer to themselves as "girls." In the summer of 1980, I lived in Waterloo. The people I hung out with there always called Fischer-Hallman Road "Fischer-Hallperson." No one does stuff like that anymore.

Still, interstellar space used to be where no man has gone before. Now it's where no *one* has gone before.

William Shatner's 1968 debut album—on which he mangles "Lucy in the Sky with Diamonds"—is called *The Transformed Man*. He won Emmy Awards for best supporting actor in 2004 and 2005, and was nominated again last year.

Nanotech, The Next Big Thing...

Ingrid Bergman calls Dooley Wilson "boy" in *Casablanca*, and no one cringes.

The year I was born, Robert was the fifth-most-popular boy's name; now it's number 47. Robin has never cracked the top 100.

My first freelance writing job was editing the CRTC license application for what became Vision TV, Canada's multifaith television channel. Back then, we called it the Canadian Inter-faith Network, or "CIN" with a soft *C;* that pissed some people off.

Used to be my books were shelved in stores next to those by Hilbert Schenck. Hilbert has disappeared; I have no idea what happened to him.

NASA has a sister organization called NOAA: the National Oceanic and Atmospheric Administration. The acronym is pronounced "Noah." A government agency couldn't get away with a Biblical pun like that today, but everybody wants to know about the faith lives of presidential candidates. Joe Biden is the first-ever Roman Catholic to become veep. *Tempus fugit.*

Here in Canada, we used to have Pierre Trudeaus. Now we have Stephen Harpers.

I collect plastic dinosaurs. My one criterion: they must have been accurate portrayals at the time they were made. *Brontosaurus* used to drag its tail; it doesn't now. And it's no longer *Brontosaurus*.

Oh, and Pluto used to be a planet. It isn't anymore.

Someday, the same thing will be said of Earth.

Robert J. Sawyer is the author of Hugo Award-winner *Hominids* and Nebula Award-winner *The Terminal Experiment*, plus *Starplex*, *Frameshift*, *Factoring Humanity*, *Calculating God*, *Humans*, and *Rollback*, all of which were Hugo finalists, and *FlashForward*, the basis of the ABC TV series of the same name. Other awards: China's Galaxy Award for "Most Popular Foreign SF Writer"; three Japanese Seiun Awards for Best Foreign Novel; ten Aurora Awards; plus *Analog's* Analytical Laboratory Award, *Science Fiction Chronicle's* Readers Award, and the Crime Writers of Canada's Arthur Ellis Award, all for best short-story of the year. He and his wife Carolyn Clink co-edited *Tesseracts* 6.

Brett Alexander Savory is the Bram Stoker Award-winning Editor-in-Chief of *ChiZine: Treatments of Light and Shade in Words*, Co-Publisher of ChiZine Publications, he has had nearly fifty short stories published, and has written two novels. In 2006, his horror-comedy novel, *The Distance Travelled*, was released. September 2007 saw his dark literary novel, *In and* Down, hit bookstore shelves. His first short story collection, *No Further Messages*, was released in November 2007. He is now at work on his third novel, *Lake of Spaces, Wood of Nothing*. He lives in Toronto with his wife, writer/editor Sandra Kasturi.

Afterword

Brett Alexander Savory

No matter what project I'm editing—be it *ChiZine* (the webzine), ChiZine Publications (the small press), or a commissioned anthology—I can't get away from leaning, quite heavily, toward the darker side of literature. Not that I *want* to get away from it, mind, but I don't think I could even if I wanted to. And this anthology is no exception.

Since you're reading the Afterword, I'm going to assume you've read the stories, so I can say with confidence that you likely noticed a rather dark thread running through most, if not all, of them. That's just the way I roll. What was surprising to me is that my co-editor, John Robert Colombo, rolls the same way. As he mentioned in his Foreword, we agreed on nearly every story in this volume. I assumed, since he traffics more in science fiction and I traffic more in horror, we'd be at odds far more often than we were. Happily, such was not the case, and I think you've just read a more qualitatively consistent anthology because of that.

Now, speaking of surprises, I thought I'd relate the brief tale of how I came to be the co-editor of this book in the first place.

A couple of years ago, Claude Lalumière asked me to write the Foreword to *Tesseracts Twelve*, which I gladly did. We got to talking about the series over lunch one afternoon in Toronto, and I decided I'd throw my hat in the ring to edit a future volume. I went home, typed up a query letter to Edge publisher Brian Hades, fired it off, and waited. And waited. And waited....

And waited some more, but never heard a word in response.

Fast forward two years to WorldCon 2009 in Montreal. I'd never met Brian before, but saw that Edge had a table not far from CZP's table. On the first day there, Brian comes over, checks out our books, says he's very impressed with them (he wound up buying a copy of every book we'd published to that point!), then says out of the blue, "Oh, by the way, I got your email about editing one of the *Tesseracts* anthologies. I have a co-editor in mind for you, if you still want to do it."

Remember, now, it'd been two years without even so much as a "Thanks for your email, am super-busy, but will get back to you soon about this," so I just kind of stared at him for a while, trying to remember if I'd sent such an email.

"Oh! Right," I said. "I did ask about that, didn't I. Well, um, yeah, sure, totally still up for it."

"Okay, I'll drop you a line when I get home, introduce you to your co-editor, and send out the contracts." And with that, he walked away.

Done deal. So yeah, color me surprised.

And I have to say, editing this book has been one of the best experiences I've ever had an as editor. The quality of the submissions was strong to the point that both John and I found it very difficult to keep the final word count down to anywhere near the 100,000-word mark. As John mentioned in his Foreword, we went over, but if we'd had our druthers, we'd have gone *way* over. There were enough good, fitting submissions to've filled close to a *second* volume.

All of the stories in this book are stories I would have taken for *ChiZine*, and I would have gladly published this collected volume under the CZP imprint. I couldn't be prouder of the anthology John and I have put together. Nor could I be prouder of the writers featured within it, as well as the writers who came close to being included. You are all deeply weird and should fly your freak flag high!

Something I've come to realize since ChiZine Publications has become my full-time job these past two years, is that Canadians can write dark, weird fiction extremely well. I can honestly say that-after editing *ChiZine* the webzine for over thirteen years-Canadian contributions are some of the best we've ever featured, always figuring prominently in our online pages, just as they figure prominently now, in print, through our press.

I've no doubt the *Tesseracts* series will continue to publish dark, strange fiction-and the writers within its pages will continue to write dark, strange fiction outside the Tesseracts and ChiZine realms. It's just how they roll.

And *that* is no surprise.

Acknowledgements

John Robert Colombo for such an easy
co-editing experience.

Brian Hades for the opportunity
to edit this book.

Erik Mohr for providing (as usual)
an incredible, eye-catching cover.

The writers featured in this anthology
for making my job easy by writing
exactly the kind of fiction I adore.

Our titles are available at major book stores and local independent resellers who support Science Fiction and Fantasy readers like you.

www.edgewebsite.com

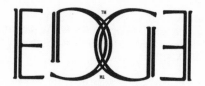

EDGE Science Fiction and Fantasy Publishing

Tesseract Books

Dreams of an Unseen Planet by Teresa Plowright (tp) - ISBN: 978-0-88878-282-3
Dreams of the Sea (Part 1 of Tyranaël) by Élisabeth Vonarburg (tp)
  - ISBN: 978-1-895836-96-7
Dreams of the Sea (Part 1 of Tyranaël) by Élisabeth Vonarburg (hb)
  - ISBN: 978-1-895836-98-1
Druids by Barbara Galler-Smith and Josh Langston (tp)
  - ISBN: 978-1-894063-29-6

Eclipse by K. A. Bedford (tp) - ISBN: 978-1-894063-30-2
Even The Stones by Marie Jakober (tp) - ISBN: 978-1-894063-18-0
Evolve: Vampire Stories of the New Undead edited by Nancy Kilpatrick (tp)
  - ISBN: 978-1-894063-33-3

Far Arena (Part Five of the Okal Rel Saga) by Lynda Williams (tp)
  - ISBN: 978-1-894063-45-6
Fires of the Kindred by Robin Skelton (tp) - ISBN: 978-0-88878-271-7
Forbidden Cargo by Rebecca Rowe (tp) - ISBN: 978-1-894063-16-6

Game of Perfection, A (Part 2 of Tyranaël) by Élisabeth Vonarburg (tp)
  - ISBN: 978-1-894063-32-6
Gaslight Grimoire: Fantastic Tales of Sherlock Holmes
  edited by Jeff Campbell & Charles Prepolec (pb)
  - ISBN: 978-1-8964063-17-3
Gaslight Grotesque: Nightmare Tales of Sherlock Holmes
  edited by Jeff Campbell & Charles Prepolec (pb)
  - ISBN: 978-1-8964063-31-9
Green Music by Ursula Pflug (tp) - ISBN: 978-1-895836-75-2
Green Music by Ursula Pflug (hb) - ISBN: 978-1-895836-77-6

Healer, The (Children of the Panther Part One) by Amber Hayward (tp)
  - ISBN: 978-1-895836-89-9
Healer, The (Children of the Panther Part One) by Amber Hayward (hb)
  - ISBN: 978-1-895836-91-2
Hell Can Wait by Theodore Judson (tp) - ISBN: 978-1-978-1-894063-23-4
Hounds of Ash and other tales of Fool Wolf, The by Greg Keyes (pb)
  - ISBN: 978-1-894063-09-8
Hydrogen Steel by K. A. Bedford (tp) - ISBN: 978-1-894063-20-3

i-ROBOT Poetry by Jason Christie (tp) - ISBN: 978-1-894063-24-1
Immortal Quest by Alexandra MacKenzie (pb) - ISBN: 978-1-894063-46-3

Jackal Bird by Michael Barley (pb) - ISBN: 978-1-895836-07-3
Jackal Bird by Michael Barley (hb) - ISBN: 978-1-895836-11-0
JEMMA7729 by Phoebe Wray (tp) - ISBN: 978-1-894063-40-1

Keaen by Till Noever (tp) - ISBN: 978-1-894063-08-1
Keeper's Child by Leslie Davis (tp) - ISBN: 978-1-894063-01-2

Land/Space edited by Candas Jane Dorsey and Judy McCrosky (tp)
  - ISBN: 978-1-895836-90-5
Land/Space edited by Candas Jane Dorsey and Judy McCrosky (hb)
  - ISBN: 978-1-895836-92-9

Lyskarion: The Song of the Wind (Part One of The Chronicles of the Karionin)
by J.A. Cullum (tp) - ISBN: 978-1-894063-02-9

Machine Sex and other stories by Candas Jane Dorsey (tp)
- ISBN: 978-0-88878-278-6
Maërlande Chronicles, The by Élisabeth Vonarburg (pb)
- ISBN: 978-0-88878-294-6
Moonfall by Heather Spears (pb) - ISBN: 978-0-88878-306-6

Of Wind and Sand by Sylvie Bérard (translated by Sheryl Curtis) (pb)
- ISBN: 978-1-894063-19-7
On Spec: The First Five Years edited by On Spec (pb)
- ISBN: 978-1-895836-08-0
On Spec: The First Five Years edited by On Spec (hb)
- ISBN: 978-1-895836-12-7
Orbital Burn by K. A. Bedford (tp) - ISBN: 978-1-894063-10-4
Orbital Burn by K. A. Bedford (hb) - ISBN: 978-1-894063-12-8

Pallahaxi Tide by Michael Coney (pb) - ISBN: 978-0-88878-293-9
Passion Play by Sean Stewart (pb) - ISBN: 978-0-88878-314-1
Petrified World (Determine Your Destiny #1) by Piotr Brynczka (pb)
- ISBN: 978-1-894063-11-1
Plague Saint by Rita Donovan, The (tp) - ISBN: 978-1-895836-28-8
Plague Saint by Rita Donovan, The (hb) - ISBN: 978-1-895836-29-5
Pock's World by Dave Duncan (tp) - ISBN: 978-1-894063-47-0
Pretenders (Part Three of the Okal Rel Saga) by Lynda Williams (pb)
- ISBN: 978-1-894063-13-5

Reluctant Voyagers by Élisabeth Vonarburg (pb) - ISBN: 978-1-895836-09-7
Reluctant Voyagers by Élisabeth Vonarburg (hb) - ISBN: 978-1-895836-15-8
Resisting Adonis by Timothy J. Anderson (tp) - ISBN: 978-1-895836-84-4
Resisting Adonis by Timothy J. Anderson (hb) - ISBN: 978-1-895836-83-7
Righteous Anger (Part Two of the Okal Rel Saga) by Lynda Williams (tp)
- ISBN: 897-1-894063-38-8

Silent City, The by Élisabeth Vonarburg (tp) - ISBN: 978-1-894063-07-4
Slow Engines of Time, The by Élisabeth Vonarburg (tp)
- ISBN: 978-1-895836-30-1
Slow Engines of Time, The by Élisabeth Vonarburg (hb)
- ISBN: 978-1-895836-31-8
Stealing Magic by Tanya Huff (tp) - ISBN: 978-1-894063-34-0
Strange Attractors by Tom Henighan (pb) - ISBN: 978-0-88878-312-7

Taming, The by Heather Spears (pb) - ISBN: 978-1-895836-23-3
Taming, The by Heather Spears (hb) - ISBN: 978-1-895836-24-0
Ten Monkeys, Ten Minutes by Peter Watts (tp) - ISBN: 978-1-895836-74-5
Ten Monkeys, Ten Minutes by Peter Watts (hb) - ISBN: 978-1-895836-76-9
Tesseracts 1 edited by Judith Merril (pb) - ISBN: 978-0-88878-279-3
Tesseracts 2 edited by Phyllis Gotlieb & Douglas Barbour (pb)
- ISBN: 978-0-88878-270-0
Tesseracts 3 edited by Candas Jane Dorsey & Gerry Truscott (pb)
- ISBN: 978-0-88878-290-8

Tesseracts 4 edited by Lorna Toolis & Michael Skeet (pb)
  - ISBN: 978-0-88878-322-6
Tesseracts 5 edited by Robert Runté & Yves Maynard (pb)
  - ISBN: 978-1-895836-25-7
Tesseracts 5 edited by Robert Runté & Yves Maynard (hb)
  - ISBN: 978-1-895836-26-4
Tesseracts 6 edited by Robert J. Sawyer & Carolyn Clink (pb)
  - ISBN: 978-1-895836-32-5
Tesseracts 6 edited by Robert J. Sawyer & Carolyn Clink (hb)
  - ISBN: 978-1-895836-33-2
Tesseracts 7 edited by Paula Johanson & Jean-Louis Trudel (tp)
  - ISBN: 978-1-895836-58-5
Tesseracts 7 edited by Paula Johanson & Jean-Louis Trudel (hb)
  - ISBN: 978-1-895836-59-2
Tesseracts 8 edited by John Clute & Candas Jane Dorsey (tp)
  - ISBN: 978-1-895836-61-5
Tesseracts 8 edited by John Clute & Candas Jane Dorsey (hb)
  - ISBN: 978-1-895836-62-2
Tesseracts Nine edited by Nalo Hopkinson and Geoff Ryman (tp)
  - ISBN: 978-1-894063-26-5
Tesseracts Ten: A Celebration of New Canadian Specuative Fiction
  edited by Robert Charles Wilson and Edo van Belkom (tp)
  - ISBN: 978-1-894063-36-4
Tesseracts Eleven: Amazing Canadian Speulative Fiction
  edited by Cory Doctorow and Holly Phillips (tp)
  - ISBN: 978-1-894063-03-6
Tesseracts Twelve: New Novellas of Canadian Fantastic Fiction
  edited by Claude Lalumière (pb)
  - ISBN: 978-1-894063-15-9
Tesseracts Thirteen: Chilling Tales from the Great White North
  edited by Nancy Kilpatrick and David Morrell (tp)
  - ISBN: 978-1-894063-25-8
Tesseracts 14: Strange Canadian Stories
  edited by John Robert Colombo and Brett Alexander Savory (tp)
  - ISBN: 978-1-894063-37-1
Tesseracts Q edited by Élisabeth Vonarburg & Jane Brierley (pb)
  - ISBN: 978-1-895836-21-9
Tesseracts Q edited by Élisabeth Vonarburg & Jane Brierley (hb)
  - ISBN: 978-1-895836-22-6
Throne Price by Lynda Williams and Alison Sinclair (tp)
  - ISBN: 978-1-894063-06-7
Time Machines Repaired Whie-U-Wait by K. A. Bedford (tp)
  - ISBN: 978-1-894063-42-5